a HUNDRED Things YOU HAVEN'T DREAMED OF

HARD BROKE SERIES, BOOK TWO

ENGLISH MICHAELS

Rash daredevils with a score to settle. Swaggering jet jocks with no regard for rules or safety. Unchecked egos battling for superiority. This is the picture Hollywood paints of the military fighter pilot— but what really happens behind the closed doors of an Air Force fighter squadron?

English Michaels knows.

Captain Davis Foster, the Scorpion squadron's Weapons Officer, is winning at life. Born into old southern money, educated at a private military institution, and now a leader in an elite fighter squadron, he's on target for the successful military career he's always dreamed of.

But one terrible moment can change everything.

Unexpected adversity challenges Davis's strength of character, placing his life and career in jeopardy—and the secret weapon he never expected could be the woman he's only recently met, the charismatic Lucinda Page.

Davis and Lucinda are inexorably drawn together and falling fast when the unthinkable happens, sending both of their lives into a tailspin. Luckie's support may give Davis the edge he needs to weather the storm he faces. She's an experienced nurse—self-assured, intelligent, and so gorgeous she takes his breath away.

She's also black.

Worlds collide when she travels with Davis to his hometown of Savannah, Georgia. The experience compels her to confront bias woven into the fabric of a culture that shaped the man she loves, as well as some surprisingly progressive attitudes—and support where she least expects it.

Strap in for an action-packed trip with Davis and Lucinda as they leave the stark beauty of Tucson behind for Savannah's lush, Spanish-moss-cloaked streets, haunting history, and historic architecture. The journey is marked with danger, heartbreak, redemption—and ultimately— proof that love has the power to overcome every obstacle.

Dedication

To Schneider, SandyPants, Pats, JDawg, CB, Terri Leigh, Dr. B, Dawnster, G8, and Miss Betty—the hardest-working girl squad/cheering section in the history of fledgling authors. Thank you for the sterling advice, everlasting encouragement, and for helping me believe what I had to say was worth the trouble to put it on paper.

and

To Chef—Profound gratitude for so generously sharing your reflections on the crucial role of the Weapons Officer in modern fighter squadrons. You are not only a wellspring of fighter pilot wisdom and a genuinely good-hearted man, but a damn fine song-writer. Not so much with the cooking thing, however.

The Hard Broke Series follows the adventures of the pilots of the Scorpion squadron and the women they love. Although each story is self-contained and does not contain a cliffhanger, the terminology unique to the fighter pilot world and the United States Air Force makes it preferable to read the series in order. Please enjoy each story chronologically—I hope you love the Scorpions as much as I do.

A NOTE TO THE READER

The concept of flight is a romantic one; and the military pilot, in particular, holds strong appeal for many women, especially romance enthusiasts. I am only one example of a young woman who was secretly taken with the raw magnetism and power of a handsome man in a flight suit striding toward his jet, helmet in hand, ready to casually stare death in the eye.

Reality invaded my overly-dramatic fantasy life when I fell in love and married a kind-hearted, ridiculously sexy, utterly flawed, devastatingly handsome Air Force pilot. While our love match has enjoyed the qualities of many long-lived marriages—the marvelous and the mundane—his military career over the first decade of our lives together also afforded me a front row seat to the fascinating world of the fighter pilot.

In July, a little over a year before we married, I took a seat in a stiflingly hot Air Force base auditorium, dressed in a black taffeta cocktail dress and fidgeting like the twenty-year-old I was. That afternoon, I watched my boyfriend stride across the stage to receive his Air Force wings, signifying his successful completion of Undergraduate Pilot Training. It was a sentinel moment in his life, as it is for every military pilot. Printed on the last page of the cheap paper program was a poem I'd never seen but would come to know by heart.

John Gillespie Magee was a young pilot in the Royal Canadian Air Force who died in the service of his country in 1941. Mere months before his passing, at the tender age of nineteen, he penned this sonnet and beautifully captured the allure and romance of flight.

"High Flight"

By

John Gillespie Magee

"Oh! I have slipped the surly bonds of earth

And danced the skies on laughter-silvered wings;

Sunward I've climbed, and joined the tumbling mirth

Of sun-split clouds—and done a hundred things

You have not dreamed of—wheeled and soared and swung

High in the sunlit silence. Hov'ring there,

I've chased the shouting wind along, and flung

My eager craft through footless halls of air.

Up, up the long, delirious, burning blue

I've topped the wind-swept heights with easy grace

Where never lark, or even eagle flew—

And, while with silent lifting mind I've trod

The high untrespassed sanctity of space

—Put out my hand and touched the face of God."

GLOSSARY

The world of the military pilot has a language all its own, as confusing as a foreign tongue to the uninitiated. This glossary is offered to assist those unfamiliar in navigating the technicalities, jargon, and buffoonery. A few medical terms are included for additional clarification. The first occurrence of each term within the text of the book is bolded.

A-10 Warthog—The Fairchild Republic A-10 Thunderbolt II. More commonly, "the Warthog" or just "the Hawg." The only USAF aircraft designed specifically for the Close Air Support mission: supporting troops on the ground in contact with the enemy. Designed around the lessons of Vietnam and the threat of massed Soviet tanks in Europe. Maneuverable, survivable, and lethal. Pilots refer to themselves as "Hawg drivers."

AGL—Above Ground Level.

AIM-9 Sidewinder—Also Sidewinders; Short range air to air missile with infrared guidance; a heat-seeking missile or a "heater"

ALO—Air Liaison Officer; an Air Force pilot assigned to any ground unit, usually a brigade or larger, to provide tactical air support expertise to the ground commander.

ATO—Air Tasking Order; the daily headquarters message in combat, either real or simulated, detailing the next day's plans: units, targets, weapons, etc.

Attached Personnel—Persons operating with or within a military unit but not directly assigned to that unit. Usually support specialists—chaplains, lawyers, doctors, etc.

Bean Counter—Marginally derogatory term for non-pilot Air Force personnel; office or headquarters staff.

Beer Call—Official but informal meeting of squadron pilots held in the squadron lounge or bar, usually on a Friday, after all flying for the day is complete.

BFM—Basic Fighter Maneuvers. The essential building blocks of air combat maneuvering. When a single aircraft is engaged in aerial combat with another single aircraft, BFM is the set of maneuvers and techniques used to move from a neutral to an attacking position relative to one's opponent. Developed in World War I and formalized by German ace Oswald Boelcke.

Billeting—Office and staff tasked with assigning housing, both temporary and permanent.

BOQ—Bachelor Officer Quarters. A holdover from a bygone era. The "Q" would be a small efficiency apartment in a dormitory-style building on base, often with a shared kitchen. Unless required to live there, most single officers elect to live off base in apartments or rentals.

CAS—Close Air Support; providing supporting air power to the troops on the ground directly engaged with enemy forces. The raison d'être for the A-10.

Chaff and Flares—Dispensable decoys carried in every fighter aircraft to spoof enemy radar-guided and heat-seeking missiles.

Clean Kill—A sure thing; a straightforward, obvious decision.

Cleared Hot—The command from a gunnery range control officer or forward air controller indicating attacking aircraft are cleared to employ weapons.

Cord Accident—Disruption of the umbilical cord blood flow supplying a fetus with oxygen and nutrients before birth; ordinarily a knot in the cord or a prolapse. A prolapse occurs when the cord becomes pinched between the baby and the mother, commonly when the water breaks and "washes" the cord into the birth canal in front of the baby. Cord accidents are a relatively rare complication of pregnancy.

FAC—Forward Air Controller; specially trained ground or airborne personnel responsible for locating and marking targets, then assigning and managing attack aircraft as they engage the target.

Flight Surgeon—Military doctor specially trained in aerospace medicine: the unique interactions between the flying environment and the human body. Responsible for pilots' medical clearance to fly.

Frag—A "fragment" of the daily Air Tasking Order (ATO) that applies to a specific unit.

Frequent Flyer—Medical slang used, especially in the emergency department, for drug-seeking patients who repeatedly visit many hospital EDs fabricating various ailments to illicitly acquire pain medications. Many hospitals maintain a list of people identified as the most common offenders for new employees who might not recognize them on sight.

GAU-8 Avenger—The General Electric GAU-8/A Avenger is the weapon mounted on the USAF's A-10 Thunderbolt II. Its unique 30 mm Gatling-type autocannon can deliver up to 4200 rounds per minute and was designed specifically for the anti-tank role against Soviet armor. The heart and soul of the Warthog.

Hard Broke—An aircraft with a maintenance issue is referred to as "broke," provided it's expected to be repaired in time to launch with only minor delays. With a longer, or even indeterminate, delay of return to status by maintenance, the aircraft is said to be "hard broke."

HIPAA—Health Insurance Portability and Accountability Act passed in 1996; long, complex, and chock-full of legalese, it most notably established a national standard to protect medical records and other personal health information.

Hog Log—A-10 specific version of a Boner Book or Doofer Log. A ledger or notebook in every fighter squadron for storytelling, name-calling, or frustration venting. Regardless of the relative rank of the author or subject, there are no rules or reprisals. The Hog Log is never seen or shared with anyone other than a squadron member.

HUD—Heads-Up Display; a projected display in the windscreen of a fighter aircraft showing flight instrumentation as well as navigational and targeting data. Enables the pilot to minimize distracting scans inside the cockpit.

Initial Point—Predetermined fixed locations used as a common basis for allocating fighter assets and coordination, communication, and attack planning between fighters and ground controllers.

IP—Instructor Pilot. Duties vary from initial flight training to mission qualification, depending on the aircraft. The A-10 is unique in that there are no two-seat aircraft. All instruction is given over the radio from another aircraft.

The Land of No Slack—Any typical fighter squadron where no quarter is asked for or offered.

LPA—Lieutenants Protection Association. A mythical association of young officers in a squadron having one another's back, protecting themselves from the OFA—Old Farts Association, aka everyone else. In reality, the LPA usually represents the lieutenants as a group when they are assigned unsavory non-flying tasks: snack bar maintenance, party planning, going-away skits, etc. A long-standing tradition in fighter squadrons.

Manual Reversion—In the A-10, a rudimentary system connecting some of the flight controls to the stick via cables. This gives the pilot basic control of the airplane during flight in the absence of hydraulics. A key survivability feature designed into the A-10 to get the pilot back over friendly territory before an ejection may be required.

Maverick Missile—Rocket-powered, television-guided, air-to-surface missile. Available with a variety of warheads depending on the anticipated target. The pilot uses a miniature joystick and a TV screen to lock the missile's camera on the target. The Maverick is a "launch and leave," meaning once it is fired, it requires no further guidance from the pilot.

Nine-Line Briefing—A standardized, "fill in the blank" format for a ground controller to pass targeting information to attacking aircraft in minimal time with minimal radio chatter. Information includes the initial point (IP), attack bearing and distance, target, threats, disposition of friendly forces, and egress direction.

Officers' Club—Also O'Club, the Club; in the past, the Officers' Open Mess. A members-only restaurant and lounge on base that is restricted to officers, their families, and accompanied guests. While membership is theoretically optional, not joining is an instant career killer. Site of most formal military functions. At a flying base, it usually includes a casual bar where the standards of decorum are somewhat more "relaxed."

Operations Officer—Also Ops O. Second in command to the squadron commander. Focus is strictly on day-to-day operations like scheduling and training. Flight commanders report to the operations officer.

OTD—Out the Door; medical speak for sending a patient home, preferably in an expeditious manner.

OTS—Officer Training School. One of the three primary commissioning sources for new Air Force Officers along with the U.S. Air Force Academy and college ROTC (Reserve Officer Training Corp). Due to the length of the course, graduates are teasingly referred to as "ninety-day wonders."

PACU—Post-Anesthesia Care Unit. The recovery room where patients are moved immediately following surgery for stabilization after the administration of anesthesia and before transfer to a critical care or regular hospital bed.

PCS—Permanent Change of Station. Military-speak for a reassignment and move.

Perch—In this context, a position for beginning a BFM exercise. The attacker is positioned above and behind the defender, figuratively "on a perch" with both an energy and positional advantage.

PROJO—Project Officer; an officer tasked with supervising a specific project, an additional duty.

RHAW—Radar Homing and Warning equipment. An onboard aircraft sensor system consisting of a small screen and audio tones designed to alert crews if they are being searched or targeted by radar. Each enemy system has a unique display and audio signature.

ROE—Rules of Engagement. The specific rules governing a military training exercise or actual combat. Some are general safety rules while others specifically apply to the exercise or the combat area of operation.

SA-8 Geckos—NATO code name for an older generation, Soviet-designed, vehicle-mounted, radar-guided, surface-to-air missile.

SA-16 Gimlets—NATO code name for a late-generation, Soviet-designed, shoulder-fired, heat-seeking surface-to-air missile.

SAREX—Search and Rescue Exercise. Leading and directing combat search and rescue of downed airmen in enemy territory is one of the primary roles of the A-10. During the exercise, various groups are able to train together in real time to recover the "survivor."

Smokey SAM—A training and missile simulation fired by ground personnel at attacking aircraft. It is both unarmed and unguided but has a readily visible smoke trail allowing aircraft to practice evasive tactics.

Socks Check—Uniform regulations require the wearing of black or blue socks with any uniform. If one pilot suspects another's socks may be in noncompliance, he may call for a socks check. The most expeditious way to perform this ritual in a flight suit (one-piece coverall) is to unzip and drop the entire garment around one's ankles. Loser of this challenge buys a round.

Squadron Tee Shirt—Tee shirt in the squadron's color, emblazoned with the squadron patch (logo). Mandatory wear on Fridays under the flight suit. Failure to wear it costs the offender a round.

Tactical/Call Sign—A fighter pilot's semi-official nickname. Generally bestowed by other members of the squadron based on some egregious or hilarious buffoonery. Glorified in the movies with names like Viper and Maverick, but, most often, far less flattering. Pilots generally address one another exclusively by their tactical, and it goes with one to the grave.

TDY—Temporary Duty; personnel temporarily performing duty away from their home base.

UNSAT—Unsatisfactory, as a grade on a training sortie. Often referred to as a "hook," it's annotated in the grade book in the shape of the letter "U."

UPT—Undergraduate Pilot Training. Air Force flight school. A rigorous course, approximately one year long, culminating in students being awarded Air Force Pilot Wings.

<u>Weapons Officer</u>—An officer in each squadron who has attended an intensive, aircraft-specific course at Nellis Air Force Base, literally a doctorate in flying fighters. The singular expert in the squadron on all weapons, tactics, and employment. Often referred to as "Patch Wearers" or "Target Arms" owing to the distinctive bull's-eye patch they wear.

<u>Wing King</u>—The Wing Commander. Typically an O-6 (Colonel), but often an O-7 (one-star Brigadier General), depending on the size and complexity of the base. Commander of all functions on a base.

Chapter ONE

"Dancing in the Dark"

Davis

I strode purposefully down the dim hallway of the **Officers' Club**; Lucinda's gloriously endless legs had no trouble keeping the pace. Our earlier introduction and the conversation that ensued rapidly resulted in a mutual attraction so powerful it must have been uncomfortable for the other bar patrons. They'd fled the general vicinity, leaving me alone with the riveting Lucinda. Flirting degenerated into blatantly filthy talk, and now I was engaged in an all-out search for cover.

This was gonna be fuck at first sight.

"Where are ya taking me, handsome?" Her voice slid over me like honey, and my hard dick hammered persistently against my fly.

I tossed her a laconic grin, allowing myself the luxury of another good, long look. She was sex on a fucking stick. Tall—five foot nine or maybe ten? All of it an endless expanse of flawless, mahogany skin I needed desperately to taste. Close-cropped hair framed her magnificent and surprisingly caramel-colored eyes that stared at me from under hooded lids. Her breath came quickly, but I surmised it wasn't so much due to our quick exit from the bar as it was the fact she was running as hot as I was.

"I need to get you behind a door, Peaches." I glanced surreptitiously in both directions. "Here we go." We finally reached the end of the hall, turning the corner. The music coming from the casual bar indicated where the action was, but I needed to do my due diligence. I yanked open one of the double doors to the empty coat closet, did some quick mental calculations on its size, and motioned her inside.

"Mm-hmm." She whispered as I closed the doors quietly, searching for the lock I knew I wouldn't find. "This is where I found your flight suit and changed into it." The party this evening had been organized as an icebreaker for the singles in our squadron, the 82nd Tactical Fighter Squadron—the Scorpions. The single men hung duplicate flight suits in this closet earlier. Women who attended picked one at random, changed into it, and used the matching name tags as an opportunity to meet and mingle.

"When I changed, I decided to go commando." Lucinda drew down the zipper of the flight suit she wore, revealing heavy, rounded breasts and just a shadow of a coffee-colored nipple.

I've hit the goddamn jackpot.

I frantically ripped the length of my cotton scarf free from my neck. It was strictly ornamental and decorated with dark red scorpions to indicate my squadron affiliation. I wound it hurriedly around the double doorknobs as tightly as I could. Privacy marginally secured, I turned and pressed Luckie's soft body against the wall of the nearly empty closet. My arms pulled her close, and I felt her soft hands brushing my lower back before moving lower to settle on my ass. Dropping my mouth to her ear, I spoke in a quiet voice laced with urgency.

"Commando, Peaches? What am I supposed to do with that?" I licked the skin of her neck, eliciting a soft moan. "You've thrown me a curveball tonight I wasn't expecting. Irresistible, exotic beauty all wrapped up in a flight suit with my name on it? Jesus, it's like Christmas and my birthday came early. I came here for a few beers with my friends, gorgeous…sure didn't expect to be drunk with need in a couple short hours."

My cock was straining against its confines and demanding exit. The air in the closet was thick with pheromones, and the whole scene screamed sex. My voice was unfamiliar to my own ears, thick and raspy with lust. "I'm a good Southern boy, Miss Page. I would never treat you—or any lady—with anything but the utmost deference, so I'll ask respectfully: may I put my hands on your naked skin while I feast on that luscious mouth?"

Only a sliver of light illuminated the closet, but I thanked every deity I knew for that scant light when Luckie stepped wordlessly from my arms, unfastened the flight-suit zipper to her hips, and dropped the garment unceremoniously to the floor. She stepped again into my space as I consciously shut my gaping mouth, and she stood on her toes to whisper in my ear.

"I'm not one to mince words or play coy when I see what I want, Davis. And I see what I want."

With that, I lowered my lips to meet her full, warm mouth and wrapped her naked body in my arms. I couldn't see her well in the dark closet, but she felt and smelled delicious. Her long body molded to mine, and she opened her lips to receive my gently exploring tongue. Considering the heat of the moment and the fact that I held a delectably bare woman in my arms, rocketing desperation should have resulted in bruised lips and torn clothing. But the opposite seemed to hold true as we tasted one another, learning and teasing. After kissing her mouth thoroughly, I nipped lazily along her jaw and under her earlobe.

"I'm going to pretend we have all night to spend together behind these doors, Lucinda, even though it's not true." I bit with a little more authority into the tender spot above her collarbone, and a more serious moan escaped her lips.

"You're making my little pussy wet, Davis." The grating want in her voice shot straight to my cock, and I pushed the hard length of it against her belly. "I know we don't have long, so I'm going to get rid of everything between that hard body of yours and mine." With no further elaboration, she pulled my zipper toward my waist, stripping the **squadron tee shirt** over my head nearly at the same time. "I hope you have a condom."

I did, although it took every available firing synapse to remember which pocket held my wallet and retrieve it. Slapping the unopened package onto the shelf above us, I dropped my flight suit to the ground and cupped the soft breasts brushing my chest.

"How much have you had to drink tonight, Luckie?" I looked into the heat of her caramel-colored eyes in the dim light. "I want you so bad my cock could break down these doors right now, but I won't take advantage of you, no matter what my dick thinks."

The heat in her eyes softened momentarily, and she sent me a small, sweet smile. "One beer, two orange juices. I'm a slut for vitamin C and a sugar rush." She squeezed my ass with both hands. "And thank you, Davis. What you just asked while holding a naked girl who wants you bad, officially makes you one in a million." She carefully pulled my boxer briefs out and down to free my aching cock and pushed them to my ankles. One finger traced the head, then the length of me while her eyes heated again to a molten gaze. "I know we're living on borrowed time here, Davis, but I do want to feel you inside me, so you'd better suit up."

"You're in such a hurry, Miss Page." I kissed her leisurely and allowed my tongue to explore again, deepening the kiss. My hands had been caressing the warm skin of her breasts, but now I moved one hand down below her flat stomach and found a soft patch of curly hair at the apex of her thighs. Wrapping one finger in the curls, I tugged gently, nipping her earlobe. "Don't you know a real gentleman will stroke your clit and finger your beautiful pussy till you're wet and then gift you with an orgasm or two before he offers his cock?"

I had to smile as she whimpered and wrapped her hand around my length. She parted her legs to allow my fingers easy access to the heat sheltered there. It seemed I'd finally rendered the lovely Lucinda speechless, and the creamy wetness my fingers found at her entrance was the reason why. She rocked her hips toward my searching fingers, and I found the swollen pearl of her clit, circling it softly with my finger.

"Wrap your left leg around my waist, baby." I helped her lift it into place for extra support, something that experience told me she was about to require. "Now curl those arms around my neck and let me make you feel good." She groaned her agreement, eyes fluttering closed, and her weight settled into my arms.

I loved fingering a woman's wet cunt almost as much as I loved eating it. Almost. Feasting between her legs afforded the additional delights of taste and smell, which were my personal favorites. But fingering a wanton pussy, its owner weak with pleasure in your arms, offered the opportunity to watch her face as she came. And I loved making a woman come.

Luckie was uninhibited and wildly responsive. Her hips moved in concert with my fingertips as I stroked along the swollen warmth of her folds, continuing to circle her clit with my thumb. Her fingers tugged at my hair, and she pressed her thigh into the heat of my erection, escalating the ache to new heights. Fuck, I needed to be inside her.

Her hands pulled our heads close, and she panted into my ear. She was barely audible when she finally spoke. "Davis, I know you said I get to come on your fingers first..." Her pussy began to tremble almost imperceptibly, and I gently slid two fingers inside, fucking her while she tried to talk. "But I want to come the first time with you inside me." One of her hands dropped to take my measure, giving my shaft a couple firm strokes. "That is if I can take all of you."

Holy shit, self-control had officially left the building.

"If that's what you want, Peaches." I helped her regain her feet, never allowing my fingers to leave her warmth, and found the condom package, tearing it with my teeth.

"Wait, baby." Her voice was smooth and low, suddenly more controlled as she took the condom from me. "Let me help you with that; I want an up-close look at what I'm about to wrap myself around." With that, she dropped to her knees and blew out a long, warm breath across the broad crown of my cock. I could see her eyes widen in the faint light as she studied my dick and reached one hand up, carefully caressing my testicles. "Fuck. This is beautiful. So thick...long. I'm going to enjoy this ride a lot." She rolled the condom onto me and stood up, wrapping one leg around my waist. Her face tilted up, and she stared into my eyes. "Take me, Davis. And don't be nice."

I pulled her close once again and fisted my cock, using the head to stroke slowly from her entrance upward, dragging the slick heat across her clit. "Jump up a little and wrap your other leg around me, Peaches." She leaned against the wall, steadying herself with both hands on my shoulders, and circled my waist tight with both legs. Once she was situated, she looked back up, gaze hooded. "Give me your eyes now, Lucinda. And take my cock." I slid myself a couple of inches into the tight heat of her pussy, studying her face.

"More please, Davis." She groaned the words as she

tightened her legs around me.

I pushed carefully, stopping when she bit her bottom lip and gasped a little. "No…give me just a minute. I can do this." She took a couple of breaths, then leaned in toward me and melded her lips to mine. Kissing me thoroughly, she pulled me further into her with her legs, groaning into my mouth as I sunk the final few inches of hard cock into her snug little pussy.

My mouth was tight against hers as I began to thrust, gently at first, then picking up speed as she continued to groan into my mouth. "Almost there, Davis…" Her hand slid from my shoulder to between us. Her hips thrust to meet my length and her fluttering fingers. "I need to feel you coming, baby; it's so much better with a throbbing cock inside."

I was past ready to come apart as I plunged in and out of Luckie, helping myself to every part of her mouth as I did. Then, in the edges of my consciousness, I heard voices in the hallway.

Fuck. That.

"Don't listen, Peaches. Just you and me. You and me."

She rode me like a drunk sorority girl on the bull at Gilley's, her voice rough. "I don't care who sees. I'm coming—let 'em watch." And with that pronouncement, her tight heat spasmed, pulsing rhythmically as she struggled to breathe. "Fill my pussy, Davis…fill it up."

My ass clenched at her directive, and I held her tight to me. As I pumped my substantial load into the condom, all I could think was how I wished I was bathing this beauty's center with my seed. My head spun, and I kissed her deeply, swallowing her whimpers and gasps with my mouth. My length still pulsed inside her, but I already knew.

I'm gonna need more of this. Soon.

A minute passed before we untangled slightly, and I looked wordlessly at her beautiful face. Illuminated in the scant light, she was glowing and sated; a small smile played around her lips. She tightened her pussy on my softening erection, still inside her, in a little hug. And then she giggled.

Actually *giggled*.

I smiled, dropping my forehead against hers, and wondered if she'd go to dinner with me.

Fuck. What just happened?

Chapter TWO

"You Really Got Me Going"

Lucinda

I turned over for the third time in less than an hour. The sun was intense, but I'd staked out my favorite pool lounger just after lunch and settled in for the afternoon. A big canvas umbrella shaded my sensitive skin, liberally protected with SPF one zillion. My oversized pool bag was stocked more adequately than usual—two erotic romances, sunscreen, two water bottles and a giant insulated cup full to the brim with vodka and grapefruit juice. Vitamin C was, as usual, of paramount importance.

It might be pushing it a bit for a lone Saturday at the pool, right after lunch, but things were far from status quo. I'd just returned from Camille's bungalow where Vivvie Travis gathered the gang to help Cami pick an outfit for her date tonight with the new squadron commander.

Vivianne, known variously as Viv and Vivvie, was one of the other nurses who worked in the emergency department with Camille and me. Her brother, Jacob, was a pilot whose squadron, the Scorpions, had hosted the flight suit party last night at the

O'Club. As for Camille, she was my forever bestie, dating back to the wild roller-coaster ride of nursing school. We were family to each other. It was nothing short of a fucking miracle that Camille was venturing back into dating territory this evening. Sure, she had done the blind-date thing occasionally in the past and a fix-up here and there, but I knew her heart wasn't in it. She wouldn't have succumbed to it at all, had it not been for the driving urge she had to please the women she regarded as her family.

Me in particular.

I was fortunate that between the lovebirds swooping through the O'Club bar last night and the confusion caused by the barrage of Cupid's indiscriminate flying arrows, Davis's flight to the coat closet with me in tow went undetected. Even with the foot traffic to the bathrooms passing the closet doors, we'd entirely escaped notice, as far as I could tell. There hadn't been a word about it this morning, and the focus stayed on Camille and Nathan—right where it belonged. Nathan Morgan was the new Scorpion flight commander who'd caught my friend's eye. He was tall and dark—the brooding, mysterious type. Very bangable.

Don't get me wrong. I'm not a girl who's shy about what she wants—or about sex in general. That much was apparent when I dirty talked my way into a coat-closet fuck in a public place with a tall blond who was hung down to his goddamn knees. A smile played around my lips as I remembered the "meet-cute" in the bar with our friends clustered around. I thought I played it pretty damn cool on the surface, but those deep green eyes and thick hair? The drawl alone had my heart pounding out of my chest. My panties would probably have been wet, had I been wearing any. He was a huge, delectable man in every way that mattered. At five foot ten, I towered over practically every woman I knew and many of the men. I was comfortable with my body and content to be the tallest girl in the room, but the price of admission was never feeling…what? Diminutive? Sheltered in a man's arms? Not that I required any of that, but it would be a pleasant change. And did Davis Payne Foster ever deliver in that department. He held me against the wall with no apparent effort and fucked an orgasm out of me in record time.

The vodka in my cup was there for a purpose. There was a very particular reason I hadn't mentioned a word about the incredible encounter to the women I also counted as my family. Unlike Camille, I dated occasionally. Nothing serious, but I'd had a few short-term men in my life and over the course of my years in Tucson. There had even been the occasional one-night stand. Sometimes hormones and alcohol and frustration combined in perfect proportions. But even that didn't explain last night.

Something unusual happened. Something passed between us that was fundamentally different from what I'd sensed with men before, even though we'd only crept off for a hasty coat-closet bangfest. And I wondered if he felt it too.

That called for day drinking. So I settled in with the second novel, enthusiastically recommended by Sam, and tried to lose myself in its pages. Sam, aka Samanthe Barber, was one of the nurses Cami and I worked with in the ED. She was gorgeous, intelligent, and knew her way around the bedroom better than anyone I knew; when Sam recommended a one-handed read, it was a guaranteed page-turner. This book was no exception— the plot was engaging, the heroine long-suffering, the sex off the charts—but I was drifting. I took a long drink of my vodka and grapefruit concoction, contemplating the wisdom of adjourning to my apartment for a nap. But the sun was hypnotizing, and I dozed. Eventually, the paperback slipped from my fingertips to the concrete.

It was difficult to say how much time passed before I roused enough to sense delicious pressure on the arches and balls of my feet. Nirvana. My eyelids were like lead, courtesy of the sunshine and vodka, but I forced them open, feeling the urge to thank whoever was responsible for the pleasure my feet were enjoying. Focusing slowly, I could just make out the immense male figure at the foot of my lounge chair. Muscular, but not overly so—and staring at me with dark green eyes, hooded and hungry. I couldn't manage a single clear thought.

"Davis. Why are you rubbing my feet?"

This was better than an unexpected day off.

"God, please don't stop." I wiggled with a satisfied groan, so he didn't misinterpret. Then a chilling thought crossed my mind.

How does he know where I live? This is creepy.

His drawl draped around me like an embrace. "Well, Lucinda, when I saw you there…I couldn't help but touch you, Peaches. I hope you don't mind."

I blinked and tried to shake myself awake. "Uh, I don't…no, I don't mind." I grabbed my wide-brimmed hat, jamming it unceremoniously onto my head and tilted my gaze up to meet his, needing clarification. "How did you find me here?"

Scratch that.

"*Why* did you find me? And what's with this 'Peaches' thing?"

His chuckle was low and smooth, and he moved to the neighboring lounge chair, giving my foot a gentle squeeze before releasing it. The bulge in his navy blue bathing suit, right between powerful thighs, was impossible to miss. I could feel my throat working as one hand blindly sought the cup of liquid courage on the concrete next to my lounger.

Davis grinned and reached just past me to hand me the cup. As he straightened, his lips hovered momentarily near my ear, and he whispered softly. "It just makes me harder when you stare at my dick, Luckie. I'm working overtime to be a good guy here, so give me a break, would ya?"

I smiled a little, looking down and sipping the frosty drink. I was usually a pretty cool customer, much more acquainted with leading than following. He was flipping the narrative on me. If I could administer a full-strength dose of Luckie, I was pretty sure I'd be back in the driver's seat.

"Sorry to make you uncomfortable, Davis. I wasn't expecting you, but being this close to what you gave me last night is giving me some pretty jarring closet flashbacks." I smiled a big, sunny grin, letting him know I was comfortable with him *and* discussing sex.

He leaned forward, resting both elbows on his knees, and regarded me with a slowly evolving smile. I wondered if the hot volley of innuendo that rapidly developed between us last night at the Club was about to make an encore appearance. His eyes danced a bit, and he shook his head, breaking our gaze and staring at the ground. The heat between us dissipated.

So no repeat performance. He wants something different from last night.

His eyes lifted again and met mine. "Last night was amazing and unexpected, Lucinda. You have to believe me when I tell you I didn't go to Happy's party looking for anything—or anyone. You were an amazing surprise, and I couldn't have predicted what happened. I'm glad you enjoyed it." His eyes blazed, looking into mine. "I sure as fuck did." He held my gaze as he continued. "Please trust me—I've never done anything like that before."

I couldn't help but smile. "You certainly seemed to know what you were doing." I sipped and waited.

He shook his head, grinning at me. "I've done *that* before. But, Luckie, all kidding aside, I don't normally operate like that." The smile faded, and a serious expression replaced it. "I'm not that guy. But you affected me in a way I haven't…I mean, I haven't felt like that before, Lucinda." He was so earnest, as if it were critical that I believed him.

Well, slap my ass and call me Sally.

I settled back into the lounge chair. "I didn't think less of you, Davis. Remember, there were two of us naked in that closet." It was a particular gift that Davis was shirtless; I tried to focus on what he was saying, but the drawl made me want to lick his face. The cadence and inflection of his words varied with what he wanted to convey. When he turned on the flirtatious charm, his voice was deep and everything seemed to slow to an agonizing crawl. It made me wet.

Good God, Luckie. Stop staring.

He leaned on one muscular arm as he spoke. "I'm acutely aware of who was in the closet, Peaches; I just want you to understand the man who's sitting here with you. And by the way, I didn't know you were at the pool—didn't know you even lived here. I don't get to the pool very often. How long have you had an apartment here?"

I extended my foot back toward him, wiggling it in his direction. "I moved in a couple months ago. My old complex had a sad little outdoor area with broken concrete that was as hot as the surface of the sun. There was only a tiny pool and no place to cook out. It was time for a change."

He grabbed my foot with one hand, kneading it like before. "Damn. I hate moving. I'd do almost anything to avoid it." He reached one hand into the little bag he'd set next to my chair and pulled out a cold beer, neatly popping the top with his one available hand.

I laughed out loud. "So an Air Force career was the obvious choice for you?"

He laughed and nodded. "Occupational hazard, I guess. But I wouldn't do anything else."

The relaxed laugh turned into silence, and we both sipped our drinks. He paused and took a couple of long slugs of his Samuel Adams. I admired his strong throat and was almost taken by surprise when he broke the quiet. "Hey, umm, Luckie? This might be coming out of left field, but I was wondering something." He seemed uncharacteristically at loose ends, rubbing his thumb nervously along the cold can. "Would you be interested in dinner with me tomorrow night? Or, you know, next weekend, if you're tied up tomorrow." His words tumbled together as he hurried along. "That's kind of soon to ask. But I was just wondering. You know." I had to rein in the urge to sigh and bat my eyelashes.

He's so fucking adorable I could die.

This was the guy who sweet-dirty talked me naked in the dark last night, fingering and filling my pussy and making me come. He'd fucked me so good I couldn't remember much about anybody who did it before him.

And now he was anxious about asking me out for dinner. It was about the cutest damn thing I'd ever seen.

I reached out and touched his strong thigh. The skin was warm, and he relaxed noticeably at my touch. "I'd love to have dinner, Davis. Just don't expect me to put out on the first date." I favored him with a cheesy grin. "I'm not that kind of girl."

He caught my hand, bringing it to his lips. "That's not what's on my mind, darlin'. I just want to get to know you a little better." He hesitated as if weighing whether to say what was on his mind. "To tell the truth, I was thinking about it while I was still inside you in the dark."

My mouth slipped open. I couldn't remember a time when a man had rendered me speechless. This could get interesting.

Chapter
THREE

"Only Fools Rush In"

Davis

Lucinda had to work a partial shift and made arrangements to meet me at a gastropub near our apartment complex in the Foothills area of Tucson. Views of the Catalina Mountains north of the city when they were illuminated by the setting sun were spectacular. I sipped my Glenlivet and signaled the bartender, ordering a Belvedere martini for Luckie. She texted me she was walking out of her apartment, having stopped by after work to shower, and would be arriving presently. I thought maybe we'd have appetizers here at the bar, followed by dinner at one of the intimate tables by the window. I'd heard good things about some of the seafood and pasta.

My eyes moved from the palette the sunset had flung across the sky, drawn to the smiling woman who approached me. God, she was riveting. She crossed the room like a trained thoroughbred with the eyes of several men and at least one woman locked on her. I couldn't blame them for that. Her eyes were light, a toffee color that contrasted beautifully with her burnished skin.

She wore her clothes effortlessly, neither showing off nor hiding soft curves and long legs I wanted wound around me all night.

Cut it out, D.

It wouldn't be cool to wind up in the closet two nights in a row. She deserved better, and I had an unprecedented desire to give her better—and to get to know what was under the stunning exterior in the process. I'd never had a serious girlfriend, much to the chagrin of my parents, so this desire to dig under a gorgeous shell was a road not yet taken, or even encountered. Something in my blood buzzed and bubbled when she was around, a sure indication that she was extraordinary. Without thought, I rose to my feet and held out a hand as she approached. She reached for my hand, and I brought hers to my lips, barely touching the soft skin.

"You look handsome this evening, Davis." Her eyes locked with mine, and the room melted away. The feel of everything with Lucinda was novel. When out with a woman, I was accustomed to being entirely in charge of the mood from beginning to end. There was something magnetic about her that made me anxious and a bit agitated. I wanted her to like me with an almost juvenile yearning. The lack of certainty was unfamiliar.

"I ordered your martini. How was work?" I pulled out a barstool, guiding her with my hand at the small of her back. Her throaty laugh made my cock thicken against the zipper of my gray dress slacks. Damn, that signaled a long night ahead for my dick.

"Work was the train wreck I've come to expect. It seldom disappoints." She flashed a wide smile, accepting her drink from the bartender. "I can't even imagine going to a workplace and anticipating a predictable or monotonous workday. Today's prizewinner was a bodily fluids situation, necessitating that shower I stopped by the apartment for—and that was my second shower since the shift ended. I won't distress you with the details."

Gorgeous and earthy in one package. I was already enjoying myself and relaxing into the conversation. "At my workplace, if bodily fluids are involved, things have already deteriorated to the point that a significant amount of intervention is required." She laughed easily and turned her barstool to face me, crossing slim legs between mine.

"Thanks for asking me to dinner, Davis. I'm glad you did." She leaned into the back of her seat, sipping the martini, and cocked her head. "It's pretty strange that we live in the same complex, isn't it?" Her gaze was direct but warm.

"It was a very pleasant surprise to find you stretched out on a lounger when I went for a swim." I felt comfortable leaning toward her and resting one hand on her knee.

Her hand covered mine and she looked away, admiring the last vestiges of sunset through the broad windows. A little smile danced over her lips as she looked back at me. I fought distraction, briefly recalling the taste of her mouth, but her voice brought me back. "You've seen enough of the show to understand that I'm a pretty open book. Ordinarily, I get what I want. I assume you've gathered that much?"

No surprise there. Anyone who hadn't already drawn that conclusion wasn't paying attention to the woman they were with. What I'd seen in a few short days told me that failing to pay attention to Lucinda would be a grievous error in judgment. She was a handful.

I removed my hand from Luckie's knee and looked softly to her beautiful face. "I see who you are, Lucinda, and I don't believe I've ever met anyone like you before. I'm pretty confident that I can guess how things ordinarily work in your world." She usually held all the cards and was accustomed to running the table.

Careful now, D.

"But you're about to learn a new game, because I'm not like

anyone you've met before either. I think we're both moving into some uncharted territory. You open to that, Peaches?"

Her eyes widened noticeably as she sipped the martini, carefully replaced it on the bar, and leaned into my space. "To be honest, Davis, I believe I'm more than okay with something new." I wasn't used to feeling this sort of connection with a woman—or anyone for that matter—so I waited. And listened.

She continued without breaking my gaze. "This is the third occasion I've had to enjoy your company, Davis. Only three times over the course of a few days and nothing has gone the way it usually does. Nothing at all." She grinned. "Obviously, I don't usually begin relationships with coat-closet sex, but that's not what I'm talking about." The smile faded, but she continued to hold my eyes. "Something here feels different. If you have a better idea about what's up between us, then you feel free. Take me someplace new—I'm a pretty adventurous girl. Hey, you never told me what's up with the 'Peaches' thing."

I grinned again. "It was a spur of the moment association. When we were introduced, I thought you looked delicious. Irresistible. Like a sweet, ripe Georgia peach. Something I wanted to pick and enjoy." Her eyebrows lifted as she smirked wordlessly. "I hope to have the opportunity, very soon, to taste all of you. I'll bet you're just as luscious to eat as the peaches I loved as a kid."

A dark blush crept across her neck and her breasts swelled gently against the material of her dress. "I think I should thank you for comparing me to a peach without using the term 'juicy,' Davis. Or 'moist,' God forbid. Extra points awarded."

We'd moved to a table and ordered dinner. Now almost two hours had passed, and my face hurt from smiling and laughing. Luckie was drinking orange juice, and I'd swapped to beer, but the conversation picked up steam like we'd known one another forever. Belly laughter punctuated our conversation, and the evening was slipping away.

"You haven't said a word about your family," Luckie protested when I asked a second time about her family's company. Her parents lived in Manhattan and traveled extensively with the family business. Luckie's upbringing in that environment meant she was multilingual (semi-lingual, she laughingly insisted) and very well-traveled. It sounded exciting by comparison to my background as a relative homebody.

"Well, I'm the only son of Emmaline and Davis Payne II of beautiful Savannah, Georgia."

Luckie's face brightened. "Savannah? What an amazing city—Mercer House, Bonaventure Cemetery, Forsyth Park? SCAD, for Pete's sake, Davis. I went with my mom when I was in high school, and we shopped on River Street until the blisters on my feet had blisters. I took my shoes off and finished the afternoon barefoot, but no one seemed to care. We stayed at this haunted hotel, but I can't remember the name." Her brows knit as she tried to remember.

"Maybe the Marshall House," I supplied. "Seriously haunted. They even found bones under the floorboards in some rooms." I lowered my voice and leaned in menacingly. "Probably amputated limbs of Confederate soldiers."

"You won't scare me off with a few dusty bones, Davis Payne. They dragged me out of town kicking and screaming." She grinned broadly. "I'll bet you can still see the marks my fingernails left at the airport when my mother made me get on the plane. You have to promise to take me when you go next time." She shook a finger at me, taking a healthy drink of her OJ. "Promise, now."

A smile spread across my face, followed immediately by a deep blush that began on Luckie's lovely neck and crept slowly until it pinkened her cheeks. The waiter arrived to replace her nearly empty glass. She pursed her lips, looking slightly embarrassed as

I caught one of her hands in mine.

"Why, Miss Page, did you just invite yourself home with me? Is it already your intention to meet my family and prepare to lock me down for all eternity?" I chuckled at her discomfort but reversed course just as quickly as she shook her head ruefully. "I'm only teasing you, gorgeous. We'd have a great time together in Savannah; my hometown would never recover."

She settled back into her chair, the embarrassment dissipating. "It's only the first date—I mean the first real date—but I'm starting to think I'd have the time of my life with you no matter where I was, Davis."

Something warm uncoiled in my gut, satisfying and comfortable. She was easy company wrapped in what appeared to be a remarkably high-maintenance package. Just more proof that appearances could be very deceiving. This woman was, in my experience, well out of the mainstream of the fairer sex.

I stroked her fingers with my thumb and spoke, hoping my tone would convey my thoughts adequately. "I feel the very same way; I can't remember having this much fun in a long time—and that includes the cockpit."

The quiet atmosphere of the restaurant was suddenly and violently disrupted by a woman's terrified shriek and a shout from behind the bar. I was immediately on my feet and moving toward the disturbance, the scene making my gut roil. A portly middle-aged man, expensively dressed, stood next to a barstool, panic washing his features. His hands clenched his throat tightly in the universally recognizable sign of choking. His face was pale and marked with ominously blue lips. Even from across the room, I could easily see the sweat dripping from his puffy face. My mind whirred and spun as I tried to recall the details of the Heimlich maneuver used with choking victims.

My anxiety ratcheted skyward, but there was no need. Luckie's long legs ate up the distance between our table and the bar in no time. She spoke calming words I couldn't hear into the choking man's ear and rapidly positioned herself at his back, her movements economical. His companion, a tiny, nervous-looking woman, wailed in increasingly distressing registers, but Luckie was unflustered. Her long arms circled his girth, rapidly found their position, and abruptly squeezed. Hard.

Nothing.

The woman's wailing escalated, but Luckie coolly repeated the motion. Her biceps flexed with surprising force, and this time the man's feet left the ground.

Still nothing. There was no hesitation from Luckie. A third attempt, and then all hell broke loose.

As the man's feet met the ground, he gasped and vomited impressively all over the shoes of his howling companion. He panted and coughed, resting his weight against the bar, and color quickly returned to his face. Luckie stepped away, checking her Manolo Blahniks surreptitiously, and smiled politely at the bartender's effusive thanks.

I was rooted to the spot. The sparsely populated room gaped along with me as Luckie made her way back across the room to our table. The manager approached, pumped my hand enthusiastically, and insisted that our check was taken care of. I handed Lucinda her purse wordlessly and offered her an arm. She steered us back to the bar and accepted the thanks of the man. His wife frantically dried her eyes, thanking Luckie over and over. She took in the man's appearance, asked a couple of questions, and shook his hand warmly. Once she seemed satisfied with his condition, I moved with her toward the door.

We didn't exchange many words on the short drive back to her apartment. I was a bit dazzled, to be frank. Fighter pilots often got more than their share of attention in public; the mystique assured that people would always ask questions and want to hear stories. But tonight I'd gotten a glimpse of my beautiful companion calmly saving the life of a stranger. It was what she did every day—maybe more than once—in the course of her work, but I'd not given it much serious thought. It was hardly possible for me to think more of her than I did after the best date I'd ever had, but what happened in the restaurant sure as hell upped the ante.

Hand in hand, we walked silently to her door on the second floor, several buildings from mine. Only a few distant lights cast a bit of illumination across her exquisite features. I usually had charm in spades and flirting was second nature, but none of that was helping me now. I leaned closer to her. "You are one extraordinary woman, Lucinda Page. Thank you for an amazing evening; I sincerely hope there will be many more."

Her hand touched mine lightly. "Normally I'd say that depends on the kiss, Davis, but I already know it'll floor me."

The words were still on her lips as I took her in my arms, pulled her close, and allowed my lips to melt into hers.

Chapter FOUR

"Who Run the World?"

Lucinda

"That was some serious fun at the bar the other night, although I think *some* of us had more fun than others." Camille arched one eyebrow comically. "Wouldn't you agree, Belvedere?"

I stuck my tongue out at her. "I had shit on my mind, so I finished my drink a little faster than I should have. Also, kiss my ass." But she was right. I tore through two martinis in short order as visions of Davis ran through my head in a jumbled, thrilling review of the last couple of weeks. My tongue had been looser than necessary, though, and that was bothering me.

Camille wouldn't be deterred. "So…a coat-closet rendezvous? You also mentioned he's, uh, pleasing. Anatomically speaking. Is this a *thing*, Luckie?" Her face softened, and she smiled genuinely. "You know I'd be so happy for you, don't you?"

Objectively, I knew my dearest friend would be delighted to know I'd found someone special. Realistically, Camille had lived a much harder life than anyone I knew—especially during the years we'd been close. She was falling fast for Nathan, the brand-new Scorpion squadron commander, and I didn't want anything, not even what was happening between Davis and me, to pull her focus from the possibility of long-overdue happiness. I wanted to be fully present to celebrate this with her; it already seemed that she and Nate were the real deal.

"Don't be silly, Cam." I picked at my nails. "When have you ever known me to mistake lust for something more?" I raised my eyebrows suggestively. "Have you seen him, girl? He's hot as fuck, but we're just hanging out." Even as the words left my lips, it felt like a bit of treason. I shook it off and changed the subject.

"This office is so small; it's an affront to small offices. Maybe even coat closets." I leaned backward precariously on the back two legs of a chair that looked unreliable on four.

Cami narrowed her eyes and smiled evilly. "I guess you'd be a subject-matter expert when it comes to coat closets." She waggled her brows. "Whore."

I pursed my lips, blowing her a kiss and adding a licentious wiggle of my tongue. "Last I checked, there's only one of us in this pathetic office getting the high, hard one on the regular, my sister. According to my calculations, that makes you the whore. Slut cookie." Easing ever backward until I felt the wall behind me, I stretched my legs and concentrated on trying to pick up a pen with my toes. It's quite a bit more difficult than it looks, at least in socks.

Camille regarded me from her chair on the opposite side of her desk, squinting her pretty blue eyes in faux irritation and adopting a haughty tone. "We'll concentrate on the important topics here, and I'll thank you not to marginalize my office, Miss Page. As you know, your Coach handbag is more spacious and has better lighting. But this office is all mine." She waved her hands dramatically, underscoring the point. "You know I had to fight for this steaming turd of a broom closet, Luckie. Do you remember when I had to keep the schedules and evaluations in my Scooby-Doo binder? This represents a measurable improvement."

Mention of a closet made my neck, then my face, heat; but I wasn't at all certain Cami was referencing my coat closet encounter with Davis. Fortunately, she seemed mostly oblivious; she just was fishing. I gave up on snagging the pen and slipped my clogs back on. "You're right, sister girl. This is the crown jewel of your shit-encrusted Emergency Department Kingdom. I'm probably just jealous."

Camille let loose with an unbridled guffaw. "Oh, yeah. Everybody's jealous of the charge nurse—the least desirable and most hated job in the hospital." She was laughing in earnest now. "But, you know, that extra two bucks an hour makes it all worthwhile." She snorted and stood up, slapping her hand decisively on the desk.

"Enough procrastination. You know what today is, so don't try to delay anymore. You agreed to this, and the group last semester loved you, Luckie."

Today was the end of the first week for our new group of student nurse interns. Three of the local nursing schools used intern programs toward the end of senior year to help their student nurses drill down into their areas of interest. This semester, eight terribly misguided young women and men had elected to spend their time in emergency nursing.

Each student was paired with a staff nurse, working her schedule alongside her and seeing real hospital nursing up close for the first time as graduation loomed. Rather than begin the six-week rotation with a series of all-day orientation lectures, Camille preferred to throw them in the deep end on day one. Each week ended with a different experienced nurse from the ED staff holding question-and-answer sessions peppered with informational bits. It was just an hour or so, but, in past years, my session had been extraordinarily popular. This was likely due to my special, unique gift.

I could swear the wallpaper off the walls.

It wasn't an ability I'd purposefully cultivated. It was truly a knack I exercised with unusual flair and one I found utterly necessary as a practicing nurse. If some of it happened to wear off on the untarnished fledglings, it would serve them well in the future.

"Okay, what do you have up your sleeve for the interns today?" Cami searched for something in her catastrophic filing cabinet. "I want you to touch on narcotic usage, medication reconciliation, and issues with our **frequent flyer** population. Opioid addiction and the like."

"No problem, Cami. I had planned to talk about how we handle our frequent flyers after that cute little redhead…"

"Lily," Camille interjected.

"Lily told the resident old Mr. Otto needed Dilaudid for his headache because nothing else worked." I shook my head sorrowfully.

"I feel certain Mr. Otto communicated that directly with Lily and in exactly those terms." Camille was grinning. "Come on, girl. We were that green once, right? Just explain about our frequent fliers and tell them about the file. We know all the usual suspects on sight, but they'll need a crutch for these few weeks while they're with us."

"Not to worry, I've gotcha covered; and I brought refreshments. I'm outta here." I grabbed my tote, overflowing with essentials like ChapStick and bottled orange juice, and headed to the little meeting room reserved for my powwow with the baby nurses. As I walked briskly down the hallway, my phone vibrated, indicating an incoming text.

Mmm. From Davis.

Davis:Afternoon, Peaches. Thinking about you.

Me:And now look what you did. I'm thinking about you too. How's it hangin', Tarzan?

Davis:A little to the left, as usual. Not hanging so much as peeking out of my shorts and asking for attention, thanks to the thought of you.

Me:Why, Mister. Foster. Speaking of your penis and its persistent erection during work hours. How indiscreet.

Davis:I'm done flying for the day. Tarzan??

Me:Hot. Manly. Hulking. I'm hopeful about the loincloth.

Davis:We can negotiate. Want to talk to you about getting away; got something fun coming up this weekend with the squadron. Time to talk?

Me:Not presently, but I'm interested. Got a thing with the students—call after?

Davis:I'll be waiting by the phone, writing in my diary like a middle school girl.

Oh, that boy made me smile. I slid the phone back into my scrubs, shouldered my bag, and swung the door open.

"Greetings, bitches. Mama Lucinda is here to pour knowledge into your empty little brains. Now, who's up for sushi?" I produced a stack of bento boxes from my bag to a roomful of grinning faces.

An hour later, I'd tidied the room and was flipping off lights with a long day in my rearview mirror. I tapped my phone to life and dialed Davis.

His smooth voice sizzled across the line. "How's the most beautiful girl in Tucson?"

His drawl made my tummy flutter—that wasn't at all like me. "Tired after a long day and interested in the fun you mentioned. I have two more long day shifts this week, and I need some motivation to make it until Friday."

Davis laughed easily. "Say no more. I'm here to save your professional reputation and light a fire under that sagging work ethic, darlin'. I'd like to light a fire in other strategic areas too, but we can talk about that later."

It was hard to believe that we'd only been dating for a couple of weeks; being with him was so easy. Everything felt unforced and stood in stark contrast to my past relationships, if they could even be called that. I wondered if my openness to Davis's suggestion of moving toward something new had been the catalyst. Even without pinpointing the cause, I was so content with the state of this new romance. I already found myself looking forward to Davis's company.

"So. You mentioned fun. Whatever it is, I'm in. These nurse interns are sucking my will to live."

"Anything serious, Luckie?" The tone of his voice changed abruptly.

I waved my hand as if he could see the gesture through the phone. "It's nothing to worry about. Three days ago, a chatty, star-struck little intern named Sharpay—that's her actual name—called in to a local morning radio program. She took that opportunity to share the pertinent details of a recent admission, a randy housewife who required surgical retrieval of the business end of her husband's rechargeable drill. She and I had a stern chat—Sharpay and I, not the randy housewife—behind closed doors about patient privacy and **HIPAA**, but it was mostly lost on her. Frankly, she's not one of our shining stars. And I can't figure out who Sharpay had to blow to get a slot in nursing school. Cami and I think it bodes poorly for the profession."

I slid into the driver's seat of my well-loved BMW. Well-loved was a charitable term for "breathing its last." Dad wanted to gift me with a shiny new Mercedes after graduation, but the beauty he was offering came with a plethora of figurative strings tied to

the shiny bumper. My parents were well-off and socially connected. They'd made no small secret of their displeasure when I
announced my intentions to be an RN. First, they cajoled. When
that didn't work, there were bribes and finally threats. I hadn't
been cut off, but stubbornness, combined with scholarships, private loans, and part-time jobs, propelled me through school. I
would've declined their help, but the offer never came. As difficult as it had been, the sense of accomplishment was more than
its own reward. I walked across the stage at commencement with
only Camille cheering me on as she stood in the long line of
graduates behind me, all awaiting diplomas. My parents' refusal
to attend graduation came as no surprise; I was so accustomed to
their disapproval, it hardly stung at all by then. My choices, my
hard work, my reward.

My life.

Davis's voice brought me back to the present. "The Scorpions
are floating the Salt River next weekend—sunshine, beer, inner
tubes. I'm trying to tempt you; is it working? We could drive up
Friday after work and spend a couple of nights in a cabin close to
the water. Can you swing the time off?"

My smile was practically audible. "Now, Captain Foster, that
sounds perfect. Let me make some inquiries and see if the scheduling gods smile."

His voice was low and rumbly; it made the butterflies in my
tummy bonkers. "Gotta bounce, Peaches. You work that schedule hard, baby. I'm craving some unhurried downtime with
you—horizontal. I need to take some time getting to know you
better, Luckie. All of you."

We reluctantly said our goodbyes, but the butterflies kept
wreaking havoc in my belly. This guy was in a class by himself. I
scrolled through my phone quickly to find Gracie's number; that
babe owed me a scheduling favor, and it was time to pay up.

Chapter FIVE

"Gonna Put the World Away for a Minute"

Davis

"Yes, sir." I worked consciously to eradicate any trace of irritation from my tone. Daddy would sense that a million miles away. "I understand, sir."

His voice exuded forced patience. "Davis, it's not that I don't respect your service to our country; I do, and it will play well with the electorate in the future. But you understand your mama and I have always known you were destined for more. Much more, Son."

If I had a nickel for every time we'd had a version of this conversation. There had been dozens, maybe a hundred, since I finally gathered the courage to tell him—one hot summer night before my junior year of high school—that I wanted to attend The Citadel in Charleston, South Carolina and become an Air Force pilot. The Citadel wasn't a hard sell; quite the opposite, in fact. Daddy was a grad, as was my granddaddy. As a legacy applicant with an enviable academic and extracurricular record, I wasn't too worried about rejection. It was what came after that became cause for concern.

"Your service commitment is almost up, Davis. It's time for you to think about getting back home and learning the ropes; that poli-sci degree will make you invaluable at Foster and Sons. With the head you've got on your shoulders and your last name, you're in the State House in three years. And your mama is anxious to begin reintroducing you to the appropriate people in Savannah. This time away in Tucson is costing you sorely in terms of meeting suitable young ladies."

He said "Tucson" like the word soured his mouth. Funny, I felt exactly the same way about the "suitable young ladies." I was well familiar with their ilk.

I'd had the best of Savannah's private education from my first day of nursery school. And the aforementioned females made every effort to sink their well-manicured talons into my hide from puberty onward. Looking back, I couldn't blame them, at least not entirely. Serious pressure was brought to bear on the younger generation in our city to keep up appearances, achieve at the highest level, and marry well. *Very* well. My family name alone would make me a desirable acquisition.

I tried not to chafe under the expectations of my parents; as their only child, the bar was high. I was frequently reminded that failure wasn't an option. But my dreams didn't include a career on the political stage. My father saw things differently, but I'd never addressed the disparity directly. I knew all too well Davis Payne Foster Junior didn't suffer alternative points of view.

And I was a peace-loving son of a bitch.

"Now, Payne. You hush." I could hear Mama tsking him; she was probably standing behind his desk and crowding his phone to talk to me. He pretended to tolerate her corrections—barely—but it was plain to everyone that the sun in his world rose and set on Emmaline Rose Abbott Foster. "Davis knows to do right by his family; there's no need to lecture him." Her voice came closer to Dad's phone. "I'm off to Savannah Women's League, Davis; I'll call later." I heard her heels tapping hurriedly across the marble foyer outside Daddy's study. The room looked like something imported directly from Batman's stately Wayne Manor. There were silk Oriental rugs and acres of mahogany garnished with sparkling Baccarat decanters. A bottle of the single malt Daddy sipped in the evening and offered to guests cost more than my rent.

"Dad, I'm going to have to table this discussion for another time, I'm afraid." I interrupted before things progressed further. "I have a date."

"A date?" His voice thundered back, humor lacing his tone. "Is that what they call it now?" He charged on as I pinched the bridge of my nose. Hard. I could feel the beginnings of a headache as we moved into the second part of this unwelcome discussion. "Nothing wrong with a man scratching the itch, Davis. Unnatural not to, frankly, especially considering the loins you've sprung from." He guffawed as if we shared a private, sexist joke. I remained silent; he didn't require my assistance with this shtick. "Why, when I was your age, no pussy was unavailable to a handsome young barrister on the prowl—the ladies of Savannah were my oyster. I may be getting a bit long in the tooth, but your old dad isn't too old to appreciate a beautiful woman."

I wasn't at all sure he would like Lucinda, though. Because for all her brains, beauty, charm, and endless appeal, Lucinda was also something my dad would never admit he didn't like. She was black. Not that I gave one fractured fuck about his archaic, racist opinion.

I interrupted once again. "Sorry to cut you short, Dad, but I'm running late." I forced a cheerful tone. "Let's catch up more sometime soon." I mumbled my goodbyes and snagged a couple of bottles of water from the fridge. Grabbing an oversized back-pack, I locked the apartment door and jogged toward Lucinda's building.

Approaching her place, I heard an ear-splitting wolf whistle and looked up to see Luckie, perched on her porch rail, waving. My gut twisted and my mouth dried as I took in the dark, long legs and lusciously curved ass barely contained in Daisy Dukes. Good goddamn, I couldn't wait to get my hands all over those curves again, this time with a big, soft bed under us and no time constraints.

"Hey, handsome," she sang out, affecting a drawl she likely imagined mimicked mine. "I heard you had some extra room in your tube—any chance I can come along?"

I took the stairs two at a time, reaching her side quickly. I leaned close to her face, taking in the huge laughing eyes and snaking an arm around her narrow waist. "I may have a little space, sugar, but it's strictly a 'rider with benefits' situation. You down?"

She pressed soft lips against my mouth briefly. Her voice was low. "I like the sound of that. Let's go." I slung her duffel bag over my shoulder, and she pulled a floppy, bright orange straw hat onto her head. On anyone else, it would have looked utterly ridiculous. She looked ready to walk the runway.

"How do you always manage to look like you're going to a photo shoot?" I blurted it out without a thought and immediately hoped she wasn't insulted.

She turned dazzling eyes in my direction and smirked. "Just a product of my upbringing, I'm afraid. My mother would have died before she left the house without full makeup, jewelry, heels, matching handbag—the whole nine. And you can bet she never let me either. I came to dinner during my last visit home without stockings and heels, and it caused a fuss that near-ly ruined the evening. If my father saw these shorts, he'd have a major cardiac event." Her grin grew wider, and she sashayed ahead with an exaggerated roll of her mouthwatering ass, making my cock buck painfully against my zipper. Thank God my cargo shorts were loose enough to afford my dick some cover. This road trip would be just what the doctor ordered.

Chapter SIX

"Take Me to the River"

Davis

I jogged to catch up and grabbed her hand, leading her to my Jaguar coupe, already parked near her building. I opened the door, helped her inside, and then lifted the rear hatch to throw our bags in. Joining her, I clicked the seatbelt and leaned over until my face was inches from hers, studying her quietly.

"Thanks for going with me, Luckie; I sure feel like the lucky one today." I leaned a bit further and kissed her warm cheek gently. The fringe of her long lashes rested against her cheeks as I pulled away. Glossy lips the color of a ripe peach curved into a luscious smile as her eyes blinked open, locking with mine.

"I've been looking forward to being with you all week, Davis. Let's get this show on the road." She grinned as the Jag roared to life and I pointed us toward I-10 and Mesa, Arizona.

"Who the hell orders a Swiss chocolate orange chip milkshake?" I shook my head in mock disgust. Lucinda had insisted on an immediate stop at Sullivan's to "take on basic supplies." It turned out that ice cream was a necessity in her universe. I took a long slug of my vanilla shake and was immediately rewarded with a brutal brain freeze. "Ugh…dammit." I grabbed my head in a fruitless attempt to combat the pain.

"Ice cream headache?" She shot me a concerned glance. "Press your tongue flat against your soft palate—hurry up." Luckie's orders came out garbled as she talked with a mouthful of Swiss chocolate orange whatever. I complied as quickly as I could, pressing two fingers against my pounding head and was surprised when the pain quickly subsided.

"Hey, how did you know that?" I turned to look and found her cheeks still full of too much milkshake. Fucking adorable. She flounced in her seat, adjusting her hat and carefully swallowing a mouthful of dangerous ice cream.

"I know lots of stuff, Davis. It's my job to know truckloads of bullshit, and it comes in handy at work almost every day. That's just one example."

"Not that I'm ungrateful, but you know I'm gonna need more information, Nurse Goodbody." I raised one eyebrow in her direction.

"Okay, okay." She nodded and slurped more of her revolting citrus concoction. "Ring stuck on a patient's finger? Gotta get it off before surgery or an MRI, so grab Windex off the housekeeping cart and squirt it good. Works almost every time. If that fails, wrap the finger below the ring tightly with umbilical tape and 'screw' the ring off." She finger-quoted "screw" with a smile. "It's almost fool-proof, and we don't have to cut the ring."

I smiled approvingly. "Impressive. What else have ya got?"

"Bug stuck in an ear canal? Shine your flashlight down there. The bug almost always makes its way out pretty quick;

they'll move toward the light. And grape juice is the best thing to mix with nasty meds to get kids to swallow them. They love chocolate milk too, but it can curdle, and then you've shot your-self in the foot. The pharmacy will buttfuck you hard if you ruin a med dosage."

I snorted at the unexpected language emanating from her beautiful mouth.

She hesitated only a second or two. "Stinky patient? Try some ground coffee in a container at the bedside and make sure to keep baking soda on the unit to put in the shoes of all your indigent patients. That's just common sense."

Ingenious. She had a thousand tricks.

"I keep a tube of toothpaste in my locker and wash my hands with antibacterial soap, then a big dollop of toothpaste before I eat or take my break. The soap cleans them, but the toothpaste does a better job of killing the smell of whatever stench is ruining my life.

"And this is for patients with a presumed heart attack—you know, crushing substernal chest pain radiating to the left arm—they sweat like whores in church." She spoke quickly and em-phasized the dialogue with hand gestures. "Seriously. We keep a stick of antiperspirant on the crash cart." She hesitated. "Well, we take it off when there are inspections or Joint Commission comes for a 'visit.'" More finger quotes. "Clean the area where the electrodes are placed, then swipe 'em with antiperspirant. Has to be antiperspirant; deodorant doesn't work. Now they can't sweat their electrodes off, and you can get a good diagnos-tic EKG on the big, sweaty guy."

I chuckled, shaking my head. "You're a wonder, Luckie. For that matter, your entire profession is, but I think you're my fa-vorite." We rode along in silence for a short time, the Jag mak-ing quick work of the trip to Mesa. I turned to take in her long form, tucked comfortably into the seat with everlasting legs folded underneath.

"I never told you how much you impressed me the other night." She turned slightly, quirking an eyebrow but never slowing her roll on that damn milkshake. "The choking thing, I mean."

She regarded me. "I guess you know the Heimlich maneuver. Probably some other people in the restaurant did too. You could argue that I saved his life, but someone else would have probably done it if I hadn't. He wasn't a particularly tough nut to crack; I've certainly had worse." She shrugged and looked out the window.

I nodded my head slowly. "I guess that might be true. I do know what to do, in theory. I keep my CPR and First Aid certifications current because I think it's the responsible thing to do, but I'll admit I was a little panicked trying to remember what I theoretically knew. I tried to will it to the forefront of my brain, but you took the situation in hand. And I'll be the first to say it: I was floored. You were cool and didn't break a sweat. He wasn't the only one who was grateful."

Her eyes were soft when she looked back at me. "It's my job, Davis. I do things like that every day I'm at the hospital, and stuff comes easier when you practice it. You know that." She turned more fully toward me. "You also know what it's like to have a job—the thing that pays the bills—that involves life and death every day. In some ways, our worlds are very similar." She lifted her eyebrows and that unacceptable milkshake to her lips at the same time.

Well, she wasn't wrong. But I was still dazzled.

"Besides," she continued, rearranging herself with bare feet on the dash of the car, "all those shortcuts and tips? Those are things you stash in your bag of tricks year after year, learning from everyone you can. And I mean everyone—not just the older RNs, but the nursing assistants, housekeepers—even the docs." She grinned. "Great hacks come from a multitude of sources. Cami and I figured that out fresh out of school."

I nodded agreement. "There's a saying in aviation about the idea that a new pilot graduates from **UPT** with a trick bag full of luck. But to be successful and presumably survive, he has to replace the luck with knowledge and experience. Luck doesn't hold out for long."

"There *are* similarities in our jobs, but yours is more likely to kill you than mine." She shot another devastating smile my direction. "But there are some days the ED will make you wonder if you're getting out alive."

We rode in companionable silence for several minutes before I sensed Lucinda tense next to me and turned to see her thinking hard. She took a breath and met my eyes.

"Camille and I are very close; you know that, right?"

"So you said. Nursing school together."

She laughed a little to herself and relaxed back into the seat. "Yeah, that's when we began our reign of terror, but there's a lot more to us than college history. We both have living parents, but we're also both essentially orphans where it matters."

I startled; this was unexpected and wrenching. "You don't have to explain," I tried to deliver the words gently because I had no idea how she might answer, "but I'd like to know what you mean."

There was another full minute of silence, and I could tell she was gathering her thoughts. "My parents are wealthy and connected, for lack of better terms. That's just the truth, flat out; to say they disapproved of my career plans would be an understatement."

My jaw was slack. "Who could disapprove of a kid who aspired to be a nurse and help people?" The words had barely cleared my lips when I thought of my own father's insistence that I leave the service of my country as soon as possible and go home to Savannah to launch a political career. It was sadly ironic common ground.

"Nursing is a professional career, to be sure, but a pedestrian one in their view. Common," she explained with a generous roll of her eyes. "We do enjoy the respect of the public, generally speaking, but there's a huge part of the job that's very undesirable in the eyes of most people. We deal with blood and other body fluids, the neediest and most marginalized people in the community. Death and dying on a regular basis. To my parents, that was all below me. They wanted me to go into the family biz."

The shared problems got stranger by the minute.

"They deal in import and export. Primarily antiquities—art, pottery, jewelry. I had no interest in it growing up, and I still don't. I went to school without their help—did it by myself with scholarships and loans and stuff."

This girl continued to surprise me; I couldn't imagine dealing with my parental issues in such a straightforward fashion. "I don't know what to say, Peaches; my hat's off. And you said Camille's in a similar situation?"

She shook her head and hesitated. "Not similar, exactly. At the risk of sharing too much, I'll just say her parents didn't want children. Fortunately, some unknown in her DNA rendered her unusually prepared to deal with everything that was thrown her direction. And it was a lot. We only had each other all the way through college, but it was enough." She laughed at a memory that must have crossed her mind. "We pooled the petty cash at our disposal on graduation night and went out for pizza and beers."

She was still smiling, but the story made my gut clench with nausea. The night I'd graduated from The Citadel had been marked with a black-tie dinner at the Wentworth Mansion for north of a hundred well-heeled guests, including the vice commandant of cadets and the mayor of Charleston.

"There's been a lot more water under the bridge since then,

and that's Camille's story to tell. I'll just say that I'm more loyal to her than to my own flesh and blood, and that goes both ways. Which brings me to something I wanted to say. Or ask."

There was more silence from her seat, but I gave her space. I knew Camille was an important friend to Lucinda, but this certainly shed more light.

"Camille has found something with Nathan, something she deserves and hasn't had before. I don't want to divert her attention from what's going on in her heart, even if I don't know exactly where it's leading right now." She sighed and turned again toward me.

"Do you think we could downplay what's going on between us, just for now? I realize we don't even know what that is, for God's sake, but I'm asking because of my friendship with Camille. From my perspective, what happens to her is more important than what happens to me." The words spilled out in a rush, increasingly hurried. "It's not that you don't have my attention, because you do. You very much do." She murmured the last words under her breath, as if they weren't meant for me. Then she reached for my hand, squeezing it, and continued. "I just want to keep us under wraps a little, until we figure it out. Camille has a history of watching out more for her friends than for herself, and I'm concerned that she might run from a good thing with Nathan if she's distracted by the two of us."

The lengthy preamble helped alleviate my confusion; in light of what Luckie said, it made a twisted kind of sense. I diverted my gaze from the monotony of the interstate briefly and lifted a hand to her flawless, anxious face. "Thank you for telling me, Luckie. You're a good friend—the kind we all hope to have. I play my cards a little close to the vest anyway, so I have no problem keeping things quiet." I poked her nose playfully. "At least until I'm so under your spell that everyone knows anyway."

She laughed uproariously. And hiccupped loudly.

"Mmmm...sorry about that." Her body relaxed noticeably in the seat. "I don't have that girlie gene thing that makes the fairer sex coy and flirty, in case you haven't noticed that already." I grinned and shrugged my indifference as she continued. "I just don't roll that way, Davis. For the most part, what you see is what you get. I don't get off on pretending to be something I'm not."

I guessed most men would profess their preference for this in a woman, but I wasn't sure it was really true. I definitely preferred getting my hands on the real thing, knowing who she was and what made her tick. Through our sometimes less-than-desirable and fun-filled experiences at a military college, my best friends always said my motto was, "It's better to know." A left-handed compliment if I'd ever heard one, but that summed me up pretty well.

"I'll keep a lid on it within reason, gorgeous, but I can't guarantee everyone within a mile won't know I'm crazy about you."

Chapter SEVEN

"Hot Fun in the Summertime"

Lucinda

The sun was already dipping, and the Scorpions swarmed two grills, rapidly turning out burgers and brats as we arrived. Davis parked the Jag and made short work of checking in before delivering our bags to our cottage. I'd already found a place in the line and was making introductions when he joined me.

I was chatting with Rock, dark and terribly handsome, when Davis's big hands slid along my hips.

"Dude, you're not moving in on my girl, are ya?" Davis's voice was full of laughter as he took the partially filled plate I offered with a grin.

"No way, D. Just playing host." Rock was curiously attired in a damp bathing suit, a hoodie, and a cowboy hat. He also held a mostly-spent bottle of Cuervo, corked, that he was apparently not drinking. His charcoal gaze returned to me. "As I was saying before we were rudely interrupted by the Incredible Hulk, I am the **PROJO** of this gig, so feel free to direct all questions to me.

Have you ever floated the Salt, Luckie?"

"Oh yeah. Camille and I borrowed a couple of minivans and drove all the new nurses up here last summer. We had a large time, but I had no idea we'd drink so much beer. We shacked up in two rooms at some roach motel right down the road, eating delivery pizza and singing karaoke in the skanky motel bar." I shrugged. "It wasn't a big deal, except there wasn't karaoke that evening." Rock and Davis dissolved into raucous laughter. "I thought we were pretty passable, even without accompaniment. But I was also pretty drunk."

We continued through the line, piling our plates high, as the men continued to grill me about my prior experiences on the Salt. Toward the end, I encountered a beaming Camille who was putting the finishing touches on a burger piled with delicious-looking fresh veggies. She seemed mostly oblivious to the piercing gaze of Nathan, who hovered nearby.

I leaned near her ear. "Happy, baby?"

She breathed out slowly and smiled my way. "Like you can't believe, Luckie."

My heart leaped for my friend; it was one of the ways I could tell what a big part of my life she was. The safety and comfort of her heart mattered more to me than that of my own. It wasn't selflessness; it was just the way our lives were inexorably woven together. Our bond had been forged in the fires of loneliness, difficulty, and tragedy; I counted her more a sister than a friend. To see the blush of new love lighting her face was the long-awaited fulfillment of hope I'd harbored. It made the weekend even better than I'd anticipated. I lifted my hand to her cheek as Davis and Nathan looked on. "Take care of you, babe. We'll catch up tomorrow."

She nodded in agreement over her shoulder as Nathan gave a half wave and a smile before taking her free hand. They walked together toward a quiet area of the expansive lawn stretching out in front of the riverfront cottages. I sighed my contentment and turned my attention back to Davis.

"Come on, Peaches," Davis swung an arm casually around my shoulder and guided us toward a picnic table where several of the pilots already sat, devouring their dinner and laughing loudly at a story one of the women was telling. She'd abandoned her meal and was spinning her yarn between sips of beer aided by effusive hand gestures.

Davis sat my plate next to hers and helped me across the bench before settling his solid frame next to me. "What kind of bullshit are you spewing, Miles? Which should I be over here defending—my character or flying prowess?" He grinned affectionately at the woman next to me as I gave her the once-over.

She was tiny; no more than five foot one, certainly, with elfin bone structure, bright blue eyes and milky skin that looked as if it'd never seen the sun. I hoped she'd brought that sunblock they used for babies. By far the most riveting thing about Miles—and what kind of name was Miles, anyway?—was the most astonishing mane of curly red hair I'd ever seen. It probably would've fallen almost to her waist had she not pinned it on top of her head in a haphazard mass.

She sniffed in faux disgust at Davis. "I'll have you know this particular story doesn't involve you in any way, Deliverance. The world doesn't spin on its axis around your pretty mug." She turned her attention to me and stuck out her hand. "I'm Charlotte Christman, but everybody calls me Miles." She laughed and shook her head. "What I meant to say was, call me Miles."

I squeezed her hand, smiling. "I'm Lucinda Page, but you can call me Luckie." I hesitated. "So, should I ask where the nickname comes from?" I might not have asked, had her demeanor been less than completely friendly, but I felt immediately at ease around her. Fighter squadrons had a habit of assigning **call signs** that functioned as nicknames. Davis's sexy Southern drawl and Savannah roots earned him the call sign "Deliverance." He could've read the dictionary, and the drawl would've still made my panties wet. I noticed everyone except me seemed to refer to him with the moniker, so I assumed he took no offense. I was curious about Miles's nickname, but there were others I wouldn't dare inquire after. Most notably, one of the flight commanders evidently answered to "Hung." There had to be a story there, but it was one I'd wait to hear in private.

Rock, whose given name was Hayes Hudson, sauntered by just then; he now carried a large, hot-pink bullhorn in addition to the partial bottle of tequila from earlier. He leaned down to stage-whisper conspiratorially near my ear. "I'll save you some time there, Luckie, because you won't get a straight answer from any of these clowns. The pocket-sized Lieutenant Christman has a spectacular set of stems." Noting my confusion, he quickly clarified, "Legs. She has long legs. Miles of legs. Get it?" He raised his eyebrows to confirm my understanding and was off, fumbling with the bullhorn.

I elbowed a still-smiling Miles. "You could do worse." She nodded her assent, and we both dug into plates full of food.

A small group of the younger pilots built a fire in the pit near the swimming pool as dinner concluded and cleanup began. I cleared plates and napkins along with Miles, chatting amiably, as Davis set to work cleaning one of the two large grills with a wire brush. There were so many helping hands that the work seemed done before it had begun. The next order of business was apparently drinking by the fire, now blazing in earnest, so we dragged folding chairs from the porches of individual cottages.

Setting up around the fire pit, I encountered Vivvie, effortlessly gorgeous in a tank and khaki shorts. "What's doin', Viv? Camille said you'd be here." I looked around the crowd quickly. "I heard you're with...umm...Hung, is it?"

A diabolical grin lit her face. "I guess that remains to be seen, technically speaking, but I'd wager the rumors are true." She grabbed one of the chairs I carried as we moved toward the fire. "That's just his nickname. It's Walker...Walker Jackson. He hasn't addressed it directly, but I've heard it has something to do with a flying story. Not how he packs his shorts." She snorted. "Anyway, I like him. What's up with you and Deliverance? That was some introduction the other night at the flight suit party."

She had no idea.

I shrugged casually. "We're just hanging out. This sounded like fun, and I knew you two would be along. So why not?"

Viv's expression was dubious. "I'll just save us some time by not calling bullshit right now, but I absolutely reserve the right to do so later. Or sooner." We set up our chairs around the outside of the gathered group just as I noticed Hung, with a beautiful guitar in his hand, exiting the cottage he and Vivvie would be sharing. He searched the crowd, obviously looking for Viv and made a beeline for us once he saw her.

Hung—maybe I'd call him Walker, too—reached us just as Davis did. Davis handed me an icy cold Stella and offered the other one to Viv. "No thanks, Davis," she smiled up at him just as Walker put a hand on her waist and nuzzled her neck affection-ately. "I'm gonna look around for something lighter."

A full-sized pickup truck, full to the brim with bottled water, beer, and ice, was parked under a tree nearby and functioned as a self-serve bar. "Well, Viv, if you need somebody to dig in the ice, I'm your man. Looks like we're in for a treat; Hung's gonna entertain the troops." He clapped Walker on the shoulder and took my hand.

The music started almost immediately, and I was gratified to hear Walker's pleasing baritone taking on Eric Clapton's "Change the World," a favorite of mine. Settling back into a folding chair, I closed my eyes and took a long drink of the cold beer. Davis lifted my hand to his lips and touched my fingertips with sweet kisses. "I'm not going to lie, Lucinda Page." His voice was quiet, the words meant only for my ears. "I've thought a lot about how pretty you are, how smart and funny. And I've thought quite a bit about how much I hope you like me and how we'll be spending a lot more time together. And about how impressed I am with your drive and accomplishments." He was quiet for a second before continuing. "But, in these past couple of weeks, I haven't thought about anything nearly as much as I have thought about how badly I want to lie on top of you on a soft bed, fucking your pretty, pink pussy and making you come all night long."

My tummy flipped over and a soft, insistent throb set up between my thighs. I picked up my head, opened my eyes, and looked into the beautiful face of the man who'd not left the forefront of my mind since the night we met.

"I guess women are supposed to play it cool and distant when it comes to attraction and sex, but I told you that wasn't me. I don't play hard to get—I *am* hard to get. But you got me, Davis, and I've been thinking of all those things, too. And I can't wait to feel you inside me again."

He squeezed my hand. "It's a perfect night, and we've got all weekend, Luckie. Let's enjoy every minute."

The music and the symphony of crickets provided the ideal soundtrack as the fire died off slowly. Something good was afoot with Davis and me. After a lifetime of nothing special, maybe I was finally going to find out what all the fuss was about.

Chapter EIGHT

"In the Still of the Night"

Davis

The fire was nearly out, and the music stopped when Hung became more interested in whispering in Viv's ear and stroking her calf than playing Paul Simon and Dave Matthews Band songs. This place reeked of the kind of romance women dug, and couples started making their excuses and saying goodnight after Hung and Vivvie's exit. We'd both finished our second beer when I stood, folded our chairs and took Lucinda's hand. I had every intention of ensuring that we both had clear heads and a very long, unhurried night for what lay ahead.

The walk to the far end of the property where our cottage was located took several minutes. Lucinda and I walked mostly in silence, loosely holding hands. The quiet was deafening; I *had* to ask, "What's on your mind, Peaches?"

She looked introspective. "I'm not the girl who has relationships. I date now and then, but…"

It was unusual to hear hesitancy in her voice; she was normally so sure of herself. "Go on, Luckie. I really want to know what's swimming around in that head of yours."

She waited a few more beats before continuing. "Again, I'll remind you that it's not in my nature to be less than straightforward." She grinned and shook her head. "Think of me as one of your male friends, but with a great rack."

She cleared her throat and continued. "I date now and then, but I can't say there's ever been anyone for me..." I waited patiently for her thoughts. "Anyone who made me feel the way you do. You know, whatever this is."

Whatever this is. I didn't have a fucking clue what was up between the two of us, but I'd never found myself so anxious to uncover the next chapter. I fumbled around in my pocket for the old skeleton key, unlocked the door, and slid my hand up to grip the back of her neck, pulling her to me. "Well, babe. Let's get busy figuring it out—whatever it is."

The cottage was old and constructed of stone; the wood floors were worn smooth from years of use. A fluffy queen-sized bed occupied the arched alcove at the far end, heaped with white linens and a voluminous feather duvet. I wondered how it would work; I hadn't slept in anything smaller than a king-sized bed since my growth spurt in middle school. My bed at home was a California king. Pitfalls of a build like Dwayne fucking Johnson. Actually, that might be a slight exaggeration.

Although it had been a very warm day, the ancient cottonwood trees that thrived along the riverbanks kept the cottage cooler than expected so the bed would be comfortable as the night wore on. Lucinda moved to turn on a bedside lamp, but I caught her hand and pulled her to my chest, tipping her face toward mine. Dim moonlight streamed in through the open window over the bed, illuminating her wide eyes and the pulse beating a rapid thrum at the base of her delicate neck.

God. Is she nervous?

"I've thought a lot about tonight, Luckie." My whisper was

soft, an unconscious effort to preserve the silence around us. "But I want you to know I'm not assuming anything. Tonight, hell—tomorrow and every day after that—I won't have any of it be more or less than you want. My body wants you more than my next breath, but nothing happens unless you say so."

Her body was so soft against mine, and there was no mistaking my erection between us. Even so, I pulled her closer and pressed several soft kisses to her plump lips. In no hurry, I trailed my mouth across her jaw and sucked gently at the warm skin of her neck. A soft moan escaped her, and it played in my ear like sweet music, but I waited for her consent before moving any further.

She reluctantly pulled away from my lips until I could see her hooded eyes. Her voice was as soft as mine had been. "There's nothing I don't want tonight, Davis. I want everything you have to give me. I need every inch of your thick cock; I want to feel you in my mouth and throat. I want to feel your mouth on my pussy. Do whatever you want with me. I'm so fucking ready for you."

It took every ounce of resolve to avoid ripping her clothes off and burying my aching length inside her, but that wasn't what was on the menu tonight. I pressed my hungry mouth again to hers, first asking permission and then sweeping inside. Our tongues tangled lazily as my hands reached under her tee to stroke her soft skin, feeling goose bumps rise under my fingers. I moved from her lips only briefly to pull the shirt over her head and quickly release the front catch of her lacy bra with one motion. Her breasts molded to my chest, in need of my mouth, and suddenly nothing was happening quickly enough.

At the foot of the bed sat an old chest, the kind used to store keepsakes. It might have been an antique, but it was probably just old. More interesting, however, was the oversized mirror that tilted against the wall directly across from the chest. I led

Lucinda by the hand, turning her to face the mirror and positioning myself behind her.

"Now I want your eyes open and watching yourself in the mirror. You can bet I won't be taking my eyes off you, baby." My mouth was against her ear, and I spoke so quietly she could barely hear me. "Now just watch. And feel." She let a small groan escape as she watched me speak to her, both of us reflected in the old mirror. "Wait for it, Peaches, and I'll give you everything."

My hands wrapped around her slim waist and stroked upward toward the bottom of her breasts, never quite reaching the sensitive curve underneath. Her slender arms twined around my neck, turning my ear toward her lips. She groaned low, and hissed, "Touch me there, Davis, I need it." Her knees softened, lowering her breasts into my hands.

I rolled one nipple in my fingers until the tip pulled taut, and carefully tightened until she grimaced. "Be patient. Take what I give you, Luckie." The other hand dropped to the button of her shorts, opening it and allowing them to drop to the floor. I pulled her backward until my legs brushed the chest at the foot of the bed. Removing one hand from her body, I made short work of my remaining clothes and toed out of my shoes. Holy shit, she was so warm; I loved feeling her melt into me. "Now sit on my lap and spread your legs wide."

I sat on the chest, studying the full-length view of Lucinda as she settled on top of me, the crease of her delectable ass hugging every inch of my heavy cock. Before she could turn to reach for me, I moved her knees outside mine, leaving her center open to my eyes and hands and only barely covered with a tiny lace thong the color of sunshine. "Reach back and wrap your arms around my neck again, Lucinda. Don't move your hands. Keep your eyes on the mirror, gorgeous, and watch me touch you. Then we can both watch you come."

I moved my lips to her neck, licking and sucking softly, all the while allowing my hands to drift upward until the backs of my fingers were stroking tight nipples. Her hips began to thrust gently, imploring me to touch. My cock felt like a goddamn spike between the cheeks of her ass. Apparently, words were mostly off the table, because she moaned and rolled her head backward onto my shoulder, eyes fluttering closed. The fingers of one hand continued to caress her breast, paying special attention to the sensitive tip with feathery light touches, but the other hand gripped an erect areola and applied increasing pressure until her thrusting hips begged for relief.

"Eyes open, Luckie." I eased the pressure on her nipple and allowed my hand to stray downward across her tight belly. "Let's see if my tight little peach is slick and ready to come. I'm going to touch you now, beautiful; watch me…let's see if my baby is wet." Her breath came in short pants as she waited for my fingers to touch her center, the folds already visibly damp with arousal. She stretched her legs wider and pushed her hips upward to meet me. I pushed the lace aside, and my fingers finally reached her slit, wet and ready to be filled. But I only slicked one finger and began to lazily circle her clit. My other hand turned her face, kissing her mouth hard with bruising lips. She attempted to pull away and moans escaped as she tried to plead for more, but I pulled her closer and continued to lick deeply into her mouth and nibble on her lips. The finger on her clit never hesitated or slowed, and I felt it swell while her pulse beat a steady rhythm against my fingertip.

"Come for me, sweet girl. Come on my fingers and watch with me." I gently moved her head until it faced the mirror. There she could see her long body, legs open and pussy beautifully displayed with my fingers on her swollen core. "When you're ready, baby."

In the dim light, I watched the mirror, entranced, as her pussy began to tighten and then contract. Lucinda's face was riveted to the sight of her body in the clutch of orgasm. Her mouth opened, gasping through the spasms of pleasure that her body rode like an ocean wave. Gradually, the panting slowed slightly, and the sporadic tightening at her center ebbed.

I was nearly speechless. Several moments ticked by, my cock throbbing and roaring its anguish at my inattention. Finally, I breathed low in her ear, "God, you are so fucking breathtaking when you come, Lucinda." She exhaled softly, shuddering slightly as she did. "If I did nothing but touch you until you came apart in my arms, over and over, until the sun came up…it would be the best night of my life."

I could see the reflection of her smile in the mirror, and her arms tightened around my neck as she turned to look into my eyes. "I'm not voicing any objections to more orgasms, so don't mistake me here, but I'm hoping my pussy will be full of that thick cock the next time I come."

Fuck. Yes.

She lifted her ass a little, and I helped her slide the scrap of lace to the ground, leaving us bare to one another. Reaching between her legs again, I found her warm and welcoming with arousal now generously bathing her lips and thighs. Slipping two fingers inside, we both watched as they disappeared into Lucinda's warmth; then I fucked her slowly with my fingers, kissing and lapping at her neck. Luckie rolled the soft cheeks of her ass as I fingered her, massaging my cock until I could feel the precum leaking from it, anointing our heated skin.

"Please, Davis. I can't stand it anymore; I need to be full of you." Her voice was tinged with pain, and she ground her pussy onto my fingers. "Please give me your cock, Davis."

My length sprang free as she lifted her body, and my fingers withdrew from her. I plunged my fingers into my mouth, savoring the salty sweetness of Lucinda's addictive little cunt and reached for my suffering cock with the other hand. Luckie stood and turned to look at me, eyes riveted on my length as I stroked it slowly for her, root to tip. The crown was nearly purple and leaking profusely.

Her voice was rough. "I need you to feed me. Let me taste your cum, Davis. I…I need to taste you." She fell to her knees between my spread thighs without invitation and opened her beautiful mouth to take my crown in with no hesitation. Her tongue bathed me, lapping and swirling, and she stopped more than once to swallow my offering. Groans in the back of her throat tortured me with the vibration, but I thrust upward carefully, savoring her warm mouth. Then, haltingly, she worked the considerable length of my cock further until the ridge encountered the back of her throat. There was a brief hesitation that made me look down. I affectionately stroked her cheek, and her eyes looked up to meet mine.

Wide caramel-colored eyes locked on mine. Lucinda took a deep breath and swallowed hard, taking the head of my swollen cock into her throat.

Oh, God. Never.

I'd never felt myself lodged in a woman's throat, and the drive to come was almost unbearable. Hard throbbing pounded at the base of my shaft, and I immediately reached below her face, tugging roughly at my balls to prevent myself from coating her throat.

"Fuck, baby." I withdrew until I felt the head of my protesting dick pulled free of her throat, and she gulped in air, her big eyes watering a bit. "I haven't ever felt anything like that. Not ever." I could barely grind the words out as I lifted her from her knees by both hands.

"You shouldn't have stopped me, Davis. I wanted to taste you." Her words should have been light, teasing, but she was intense, and need tinged her voice. "I wanted to feel you come in my throat and swallow everything you'd feed me."

"I'll feed you a nice, warm load from my cock someday soon. Stand in front of you while you're on your knees, and pump myself into your mouth. Then I'll lick your gorgeous cunt and tongue your clit so you can come with my taste on your tongue." It took every ounce of focus to grab the condom I'd dropped on a side table and sheathe myself with the mental picture of Luckie on her knees, taking me.

I returned her to my lap, thighs spread, and began to lower her body, steadying my shaft with one hand until it spread her lips. The arousal from her pussy ran down my dick, wetting my length first, then my balls. Both our eyes were fixed on the reflection in the mirror as I lowered her steadily, filling her snug little cunt. I pushed to position myself firmly inside, my ass cheeks lifting from my seat.

There was a groan from low in her throat, and she balanced a bit of weight on her toes, avoiding the last inch or so of my shaft. Reaching around her, I dampened one finger in her slit and caressed a nipple softly. "Come on, Peaches, take all of me. Try to relax and let me give you what you need." I added the other hand, circling her swollen clit, and watched her face carefully in the mirror. The walls of her pussy clenched as she relaxed into my chest, very slowly allowing me in. "That's it, sweet girl. Let me fill you up; relax now."

The groans returned as soft moans, all her weight on me now, and her hips began circling again. I recited the alphabet backward, so close I could barely manage to hold off for another second. "Gonna fuck you now, pretty baby…easy does it." I moved one hand to her waist and took some of her weight while relaxing my thighs and pulling several inches from her. Sliding my cock in and out of her welcoming body, I settled enough to stroke her clit rhythmically and quiet the distractions.

God, she was so fucking beautiful, taking me. I'd never had

thoughts like these when I was with a woman before. I was no man-whore; I liked and even cared about the women I'd been with in the past. But this? The awe I felt watching her body take pleasure from mine was like nothing I'd ever experienced. Thoughts that crowded my mind during sex normally flowed along the lines of how good it felt and how much I wanted to come. But her beauty stunned me. The way she let herself feel and enjoy me. I couldn't look away as I gradually coaxed her opening with long, slow strokes.

Luckie's increasingly desperate moans snapped me back into the moment. "I'm close, Davis…you feel so good." Her eyes alternated between closing blissfully and studying the reflection of our bodies where we were joined. "Goddammit, baby, I love watching you fuck my pussy. I want to feel that big cock of yours coming inside me, Davis."

Need bubbled rapidly to the surface, building faster and harder than before. I stroked her clit with more purpose, gently teasing the bare knot that had grown more swollen under my finger. "Once more, Peaches. I want to feel your little pussy milking the cum out of me. Don't hold back, sugar. Let me feel your pussy sucking my dick." The throb in her clit increased under my fingertip first, followed quickly by the tightening muscles of her tummy, and finally, the strong cadence of her orgasm around my cock as she came.

The room was perfectly silent except for the sound of Lucinda's heavy breathing, and I couldn't wait a moment longer. My hips snapped up, and the wide crown of my cock found its home wedged against her cervix, releasing volley after volley of warm seed. My vision blacked momentarily as I filled her, pulling her close and gasping.

Our bodies thrummed together for a time until our breathing finally began to slow, and her soft form relaxed gradually against mine. She shook her head a little as if clearing it and spoke softly. "Oh, Davis, I never…" She swallowed and hesitated. "Well, I just never."

I peppered her damp neck with little kisses. "So good, baby. So damn good. Thank you for letting me give you that. For giving *me* that." I lifted her carefully, made short work of the condom, and led her by the hand to the soft bed. Tucking her close to me, I covered us both against the encroaching cool of the night. "Sleep tight, beautiful. I'll be dreaming about tonight for a long time."

Chapter
NINE

"Down by the Lazy River"

Lucinda

S leeping in Davis's strong arms was my idea of heaven on earth. I woke several times over the course of the night, marveling at the contrast of his hard, muscular body to my soft one. I was unaccustomed to the way his six-foot-three frame made me feel almost petite and totally feminine. He slept soundly almost throughout the night, awakening only once. It was then, around three a.m., that I woke to the rough scrape of whiskered cheeks gently nudging my legs apart. He didn't speak, but only groaned my name softly as he lapped at my pussy and fingered me gently until I came on his tongue. Then he crawled up the length of my limp body, kissed me thoroughly, and tucked me back into the curve of his hard form.

I had never been a great sleeper and woke with the sun. Davis slept peacefully beside me, so I took advantage of the opportunity to admire the hard planes of his nakedness. The sheet had slipped to the foot of the bed, and he stretched nearly the entire length of the mattress. His cock was glorious, even as he slept, wide and thick at rest on his thigh. His arms extended over his head, impressive biceps apparent, and his face took on an innocent, almost childlike appearance in sleep. I debated making a pot of coffee but opted instead to brush my teeth, dress quietly in shorts and a tee, and slip outside for the short walk back to the lodge.

Near the spot where we'd gathered last night, a small building stood apart from the cottages. The door was propped open with a chair, and the unmistakable aroma of strong coffee greeted me.

Yes, child.

I peered cautiously inside and found a small group of Scorpions around the coffee pot, pouring and doctoring their brew. True believers.

"Morning, everybody," I greeted the group and was relieved to see them similarly and casually attired. All, that is, except Miles, who evidently decided to take her chances with a coffee run in PJs. Lieutenant Colonel Chuck Ditka, aka Coach, the Scorpion **operations officer**, was there with his wife, Bibi. They were joined by Miles, Rock, and a couple of younger pilots I hadn't met. The entire group turned and called out greetings, motioning for me to join them.

Miles was barefoot and sporting a stunning case of bed head; she raised a mug as I approached. "Good. You're here. The peanut gallery here has decided to place themselves in charge of the dress code. Make yourself useful and defend my hungover ass."

I filled my cup and drank deeply, welcoming the jolt of caffeine. "I can't see where you're in need of defense, Miles. My services as a jailhouse lawyer are pretty worthless, especially if we were supposed to dress to impress."

Coach was all smiles and found a seat at the old wooden table, pulling Bibi onto his lap. "Aw, don't you worry about these boys, Miles; you know all their taste is in their mouth. They're just flipping your shit to see if they can get a rise out of you before breakfast."

Bibi nodded her agreement. "Yeah, Miles. Joke 'em if they can't take a fuck."

Coach whistled low. "Nice mouth, babe. Come give Daddy a kiss so I can clean that up." It was very early in the morning for the way Bibi kissed her husband. Apparently, they hadn't gotten much sleep either.

Miles's voice was whiny and loud. "Gross! Stop it, Dad. I hate when you and Mom do yucky kissing."

Bibi broke away from Coach and turned to regard Miles with one brow arched. "When you're not around, Daddy and I do a lot more than kiss. And if you think this is yucky, you should see how he…"

"Too much information, Bellamy Bennett Ditka." Coach interrupted Bibi with an indulgent chuckle. "You're the goddamn queen of oversharing."

Bibi stood and moved to refill her coffee. "I just think everyone should benefit from your, um, skill set. Maybe you should offer classes, babe." Her smile was wicked and made everyone laugh.

A very familiar voice spoke from the vicinity of the door behind me. "Morning, campers." I felt the width of his hand wrap the back of my neck before I could turn, and his lips met mine for an unhurried kiss. My tummy flipped like a teenager getting her first smooch. When he broke the kiss, his voice was like gravel. "Peaches."

He walked over to the coffee pot, pouring a large mug. "Morning, Bibi. Beautiful as always." He lifted his coffee in salute. "When are you gonna leave that old man and let me make you happy?" The gaggle guffawed, and Coach rolled his eyes in mock disgust. Davis turned his attention to the remainder of the group. "Did I wander into an early morning **LPA** meeting?"

Rock, the sole member of the breakfast club who was

dressed for the day, shook his head. "No, man, we're just up to help Bibi get breakfast ready; the Scorpion army travels on its stomach."

Bibi stood. "Speaking of breakfast, we'd better get going. We're on a schedule. Buses pick up at eleven, and people will be up and ready to eat soon."

The group dispersed with the majority following Bibi to unload coolers from Coach's truck, but Davis and I refilled our coffee mugs and walked back to the cabin. His voice was low and quiet. "Did you get enough sleep, Lucinda?"

I nodded affirmatively and caught Davis's hand as we walked along at a leisurely pace. "Last night was amazing, Davis. Thank you for taking care of me."

He squeezed my hand. "You're very much worth it, and I love taking care of whatever you need, gorgeous. I hope you know that." We walked back to the cabin, soaking in the quiet beauty of the desert landscape and the placid rushing sounds of the river passing nearby. I didn't doubt my worth, but his words were a treasure, and they played on a loop in my head. I wanted to tell him how much his simple expression of how he valued me meant. The lesson of my young life had been that material things—and the opinion of those who had plenty of material things—mattered more than the people closest to you. I wondered what someone like Davis would think of my family.

Instead of diving into that deep pit, I stepped closer to him as we walked along. "You're pretty special yourself, you know. Thank you for inviting me; I'm having a lot of fun." I turned to him, grinning. "And the party hasn't even started."

We changed into bathing suits, shorts, and sandals and quickly made our way back to the gathering place where Scorpion Breakfast Central was humming with activity. The ingredients for breakfast tacos were spread out across a couple of tables, and small bottles of milk and orange juice chilled in the dregs of ice in the pickup truck bed that was now pulled along-side our breakfast area. Rock called the curiously hot-pink bull-horn into service for an announcement.

"Attention in the area. Stingers: breakfast is served, and bus-es depart at 1100 hours. Cleanup must be accomplished by that time, so eat up. That is all."

I had already recharged my coffee cup and joined Miles and her cohorts to compliment them on the excellence of the break-fast tacos I had enjoyed. "Was that salsa homemade?" I was engaged in grilling Miles when Davis joined me. "Because it doesn't taste like any I've ever had."

Miles must have found time to sprint to her cabin and tidy her appearance; she was barely attired in a skimpy bikini, a cover-up, and serviceable sandals. Her hair had been brought under a modicum of control as well. "I would have no way of knowing about such matters," she informed me with a wave of her hand. "I don't make anything, from scratch or otherwise. Cooking is accomplished with smoke and mirrors. PFM." At my questioning look, she explained. "Pure Fucking Magic. It's how airplanes fly, among other things. She continued while stuffing her mouth with one of the delectable tacos her team had produced. "I don't make food; I buy food. I love a good meal as much as the next gal, but I'm no domestic goddess."

Bibi climbed onto a picnic table and used Rock's bullhorn to address the group. "Scorpions…twenty minutes. Everybody pitch in, and let's clean up quick. We need to pack the coolers and be ready for the buses. Don't forget water and sunscreen—and hats."

The group dispersed, readying for departure according to Bibi's directions, and the time flew by. Buses arrived as adver-tised, and the group loaded up coolers and equipment.

Along the road to the river, gallon jugs of homemade Bloody Marys were passed around and rapidly depleted by the group. In no time, the short ride was over, and we unloaded the buses, laughing and already a bit buzzed. Rock emerged from the back of the second bus with another dark-eyed hottie bearing a huge hot-pink monstrosity down the hillside. I was informed that he was yet another member of LPA, Radley "Boo" Harper. The pink thing was not much smaller than a Volkswagen Beetle and utterly defied description. I turned to ask Davis what the hell was accompanying us into the river, but he was already knee-deep in the frigid water, holding both tubes. "Move your cute ass, Lucinda Page. I'm freezin' my balls off over here." His drawl was punctuated with chattering teeth, and I broke into a jog. He looked good enough to eat with his wide, muscular chest bare and the sparse trail of golden hair dusting his flat stomach and then trailing downward—a very happy trail that led to what I now knew was heaven on earth.

He pulled my face to him as I approached, kissing me sweetly, and pushed my inner tube toward me. "No surrender, no retreat," he yelled, pumping his fist as he leaped, landing on his tube with a mighty splash. I followed him, screeching like a kid as I waded deeper into the icy water, and plopped awkwardly into my tube.

Once everyone was in the water, the mysterious monstrosity was floated out among us and boarded by Rock. We formed a loosely-held flotilla precariously connected with nylon cords, hands, and feet. Five or six oversized tubes held big coolers of ice and drinks, and cold beers were distributed without delay.

"Rock really knows how to throw a party." I took a long drink of my icy Stella and relaxed, arms and legs sprawling wide. "But I still don't know what that ugly pink thing is."

"All will be revealed in due time." Davis's voice was solemn, but his wide smile canceled the effect. "Did you grease up, my dark-skinned princess?" He produced a tube of sunscreen, applying it liberally to broad shoulders.

"You betcha. I cannot live without sunscreen; I'd be a crispy critter in...what the hell?" The hushed canyon was suddenly alive with the raucous opening guitar solo of Boston's "Rock and Roll Band." The sound emanated, inexplicably, from the pink monstrosity; I raised my eyebrows wordlessly in Davis's direction.

"Courtesy of our all-purpose LPA. It's been handed down for a decade or so, but Rock painted it that intolerable fuchsia last week out behind the squadron. He'd been at **beer call** a little too long and decided the river sound machine needed an up-grade. For some unknown reason, there were several cans of spray paint left over from a project, and hot pink was what was available. I can't fathom what that color would be used for in a fighter squadron." He grinned as he finished applying his sun-screen and popped the top on his beer.

We floated along in amiable silence, draped bonelessly over our inner tubes and holding hands loosely in between. The sun and alcohol combination, along with the gentle rocking of my inner tube, had a sedative effect. I drifted in and out. Davis's voice was low and seductive as it floated through my quietude. "I like you a lot, Lucinda. Just...a lot." He seemed to search for words, so I waited with my eyes closed and pulled closer to his voice with our clasped hands. "I know we've both said it, at one time or another, but something here feels...real." I opened my eyes and turned to see his face, the expression earnest. "I don't have better words to express myself, and I'm sorry that I don't, Luckie. But I think you deserve to know what I'm feeling."

His eyes were soft, looking straight into me, and I felt a lit-tle lump in my throat. "I've never met anyone like you, Davis, and I know something's going on. I just feel really thankful for whatever reason fate dropped you into my life." It occurred to me that a couple might normally kiss after this kind of ex-change, but I couldn't tear my gaze from his beautiful eyes, full of affection.

We fell silent again, allowing the water to carry us along. Then he spoke again. "Since I'm falling for you, Peaches, I think we need to get to know one another better. No time like the present."

Chapter TEN

"Talk Dirty to Me"

Lucinda

"So I'll interrogate you on a variety of topics for my amusement, okay?" Not waiting for my consent, Davis hurried along. "We all know that everyone is blessed with a special skill, a gift that sets them apart from the rest of the human race."

I smirked and wiggled my eyebrows. "I think I may have found yours around three a.m., Mister. Foster."

He admonished me with a frown. "Don't be such a dirty birdie, Lucinda. A cultured lady like yourself shouldn't entertain filthy thoughts about me licking your perfect little pussy and tongue fucking you last night." He broke into a wicked grin. "Although it was my pleasure. Now look what you've done; I'm thinking about doing it some more."

Even though we were teasing, my clit beat a happy little tempo at the thought of coming against his lips again. "I'm going to ignore your discussion of my pussy and answer your question. As a matter of fact, I do have a unique gift that sets me apart from everyone else. It's a skill that's highly prized among nurses, yet the level of expertise I enjoy cannot be learned. It is a gift, and I am its caretaker."

He wrinkled his nose and looked at me suspiciously. "This doesn't have to do with blood or needles, does it?"

I laughed aloud. "No, it doesn't, Tarzan, and from the expression on your face, I'd say that's a good thing." I lifted one brow. "It's much more interesting than that."

He settled back in his tube and regarded me with interest. "I'm breathless with anticipation."

I looked away from him before replying. "I possess a startling aptitude for profanity."

He was obviously skeptical, and I knew why. He shook his head, eyes narrowed. "I don't believe it. You rarely swear at all around me, except when we're doing some particularly dirty fucking. I'm gonna need evidence to back up this outrageous claim."

I gave it some thought. "Doesn't do as much good to reel off a list of insults and go on a name-calling spree. It'd be better if there were someone who could vouch for my abilities. Like a third-person confirmation." I'd already clocked Viv, all fuck-hot in the teeniest of bikinis, sprawled in her inner tube while Hung paddled industriously in our direction, my girl in tow. I gestured toward them. "Now, see. This is fortuitous. Here comes one of my favorite cum-guzzling thundercunts now."

Davis choked on the beer he was drinking and stared at me, agape. He didn't break the stare until Hung and Viv approached and greeted us.

I puckered up, throwing Viv an air-kiss. "Vivvie, I'm so glad you dropped by. Davis and I are having a discussion, and you're just the person to corroborate my story. The thing is, he thinks I'm fibbing about my super-special talent."

Viv sucked down the remainder of her beer, nodding her

head emphatically as she swallowed. "Don't you doubt it for a minute, Davis. Lucinda Page is the world's preeminent authority on swearing and name-calling. Her abilities are unparalleled, and everyone at the hospital knows this. *Everyone.*"

Davis's dumbstruck expression and inability to respond were hilarious, especially to Hung. He shook his head, laughing. "I don't know that I've ever seen Deliverance at a loss for words. This is good stuff, Vivianne."

Viv continued her thought while searching Hung's tube, eventually producing and popping the top on another cold beer. "Example: last week, there was an undeclared war between the ED and blood bank. One of the assclowns who answers the phone up there scared the ever-living fuck out of one of our sweet little student nurses during the first week of her internship. He called her incompetent and threatened to get her thrown out of school. As if *that's* a thing." Amusement showed on Hung's face as he watched Vivvie prattle on. "Anyway, the poor lamb was sobbing in the linen closet, and it took me forever just to drag the story out of her. But when I finally did, I launched the Enola Gay and sent Luckie up to deal with the dickhead. Fifteen minutes later, he called the charge nurse phone—that was me 'cause it was Camille's day off. He was all contrite and quiet. Called me ma'am and apologized. Then he asked to speak to the student and did the same thing. *Bam.* Nobody fucks with Lucinda Page."

She garnished the tale with dramatic hand gestures and hilarious expressions. Hung looked at her like a starving man who'd found a bathtub full of ice cream. I guessed if he could've figured a workable way to strip her naked on that inner tube, he would've gotten busy.

Davis was belly laughing by the time Viv finished her diatribe. "So, Luckie, how did you subdue this…difficult co-worker?"

I tried to sit up straight in my inner tube—no easy task—and answered primly. "It's like children are taught to do; you simply use your words. I told him the next time he wanted to throw his weight around and pretend to be more than a pencil-dicked, window-licking ass taxi, he should mightily resist the urge to do so in front of our impressionable students. Then I threatened to rip his tiny ball sack off with my hemostats and strangle him until his eyeballs popped out of his head if he didn't fix things with the student." I thought for a second. "And I think I called him a turd-polishing shitlord. Or a weapons-grade douche canoe."

Deliverance and Hung stared, awed looks on their faces. Viv picked up the conversation again. "She's legendary. And, like Porsche—there's no substitute." She puckered up and sent an air-smooch back in my direction. The girls were completely at home with my intermittently lewd vocabulary; we all put it to use on occasion. Skillful swearing was a known requirement of being a nurse. Well, Grace Marshall was the exception there. The poor thing couldn't curse in context or on demand, and it was unacceptable. We forgave her because she was so sweet and shy; in other words, completely unlike the rest of us.

Davis settled again into his tube, a big smile on his face. "Well, I *did* ask. And now I've learned more about you than I'd expected. Can't top that one, Luckie; I'll have to think on something I can share."

The afternoon flew by. The sunshine, cold river water, and good company wrapped around me like a familiar companion; I loved seeing Davis surrounded by people who liked and respected him. His position as the squadron **weapons officer** meant he brought to the table expertise critical to the Scorpions' success. It also meant that he was frequently called upon to instruct the pilots, especially the younger ones who were new to the mission.

It was just another way our careers and passions seemed to parallel. Although both nurses and pilots received extensive education, practical experience, and ongoing training, there was a crucial element of apprenticeship that happened on the job. And there was no way to negate the importance of learning at the hands of those who knew the job because they did it every day. Experience is an exceptional teacher. That was one of the reasons Camille and I loved spending time with the younger nurses and sharing our expertise.

As Davis talked with Walker about the younger pilots, Boo and Miles in particular, I could see the devotion that informed his work. Both of them valued excellence in a way that lit me up.

I recognized within myself the first blush of serious infatuation, possibly even new love. I liked what I saw in Davis—a genuine, easy-going man who was well regarded by his peers and superiors. Hardworking and respected. Behind closed doors, he exposed a more dominant side, protective and a bit domineering. And he was so affectionate he took my breath away. I loved everything I saw.

My diminished judgment told me to pump the brakes and protect my heart. But that was increasingly difficult with every passing day.

Chapter ELEVEN

"Living on a Prayer"

Davis

The float trip was a game changer. Two relaxed days in the middle of nowhere learning about Luckie convinced me that I wanted to know more. I was stumbling awkwardly along in uncharted territory, heart and head happily confused. I thought about her almost constantly and spent downtime plotting ways to get the two of us together. Naked or otherwise.

Then life intervened with a vengeance.

Special projects at the squadron, along with flying, made for long days. Happy was hell-bent on whipping the Scorpions into fighting shape, and I supported his goals enthusiastically. Flight discipline had been sloppy in recent history, and record-keeping was barely passable. I waded in to help in every way I could, but it resulted in long days and sneaking into the squadron building to comb through paperwork on the weekends.

Lucinda's schedule was at least as hectic. The new nurse interns apparently required quite a bit of what Camille and Luckie referred to as "breastfeeding." That meant at least one of them needed to work with the fledgling nurses every shift, every day. Luckie insisted on working so Camille could attend the only big squadron event on the calendar—Bibi's surprise birthday party—and our days apart stretched into weeks.

Not that we didn't talk and text. After hours, much of it wasn't fit for public consumption, but that was the fun part. Luckie's filthy mouth was put to good use almost every night, and we even tried our hand at phone sex.

On that evening, as I lay on my bed, panting in the aftermath of a very respectable orgasm, I heard Lucinda sigh on the other end of the line. "What's wrong, Peaches?" I had gotten her there before me courtesy of some vivid descriptions of what I wanted to do to her the next time I got her under me.

I could hear the smile in her tired voice. "Ready for the real thing, you sexy motherfucker."

The irony, of course, was that we lived in the same apartment community, probably only a few hundred yards apart. Although we hadn't discussed it, we knew we'd both be exhausted and ill-prepared for work in a critical environment if we spent the night together the way we longed to do. It was new for me to keep company with a woman who took her career responsibilities as seriously as Luckie did.

And the hits just kept coming. I had a huge shit-eating grin on my face as we exchanged dirty, affectionate tidbits and said goodnight, vowing the coming week would be the one that changed our fortune.

How right we were.

Among the problem children who populated the Scorpion roster, arguably the most concerning was Miles Christman.

She possessed a charismatic personality and wit that drew

everyone around her. Yet no one seemed to know Miles. Her darker underbelly came out to play with startling regularity and manifested in a stunning disregard for consequences. She was an excellent young pilot with real natural talent in the cockpit, but risky behavior endangered her and anyone who flew with her. Happy already recognized the problem and had discussed a need for me to zero in on the cause while keeping a tight leash on her.

The annual base **SAREX** began first thing this morning, and I expected Miles to be a foul-tempered little beast. She'd counted on a Sandy checkout during this exercise, one of the most important missions the **A-10** performed. And it performed the fuck out of it. During the Vietnam War, a "Sandy" aircraft flew into enemy territory to defend downed aircrews, suppress the threat, and coordinate a rescue by helicopter. Rescue helicopters, call sign Jolly, dated to the same time in history.

A Sandy checkout was not in the cards for Lieutenant Christman today, though, and she sure as hell knew why. There would be no good deals for one of the ringleaders of the shitshow at the O'Club a few weekends ago. The version I heard had a spectacularly overserved Miles, Boo, and Torch dropping their flight suits in an old tradition called a **socks check**. It was not a big issue in itself, but add the fact that they showed their asses—literally—right in front of a table where the **Wing King**'s wife and her mother were seated? Big problem. General O'Cherry had Happy's head on a platter for that one. Ergo, no good deals.

I settled into a chair in the briefing room early to prep for my **BFM** ride with Miles. She arrived only a minute or two late, but pissy as all hell. I'd determined I would play it strictly by the book and demonstrate friendly professionalism.

Lead by example, D. Kill her with kindness.

"Morning, Miles." I kept the ire out of my tone, just barely.

She sounded irritable and tired, calling to me from the next room. "Coffee, Deliverance?"

"Hell, no. What—are you trying to kill me?" Scorpion snack bar coffee was so bad its reputation was well known base wide. When the engineering squadron moved in for a couple of weeks last spring to do roof repairs, they made a big show of bringing their commercial coffee maker and setting it up next to ours with a sign proclaiming it was "Engineer Caffeine/Secret: No Pilot."

Miles reappeared, flopping into a chair with her coffee, and rested her chin on one fist. "Okay, let's get this show on the road, D, I'm ready. Hit me."

The briefing proceeded predictably. We were flying together more than usual, and I doubted this was lost on Miles. Despite her issues, I liked her. My gut told me there was more to the story than the Hard-Hearted Hannah routine she liked to project. I continued to hold out hope that my observations and instruction could make a difference, but we were at the point of needing a breakthrough. Maybe today was the day.

Miles was much quieter than usual as we walked to the jets, taxied, and took off. There was no banter on the way to the area where we'd work, and her voice was unusually tight as we worked through warm-up maneuvers; first at three G's, then five. She voiced no protest, so I determined we'd start slowly.

"Okay, Miles. Why don't you set up on the **perch** first?" I kept my voice relaxed and confident. Flying was a fucking amazing job, and the whole sky stretched out—blue, clear, and a million. "Lead's ready."

Come on, Miles. Get your head in the game.

"Two's ready." Her voice through the radio, flat. She sounded pissed. Or bored. I set her attitude and my response to it on a shelf in my head. No place for distractions up here; we'd talk about that in the debrief.

But she wasn't helping me. She fucked up the first two engagements, resulting in two easy, quick "kills" for me. Made exactly the same damn mistake twice. Shit, I was gonna have to sit down with the boss when this sortie wrapped; Miles usually fought better than this. I took a deep breath and tried patiently to use the errors as teaching opportunities.

While she acknowledged my instruction, the pissed-off quality multiplied. I realized she wasn't irritated with me but herself. Maybe the third time would be the charm.

Miles was all in this time. I could tell by the way she set herself up to maximize airspeed, but something in my gut roiled. I could hear Happy when we'd talked behind closed doors a couple of weeks ago about the issues we faced with Miles. "When I took command, Coach called it NAFD: No Apparent Fear of Death." Nate had chuckled a little as we both tried to choke down our coffee. "I'd never heard that one."

But I wasn't laughing now. I increased my turn rate toward Miles, setting up the same scenario she'd seen twice already. I expected her to roll toward me and climb, searching for room to maneuver. Instead, I watched as she inexplicably rolled into more bank and tightened her turn. Too late, the awful realization dawned—she could no longer see me. Worse still, she wasn't taking corrective action. By the time my brain processed the imminent danger, there was simply no time to move my jet out of her path.

The mammoth aircraft shuddered powerfully as we collided, and my big frame jolted violently in the harness. "Deliverance, knock it off." I made the radio call automatically; training had already taken over. Time slowed to a near standstill and I watched, almost detached from the surreal scene that unfolded, as the fuselage and wing of my **Warthog** fell away from the cockpit I remained strapped into.

It took no more than a second or so to position myself in the seat as I'd been taught, back straight and erect, elbows tight to my sides and feet back. "Time to give it back to the taxpayers," I mumbled, reaching down and firmly pulling the ejection handles on either side of the seat.

In an instant, air roared in my ears and blue sky rushed in my face as the rocket motors under my seat fired and hurled me from the jet. The sensation was disorienting, despite my years in the cockpit. The flight upward lasted much longer than I'd have guessed, but I also figured my perception was for shit. The trajectory upward finally slowed, and the trip down began in earnest, toward the wide desert floor far below. Altitude was burning away fast, I noted distractedly.

I should probably feel serious concern about that.

The loud pop of my parachute automatically deploying snapped me back to the present, and I began to consider options for landing. There were a few relatively flat spots that looked like good candidates, but the training we received for landing after ejection was understandably brief. I picked my favorite and tried to steer in that direction. The ground came up to meet me rapidly, and I attempted to land as I'd been taught: on both feet, rolling immediately to my side to dissipate the energy across the length of my body.

The idea exceeded its execution, and time lurched into fast forward. I could hear it before I felt it—the sound of my left femur snapping was louder than the deafening crash of my jet colliding with Miles's. Fighting blinding pain, I dug a boot into the landscape as it flew by and tried to slow my movement across the ground. I flailed, trying and failing to engage the release that would separate me from the parachute. Despite my meager efforts, the desert floor continued to roll past. After what seemed forever, I finally tugged the release mechanism and the chute disengaged, floating away in the breeze. I tumbled along the ground for several yards further before stopping, my leg resting at an unnatural angle. The pain was indescribable; my leg was bloody and obviously very, very broken.

Mother. Fucker.

The pain was excruciating, much worse than any I'd ever experienced, and the nausea was almost as bad. Retching only made everything worse, and I put all my mental energy into finding some way to staunch the bleeding while staying stone fucking still. Tying my scarf above the wound, I tightened it until the bleeding slowed to a trickle. Holy fucking mother, I was pretty sure it was my bone I saw protruding from the wound. Time to move on to the next activity, pronto.

Locating the emergency radio on my harness, I came up on the emergency frequency called Guard and tried to steady my voice. "Any aircraft, any aircraft, Deliverance lead on Guard."

The obviously relieved voice of Colonel Nathan Morgan answered me after less than a second of delay. He asked about my condition, assured me that rescue helos were en route, and questioned me about location. Nausea and pain washed over me like ocean waves, coming too close together to control. I vomited repeatedly between snippets of radio conversation with Happy, using every dollop of clarity to formulate accurate responses. Ironically, Happy's position as "Sandy" today meant he was coordinating my rescue. I was able to piece together, from the additional conversation on frequency, that Miles was limping her busted-ass jet back toward Davis-Monthan. Jacob "Bashful" Travis was on her wing and would walk her through options and procedures she needed to follow. Bashful would be one miserable bastard and in almost as much pain as I was by the time this was over. Miles was a fucking handful.

My vision was increasingly fuzzy, and a loud hum in my ears drowned out pieces of the radio conversation. Even in my diminished condition, I could pick out the easily recognizable whine of big GE engines overhead. I looked up to take in a sight that had lent comfort to countless of our friendly troops pinned down in enemy territory. A beautiful, hideous Warthog, with a swath of Scorpion red adorning the tail, circled in a lazy orbit above me.

Happy. He'd found me, and help wouldn't be far behind.

"Hey, boss, looks like you lost your wingman," I cracked, wincing as my leg moved slightly. "Mine bugged out, too." I sounded drunk, even above the loud buzz in my head.

Happy's voice was strained. "Yeah, D. We must be a couple of real assholes, huh? Listen, man, you're gonna hear Jolly any minute. They're coming for you, buddy. Hang tight, right?"

I couldn't answer anymore. The fuzziness in my head was turning a progressively darker gray, so I leaned my head against the arm nearest me and prayed for Jolly.

Chapter TWELVE

"If You Leave Me Now"

Lucinda

It was a rare day in the ED. Nothing disastrous had happened. Not yet.

It was only a matter of time, as we were all aware. Nurses are a wildly superstitious lot, especially considering we're educated professionals. A nurse on the clock would never utter the word "quiet" as it referenced how the shift was progressing. It was a foolish temptation of the Fates that would result immediately in the arrival of a busload of admissions who did not speak English, each with uncontrollable diarrhea and a weeping rash on their ass.

The nursing staff carefully tiptoed around the well-behaved elephant in the room, taking coffee breaks and running to the cafeteria to pick up breakfast, just like real people did. We'd heard about those in other professions who were regularly afforded breaks and meals at appropriate times. Perks like those weren't guaranteed when there was no predicting what would walk through the door in the space of the next sixty seconds.

I'd already enjoyed coffee and a bagel, and it wasn't even noon. In room six, I wrangled a cantankerous octogenarian with a probable fractured hip. All had gone smoothly until I administered pain medication to keep her more comfortable until we could obtain an x-ray. Then we'd get ortho in to hammer out a plan of care, no pun intended. The morphine transformed the tiny, pearl-clutcher into King Kong, and her harried daughter and I had our hands full as we attempted to keep her in bed.

"You bitch!" she roared, pointing a shaky finger at me. "You can't keep me in this prison. I'll carve you up like a Thanksgiving turkey." She scratched at me with sharp little fingernails. This wouldn't do at all; she likely had what we liked to call "a reaction" to the morphine. Fucking understatement.

Sam stuck her head through the door with a dazzling smile and thrust a sterile, packaged syringe and a vial in my direction. "Valium two milligrams IV, Luckie Lady. I took the liberty of getting you an order. Do you need me to draw it up?"

"Thanks, pumpkin pie. This is just what the doctor ordered. Literally. You're a gem, Sammie." I sent a little air-kiss her direction as her eyes narrowed at my use of the despised nickname.

"So welcome, Luckie. Sing out if you need anything else; I'm around." And she was gone.

I drew up the medication quickly and administered it, explaining to Mrs. Roosevelt's daughter that it would help calm and keep her from further injury. We chatted as the elderly lady calmed and her fragile features finally relaxed in sleep. I sat next to her bed, stroking her hand softly, and tried to comfort her distraught daughter.

The relative peace of the ED was rudely interrupted by the unmistakable thunder of a medivac helicopter. It seemed even more intrusive than usual, and it usually scared the bejesus out of every patient and family member in the department. Not a good look for a place that was only three seconds from utter chaos at any given time.

I extricated myself from the conversation in case Camille needed extra hands. Patients who arrived via medivac were normally trauma victims and frequently critical. Thrusting my head through the door, I encountered Camille and Grace hurrying through the nurses' station. Camille was stuffing her pockets with gloves, her favorite pen, and alcohol pads as she moved quickly toward the stairwell to the roof. I shot her a questioning look.

She shook her head, not stopping to chat. "Got it covered, Luckie. Hang here and keep an eye on exam three and four. The resident may need to suture."

Nobody had to invite me not to attend the trauma of the day. I'd had more than enough to last a lifetime. I nodded my agreement and disappeared back into Mrs. Roosevelt's room.

Our invaluable unit secretary, Josie, sent me to assist the resident who was suturing the leg of a young man, cut on a broken PBR bottle. Fortunately, my fiery little senior citizen slept like a baby throughout, and my controlled grip on the shift continued uninterrupted. I felt mildly guilty for avoiding Camille, but Josie was keeping my dance card full.

I completed dressing and discharged the beer-bottle victim, and then sent Mrs. Roosevelt to radiology. While stripping dirty linen in the now empty rooms, I contemplated making a donut run for the staff. There had been no further admissions, and it wasn't often we had the chance to treat everyone.

I sensed someone in the room with me and turned to see Vivianne. "Vivvie, give me a hand with this linen…" She didn't move or respond, so I stopped and looked, meeting unusually serious emerald eyes, shiny with tears. She swallowed hard but didn't explain.

"Hey, Luckie, I'll finish this later. Come down the hall a minute; Camille needs to talk to you." Her voice wobbled, but she cleared her throat and turned away, fidgeting with something in her pocket. Without waiting for a response, she grabbed my hand and pulled me behind her out of the room and toward the trauma rooms.

Her face turned away from mine as we started up the hall, but I pulled her arm, my heart racing. "Wait, Vivianne, what is it?" She seemed to ignore me, her long legs striding up the hallway. "Dammit, Vivvie, tell me...what's wrong?" I was barely damming up the panic, and my stomach churned with uncontrolled nausea.

Viv whirled on me, unshed tears threatening to spill from her eyes. "Luckie, it's fine, I promise. He's...it's okay." I could barely keep the contents of my stomach from erupting everywhere.

He?

There could only be one. Viv's hand firmly grasped mine and led me around the corner where I saw Camille's face. Her eyes were soft, and she rushed toward me, holding out both hands. She spoke calmly, looking into my panicked eyes. "Luckie, Davis is alive and stable. The medivac transported him here; Vivvie and I have been taking care of him. He's going to be okay, but there's been an aircraft accident, and he had to eject."

I'd heard people say shock felt like a punch to the gut; and, at that moment, I understood exactly what they meant.

Camille squeezed my hands until I returned focus to her and she continued. "He has a nasty compound fracture to the left femur. Viv's just about to take him for surgical reduction. He lost quite a bit of blood, but we're replacing with packed cells and volume. He's been unconscious since he got here, but they got to him quick, honey. He's gonna be okay."

A big sob tore from my throat, shoulders shaking uncontrollably. I had to go to him—how could they have kept me from him? I tried to break from Cami's grasp, but she pulled me close to her.

"Look at me, Lucinda. *Look*. Babe, this is why I didn't tell you right away; you have to pull it together. Davis is gonna need you, just like I needed you, Luckie. Do you remember? Viv and I took care of him just the way you'd have done it. We gave him the very best of everything, just like you would have. But now you have to make sure he gets his best girl, do you understand? Dry those tears; you know he may hear you." She met my eyes, and I lifted my chin. "Get your shit together, Luckie, and go talk to Davis. He's waiting for you."

I wrapped Camille in my arms. Thank God for this woman. She was more than a sister. "Thank you, Camille. I don't know what I would've done if…you hadn't been here.

She pushed me in the direction of the trauma room. "Shut up, wench. Dry your face and go see Davis."

A few more words were exchanged, and I was gone, pushing the wide door open. My heart skipped a beat. His muscular frame and beautiful face were relaxed as if sleeping, but the dual large-bore IVs in each arm and long trauma cast holding his leg stationary told a different story. I pulled up the high stool nearby and took his hand in mine, laying my head on his pillow.

"I'm here, Davis; it's me. Luckie. Everything's gonna be just fine now. Just fine." I kissed his stubbled cheek and wiped tears from my face with the bed sheet. His breathing was deep and unlabored, hopefully indicating he was comfortable. "We're all here to make sure you get out of this good as new, and I'll be waiting when you come out of surgery."

I don't know how long I lay next to him, our faces close, counting his respirations, and feeling his pulse with my finger. My tears wet his pillow, then my scrub top. Time slowed, but I couldn't have been with him more than a few minutes; he was a priority surgical case. Finally, my eyes turned to take him in, quiet and beautiful. And in that sliver of time, every ounce of the confusion and fearful anxiety fell away. All of the parts of me wondering what would happen to him—to us—faded in silence into the background. In their place was confidence. Peace. As certainly as I'd ever known anything, I knew this. Moving closer, I felt the warmth of his body and whispered near his ear.

"I didn't know until today, Davis, but I know now. When I thought something might have already taken you away from me. When we'd just started. When I'd just found you…" The words were so hard to force from my swollen throat, even at a bare whisper. I swallowed hard and continued. "It's just too important not to tell you, Davis, and something in my gut says you can hear me. I love you so much." The sweet weight of that revelation was an easy burden to share. "I don't know everything that means, but I want you to carry it with you for the next few hours. When you go into surgery and during all the days that you recover, I'll go with you. There's no obstacle we can't get past. I do love you, Davis, and you're not alone. So I'm ready to get started when you are."

The surgical transport team was outside the door, and Viv stuck her head in. "Ready, Luckie?"

I helped Vivvie disconnect the monitors, affix the leads to transport equipment, and they were gone. I looked around the empty trauma room and willed the lump in my throat to recede. Warm arms wrapped around me from behind, and Camille squeezed hard. "We're gonna get through this, Luckie. It's what we do."

I nodded, grasping her for support. This road would be a long one, but she and I had walked long, rocky roads together before.

"Come on, Chiquita." She spun me around and grabbed my hand. "Let's get you off the clock and into the **PACU**. You need to be ready when your bionic boyfriend rolls out of surgery."

Chapter THIRTEEN

"Coming Out of the Dark"

Davis

It was dark, much blacker than I ever remembered and very cold. That was about the limit of what my sluggish brain could process, but I did gradually begin to wonder where I was. There was movement and quiet conversation in the room. Friendly voices I didn't recognize. Someone covering me with something warm. Unable to muster any cohesive thought, I allowed the darkness and warmth to settle again, like an embrace.

The dark remained. Not as cold as before, and I heard a low, familiar voice. Lucinda was calling me from someplace far away. I tried to stretch or turn my head, but no dice. Even opening my eyes was impossible. I could sort out relatively normal feeling in my arms, hands and right leg; oh, but that left leg throbbed like a motherfucker. The puzzle pieces began to drop slowly into place as Luckie's voice came into focus in my head.

"Davis, it's me…Lucinda. Wake up, Tarzan." Her hand was firm on mine, and I could sense the warmth of her body near mine. Struggling a little, I peeled protesting eyelids open briefly and could make out a fuzzy outline of the only face I wanted to see. "There was an accident, Davis. You and Miles…Miles is just fine, and you will be soon. Open your eyes, handsome." A few minutes passed, and Luckie continued the patter of quiet conversation, rubbing my hand and touching my face gently all the while.

I was pretty disinterested in anything but sleep until the words she'd said gelled in my foggy consciousness in a rush, and the accident flashed through my head like disconnected bits of a movie.

The wing of my Warthog falling slowly away. The sensation of speed as the rocket motors flung me and my ejection seat from the useless fragment of aircraft. The pop of my parachute, and the gut-wrenching pain of gravity flinging me onto the unforgiving earth. I forced my eyes open once again.

"Davis." Her voice was a rough, teary rumble. "There you are." I swallowed painfully and tried, unsuccessfully, to ask for a drink.

"Shhh. Don't try to talk right now; suck on these." She placed two ice chips between my parched lips and reached for a damp cloth, wiping my eyes and face. "The tube they place in your throat makes it possible for you to breathe during surgery, but the memory lingers like a bitch after it's gone." Her sweet, soft mouth touched mine in a kiss, and her long lashes fluttered closed against my cheeks.

"You're like a beautiful dream." I barely recognized my broken growl, and Luckie knit her brow as she broke the kiss and pulled away, regarding me with mock disapproval.

"No. Talking. None, Davis, until your throat doesn't feel like it's on hellfire." She shoveled two additional ice chips into my dry mouth. "I'll tell you everything you always wanted to know about your crash—but were afraid to ask."

I smiled a bit at her teasing tone. If she was treating the accident with any humor, it meant everything was okay—or it would be. Miles was my most pressing concern, and I croaked her name at Luckie as she fed me more ice.

"Shut up, dammit. You can ask Cami what I do to recalcitrant patients." Her eyebrows shot up. "You don't want to know, Davis Payne. *You don't.*" She settled back into the chair pulled up next to my bed, still holding my hand. "Okay, like I said, Miles is just fine. She flew her airplane back to the base with Jacob's help. And he said I'm to tell you when you wake up, that she…" She fished in the pocket of her wrinkled scrub jacket, retrieving a scrap of paper. "…landed it in **manual reversion**."

Holy fucking fuck. She landed in manual reversion? With no voice to speak of, pun unintended, there was not an expedient way for me to communicate to Lucinda the minor miracle Miles pulled off. There were rare occasions it was successfully accomplished, under battle conditions, but it was a "walking on water" moment. My shocked expression must've told the story because Luckie tossed the paper on a nearby table with a grin.

"Jake said that would drop your jaw. She's uninjured, at least physically, and by all accounts, the airplane is a complete mess. Nathan returned to the base after you were loaded onto the rescue helicopter to make sure Miles made it home alive; he's in the waiting room along with a billion other people." She grimaced comically. "Pilots. In my hospital—can you imagine? Camille sent Samanthe Barber to pick up Miles and get her home after the clinic completed her medical workup. She's one of the nurses who works with us in the ED. Sam will stay with her tonight; she has some psych nursing and counseling background, so she's the best candidate for that job."

The pressure in my chest eased as I accepted that Miles was

okay. This would likely be the beginning of a long road for her. She would need to face down whatever demons left her in the perpetual cycle of self-sabotage. Sometimes stubbornness left no option but dramatic failure to grab our attention. At least we both lived to fight another day.

"As for you, Mister Foster, you have a bit of a road ahead." Luckie sighed and gave me a tired little smile. "You're pretty banged up all over, almost like you jumped out of an airplane. That's going to make you feel like you've been on the losing end of a bad bar fight for a couple of weeks. The real star of the show, however, is this left femur." She gestured like a game show hostess to my leg, strung up with a complex set of pulleys. There was a cable protruding, in a disconcerting manner, from the cumbersome-looking cast that started at my toes and extended all the way to my upper thigh. "Dr. Taft is the biggest son of a bitch and best orthopedic surgeon in Tucson, maybe all of Arizona. And your internal repair, complete with an intramedullary nail, is the finest piece of femur repair it's ever been my pleasure to see on x-ray. Brought tears to my eyes, swear to God."

I had a lot of questions and not much voice. "But the bone was...sticking out." I croaked out my concern and felt my stomach churn with nausea. Blood and guts were definitely not my long suit.

Luckie waved her hand and fed me more ice chips. "There will be lots more details to come, but suffice to say, things could've been worse. The doctor was able to stabilize your bone and repair the skin before he applied the cast; that's not always the way it goes down. The fracture was in a decent location on your femur to help it heal well, and the way the doc repaired it is the best-case scenario. You're out of bed by tomorrow night, max." It all sounded overwhelming, but Lucinda seemed to have confidence that everything was going to work out. I was waking up from the anesthesia rapidly now, and the growing agony in my upper-left leg caused my confidence of a rosy outcome to flag. "Push your button, Davis. This one, the painkiller button." She brandished a button on a cord affixed to something flowing into my IV. "This is the magic sauce, baby. Don't spare the horses; you can't overdose. I programmed the pump myself." She gave the blinking machine hanging on my IV pole the Vanna White treatment again before continuing my update.

"In other news, I spoke to your mother on the phone and gave her the 411 on the accident and your condition." I knew the Air Force chaplain would ordinarily notify next of kin in the event of any accident resulting in a casualty, fatal or otherwise. I hated to think of my mother receiving news of the crash, partially because her response would likely be wildly inappropriate, but Luckie continued. "Before you worry about your family, you should know that Nathan got me their contact information and I was able to call before the official notification." She smiled again. "Your mother invited me to visit with you next time you go to Savannah. She was surprised to hear you were seeing someone."

Well, hell's bells. I'll bet she *was* surprised. She'd be a fuckuva lot more surprised if she met my gorgeous Luckie, but that was a problem to tackle on a different day. Not to mention my dad.

Again, Deliverance, another day. One fucked-up thing at a time.

Then Lucinda sat on the edge of my bed, her kindness cutting through all the worry and pain wracking me. She leaned close and kissed me, pushing the painkiller button on my machine. "We'll discuss Savannah later. For now, I need to head to the waiting room and update your adoring public on the beginning of your astounding recovery." She stood and fixed me with her caramel gaze. "Don't you worry about a thing, Davis. We're gonna do this together, do you hear me?"

She left with a little wave, sliding the curtain of my cubicle almost closed, and the effects of the morphine began to settle in.

My eyelids grew heavy, and another nurse slipped in to check vital signs. I felt oddly at peace and heard the reason for my tranquility just as I drifted off. That was the sweet voice of my Luckie whispering just before I woke.

"I love you so much."

Chapter FOURTEEN

"Fix You"

Lucinda

It had been almost two weeks since my world, along with Davis's, was turned upside down. He began the road to recovery with enthusiasm and surpassed all expectations during the first hours and days in the hospital. On day three, however, cabin fever set in and his patience wore dangerously thin. He demanded discharge and a return to the comforts of home. The orthopedic charge nurse doubted the attending doc would be impressed with Davis's plan and suggested I channel all my powers of persuasion and any available charm toward the good doctor when he next rounded.

The days at Davis's bedside had taken a toll I was glad to pay, but a toll nonetheless. I declined to go home, opting instead to shower in the ED nurses' lounge and make use of the bag Camille brought from my apartment. Hygiene at its most basic and a nice, fat sleep deficit had rendered me ill-tempered and grubby. I was grateful to be at Davis's side and able to make him as comfortable as possible. But that left precious little energy to suffer fools, and a spectacular fool stood at the ready to cross my path.

Dr. Stuart Humphrey Taft was an Ivy League-educated surgeon, widely regarded for his extraordinary technical skill. As both the hospital's chief of surgery and the medical chief of staff several times over, he was known as a gifted genius in the OR. He was also the most disagreeable malcontent in the hospital, an angry little man in dire need of a personality transplant. The staff knew to avoid crossing him or risk being sliced to ribbons in one of his signature tirades.

He was strictly punctual, never straying from a ten a.m. rounding habit. He did not make a practice of answering questions or holding court with patients or their families. A thorough exam of each patient was conducted, followed by a brief and silent study of the chart. Then a few statements about the patient's condition were uttered, and he was gone. Nurses followed him on rounds to clarify or comfort, but he did not entertain the queries of laypersons.

And so it was, at nine fifty a.m. on day five, I found myself leaning on the wall outside Davis's room, awaiting the arrival of Dr. Taft. He arrived promptly, attired in a starched lab coat, perfectly shined wing tips, and a Patek Philippe watch. He was attended by his physician's assistant and four beleaguered-looking medical students. He didn't address the students—I guessed he would eat them for lunch—but instead barked a steady and impatient stream of orders at his PA. I noted idly that the PA didn't seem the least rattled by Taft's manner and endless demands; I hoped Taft made it worth his while. Charts were stacked in the waiting arms of medical students, and the train left the station, headed to Davis's room first.

"Good morning, Dr. Taft." I smiled, none too brightly, as I stepped into his path and blocked the doorway. I held a strong resemblance to something the cat had dragged in, rocking my "day five hair" and wrinkled scrubs from the lounge. His head snapped up, lip curled.

"On rounds, Miss..." He waved an irritated hand, dismissing me.

"Yes, I'm aware. I'm Lucinda Page, one of the ED RNs, and I..."

His voice held a sharp edge when he interrupted. "I'll not be taking ED call today."

"Again, I'm aware, Dr. Taft. I'm here to speak to you about Captain Foster, the active duty pilot trauma from the accident earlier this week." Now it was my tone that sounded cold. "I know you don't make it a practice to speak to family, but you'll make a few minutes for me." My tone was more strident than I'd intended.

What. Ever.

Eyebrows shot into his silvery hairline, but he remained silent. One of the medical students took a step backward, and I soldiered on.

"I'm Captain Foster's significant other, as well as an experienced nurse, and I've been assisting with his care since he arrived. His post-op progress has been excellent, well ahead of expected, and he'd like to be discharged today."

"Post-op day five? Out of the question," Taft harrumphed.

I stood a little taller, putting all five feet, ten inches to work, and looked him straight in the eye. "All the behavioral and educational metrics set out by your PA on admission are met. And he'll have 24/7 skilled care for the first two weeks minimum, as well as daily home visits from a licensed physical therapist."

His eyes narrowed, and I was treated to the fire-breathing, hell-on-wheels version of Taft I'd heard about. "And I suppose you would be providing the 24/7 nursing?" He practically roared the words at me. "Skilled care and conjugal visits are not one and the same. I envision actual nursing care for my post-op patients, Miss..." He stumbled, having forgotten my name in the rush to embarrass me into silence, so I stepped quickly into the void.

"I'm a skilled nurse, completely invested in the successful recovery of this patient, Dr. Taft. I have trauma experience and certification, excellent ability to follow physician orders and all the necessary ancillary services lined up and standing by. And I strongly suggest you refrain from disparaging my professional abilities—or was that sexual harassment?"

We stared at one another like a couple of gunfighters, neither blinking. Finally, he grunted and rolled his eyes. "If he meets the requirements for discharge…I'll consider it."

"The staff will need discharge planning and orders. Let's go in so you can examine the patient." I opened the door and stepped in front of the entourage, meeting Davis's shocked expression with a smile. He'd clearly heard our conversation. "Good news, Davis. Dr. Taft is planning to send you home."

So here we were, at home in Davis's apartment, fortuitously located on the ground floor, and settled into our routine. I'd moved into the second bedroom, sleeping with the door open in case he needed me during the night. I managed to work a couple of shifts a week with Camille picking up the lion's share of the slack. She seemed so grateful to give back in light of what she felt I'd done for her. I never felt a debt was owed, but there was no reasoning with that broad. Vivvie, Sam, and Grace dropped by with food, magazines, and paperbacks almost daily, but it was their company we welcomed most of all. Truth be told, anything at all—including cholera—was more welcome than Vivianne's cooking. She was a danger to herself and others in the kitchen, but she fancied herself Tucson's own Julia Child. When Viv brought dinner, we had take-out Chinese or delivery pizza. No exceptions.

Bibi Ditka, a pediatric physical therapist at Tucson Medical

Center, had been an acquaintance before our social introduction at the now-infamous flight suit party, and she came to Davis's bedside a few hours after he was moved from the recovery room. She was not only Coach's wife but a respected friend and confidante to the Scorpions and their spouses. She met with the fearsome Dr. Taft and discussed his goals, ironing out an individualized plan for Davis before his discharge.

"Hump is just an asshole, Luckie, pardon my French. He's utterly devoid of self-awareness, so he has no idea how intolerable he is." Bibi stood at Davis's bedside, taking his mending leg through its paces with a watchful eye and practiced hands.

"Hump?" Davis paid attention only vaguely, his focus much more attuned to the leg in Bibi's hands, as it was his.

"Dr. Taft. His middle name is Humphrey, and that's what the other docs call him. Among other things. That's what I call him too." She grinned at her patient. "Among other things. You're doing great here, Davis. This leg's range of motion is better than I'd expect at two weeks. But then, you're so young and strong. And sooo handsome."

"Ahh, Bibi…you're a sweetheart. With the black heart of a demon." He returned her smile and then grimaced as she continued to extend and flex his leg.

I watched the proceedings from the door of his bedroom. It was genuinely encouraging to see him progressing. "I'm sorry you had to tie up with Dr. Taft, Bibi. That man's a trial for the purest of souls."

She tossed fiery red hair over her shoulder and hit me back with her million-dollar smile. "My soul is anything but pure, Luckie, and I have quite a bit of experience with Hump and his ilk. They're a dime a dozen and easy as pie to manipulate. We have history, me and Dr. Assclown."

I busied myself cleaning up the kitchen, still a mess from dinner the evening before. I'd worked a night shift last night after arranging an elaborate scheduling swap with the nurse who took care of Davis during the hours I was away. Bibi offered to spend the morning with him, allowing me five precious hours of shut-eye. It'd been years since I'd worked night shifts consistently, and it never failed to amaze me that they had been a regular part of my life for three years.

Davis was young, healthy, and accustomed to independence. I was unsurprised at his restlessness. It was completely normal under the circumstances. The progressive nature of the recovery, however tedious, would be enough to buoy his spirits and ward off discouragement—hopefully. Bibi was especially gifted at setting attainable goals and showing him progressive independence with almost every visit.

But I saw signs of mild depression as Davis looked at the long road ahead. His appetite was off, and I found him distracted and a bit dispirited over the past couple of days. The repetitive schedule of rest, PT, doctor's visits and household routines was wearing on him. I needed to shake things up and remind my hot boyfriend that this season of our lives was only temporary. I'd called Nathan when these thoughts began crowding my head and asked him to consider work Davis could effectively do from home and eventually from his office at work. With some luck, he might be able to use a walker or wheelchair within a week or two for more than short jaunts inside the house. That would open up possibilities, and Nathan promised to give the idea thought and get back to me.

In the meantime, however, I needed to pay a visit to Samanthe. Specifically her closet. Some good old-fashioned debauchery was called for, and she was just the brand of twisted I needed to help me carry out my plan.

Chapter FIFTEEN

"Take You to the Candy Shop"

Davis

To review: I'd survived an aircraft accident that could easily have taken my life—and had only one terribly broken limb to show for it. Bibi said the leg was healing well ahead of schedule, and the charming Dr. Taft even managed some surprise and optimism at my two-week checkup last week. I had the full attention of a highly skilled professional who catered to my every need, kept me company, and was a welcome and constant reminder that I was probably already in love with her…even if I wouldn't fully admit it to myself.

But I missed the Scorpions, hanging out with the squadron, and flying. *Especially* flying. I missed my work, even the paperwork, for God's sake, and the camaraderie. I sure as hell missed my independence, although it was slowly coming back. Even driving and walking without asking for help was a fond memory.

Oh yeah, and I was horny as all fuck.

Luckie was sweet and attentively affectionate. She touched me often, rubbing my shoulders and back as best she could under the circumstances and made sure I knew she still cared deeply for me. There was lots of making out, especially at bedtime, and cuddling while binging on *Arrested Development* and *True Blood*.

Lots of Netflix, but no chill.

I sensed it was her professionalism that held her back, not a lack of desire. But the net result was that I hadn't felt the tight grip of her wet pussy in three and a half weeks, almost four. It was utterly unacceptable.

She'd been gone all afternoon, running errands and hitting the grocery store. My dick was an iron spike making for the exit in my shorts, but I couldn't even be bothered to milk the purple-headed lizard. The thrill was gone. I shook my head in disbelief at this sad new milestone. Willing my kickstand to stand down, I fished around in the well-stocked cooler Luckie had thoughtfully prepared before she left. She supplied lunch as well as plenty of healthy drinks and water bottles—all gone now. And, there in the melting ice at the bottom, lay the highlight of my dreary day. An icy cold Blue Moon adorned with a tiny ziplock bag containing an orange slice. The woman was a national treasure.

Popping the top and stuffing the orange through the long neck, I fished through the tangle of bedclothes and retrieved the remote. Tuning in to an old *CSI* episode, I willed my brain off and hoped the little head would follow. The action was just getting intense when I heard the door open and noise from the living room. Luckie was home, I was sure, so I called out a distracted greeting.

No response.

Well, there was certainly no getting up to find her; she was probably bringing in groceries and packages from her errands. As if I didn't feel helpless enough, I couldn't even—

Holy sweet merciful fucking Mother Mary on a toasted Ritz Cracker. With peanut butter.

In the doorway of my bedroom stood a tall vision of glossy, caramel sex. My mouthwatering Lucinda was barely clad in the filthiest version of a naughty schoolgirl getup I'd ever laid my pathetic eyes on. I let my eyes sweep disbelievingly up and down the hottest fucking fantasy girl I'd conjured in any dream, unable to formulate a word. A navy cardigan, easily two sizes too small, was held precariously together by one overworked button; underneath, soft breasts strained against a demi-bra that pushed them from its confines, revealing dark, taut nipples. A pleated, plaid miniskirt, no longer than eight or nine inches *almost* covered her pussy, the little tuft of soft hair she maintained at the apex peeking out at me when she moved. Long legs stretched out forever in black thigh-high stockings trimmed with bows at the top. And, on her feet, impossibly high black heels. Her mouth formed a perfect "O," and she sucked on one long, red, manicured nail tip while silently regarding me with wide, innocent eyes.

The air was thick. The lizard peeked out of my waistband for a look and began to weep.

After a long moment, she blinked ridiculously long, curly lashes. Twice. Then she spoke in a soft, breathy voice.

"Hiya, Mister Foster." The tip of her tongue poked out and licked her pouty mouth.

Okay. "Hi there...umm..."

The breathy sigh was back. "It's Lucie. From next door. I hope you don't mind that I dropped by after school to see how you're feeling."

"Not at all, Lucie; come on in and sit down." My dick was hard enough to cut off my cast. She didn't sit but instead swaggered a couple of steps closer, popping a hip and resting one hand on her thigh. The skirt pulled up slightly, and I could just make out the intoxicating fragrance of her arousal.

"I need to talk to you about a problem, Mister Foster. I hope

you don't mind." The wide eyes blinked again. "It's a little…
embarrassing."

Ahh, fuck yes, wet-dream girl. Let's talk.

"Of course, Luck…Lucie. I'm here for whatever you need."

Heh heh.

She moved the rolling stool Bibi liked to have handy from the
corner of the room, and I made a mental note to wipe it down before my next physical therapy visit. Pulling it alongside my bed,
she took the time to bend over and adjust one of her stilettos. The
superfluous skirt rode up to the apex of her heart-shaped ass,
revealing both juicy cheeks and the glistening sex between them.
I reached out to run a hand over the smooth skin of one cheek.
"Now you don't have to be embarrassed around me, Lucie. You
just tell me how I can help you." My voice sounded like I was
being strangled.

Holy fucking fuck.

She settled herself on the stool, spreading her gorgeous legs
wide and revealing obviously wet thighs and a glimpse of pink.
"It's like this, Mister Foster," she said, hanging her head a little.
"The other seniors are making fun of me at school." She blinked
those big eyes at me sadly. "See, I'm a virgin." She looked right
into my eyes, and a big fat tear rolled down her cheek.

Holy shit. The girl was an Oscar contender.

"I turned eighteen last summer, and the other kids say now
I'm the only senior who still has her cherry. I don't even know if
any of those boys who want to see my pussy even know what to
do." Her lips slid into a little pout and she rolled closer, leaning
forward to give me a generous view of her tits. A rosy blush on
her chest and the racing pulse at her throat told me I wasn't the
only one having fun. Her voice was almost a whisper, and she
looked right at me for the next part. "I think it would be better if
I had a man—a real man—to be the first one inside me. A man
like you would know what to do."

My cock was leaking in earnest, cum wetting the crown and beginning to soak my shorts. "Well. Lucie, I…"

She pushed the stool away suddenly and whirled away from me. "But I'm afraid. You're so big and tall, and I'll bet you're really big. My little pussy is so small, Mister Foster. I can barely get one finger inside it." She turned back to look at me, sucking on that damn finger again. "Is your penis really big? Will it fit inside my tight little hole? I'm so afraid it'll hurt the first time."

This was fun role play sex, and my head knew that, but it was also about the hottest thing I could imagine happening to me while I lay in bed with one leg in a cast. And my dick had zero fucks to give about whether we were playing or not. He and I were all in.

I reached for her, pulled her close and kissed her hand. "Don't be afraid, Lucie. I'll take my time and show you how your sweet pussy can hug my big, thick cock so tight and make both of us feel good. Real good, Lucie, over and over. Do you want me to show you how?"

She nodded her head, reaching to release the front clasp on the scrap of lace that passed for a bra. I pulled her to me and sucked one peaked nipple into my mouth, nursing it gently. She dropped the skirt to the ground and went to work on my shorts. Fortunately, she'd modified some of my clothes with side access to help in moving the process along, and I was soon naked and ready to fuck her delicious body. Finally.

"Come sit on top of me, Lucie." She stretched one long leg across me, settling her center directly onto my shaft. I took a couple of deep breaths, thinking about our last family reunion and my auntie's potato salad because these were desperate times. She did as I asked, allowing the sweet softness of her folds to surround my cock and slide slowly back and forth while she rubbed her clit against me and moaned deep in her throat, eyes fluttering closed. Her fingers found the tips of her nipples, pinching cruelly with those long, red nails.

I was mesmerized.

The glossy bubblegum-scented lips, the dragon-lady nails, this wide-eyed, virginal persona…it was all concocted for me. But it was really an escape from the long, steep road we were walking together. She was so full of surprises and generosity; for a split second, my angry cock was forgotten. All I felt was warmth and grateful affection for the little fake-virgin/deviant I was about to impale with my dick.

"Let me rub that clit for you, Lucie. I'll help you come and get your little cunt slick and ready for me. When I open you with my cock for the first time, it'll feel so much better if you're creamy wet." I ran my thumb through her slit, unsurprisingly soaked and more than ready, and gently circled her clit with it as she bathed my shaft with her pussy. Pinching one nipple a bit harder than necessary, I pulled her toward me. "Open your mouth, Lucie, so I can taste you while I finger your pussy." I coaxed her mouth open, exploring with my tongue, and continued slow circles of her blossoming clit.

She pulled away from me, panting. Several tiny beads of perspiration had bloomed on her lip and brow. She whispered against my lips, eyes still closed, "I'm going to come while you finger me, Mister Foster. Is that okay?"

I was careful to keep a steady rhythm, pinching and stroking her tight nipples in turn with my free hand. "Come on my finger, Lucie, and then I'll stretch your pussy with my cock. It'll feel so much better to come when you're all full of me, baby. You'll see." Her arousal flowed freely now, wetting the lips of her pussy and lubricating my fingers liberally. "Come now, Luck…Lucie."

I hadn't yet finished saying her name before the throbbing began in her swollen center, and she gripped my chest with both hands, groaning and gasping hard. "Don't stop…please. Don't stop." Her orgasm, so obviously not that of a virgin, lasted a couple of measures longer than I'd come to expect, and my hot-as-the-fucking-sun faux schoolgirl forgot to stay in character as her belly rippled and she struggled to stretch it longer. It occurred to me that Luckie had probably had no time or energy for extracurriculars in the next room after dark. She was burning the candle at both ends by taking care of me and doing her part at the hospital.

I was enjoying the fantasy and decided to continue the charade. I took my dick in my fist and lifted her bottom a bit as she came down from her orgasm. "Relax now, Lucie. I'm going to push my cock inside you nice and slow while you're still throbbing from coming. Don't worry, baby, I'll make it good." Sliding the thick head back and forth through her slit, I took time to rub her still-throbbing clit, eliciting a moan each time. This was no acting job; Luckie needed this as much as I did. I was leaking precum so copious it wet my hand and dripped onto the tense abs below.

Oh, fuck.

"Condom, Luckie. I'm so sorry, babe…condom." I had almost forgotten—shit, I *had* forgotten.

But it was Luckie, not Lucie, who smiled gently at me, still panting a little. "I didn't forget, Davis. I'm clean. On the pill. Saw your lab work when I was cleaning up yesterday. Still clean?"

I nodded numbly. "Really, baby…bare? Are you sure?"

She slipped easily back into character. "I want to feel you inside me, Mister Foster. Will you take my cherry for me?" She pouted. "I *want* you to take it."

I nodded again, head reeling. "Look at me while you take my cock for the first time, Lucie." I pushed the broad head through her folds and just inside the welcoming warmth of her delicious pussy. Her eyes were locked on mine as she relaxed and allowed all of me to fill her.

Ahh…heaven.

"God, I missed you, Davis." Lucie was gone for good, and Lucinda's mouth was on mine as she rode the whole length of me steadily from root to tip. "That thick cock feels so good, baby. Give me all of it, honey. Lucie might not be able to take it all, but Luckie needs every inch of her man."

My little virgin had developed quite the dirty mouth.

I stared at the juncture where our bodies met, her folds glistening and opening to receive my straining length. "You're so long, Davis...does it feel good when you push your cockhead against the end of my pussy? You wanna fill me with all that hot cum you've been saving for me?"

Holy fuck, the dirty talk. I thought the end of my dick would explode, but I was desperate to make it all last. "I need to milk you, baby...need you to shoot that hot load inside me now..."

She sat straight up on top of me, working tight nipples with her manicured fingers, groaning to let me know she was subjecting them to abuse for my viewing pleasure. Then her pussy began to squeeze me rhythmically as she rocked her hips slowly back and forth in time.

I groaned and clutched the smooth curve of her ass with both hands. "Holy fuck, Lucinda. You're so tight. You're gonna make me come too soon, baby."

She shushed me and dropped a hand between her legs, fingering her wetness. She fixed me with a stare and spoke with a low voice. "When could it possibly be too soon to feel you pumping me full of your seed, Davis? I need that warm cum inside...love to feel you throbbing...coming inside me. Give me everything you've got, Tarzan. I'm ready, baby."

Gawd. My dick stood up and cheered as the orgasm coiled and spun in my balls. I couldn't hold it off long, but then Luckie unexpectedly delivered the goods. Reaching behind her with a free hand, she parked two fingers on my taint and massaged firmly.

"Come for me, Davis. Fill me up, baby. I wanna feel that fat dick throbbing. Fill my pussy, honey…"

Done for, I let go with a hard thrust upward and a roar. My vision faded briefly as I focused on the delicious sensation of Luckie's perfect cunt licking at me and sucking everything from my balls. Her voice seeped into the frayed threads of my consciousness.

"Feed me, Davis…my little pussy's so thirsty, baby. Let my cunt milk those big balls dry…"

I could barely catch my breath as the last vestiges of the orgasm gradually faded away, and the firm massage of Luckie's fingers below my balls became softer, affectionate stroking. Sight slowly returned, and I gazed in open amazement at the "despoiled virgin" straddling what was left of me.

I meant to whisper seductively, but it emerged as a desperate croak. "Fuck. Such a beautiful girl. My gorgeous, filthy Luckie. Thank you, baby. Thank you…"

She leaned into me, and we held one another, breathing hard. I had to chuckle when there was enough spare energy. "Peaches. A virgin schoolgirl. Really?" We both smiled and laughed, enjoying the shared moment. Then she sat straight up, still full of my softening cock, and pushed her soft breasts together. Her eyebrows cocked upward, and she ran slim hands over her body, feigning seduction.

"I warned you about the potty mouth…and thanks for popping my cherry, Tarzan." She bent close to my ear. "You're really something special."

Chapter SIXTEEN

"Man in the Mirror"

Davis

"So much better, boss. Things are moving right along. How is everything in the squadron? I can't believe I'm admitting I miss work. Who does that?" I was catching up with Happy on the "almost six-week anniversary" of the accident. Progress was amazing in many ways, but there were still many miles to go. Bibi helped me learn to transfer independently from my bed or chair with the assistance of crutches or a rolling walker. Compared to the prison my bed had become, it seemed like freedom, but I longed to rejoin the Scorpions—or at least to be serviceable in moving the mission forward.

Nathan seemed glad to hear the good news, and his tone was encouraging. "We sure miss you, Deliverance. The place isn't the same without you here; the LPA is getting slack. But I'm planning to keep your nose to the grindstone. You interested in doing a little traveling on the Air Force's dime? I have an errand that would otherwise have tied up senior staff, but you'd be a better choice as long as you're able. I think I could probably work out a paid travel companion to take care of the logistics. Just a couple of weeks to scope out a **TDY**. How's that sound, D?"

Hell, yeah.

I couldn't wait to get out of this apartment and back in the game. "Put me in, coach; I'm ready. Where am I headed?"

He spoke briefly to someone else in the background. "It's Hunter Airfield in Georgia, D. Don't you have family in Savannah? Hunter's not right in town, but not very far away." He was distracted by the secondary conversation but continued after a short break. "Good. I'll get with you soon, Deliverance, but I've got a thing right now with Coach. And don't forget the 'Hail and Farewell' Saturday night at our house. I mean my house. For now. Bibi says you're **cleared hot** for exterior transport as long as Lucinda's with you." He hesitated, and his "official commander voice" dropped lower and morphed into something more personal. "Thank God, man. When I saw them load you onto the Jolly from my seat at ten thousand feet, I was physically sick. And I'm not ashamed to admit it—scared too. I've never felt anything exactly like that. I'm not a religious man, but I prayed hard. Now I'm confident you'll be a hundred percent in no time." Happy's voice may have broken a little as he wrapped up. "Good job, D. Keep it up. We all miss you, man."

"Miss all you guys, too, boss. Send my best to Camille, and I'll see you Saturday night."

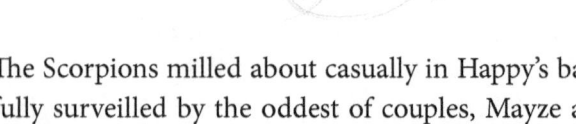

The Scorpions milled about casually in Happy's backyard, carefully surveilled by the oddest of couples, Mayze and Solomon. Mayze was Happy's endlessly moody English bulldog, and Solomon, a stunning Maine Coon cat, belonged to Camille. The two got on exactly like the dog and cat they were, except for occasions when their borders were breached. The strangers in their house were cause for the suspicious joint patrol they were conducting when I arrived. My crutches sent Sol into a feline rage, hissing and hiding behind Mayze's rotund form. I reached down for an ear scratch. "Aw, don't worry, Sol. We're friends, remember?"

Luckie regarded me with an arched brow. "He does not remember, clearly. That animal is mental, Tarzan, no shit. Sam was the only one who could reason with Sol when Camille was… away. The rest of us did all the cooking, cleaning, and appointments, but Sam had exclusive feline duty." She knit her immaculately groomed brows. "I didn't mean to intimate that Vivvie cooked at our request during that or any other time. There's no cooking for Vivianne. Ever."

Chips and salsa were in evidence as well as the ever-present coolers of drinks. The Scorpions and their significant others gathered with hugs and hearty handshakes although it had only been a short time since I made an appearance at the end-of-summer picnic. I had been confined to a wheelchair and sporting a bulky, complex cast that made the short trip challenging. Luckie and I had only stayed an hour, but the outing left us both exhausted.

Now I was practically nimble on my crutches and sporting a high-tech cross between a cast and a surgical boot. The noise level approached deafening as almost fifty pilots, wives, husbands, significant others, and **attached personnel** laughed, gossiped and got a head start on well-wishes for the two couples who were leaving the squadron at the end of the month. Rock, the unofficial leader of the LPA, huddled with the half dozen Scorpion lieutenants in the rear of the lush, fenced yard, readying the evening's entertainment.

In fighter squadrons, the monthly "Hail and Farewell" was an informal party to welcome newly transferred members and to say goodbye to those who were leaving. Our LPA traditionally presented an amusing skit, roasting the outgoing Scorpions by reviewing the highlights of their time with the squadron. If buffoonery had occurred—and it typically had—it was lampooned by the lieutenants in their tribute. Now they huddled under a big shade tree, rummaging in a garbage bag containing their shoddy collection of props. An absurd floral housedress and long, black wig à la Cher indicated the person wearing them represented a woman, most often the spouse of the pilot who was leaving. The woman may have had red hair or been blond, but she would always have long black Cher hair in the LPA skit. Their resources and interest in shopping for anything better were limited. Additionally, there were oversized name tags so various lieutenants could take on the roles of other pilots, commonly Happy. He was good-naturedly parodied as a terrifying and inflexible hard-ass one minute, and an obtuse **bean counter** the next. As the weapons officer, I was a frequent target for LPA abuse, as well as Coach, our Ops Officer. After a short period of socializing, Camille snagged attention with an ear-splitting wolf whistle.

She stood on the back patio of Happy's house, soon to be her house too, glowing under the gaze of an obviously smitten Nathan. He grinned at her, his arm around her waist, urging her to speak to the crowd.

"Scorpions! 'kay, listen up now…this Hail and Farewell begins with a 'Bigger and Better Hunt' benefiting the South Tucson Women's Shelter. **ROE** is as follows: competitive groups are flights with attached personnel. You have three hours and must present your treasures for judging at 2000 hours. You will begin with the paper clip that's being distributed to flight commanders presently. Flights are to assemble in the corners of Happy's yard for ten minutes to strategize before departure. Pizza, beer, and LPA skits with farewells will begin at 2030. It's for charity, Stingers, so leave it all on the field—huddle in your corners and prepare to depart at my signal. And…go!"

The group scrambled as if their lives depended on the

outcome, fervently yelling ideas to their flight commander and scribbling notes on scraps of paper. I explained to Luckie that a "Bigger and Better Hunt" entailed beginning with a meager object and rapidly visiting the homes of friends and acquaintances, requesting something "bigger and better." Adding the goal of assisting the women's shelter would light a fire under the teams, although their naturally competitive natures were enough to make the contest a bloodbath. In my current, slightly disabled condition, I would bring no advantage to a fast-moving team. Luckie and I planned to stay behind. She could help Camille and Happy put final touches on the party while I drank beer and got underfoot. These days, I was exceptionally good at being in the way.

Camille looked at her phone for the time, and then placed her pinkies at the corners of her mouth and let loose with another piercing whistle. The backyard erupted into bedlam as the group charged the gate, flight commanders yelling directions as they ran. They loaded into every large vehicle available, packing several SUVs and pickups, and departed rapidly in every direction.

Camille motioned for us all to relax in the deeply cushioned outdoor sectional that took up the far corner of the large patio. Luckie helped me get comfortable, propping my leg on an ottoman cushioned with pillows, and Nathan emerged from the kitchen with four cold longnecks. While he popped the tops and distributed drinks, the girls came to an agreement on the pizza order. Camille phoned in the order, specifying a delayed delivery and making arrangements to meet the driver at the security gate in a little over two hours.

The heat of summer was relaxing its grip on Tucson, and the lack of humidity made the late afternoon pleasant as soon as Nate adjusted the monstrous umbrella to shield our party from the setting sun. Mayze lumbered over to settle at Cami's feet with obvious effort, and then panted affectionately as she fed her ice chips from a cup on the table. "They're both so jealous,"

Camille grinned, petting her sleek coat. "It won't be long before Sol throws a tantrum to demonstrate how pissed he is about this cuddle session. King Solomon is accustomed to being the prettiest one in the room." Glancing around surreptitiously, I could see Sol crouching behind a shrub at the foundation of the house, his glorious tail angrily slicing the air. He was biding his time.

Nathan leaned back, stretching his arms along the back of the cushions and pulling Camille toward him with a smile. "I think we're all set for the Hunter TDY on our end, D. You'll have orders on Monday with departure set for Thursday. It's a damn good thing Lucinda and Cami worked things out for Luckie to go along; the clinic on base denied my personnel request. They're running short-handed themselves because of the big summer TDY. Not enough bodies to go around, per usual. At any rate, we're looking at almost three weeks off station. That work for you?"

I tamped down the creeping unease that had begun to take root in my gut from the outset of this plan. There was nothing I wanted more than to have my life back in order, and that included work. Flying wouldn't be in the cards for a couple more months at minimum, so being an asset to the squadron meant non-flying duty. But that wasn't the issue.

Savannah was the issue—more to the point, my parents.

I loved them and appreciated the life and advantages they'd afforded me, but their world was a small, privileged place. And as much as it pained me to admit the truth, their minds matched their narrow worldview. My dad saw the world through the lens of his desires and values, largely unaffected by the struggles experienced by many segments of society. He viewed his accomplishments and pedigree as the result of being truly self-made, not the product of wealth and entitlement that more clearly represented the truth. And, as much as I loved Mama, it was her prejudices that were more stubbornly ingrained and, arguably, more offensive. Her charitable, gracious exterior with its genteel polish concealed a woman who truly believed herself superior to others. It wasn't until I joined the Air Force and extricated myself from that insular environment that I saw the glaring discrepancy between my experiences and the real world. More than simple exposure, a bone-deep kinship with people of differing economic backgrounds, political and religious convictions, and ethnicities had molded me into a different man than the one who'd left Savannah only a handful of years before. My world was a larger place now, thanks to the richness and texture so many friends brought into my life. Stepping back into my father's realm would render the differences painfully stark.

I could frankly not imagine how he and my mother would react to Lucinda and to the fact that I was seriously involved with a black woman. The possibilities were endless; none of the scenarios I could imagine were good.

Sol's sneak attack on Mayze from the bushes, with a bizarre combination of hissing and meowing, yanked me into the present. "It sounds great, Happy. I'll be glad to get back in the saddle. Sitting on the bench is wearing on me, no matter how good the company is." I smiled at Luckie, giving her shoulder an affectionate squeeze.

"I didn't think I'd be able to take Davis up on his offer of a Savannah visit so soon." Luckie fussed with the pillows cradling my leg, and then settled herself again in the circle of my arm, snuggling in tighter. "I'm sure he's looking forward to spending time with his parents, right, babe?" Her eyes smiled brightly, then clouded as she studied my face. I was telegraphing every concern plaguing my mind, judging from the look she fixed on me. So I overcompensated.

"Absolutely, Peaches. Can't wait."

Happy's eyebrows shot up, and he took a quick slug of beer to conceal his expression.

Camille made no such effort, breaking into a huge shit-eating grin and chortling. "Peaches? Peaches? Is that because you're so juicy and luscious, Lucinda? Or is there some nasty dripping we need to address with antibiotics?"

Luckie assumed a haughty expression, smiling sweetly at her friend. "Go fuck yourself, you gross bitch. And the horse you rode in on. You know you don't have the stomach to wade into a war of insults with me and my debauched vocabulary."

Cami blew her a kiss, laughing. "You are my original true love, and I would never skewer you with words. But only because I can't."

I was glad for the diversion and laughed along with Cami and Luckie. "I can't wait to see my parents, baby—can't wait for you to meet them." The sound of screeching brakes, crumpling metal and shattering glass painted an immediate picture in my head of the *Guess Who's Coming to Dinner* moment I'd just conjured. There was no way this was going to be anything but a turbo-charged shitshow.

Chapter
SEVENTEEN

"Big Fun"

Lucinda

Now, I had to admit I had some unanswered questions. Once Davis was in surgery following the accident, I'd asked Nathan for his next-of-kin contact information. I placed the call to his parents with Nate's blessing and explained that he'd been involved in a serious aircraft accident, detailing his injuries as best I could. His mother answered the phone, but her response was more detached than I'd ever heard after breaking bad news to a family. There were no frantic plans to travel to her injured son's bedside. His father's reaction was similarly cool, and he interrogated me with terse questions about the particulars. From the outset, it was apparent they had no intention to travel to Tucson, and Mr. Foster's tone with me bordered on condescending, as if he was talking to the hired help. He even went so far as to mention how his law practice consumed most of his time with work too critical to abandon. When his curiosity about Davis's condition was sated, he brought our conversation to an abrupt conclusion, assuring me he'd be in touch later to hear the outcome of the surgery. To say their reactions were atypical didn't begin to cover it.

I never mentioned the content of my conversation with his parents, only the fact that I'd briefly spoken to them. Fortunately, Davis never questioned me further on the matter. I wasn't sure I'd be able to conceal the distaste I'd immediately developed for his father. Although my exposure to them had been brief and had occurred under terrible circumstances, it wasn't a promising beginning. It was disquieting to think of the man I'd come to deeply care for growing up with parents like that.

The noxious beeping of Cami's phone alarm derailed my unpleasant train of thought and interrupted Nathan's conversation with Davis about the Savannah TDY. She stood, stretched, and left to meet the pizza delivery driver at the front security gate. I busied myself, pouring more bags of ice on the coolers of drinks and stacking paper products along the long table situated under two shade trees at the edge of Nate's yard. Solomon accompanied me, swatting my calves with his fluffy tail and meowing complaints about Mayze. With everything ready, I checked my phone to find the eight p.m. deadline looming a mere twenty minutes away. I could see Cami's MINI Cooper wending its way back toward the house, so I let myself into the front yard, careful not to allow the livestock to escape, and began helping my friend unload stacks of warm pizza boxes.

Camille groaned as she stowed half a dozen boxes in the oven. "Dude. I'm starving. Where are the treasure hunters? I need a feeding."

Cam's complaints were interrupted by boisterous laughter as the first group pounded on the front door. Rock opened the door, striding into the kitchen. "Just tell us where we go to claim our prize; B Flight has kicked ass again." He exchanged congratulatory high fives with the other B Flight team members and an intricate handshake with Hung, their flight commander.

Camille stacked the last mountain of pizza boxes on the countertop, grinning at the assemblage, and I covered the boxes with two heavy beach towels. These would be consumed in record time as the teams arrived in the next few minutes, so they didn't need to stay warm very long. "Okay, B Flight. Congratulations on your premature declaration of victory. I assume you prefer to keep your treasure under wraps until judging?"

Hung nodded. "Yep. We've got the winner, hands down, but we'll administer the shock and awe once everybody gets back. Come on, guys and gals. To the victors go the spoils…beers in the backyard, Cam?"

Camille shooed the group out the door and into the yard just as the sound of trucks pulling up heralded the arrival of more competitors. The yard quickly filled with trash-talking pilots, spouses, attached personnel, and significant others. The pizza disappeared, box by box, along with cold beverages, and the squadron settled into companionable conversation punctuated with laughter.

The whistle sounded as Happy stepped onto a chair, motioning the group to settle. "Welcome to the September Hail and Farewell, Stingers. Miss Sullivan will officiate the judging of the Bigger and Better Hunt, and then we'll get along with the business at hand. Please welcome the lovely Camille."

Nathan pulled Cami in for a kiss and stepped down. She smiled at the group and asked the flight commanders to join her at the front. "Alright, everybody. As you're aware, tonight's haul benefits the South Tucson Women's Shelter. You've had three hours, starting with a humble paper clip. So, without further ado, let's see how you all did. Bash, get up here and let's get started."

Bashful moved to the front of the crowd, inciting the C Flight team to cheer frantically. Eventually, everyone found places in folding chairs, on one of the two picnic tables, and along the fence on big beach blankets. Then Bash addressed the group.

"C Flight is glad to lead the fight, as usual. So, it turns out that Boo lifts at the same gym Randy Johnson uses. *The* Randy Johnson—formerly of the Diamondbacks All-Star, Cy Young, whole nine. So we have procured an autographed ball from the one and only Big Unit—Randy Johnson—that can be auctioned online. All of this with his blessing, of course, to benefit the South Tucson Women's Shelter."

The cheering was enthusiastic, and C Flight celebrated their presumed win while Camille took the floor. "Everybody welcome Marilyn to let us know about how A Flight fared this evening. Come on up here, A Flight…"

Pete "Marilyn" Manson toasted the cheering crowd with his beer, took a second to pump his fist toward one of his lieutenants, Torch, and shook Happy's hand heartily. After the noise had dulled, he shot a dazzling smile at the crowd and roared, "Scorpions!" The group again erupted in cheering and hilarity.

Marilyn's rumbling baritone broke the relative quiet as he began. "A Flight has already had a blast tonight, so big thanks to Happy and Camille for hosting this Hail and Farewell. A Flight is saying a sad goodbye to everybody's favorite crew chief, Skeeter, and his beautiful wife, Sonia, as well as welcoming Chaplain Larry Creed and his lovely wife, DeAnne. Larry's **tactical** is "Apollo," although I'm told he tried to snag "Apostle.""

A tall, smiling man seated on the picnic table sang out. "That's true, Marilyn. But I'll gladly answer to Apollo. Thanks for the welcome to A Flight and the Scorpions, everybody."

"Now, on to the hunt. It took the full three hours and all the combined skills the brothers of A Flight could muster to ace this challenge. In the end, we prevailed because of the wisdom, the connections, and the complete lack of shame exhibited by…" At this point, every member of A Flight broke into a collective drum roll, using any surface available. "…the newly attached Chaplain Apollo." The group cheered loudly again, enthusiasm increasingly fueled by alcohol, and Torch, who stood near Larry, punched his shoulder in congratulations.

Pete continued his explanation. "Seems that Command Chaplain Simmons and his family are **PCS**'ing to the UK and expecting significantly smaller accommodations on base there. They donated their big sectional sofa to the chapel annex rather than opting to store it, and that left two large—and nearly new— U-shaped sectionals in need of a good home. Chaplain Simmons was very interested in the two electrical transformers we'd acquired from Sergeant Young who works over at the Post Office. He and his family just moved here from RAF Lakenheath," he said, referencing the Royal Air Force Base in England. "I called the director of the shelter to double-check dimensions, and she said they'll be perfect for the large group counseling room at the facility. The sectionals are strapped onto a trailer we borrowed from Chaplain Simmons and will be delivered tomorrow to the shelter by the finest flight in the best squadron on base." He joined his flight in chanting, "A Flight! A Flight! A Flight!"

Nathan moved forward, shaking Marilyn's hand and joining the applause for A Flight. "Well done, A Flight. You are all very fine examples of…something. In all seriousness, great creativity in procurement for a very worthy cause." He lifted a beer to the new chaplain and his wife. "Looks like Apollo is our kind of people. Welcome to the Stingers, both of you. Let's hear from B Flight."

He stepped back as the group strung along the fence began shouting, "B Flight! B Flight! B Flight!" Hung stepped forward and gestured at B Flight. "Quiet, you animals. Hey there, everybody, and another big thanks to Happy and Miss Camille. First off, a great job by both C and A Flights—fantastic effort, really." He led the applause briefly, then resumed speaking. "From the heart of my bottom, it tears me apart…" He feigned wiping away a tear. "…it really does, to destroy your efforts with our trademark B Flight superiority."

And the crowd, at least the B Flight portion, went wild. This fake-cutthroat competition, obviously good-natured, had a big smile plastered on my face, and my jaws hurt from laughing.

"After making plenty of visits to friends all over base, and nearby off base, we had managed to get our grubby paws on some pretty choice odds and ends. But it was Anna Kate who upped the ante." Davis leaned over where I sat to indicate a pretty young woman sitting near a huge man I'd met earlier nicknamed Bugs, another of the Scorpion crew chiefs. "AK's brother is an electrician who has his own business and lives right outside the back gate. When we dropped by to see him, he was so taken with the Makita reciprocating saw we'd gotten from Chief Saunders that he offered us a deal we couldn't refuse. Our next stop was the big laundromat about a half mile down the road where he'd been working on a renovation. With AK's brother coordinating the effort, the owner met us there and delivered into our cunning and capable hands today's winner: ten sets of washers and dryers."

A collective gasp arose from the group.

Hung held up his hand. "Let me explain a little further. The appliances are used but in mostly decent condition. Several need new rollers or idlers, so AK's brother agreed to meet with all available B Flight personnel tomorrow afternoon at the laundromat, walk us through the repairs and help us get the appliances delivered to the shelter tomorrow evening. Thanks for the great teamwork exhibited today, guys and gals." He used his empty beer bottle to mimic a mic drop on the grass and shouted, "B Flight out!"

Happy rose, laughing and shaking his head. "You folks dropped my jaw today, Scorpions. This is a whole squadron of winners, but I think we can all agree the prize goes to B Flight. Free beers next Friday at the Club for you guys."

I turned to Camille, shaking my head in wonder. "How the

hellfire did those people leave here with paper clips and return with collectibles and appliances?"

Davis pulled me close enough to steal a kiss and drawled in my ear, "Same way I got you naked and coming on my cock in a closet, Peaches—a little luck and a lotta bullshit. It's one of the many gifts fighter pilots have."

I threw back my head and laughed as everyone surged toward Camille, bearing a stack of pizza boxes fresh from the oven. "Seems to me you may have more gifts than the average fighter pilot, Tarzan. Anatomically and otherwise."

Davis's eyes softened, transforming from laughing to a dark, appraising stare. Then he whispered so quietly that only I could hear over the noise in the backyard.

"Lucinda Dominique, I'm gonna fall in love with you."

Chapter EIGHTEEN

"Leaving on a Jet Plane"

Davis

The pilot dropped the brakes on the 737, and we rolled down the runway on a collision course with a destiny that made my stomach ache. It had been a long morning already. Luckie did the work of two people, packing and loading everything we needed for a three-week trip as well as the supplies required for the care and feeding of my rapidly mending leg. Under normal circumstances, I'd have been searching for any excuse to introduce this extraordinary woman to my family. But the increasing anxiety I felt about exposing Luckie to the racism I'd been reared around stained what should have been an enjoyable trip. This four-hour flight from Tucson to Atlanta was my final window of opportunity to air my family's dirty laundry with Lucinda.

Luckie was exhausted in the aftermath of her marathon morning. She'd loaded a mountain of luggage into her car along with my crippled ass, then wrangled the entire rolling train wreck through the airport. She was breathing deeply, eyes closed, before we even leveled out. I stared at the fringe of dark lashes fanning her cheeks. For the first time, nothing stood between me and leisurely admiration of her beauty. I sank back into the seat, jumbled thoughts crowding my mind.

I awoke reluctantly and felt Luckie's hands gently repositioning my leg and feeling my toes for warmth. She smiled, sitting back, and offered me a cold carton of orange juice. "Vitamin C and sunshine, Tarzan. Good for what ails you."

"Thanks, Peaches. Did you sleep?" A quick check of my watch told me we were just over two hours into the flight.

"Yep. That doesn't seem to be a big problem these days." She squeezed my hand. "I'm so proud of how hard you've been working in PT and how well your recovery's going. I know there's pain, and you probably feel like you'll never get there. But you will. I *know* you will, Davis."

Damn. She was the hottest cheerleader I could've asked for, all rah-rah encouragement and optimism with a big helping of "I'll kick your ass if you step out of line." Because of the regrettable timing—as if there was a good time for an aircraft accident—Luckie had been cast in the role of caregiver and advocate-in-chief when our relationship was in its infancy. But she rolled with it like a boss. Now she was taking unpaid leave from work to travel with me. And, thanks to my silence to this point, she had no idea of the potential conflict waiting. There had been real progress in so many parts of the South, but not so much in the hearts or minds of my parents.

I studied her lithe form as it stretched across the inadequate airline seat. "Lucinda." I cleared my throat, beginning again. "Luckie, I need to talk to you about something serious." Her brow knitted abruptly, and she wordlessly scanned my face. "There are similarities in the way we were both raised. Money. Privilege." I pulled my gaze away from her and stared at the blank video screen on the seat back. "But some of the qualities my parents have…some of the things they believe, well, they don't reflect positively on me. And they aren't the things I believe." I swallowed hard and tried to formulate my next move.

Luckie's face was more somber. "Just tell me, Davis. I can't imagine you're going to say something I haven't heard before." Her tone was forthright, but it didn't hold judgment.

"They're racists. There's not a better word to use or a way to frame it more elegantly." The words tasted bitter in my mouth. "They would tell you it's not true. They would tell you they have lots of black friends." I finger-quoted the comment, feeling suddenly angry that I had to play apologist. "But the ideas are ingrained. Dug in deep, and that's how I was raised." It was quiet between us for a beat or two. Then she spoke.

"It's sad they feel that way, Davis, but that doesn't affect you and me. We care about each other. We've already been through so much together, and that's beginning to make you and me into an 'us.'" She looked away. "Or am I wrong about that?"

I didn't recognize my voice when I finally spoke. "You're not wrong, gorgeous. I can't imagine having made it through the past few weeks without you next to me, holding my hand through the hardest parts and pushing me when I didn't want to try. I never thought I'd face a challenge like the one I'm staring down, and now I can't imagine doing it without you. A couple of months ago, I hadn't given any thought to letting a beautiful, headstrong woman into my life. But look what's happened. Now I could never have made it this far without you." I crumbled unexpectedly toward the end.

I reached across her seat, stroking the smooth, dark skin of her face. She looked down into her hands, now clasped in her lap. "I don't want to make it worse, Luckie. This has been so hard for you already. You've put your life on hold for someone you barely know, if we're being honest."

Her laugh coated both of us like honey. "Oh, Davis. No...no. Don't cloak this drama in something bigger than it deserves." She relaxed visibly and traced the veins that formed a road map on my forearm. "Everyone has a different hill to climb. If this is ours, and if we're meant to get across it, we'll see the other side." We sat in the stillness, soaking in the comfort from each other for a time.

How could someone like Lucinda Page—strong, independent, driven—understand the complicated relationship I had with my father? When her parents refused to support her choices, it seemed she'd shaken them like water off a duck's back and walked her chosen path with complete confidence. Studying the situation, I had to admit I was feeling weak—maybe even duplicitous. I'd never had any intention of following the path my parents laid out. The idea of squiring around legions of vacuous socialites while sucking Savannah's collective dick? Of building business contacts on the strength of my alleged charm, family name, and connections?

Yeah, no thanks.

I'd found my biggest strengths, almost by accident, hands on the stick and throttle of the hulking Warthog. What was more, I'd found I had a real knack for teaching less-experienced pilots. With an instinctive combination of supportive encouragement and heavy-handed critique, I could consistently draw from them a better performance than they thought themselves capable of.

Armed with the confidence of a man who'd found his life's work and was fucking great at it, why would I hesitate to approach my father candidly? The answer wasn't easy, but my subconscious knew the uncomfortable truth.

I genuinely loved and respected my father, despite the vast ideological gulf that separated us in many ways. Daddy was

a product of a time and generation I didn't begin to compre-
hend. My granddaddy, Davis Senior, was a hard man. He'd never
shown compassion or affection to anyone, least of all his young
son. His discipline was harsh, his standards impossibly high, and
his approval nonexistent. I remembered being frightened of the
man with his severe mustache and heavy eyebrows. His trademark distant formality kept him from the hugs and laughter my
friends enjoyed with their grandparents. No ice cream parties on
the porch. No fishing trips.

But in comparison to the childhood my father must've endured—and there was never a hint of discussion on that topic—
my upbringing was a virtual walk in the park. Daddy was hardly
demonstrative, but there was plenty of that from my mother. He
was intensely interested in the achievements and abilities of his
only child, engaging me in all manner of sports as well as academic and social pursuits. Central to my rearing from a young
age, I'd been thoroughly trained to know I was expected to join
Father in the family business, just as Davis Junior had done with
Granddaddy and my great-granddaddy before him. In some
ways, the Old South that was immortalized in tomes like *Gone
with the Wind* had changed very little in intervening generations.
In the shiny, distorted bubble that was Savannah society, tradition and respect trumped everything else. But I suspected the
same story was true in places other than the South.

How could anyone understand the struggle without the dubious benefit of having marinated in the culture for a lifetime?
In the end, Luckie couldn't be expected to sympathize. When
she found herself at odds with her family and upbringing, she
stepped past it without hesitation. Surely she would see my
incomplete independence as flawed. Staring out onto silvery
clouds, it sure looked that way to me. I turned to find her watching me.

My eyes burned into hers, willing her to believe the words I said. "I would never have willingly dropped you into a situation like this one so early in our relationship, Luckie. This is not beginner shit. It's a smoking stick of dynamite, ready to blow us all to kingdom come."

Luckie smiled indulgently. "I *know* you didn't just call me a neophyte. You didn't do that, did you, Tarzan?"

"No. No, that's not what I mean. You believe me, don't you?" I grabbed her hand, searching for words. "I care for you, and we're just getting this thing off the ground together when I find myself swinging under a parachute and wind up sending us both down a path we didn't see coming. Now I'm getting ready to pull a Sidney Poitier with two loving but very unevolved people."

And probably blow the best thing you've ever had sky-high, dumbass.

Luckie chuckled a little and patted my hand. "Try not to be so dramatic, Davis. I'm a black woman. This won't be the first time I've encountered racism, if that's how it goes down. I do have some ability to cope and communicate, and I've even been known to win people over on occasion."

I felt some relief at her words, along with a heaping helping of doubt. Luckie had probably never met anyone like Davis and Emmaline Foster. On the other hand, she was a force even I had not learned to reckon with, and I suspected I was in love with her. The Fosters of Savannah might well be no match.

Chapter NINETEEN

"The Real Thing"

Davis

"It's just like I remember, Davis. So lush and romantic." Luckie's eyes shone and twinkled under the streetlights along Bay Street. The live oak canopy cloaked the meandering sidewalk, wrapping us in its arms as we roamed along. When we turned up Bull Street, Luckie peered into store windows chock-full of old jewelry, art, and china, and we ducked in and out of several shops. She studied several small baubles and jewelry pieces, finally selecting a fine silver chain, dusty and tarnished. After slipping some cash to the elderly shopkeeper as Luckie rummaged in her purse, I fastened the clasp at her nape, touched my lips to the smooth expanse of mahogany skin there, and watched goose bumps bloom. She turned and smiled her little smile, her downcast gaze causing the fringe of dark lashes to fan against her cheeks. Her beauty was in a class of its own, and she left me breathless during the rare, unhurried moments I was able to take it all in.

She reached for my hand as we meandered out of the shop

and slowly made our way back onto the cobblestone path near Bay Street. It led down a steep hill toward River Street, alive with crowds taking in the pubs and restaurants there. "I love the chain, Davis. I didn't expect you to pay, but thank you for giving me something beautiful to remember tonight by." Her fingers toyed with the fine links, rearranging them. "It's very typical of things I'm drawn to. There's this imperfection to it; for me, it implies age and maybe history. When something is polished and perfect— all shiny and symmetrical—I lose interest. It doesn't seem authentic." We walked in silence, awash in the music coming from the bars and the conversation of the customers. She seemed deep in thought. Then she turned back to me and squeezed my hand.

"It's like us, isn't it? The imperfection and the lack of polish." The fact that I didn't follow her must have played plainly on my face because she laughed when I looked at her, blank and questioning. "If you were hearing the story of how two people met and dated and began to build something together, would it look this way?" She waved her hand in the air, indicating the two of us. "I mean, would it start with a memorable encounter in a closet?"

I laughed. No one would ever begin a bona fide love story with a hot fuck in a public place. And wasn't that what this was—a love story? "No, Peaches, I'll grant you it wasn't the most sentimental beginning." I pulled her toward a quiet corner of the street and turned to take her in again, sobering. "And you deserve the romance. All the wine and roses. But what happened between us that night was one of the most staggeringly beautiful things that's ever happened to me. I felt things I never had that night after we said goodbye. I couldn't explain the urgency to see you again. I was spellbound, Lucinda." I lifted her hand to my mouth and turned it over, kissing her palm gently. "And you've continued to captivate me every moment since."

Her face said everything even as her mouth remained silent. She studied me, moving her palm to rest against my cheek.

Finally, she stepped closer and spoke. "I knew you were different from the very first time I saw you leaning against the O'Club bar. And everything that happened has been interesting and imperfect—nothing polished or posed or stilted. Everything I see in you and everything I feel for you is perfectly genuine. Whatever it is right now and whatever it becomes, Davis, it's the real thing."

Before the words fully passed her lips, I'd captured them in a soft kiss. My words weren't enough to tell her what I already knew about us. So I allowed my mouth to say it for me, letting her feel the depth of the longing I'd been carrying since the first night. She softened against me, wrapping long arms around my neck and melting into the kiss. I had only one arm available to feel her softness, the other leaning precariously on the crutches, so I settled one hand against the curve of her hip. After an unhurried exploration of her full lips and warm mouth, I pulled back, allowing our eyes to meet and lock. Her breath was shallow and came quickly, but a small smile decorated the perfection of her face, and her eyes danced.

I kept my voice quiet despite the crowds and noise nearby. "I have a confession to make. Are you ready?" I grinned a little to signal that the news was all good. Her head tilted suspiciously, but she nodded. "Do you remember when I woke up in the recovery room after the accident?" Another little nod. "It was so cold, and I was disoriented, but I was so fucking happy your gorgeous face was the first thing I saw. I can't even tell you how glad." It was surprisingly difficult to talk about the accident though the aftermath could've been so much worse. I continued, still only a couple of inches from Luckie's face.

"Anyway, I remember you telling me that Miles was alive and alright. You also said you'd spoken to my family, which surprised me. I'm pretty sure you told me some details about my injuries, but I can't be sure. The morphine makes the finer points pretty fuzzy." The hand splayed on her hip tightened and pulled her warmth firmly against me. "But before I fell asleep again, there was one thing I remember as clearly as I remember anything that's ever happened to me."

Her eyes shot me a questioning look before recognition suddenly dawned. She looked a bit frightened, but I forged on. "You whispered it right before you left the room: 'I love you so much.'"

She swallowed hard, but her eyes never wavered from mine. The commotion of nearby crowds, the heat and oppressive humidity along the riverfront, all the activity and lights and distraction—it all faded abruptly as if Lucinda and I were the last two people on earth in that shadowy corner of River Street. She spoke first. "It's true, Davis, and I was sure when I whispered it to you that day. It wasn't just the fear that you weren't coming back or the way my heart ripped open when I saw you unconscious in the trauma room. I don't want you to think it was just my emotions driving me to say something dramatic that I didn't mean." Her breath came fast, but she didn't pull away. "I've never been in love before. To be honest, I wasn't sure I'd recognize it if it ever did come along. But I did know, and I'm even more sure of it today than I was then." Her voice broke uncharacteristically. "I do love you, Davis—so much. I didn't plan it, but here we are. Sometimes I can't believe you're in my life."

Again, my mouth covered hers, thanking her over and over for baring herself to me. When I finally pulled away, the enormity of the great gift Luckie had given me settled around me, not like a burden, but an embrace. "What could I ever have done to deserve you? I didn't expect to tell you on a busy street in Savannah, but I love you, Lucinda Dominique. I didn't plan it either, but it was so inevitable. And there's nothing that could make me happier than walking the road and figuring out the next step together."

A smile lit up her face. "You love me too?"

I leaned toward her until our foreheads touched. "Yeah,

gorgeous. I'm in love with you. How could I not be?"

We both laughed, all the heaviness dispelled like balloons flying off into the sky, and she helped me arrange my crutches again for walking. She searched in the depths of her tiny bag, finally retrieving a tissue after an exhaustive search. My girl dabbed her eyes, then sighed happily. "Then, let's walk. How about a drink, Tarzan?"

Even hobbled by crutches, I felt elated as we picked our way along the cobblestone walk toward our destination. The bar was perched on the roof with a dramatic view of the Talmadge Memorial Bridge. We settled onto stools near the outdoor fire pit, and I ordered—a Belvedere martini for Luckie and a Hop Dang Diggity from Jekyll Brewing for me. Sighing contentedly, I stretched an arm across her chair, and she rested her head on my shoulder. A welcome evening breeze cooled the thick air, and we surveyed the beauty of the city.

"Don't even think about making it weird, Tarzan." Lucinda's voice held a teasing tone. "Just because we confessed our undying devotion for each other doesn't mean we aren't going to keep giving each other shit all the time and hanging out like best friends and fucking like horny little bunny rabbits." She took a healthy slug of her icy martini and sucked seductively at one of the skewered olives floating in the glass. "I'm going to insist that we christen that big bed at the fancy hotel you're paying for with some truly perverse sex on this very night. And maybe again a couple of times in the morning. Making love isn't the only way to seal the deal once you're in love." She put her martini down only long enough to finger-quote "making love." "In fact, we're gonna play hide the salami in such a depraved manner, it'd embarrass the pros in Amsterdam." She leered evilly at me, sipping the martini and warming to her subject. "And before we actually get to it, I'm planning to go downtown and address the court with enthusiasm normally reserved for ladies who are paid pole smokers."

My dick enjoyed her proposal and started to make his way north for a breath of fresh air. I snorted. Go downtown and address the court? The girl definitely had a way with words.

"I know from experience you can deliver on the dirty mouth and the dirty everything else." I paused briefly to signal the waiter for a second round, then took a long drink of my beer, making Luckie wait to hear what was on my mind. "What I don't know, Peaches, is how you'd react if I were…" I paused again, pretending to search for the words I needed. "If I were more domineering when we're alone." I narrowed my eyes and leaned close, dropping my voice. "More controlling. If there were things I wanted to do to you? For you?" She set her martini glass on the tabletop and regarded me with a hooded gaze.

"What kinds of things, Davis?" I could see her pulse skittering faster at the base of her throat, and the husky whisper made my cock thicken further.

"A variety of things, Lucinda. Ways I want to enjoy the woman I love and make her body need me." I paused again, leaning back in the chair this time and allowing myself a leisurely survey along the length of her mouthwatering body. Noticing that I was indulging myself, Luckie put herself on display, lazily uncrossing then crossing her everlastingly long legs and allowing the hem of the short skirt to ride higher on her thighs. One manicured finger stirred the cold martini, then traced a wet path from where her pulse thrummed at her neck and down across her chest and to the spot where the tops of soft breasts peeked from a snug V-necked tee shirt.

"I might feel the need to coddle you. To spoil and pamper your delicious body and give you more pleasure than you thought you could feel. Might want to lick and taste literally every inch of your soft skin or spend an entire night between your thighs. While away a couple of hours feeding on your soft, sweet pussy."

A moan escaped Luckie's mouth, and she swallowed visibly.

Then she grabbed her drink and took a long swallow. "Now, that sounds…wonderful, Davis." She cleared her throat nervously. "Really, just wonderful. Is there more?" She took another drink, forgetting to set the glass aside this time.

I stretched an arm back across her chair and looked my fill once more. "There's no end to the pleasure I could take between your legs, Lucinda. Quite a bit of who I am in the bedroom is a little more aggressive than I've probably shown you." I allowed a steelier tone to undergird my words and continued to explain. "In general, I have a reputation for being friendly and easy-going. There are times, when we're naked and alone together, that I'll want to take care of every need you have and tell you exactly how to take care of me." I paused to see if I'd made her uncomfortable or anxious, but there was only undisguised desire burning in her eyes. Luckie leaned into my space again.

"So let me see if I understand you clearly." She paused, allowing her eyes to soften. My cock throbbed in earnest against the constraint of my zipper. It took great focus not to readjust the length stretching in my pants. "You're saying there will be occasions when you want to let your inner dominant out to play. You'll want to demand I take a subservient role and that I acquiesce to your direction." I nodded once, and she continued. "That I'll take whatever pleasure you give me—or don't—and that I'll give you whatever you request."

I raised my eyebrows a little. She made it sound like I was rolling the dice, and I probably was. "That's about the size of it, Peaches." A beat or two of silence passed between us, and then Luckie raised her hand, signaling the waiter.

"Check, please."

Chapter TWENTY

"Down and Dirty"

Lucinda

The River Street Inn was a lovely old historic hotel that boasted views of the Savannah River, wonderful period furniture, and even a ghost. According to Davis, it was a favorite of his family's; they had hosted many events there when even the voluminous family estate proved too cramped. I was overwhelmed by the Southern charm oozing from every detail, design to furnishings, along with the easy hospitality of the staff earlier when we'd checked in. Davis had decided to forgo the more modest accommodation offered at Fort Stewart and spring for lodging that was quintessentially Savannah.

Now I was utterly blind to the considerable magic of our surroundings, helping Davis as we hurried through the stately lobby and into the elevator. When the door closed, I gathered the front of his shirt into my fist and moved in to devour his mouth. To my surprise, however, he slowed my roll with a firm hand at my waist. "Be patient, Lucinda. I'm calling the shots now." He nuzzled into my hair and chuckled, probably hearing my desperate little whine. "I'll make sure the wait is more than worth it. I promise." He squeezed me, then pushed me away gently.

The elevator finally arrived at our floor, and I hurried ahead of Davis, searching frantically through my purse for the room key card. Pulling it triumphantly from the clutter, I held it up with a smile. "Got it! See?" Davis smirked and continued making his way deliberately down the hallway.

He closed the door behind us and pushed me gently against it without turning on any of the lights. Streetlights along River Street glowed through the windows, lending an otherworldly appearance to the darkened room. My mouth was hungry for his, and my pulse picked up as I sensed his face nearing mine. At the last moment, though, he bent his face to my neck and inhaled, groaning. "You're going to be so fucking delicious when I taste you tonight, Lucinda. My mouth is watering thinking about licking and suckling at your sweet cunt. Feeling your clit throb against my tongue." He couldn't stop another groan. "But we have some work to do first. I need to earn the taste of you in my mouth. And you have to earn my fingers and tongue and my cock filling you." He pulled away, and his beautiful eyes bored into me. "Let's get started, beautiful. It's gonna be a long night for that wet little pussy of yours."

Okay then.

"Take all your clothes off, Lucinda." Davis's voice was gruff and deeper than I was accustomed to. "Kneel in front of the padded bench at the foot of the bed with your knees spread. I have a few things to take care of in the bathroom, and then I'll be back to enjoy you. I want to see your knees open and your pussy wet when I get back." He turned away, moving without hesitation into the bath and closing the door without a backward glance.

I throbbed and hurt for want of Davis's thick cock. Quickly stripping away my clothes, I couldn't think of a single thing other than the feeling of his length filling me. But this was uncharted territory. The idea of allowing Davis to use and pleasure me? In the past, I would have pushed back in a second; it would have felt too close to selling out my emotional independence. But we were definitely exploring new places together. This was the two of us, stripped bare physically and emotionally, left open to possibilities I hadn't experienced. That didn't assuage the butterflies beating the hell out of my stomach as I unhooked my bra and stepped out of my little panties. He said he wanted to see my pussy wet, but I guessed that wouldn't be an issue. Just to be certain, I ran one finger through my labia and gently brushed my clit. Swollen, wet, and needy as fuck. I swore under my breath.

"Are you touching what's mine, Peaches?" Davis stood in the door to the bathroom, backlit in the light from the window.

"N—no. Just checking. I mean, I'm getting ready." I quickly crossed the room. At the foot of the bed sat a Queen Anne style bench, thickly padded and upholstered with damask. I dropped to my knees there and wiggled my legs apart. Cool air caressed the wet of my exposed center, and I looked up at Davis for his approval.

"So pretty, baby." He still stood in the doorway, and I couldn't tear my eyes from his nakedness. In the dark, his powerful build was even more jarring, the interplay of light and shadow. He moved toward me, stopping only a couple of feet away. The angular jaw was more pronounced in the absence of the smile that usually softened it. He looked serious as his eyes swept over my kneeling form, and it colored the air with something unfamiliar.

"Are you going to tie me up, Davis?" I wasn't afraid, just interested. If that was his kink, I could give it a try. I couldn't imagine there was anything he'd want to do with me that I wouldn't enjoy.

A little smile curved his mouth but didn't reach his eyes. "No ties; not tonight. I'll let you know what I want from you, and you'll do the things I ask. And if you want to try it, we can put the shoe on the other foot some other night. You can have your way with me and be in charge. I'll let you have things any way you'd like if that's what gets you off." He raised a brow in question, but I didn't have any idea what to say. That would have to be the subject of some thought. For now, all I could focus on was the broad crown of his steely cock, and its heavy length stretched out a short distance from my mouth. I contemplated the thick vein running the considerable distance from root to head with several branches decorating the length. The largest of the veins pulsated obviously, even in the shadowy room.

My eyes darted back to his face, and it occurred to me I could be in trouble in role-playing land for staring at his cock without permission. Or was it the floor? I should've paid more careful attention to *Fifty Shades of Grey*. I was probably already in deep shit for being a subpar submissive. Sub-par sub-missive. Great. Now I was probably smirking.

"Do you like what you see, Peaches?" The low rumble of Davis's voice cut through my jumbled inner dialogue. "Maybe you'd enjoy an extended taste of my cock." My heart rate picked up at this news, and a low-key ache set up between my legs in anticipation of what was ahead.

"Mmmm. Yes, please, Davis. I'd love to suck your cock." I opened my mouth a little and batted my eyelashes, but his brows knit together, his face becoming serious again.

"I didn't say you could suck it, Lucinda." He moved closer and carefully settled himself on the bench in front of me, leaning back with his legs deliciously spread. With his knees open, his beautiful length lay against his flat stomach, straight and hard. The pulsing veins were still gloriously in evidence, and his balls hung below, generous and heavy. "I said you could enjoy an extended taste, so you may lick and taste me. But no sucking unless I say so. And you'll ask permission before you swallow any pre-cum leaking from the head. Understand?"

This was unexpected. Who didn't want his dick sucked? I

could play along though, so I leaned forward and extended my tongue toward the length of his cock, at rest along his muscled stomach. As the tip of my tongue contacted his skin, his head relaxed backward, and he exhaled hard with a, "Yesss, baby." I toyed with the head, pulsing in earnest against my tongue, then gradually relaxed the pointed tip of my tongue until the flat side of it bathed his hardness, occasionally swiping toward the tip. I looked up through lowered lashes with my tongue laving his dick and used what I deemed to be my best "breathy, submissive voice."

"May I taste you, Davis? Your cock is wet, and I'm thirsty for it." His eyes met mine, and his mouth curved up on one side in a devilish, crooked grin. He nodded quickly, only once, and I didn't hesitate to allow my tongue to sweep over the head of his cock, swiping away a couple of clear drops that collected there. I made a bit of a show of enjoying the taste on my tongue then continued bathing his length thoroughly. Eventually, Davis's slim, muscular hips began to rise involuntarily, thrusting toward my mouth, and I had to remind myself not to suck him in. Those were the specific instructions he'd given, but I wanted him to regret every syllable. Cautious to follow his direction, I lapped at his length like a lollipop.

I hoped the minutes were passing in slow motion for the man whose dick was taunting me, but I worked to pace my anxious tongue. He patiently accepted the ministrations of my mouth. Then, without warning, he groaned and tipped my face up with a finger under my chin.

"I love your sweet mouth on my cock, Luckie. I couldn't want you more than I do right now." He sat up on his elbows and pinned me with an intense look. "But I need to feel my tongue against the wet of your pussy. Good with that, baby?"

He thrust suddenly upward into my mouth, staring into my eyes. Never breaking the eye contact, he pumped his entire length in and out of my mouth, from tip to root. Once, slowly. Then a second time, even more slowly. And a third time. This time, the ridge of his cockhead slipped past my soft palate and into my throat; then he held it there until my eyes watered a little. He pulled his hips back quickly, allowing me to breathe, and spoke in a rough voice. "Take that beautiful mouth off me, gorgeous. Get off your knees and lie down on this bed with your legs spread open wide. I need to eat your wet cunt. His eyes met mine, his gaze glittering dangerously.

"And Lucinda? Hang on to something."

Oh, hell yes.

My thighs were shiny wet, and I was pretty sure that was a first. I scrambled onto the foot of the bed near the bench he'd reclined on and waited for him to carefully reposition himself, cautious to take the leg into consideration. I slid involuntarily back into "nurse mode," watching his movements and ready to correct him if he seemed about to overdo. But he was ahead of me, placing strong hands on the inside of my knees and slowly pushing my legs apart. The low light in the room made seeing him a challenge, but I could make out his darkening eyes as he studied my spread legs, wet thighs, and labia. He looked carefully for several seconds before a grin blossomed on his beautiful face and he glanced up at me. It was the most exposed I'd ever felt, naked and wet in the presence of a man who loved me. And who was toying with me like a cat with a mouse.

I spoke in a small voice. "What are you going to do, Davis?"

He stared at my pussy, tongue wetting his lips. "I'm going to eat you, Lucinda. I'm going to enjoy your pussy until I decide to fuck you. You can come in my mouth if you like, or you can wait until I'm ready to fill you with my cock."

With that, his face was between my legs, big hands pressing backward on my knees, and his tongue began to idly circle my clit. He alternately licked and tongue-fucked me, seemingly immune to the moaning and the way my legs pressed against him. I felt myself swelling against the work of his tongue but wanted to delay coming until he was inside me. I didn't want to allow him to break me so easily, but my orgasm was bearing down fast, and control was in short supply. I tried to squeeze my legs together to hold off the orgasm, but Davis easily held me open and lapped mercilessly. There was no stopping the force of pleasure that broke across me, and I thrust myself helplessly against his face, crying out without words.

He continued to lick and suckle me gently, carefully decreasing his attentions as the orgasm waned. I was a little disappointed I'd come so quickly. When I tried to sit up on my elbows and control my breathing, Davis lifted a hand and pushed me back onto the bed. His tongue continued to bathe the still-sensitive bud, lapping and stroking me gently. Only when the throbbing had entirely subsided did he stop and raise himself to meet my eyes. His eyes were as dark as the night sky, and he licked his lips salaciously before he spoke. "You're glorious when you come, Lucinda. I can't think of a single thing that compares to you in my mouth."

His big, powerful body was enthralling. All pretense from earlier was gone. I thought I had the upper hand when his shaft was at the mercy of my tongue, but that was an illusion. He'd allowed it for a time, then turned the tables—and now I couldn't even form a proper sentence. All I could think of was the way he'd stretch me. "Please, Davis. I need you." My whine sounded pathetic, even to my own fuck-drunk ears. "Please take me, baby." When he didn't move right away, I stared at him, incredulous. "You're going to give me your cock, aren't you, Davis? Please?"

He grinned. "In a manner of speaking, love." He pulled himself alongside me, settling me between his legs and careful not to hurt me with his cast. A long ray of moonlight spilled through the window, illuminating his face so I could see the emotions at play there. Arrogance, lust, unadulterated passion. "Why don't I enjoy another dose of the woman I love? You can come again while I watch; open your legs, Luckie."

I whimpered and did as he asked. He wedged a knee between mine, fisted his hard shaft, and began to stroke my swollen clit. "Eyes on me, baby—the whole time. I want you to come looking at me and saying my name." His face was dark, but his gaze burned with the love he'd confessed earlier.

"Whatever you want, Davis…anything you want." I groaned at the way he worked my slick cunt, escalating my pleasure and rocketing me toward another peak. Looking into his eyes while he used his cock on me was almost painfully intimate and stripped me even more emotionally naked than before. He whispered as he stroked me, relating in filthy detail how he loved the feeling of his tongue *inside* my pussy, how delicious I tasted, how hard his thick cock was as he waited to fuck me. He talked about the moment he'd seed me, flooding me with ropes of cum and fucking it deep into me until we were both too exhausted to continue. The orgasm was building again in my belly, tight and inescapable.

"Are you ready to come on me, beautiful?" His tone softened, and he pulled me closer. Our eyes were still locked together, and I whispered his name over and over, like a chant. Tonight started like a power exchange of sorts, but, the mood had shifted. His arm cradling me and the careful attention to my pleasure felt suddenly sweet and heartbreakingly sensual. I loved this man.

"Davis…I love you so much."

He pulled me closer to his chest and buried his face in my neck, whispering hoarsely in my ear. "Come for me, beautiful. Come…"

Davis groaned as he doubtless felt the strong pulsing while I came, sobbing quietly into his neck. The throbbing hadn't subsided when he pushed himself into me, filling me even as I continued to ride the magnificent orgasm he'd given me. "Love you, Davis." I couldn't stop the words spilling from my lips and heart. "Please fill me up; I need you to come inside me."

He slid deep, whispering in my ear all the while. "I love you, Lucinda. Open for me; take all of me, baby."

With that, I spread my legs as wide as I could, wrapping them around his waist and pulling him into me. The fullness was a painful pleasure, almost too much. Then I drank in the moment as the man I loved thrust hard against me and gifted me with all of himself.

Chapter
TWENTY-ONE

"Celebrate Me Home"

Davis

I was bent nearly double over the ancient metal desk, balanced on one crutch, and squinting under the saddest excuse for fluorescent lighting I'd ever seen. Or not seen, as the case was, all while trying to make sense of the schedule and manning for our planned **CAS** exercise. It was a damn good thing Bibi didn't see me like this, using only one crutch and putting what she referred to as her finest piece of charity work at risk. Luckie wouldn't be too thrilled either, for that matter. She'd taken up the mantle from Bibi, making certain my PT was accomplished as prescribed and calling to consult Bibi every other day. They continued to feel my recovery was progressing ahead of schedule, but I wasn't ready to climb back in the saddle. At least my body wasn't ready. And that was a damned shame, as I was in dire need of some quality time with the **GAU-8**, the sooner, the better.

In the meantime, the Scorpion TDY party would be arriving the day after tomorrow with the training exercise scheduled to begin only a week from today. I was anxious to iron out final details before a conference call later this morning with Happy and Coach. They would be accompanying Hung, Marilyn, and Bashful, along with the LPA representation—Rock, Torch, and Boo—and a small cadre of our maintainers, arriving tomorrow afternoon. I had worried that Miles's name wasn't included when I received the list, but later found she had follow-up visits with the **Flight Surgeon**. I hoped Miles would be able to move past the mid-air without too much embarrassment. I sensed she'd been wrestling with some hard truths and tough decisions.

The Savannah TDY thus far had been nothing but fun and games in the form of worshiping the glorious body of the woman I loved, interrupted briefly with a few truly lightweight workdays at the base. The Army commander was an easy-going guy, glad to offer help and excited about having real CAS for the upcoming exercise. But life on an Army base was hardship duty when compared to the "Chair Force," as some liked to call it. If the lack of light in this coat closet I'd been assigned as an office was any indication, the rumors were correct.

My phone buzzed, and I smiled, expecting to see Luckie's name. She'd taken the morning to sleep in and had informed me she'd spend the remainder of my work hours picking methodically through the SCAD retail shop on Bull Street. The Savannah College of Art and Design was one of my hometown's crowning jewels, but I was glad to be off the hook. Luckie's retail spidey senses were more finely honed than my own. Surviving a shelf check at SCAD with her was well beyond my shopping abilities.

It didn't matter at the moment, though, because the name on my phone wasn't Luckie. What I'd awaited with a sense of impending doom had come home to roost, as it always did.

Mama.

Emmaline Rose Abbott Foster—the most beloved and feared female in my life from the day she gave birth to me, probably wearing Chanel Rouge Allure lipstick and a triple strand of pearls. I loved and respected her fiercely, and I was surprised she was calling rather than my father. I was equally certain that no matter which one was calling, they wanted something.

Man your battle stations, D.

I touched the button and answered. "Hi, Mama. How are you?"

"Darling boy. I'm just lovely, and how are you?" Her voice was smooth and elegant, the same one she favored everyone with. "Enjoying reacquainting yourself with your hometown?"

With every inch of Lucinda's body, more like it.

"Yes, Mama. I'm sorry I haven't called yet. I've just been so busy with the preparations for the squadron, and it's a little bit harder than usual to get around."

She tsked. "Yes, sweetheart. Yes. I can't tell you how it broke my heart not to be there with you when you needed me. I was so terrified when that young friend of yours called and told us about the crash."

"Aircraft accident, Mama. It sounds a little less horrifying than 'crash,' don't you think?" I laughed it off, but I'd wondered about this since the accident. If it broke her heart, and if she really was so terrified, why didn't she get on an airplane and come to my bedside? Resources were certainly no limiting factor. That's what most parents would've done without hesitation under similar circumstance.

Young friend?

She had no way of knowing who Luckie was or what she was to me. And the clock was ticking ever closer to the moment when I'd have to face what I'd studiously avoided: the near-certain fear that my family would embarrass me and—much worse—attempt to diminish Lucinda. The woman who'd recently overtaken Emmaline Rose Abbott Foster as the most important female in my life. My mother would be supremely unhappy to learn of her displacement—and she would know. If women had a sixth sense about such things, my mother surely possessed a seventh and an eighth, as well.

"Well, you won't have to wait much longer. I've freed up some time this weekend; would Saturday work? Is Daddy busy?"

She tsked again. "Not at all, Davis. That's why I phoned in the first place. I've put together a small gathering of our dearest friends on Saturday evening; nothing ostentatious, darling. Thirty or forty people, fifty at most. We just want to celebrate your heroic escape from a fiery death." She let out a dramatic little sigh. "It frightened me, Davis. You just don't know."

I was glad we were separated by a dozen miles so she couldn't see my atomic eye-roll. A fiery death indeed; what an inappropriate observation. But it was all about her, after all. "Fifty dear friends, Mother. Do you really think that's necessary? I assume there's a caterer? Please tell me there's not a band."

She undoubtedly returned my eye-roll over the miles. "Of course there's a caterer, Davis. Do you really think I can manage a seafood buffet for seventy on less than a week's notice? And a full band would be far too showy for an intimate gathering." I forced myself to maintain radio silence so she could complete the irony. "It'll be a jazz trio. Perhaps a quartet."

There it was. That train was never late.

Immediately following the comic interlude my mother had inadvertently dealt me, reality intervened, and I realized the important detail I'd left out of my thought processes. My parents would need to meet Luckie so I could deal with the consequences they would surely send my way. I forged ahead.

"If I'm to be put on display like a zoo animal on Saturday, Mother, I'd like to see you both before then. May I take you both to dinner, say Thursday? I'll get reservations at The Olde Pink House. Or Mrs. Wilkes Dining Room, if you'd rather—"

"The Olde Pink House will do nicely, Davis, but you know

you'll not be on display. That's simply ridiculous. These people are our lifelong friends and neighbors. There's no requirement to meet before then, you know; I have a busy week ahead." She prattled on a bit in an effort to carefully extricate herself from an additional dinner commitment, but I interrupted with something I knew would immediately garner her attention.

"I've met someone, Mother. She's special, and she's here in Savannah with me. I'd like to introduce you without dozens of onlookers."

There was silence on the line as Mama sorted the possibilities. This was almost certainly a disaster in her mind, chiefly because she hadn't been given carte blanche in the vetting process. She was surely weighing the idea that anyone I'd met in Arizona wasn't from the South, much less from Savannah. Pedigree, family bloodlines, and appearances were everything to the Fosters. I'd broken the rules.

Speaking even more formally than usual, she carried on in a voice I knew she employed to hide her distress. "Well, now, that sounds just wonderful, Davis. Your father and I will look forward to meeting the young lady who's your…travel companion. You can leave me a message about the arrangements once you've made reservations. Oh, and Saturday evening is black tie, darling. If you didn't have the forethought to travel with your formal wear, you still have a couple of tuxedos here at home. I can have one delivered to your hotel."

Yes, I thoughtlessly neglected to bring along a tux on a work trip. Careless of me.

Another eye-roll. "Yes, Mother, if you'd be so good, it would be helpful to have one from home. Although I have no idea how I'll get it over my cast."

I could virtually see the stiff upper lip appear over the phone. "I have no doubt you'll manage, Son. You were raised to know the proper way to handle things. I should run along now, Davis.

Until Thursday, darling."

She hung up, and I was left staring at my phone. The problems with this scenario existed on several levels. It had been foolish of me not to do thorough diligence in advance of a meeting between Lucinda and my parents. My years in the Air Force had shaped me into a different man than the one I'd been reared to become, thank God. But Mama and Daddy remained ensconced firmly in their bubble, allowed to indulge in antiquated and frankly, offensive beliefs. I should have challenged them years ago when my own views began to evolve, but it just didn't seem necessary. I didn't expect them to change, and I hated the thought of a confrontation. It was a huge mistake, and now I'd pay dearly.

It would be easy to fall down an endless well of regret. I needed to remember I was a lucky bastard who had somehow garnered the attention of a stunning, whip-smart, hilarious woman who was equal parts compassionate caregiver and formidable ass-kicker. We were enjoying new love, and nothing trumped that. It was time for my parents to meet the man I'd grown to be.

But they weren't gonna be happy about it.

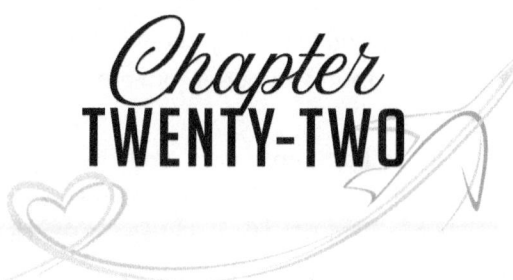

Chapter
TWENTY-TWO

"Don't You Worry 'Bout a Thing"

Lucinda

Davis and I picked our way carefully along the sidewalk of Congress Street, ever mindful of the pressing need to avoid fucking up his leg. If Davis lived in mortal fear of Bibi, it was with good reason. Her protectiveness toward him sprung purely from affection, but she was ruthless with her physical therapy patients—whether a fifth-grade Little League star or a burly fighter pilot. Her word was law, and no one disputed it. It was for this reason Davis and I had a rather terse discussion about this evening, a night out on the town we'd both looked forward to since our arrival over a week ago. The Scorpion contingent arrived earlier in the afternoon, parking their four A-10 Warthogs on the ramp at Hunter Army Airfield and making their way the few miles into town to join us for an evening of merriment, Southern style.

Davis insisted he was able to walk the half mile through town to our agreed meeting point, but I argued the possibility of injury made it a bad idea. In the end, of course, he won by playing the ultimate trump card. His body, his decision. No registered nurse would argue that point, consent being the biggest of deals in the medical community. After he won the argument and we'd navigated almost the entire half mile, I was relieved to see the black and white sign of the Congress Street Social Club come into view. I quickly found the door, opening it so Davis could make his way inside.

Moving past the bar, pool tables, and the stage that hosted live music, I could hear a lively crowd populating the outdoor patio. "Bet they're outside." Davis led the way. The patio was filled with people on barstools and benches, but a bellow that could've belonged to a wild animal drew my attention to a couple of tables pulled together at the back corner. The voice was deep and rough, like a Brahma bull who'd been gifted with voice.

"Deee! Yo, Deliverance! Back here, man!" The group of good-looking men crowded around the two tables and waved to Davis and me as if there was any possibility of missing that howling salutation. Approaching, I could see a mountain of tacos on a huge platter and large mugs of beer that were being rapidly consumed. Rock pulled two chairs from a neighboring table, offering one to each of us, and the man with the incredible voice, who I recognized as Marilyn, wrapped his muscular arms around Davis. It was unusual to see anyone who rivaled the size of my boyfriend, but this table had several fine members of the male species who could give him a run for his money. From the looks coming from several women nearby, their presence hadn't gone unnoticed.

I helped Davis into one of the chairs, carefully laying aside his crutches. "Dude. We've missed you at the eighty-two. It's a shitshow, I kid you not." The group erupted into laughter, and greetings were offered up from everyone.

Davis laughed and pounded Bellowing Man on the back in greeting. "Marilyn, you lying fuck. No one's noticed I'm gone, but the sentiment is appreciated all the same. Hey, guys, does everyone know Luckie?" He wrapped my waist with a protective arm and pulled me onto the arm of his chair. "She's been my one-woman transportation coordinator, PT dominatrix, and entertainment committee."

The darkly handsome younger pilot I remembered as Boo stepped forward and took my hand. "Isn't Deliverance a fortunate son of a bitch? Pardon my French, Luckie. But I'm just sayin.'"

I laughed, already feeling comfortable. It meant everything that they were excited to see Davis; I knew this banter was their way of expressing affection. I had no doubt they missed him nearly as much as he missed them—and flying. Nothing more than the flying, of course.

Coach stood from across the table, leaned my direction, and brushed a kiss across my cheek. "Bibi sends her best, Luckie. She has so many complimentary things to say about the way you've been taking care of our guy here. Thanks for that." He motioned for the ponytailed waitress. "How about a beer, you two?" He rolled his eyes toward the ridiculous pile of tacos. "Looks like we might be able to spare a little to eat, too. If you're hungry."

It was easy for me to assimilate into the relaxed group and the spirited, sometimes off-color conversation. I didn't feel a need for Davis's involvement in whatever group held my attention. Everyone seemed at ease together. A couple of hours flew by, filled with laughter and beer and tacos. Walker Jackson, introduced again by Coach, was the B flight commander. I'd seen him at the Salt River float and again at the Hail and Farewell at Happy's house, but we'd never spoken. He was tall, like nearly everyone in the group, and the way he moved with loose-limbed grace made his presence utterly non-threatening.

"You have a wonderful voice, um…Walker. I hope you don't mind, but I don't think I can call you 'Hung' like everyone else does—at least not until we get to know each other better." I laughed.

He raised his beer with a smile. "No harm, no foul; you can call me whatever you like, Luckie. I'm sorry we didn't get a chance to talk much at the Salt float; that was a lot of fun. It's great you're able to take care of D right now; he's our man." His voice dropped lower, and he tossed a quick glance over his shoulder where Davis laughed at an outrageous story one of the lieutenants was spinning. "It was pretty fucked up to sit by, powerless, and hear that someone I look up to was hurt. And maybe worse." He was silent in the middle of the melee of the bar scene, staring down into his beer. Then he met my eyes. "I'm glad you two found each other." I smiled, having nothing to add, and refilled both our beers from one of the pitchers the waitress had delivered. I was comfortable in the silence, but Walker was suddenly anything but. He leaned back in his chair, affecting a pose meant to appear relaxed but resulting in the opposite.

"So," Walker studied my face, "Vivianne's a friend of yours? I mean, you guys work together...sometimes?"

Ah. There it is.

"Oh, yeah, Vivvie's my girl. We've known each other, you know, forever." I smiled to let him know I was good-naturedly enjoying his discomfort. "I saw you with her up on the river, and it looked like you two were having a good time. She's an amazing woman, but she's not for the faint of heart. You should see her run the emergency room, Walker. Seriously, she's a force of nature. Nobody fucks with Viv." His eyes widened a little, but he smiled too, taking another swallow of his beer.

"I can see what you mean, and I assure you, I have no intention of treating Vivianne with anything but respect and...you know, affection."

I could tell the alcohol was working on the big man, so I gave him a break. "Look, Walker. Whatever's going on, if anything, between you and my girl, it's your business. I'm just sending a warning shot across the bow. She's a lot of woman, in case you hadn't figured it."

All the posturing melted away at once, and I saw the self-assured man I'd originally met. "You're absolutely right on that point, and I saw that almost from the beginning. I may not strike you as that guy, Luckie, but I can hold my own with Vivianne." He lifted his beer and murmured under his breath, "And I'll make sure we both enjoy the ride."

I'd have to grab a drink with Vivvie to catch up. This Walker character was unpacking a lot more than I'd expected. He might very well be a good match for Viv. Walker stood to make a bar run as the patio became too crowded to find our waitress. He reached over and touched my arm with a smile.

"One more thing, Luckie. Don't worry too much about the whole 'Hung' thing; it's a flying reference." His grin widened. "If it's more than that, you and Vivvie are close enough that I'm sure she'll clue you in eventually." He chuckled as he sauntered toward the bar.

The man across from me had a "Prince Harry in a bad fucking mood" look: low-key red hair and dark green eyes that seemed to be guarding something secretive. He wasn't unfriendly but gave off a mysterious vibe. At the very moment I realized I was staring, he turned from his conversation with Coach and leaned toward me.

"Hi there, Luckie. I'm Jackson Thomas, but everyone calls me Torch." He rolled his eyes upward and pointed at the thick head of hair. "Obviously, there's a method to the madness." He favored me with a crooked grin and turned to Davis who remained seated next to me.

"So, D, has anybody let it slip when they're turning you loose in the sky again?" Torch struck the classic male pose— manspreading muscular legs and leaning forward onto his elbows. The frown was back. "Things are better back home, since Happy's change of command, I mean. Morale has improved, and I think there's a feeling we can be the premiere Hawg squadron again like we used to be." Torch seemed to be an old soul. The seriousness of the conversation in this environment was unexpected, but Davis warmed to the subject.

"I agree with you, man; there's been a legitimate change for the better over these past months. I think the individuals who make up the squadron are quality people, that all of us *want* to perform better. Find the untapped potential." Davis turned to Nathan, seated next to him and laughing with Coach, and gave him one of those patented claps on the back men seemed so fond of. If he'd hit me that hard, I'd have kneed him in the balls. "We've got this guy to thank for showing the way. And kicking our asses back onto the straight and narrow."

Nathan grinned easily. "You may be giving me too much credit there, but thanks, D. I think we're going the right direction, but it takes a village." He toasted the group with his beer.

"That's kind of my point." Torch's demeanor had relaxed incrementally, but he was still the most serious face at the table. "To continue the progress, it's important to have you back in the cockpit as soon as it's feasible."

"No worries there, Torch." I threw my two cents into the conversation. "I haven't known enough pilots to speak with any authority on the subject, but I know Davis's left femur better than my own. He's been doing the work of ten grinches, plus two in physical therapy, first with Bibi and now with me. His bone strength is way above average at this point in his recovery, and the," I squeezed his arm affectionately, "well, I won't bore you with the medical jargon, but he's doing great. And he misses flying like an idiot misses the point. I'd wager my virginity he'll be back at the first opportunity."

My boundaries were loosened with the assistance of alcohol,

and that made me a funny girl. Even Torch apparently thought so. In this company, that gave me standing as a peer, high praise from a bunch of fighter pilots. Davis was more relaxed than he'd been since our arrival in Savannah, though I sensed his carefree facade was temporary.

Coach was thoroughly lubricated and not alone in the state of pleasant intoxication. Jake Travis stretched his athletic frame out in the wrought iron chair, balancing precariously on the two back legs. His blue eyes twinkled. "Coach, my friend, looks like you're bunking with us tonight. You'd better call Bibi's aunt and tell her what a bad boy you've been." Coach was the only one of the pilots who wasn't staying downtown, having been instruct- ed by his wife that he was expected for the week at her wealthy aunt's home on Wilmington Island. Coach winced.

"Yeah, that's a **clean kill**. I'll leave her a message; she's prob- ably been in bed for four or five hours by now. But, by damn, the woman can cook for me any day of the week and twice on Sundays. Where are you lowlifes staying? Not at the Hunter **BOQ**, I'd wager."

Rock and Boo whooped and high-fived. "Thunderbird, Dude. It's the only manly place to stay in this girly-ass town. Walking distance from here. MoonPies and RC Cola in your room, man. And Krispy Kremes for breakfast." Boo indicated Rock with a dramatic sweep of his hand. "Rock is the motherfucking king of **billeting**. The Thunderbird is the dog's balls." More high fives.

Rock stood and took a bow. "Coach, you can sleep in Happy's room."

Coach and Happy groaned in concert, and Happy signaled the waitress. "Old Ezra, please. Coach?" Coach nodded. "Scratch that. Two Old Ezras, and make mine a double."

Chapter
TWENTY-THREE

"You Don't Know Me"

Lucinda

Ipaced the length of the luxe hotel room, sweating bullets. Then I took a short break to meticulously examine the contents of the minibar. The petite bottle of Grey Goose was just the ticket. I stole a quick glance at the bathroom door where Davis was showering in advance of our dinner with his parents. It took him a little longer these days, but I normally outpaced him in primp time required.

Not tonight.

I'd been ready over half an hour before Davis even meandered into the bathroom. He'd done his due diligence, busy tongue between my legs, over the course of the afternoon, trying to calm my anxiety. But I could hardly envision a scenario where tonight went smoothly. I hadn't yet gathered the intestinal fortitude to ask Davis if he'd actually told his parents I was black. I told myself it didn't matter. They'd figure it out on their own soon enough. (Cue the inappropriate laughter.) Meanwhile, I was working at burning a tremendous amount of excess emotional energy, and the Grey Goose was in my corner. I unscrewed the top, careful not to mar my new manicure (a conservative nude shade), and chugged the contents, sans mixer. Ugh. That burn.

"Taken up covert drinking, I see." Seeing Davis nude in the bathroom doorway was enough to cure everything ailing me and wipe my anxious frontal lobe clean. The towel that should have been wrapped around his waist was instead drying his blond hair, and the flexing biceps were mesmerizing. The expanse of chest, interrupted by his hard, little nipples, seemed to fill the entire doorway, and I watched errant water drops cascade down his pecs and over the rippled surface of his belly. His cock was just beautiful, I noted as my pulse picked up. Even in its currently unaroused state, it was weighty and thickset, hanging between his thighs. Holy God, I just wanted to forget about dinner and drop to my knees. A night of cock worship would be the ideal antidote for my churning belly. But I needed to prioritize not looking like a complete asshole to the man I loved. Skulking around, sweating, and drinking furtively was not my best look.

"I'm a little nervous." I straightened, smoothing my silk blouse and navy pencil skirt. It was as close as I could come to looking demure. "How do I look? My goal is invisible." I tried to inconspicuously drop the empty Goose bottle in the trash. Davis dropped the damp towel at his feet and motioned me toward him, holding out a free arm while steadying himself in the doorway. He gathered me close to his warm, hard chest and stroked my hair.

"Goddamn, Lucinda. You could never be invisible. You light up every part of me when we're in the same room." His finger tipped my chin up, and deep green eyes met mine. "I know you're feeling nervous; I've been feeling it, too, Peaches. But what we have here is real and worthwhile. I love my parents, but I've come to realize that I hate many of the things they believe and cling to. I need you to know you can depend on me. *We* decide what's real. I choose you—and us."

Before the last word left his lips, my mouth was on his. I teased him with my tongue, opening and tasting him, all toothpaste and sweet male. We spoke all the words with our bodies, allowing me to abandon my verbal efforts. Finally, pulling away, I looked at the beautiful man in front of me. "Thank you, Davis. I'll be fine, I promise. You don't need to worry. Now get your naked self dressed, and let's get to the restaurant before I change my mind. I've been having some thoughts about spending the entire night between your legs with that long cock sliding up and down my throat."

Davis groaned and kissed my forehead. He was hard now and pressed the palm of his hand against his erection. "You're killing me, girl."

I helped Davis as he moved from the Uber onto the sidewalk and situated his crutches. Again I reflected on the people I was about to meet. I didn't understand why his parents hadn't traveled to his side in the aftermath of the accident. I'd never given much thought to having a family, or the tie I might eventually have with a child, but I couldn't imagine *not* being with my child after a trauma like Davis had endured. I must have been entirely checked out and staring because Davis took my hand and squeezed it affectionately.

"I don't want you to feel anything but loved by me tonight. Don't forget that. My parents are wild cards, but I'm not, Luckie."

I gave him a peck on the cheek, careful not to smudge my tasteful deep red lipstick. We ascended the half dozen steps into The Olde Pink House and ducked inside, stopping at the hostess stand. A tiny woman with an impossibly large ballerina bun and black clothing from head to toe greeted us with a warm smile.

"Welcome. What's the name on the reservation, sir?"

"Foster." Davis smiled at the woman then swept the down-stairs dining area with a brief glance. "We'll be joining my parents." As the hostess scanned the book in front of her, I saw an older couple at a table in the back corner looking our direction, the woman raising her hand in a half-wave. Davis smiled and returned the gesture, addressing the hostess to let her know we'd found our party. We meandered through the white-linen-clad tables, stopping once so I could move a tray and allow Davis to pass. As we approached the back of the candlelit dining room, the imposing gentleman there rose to greet us. He smiled at Davis although it seemed a foreign gesture to what I was sure was a serious countenance. Mr. Foster wore an impeccably tailored suit with French cuffs, beautifully polished wing tips and a Piaget watch. He extended his hand, shaking Davis's offered one, and Davis set his crutches against the table, leaned toward his father, and embraced him. His voice was deep and quieter than usual. "Daddy. You're looking well."

I stole a glance at his mother, still seated. She was the most petite version of a Southern belle I'd ever seen. She wore a sleeveless ivory silk sheath, and a matching cardigan draped the back of her chair. Three perfectly matched strands of pearls adorned her neck, and slim hands played restlessly in her lap as she watched her husband and only son greet one another.

He leaned on the table in front of me, supporting himself with one hand, and looked affectionately at his mother, brushing her cheek with a kiss. "Hi, Mama. You're looking beautiful, just like always." She smiled at him, momentarily the only person in the room.

"Sweet boy. You do go on." Unless I was mistaken, she blushed as if genuinely flustered.

Davis retrieved one of his crutches but reached for me with his free hand, smiling reassuringly. "Mother, Father...may I present Lucinda Page, my girlfriend." My heart skipped along excitedly at his use of the label. Funny, considering everything else on the proverbial table.

I pasted on what I hoped was a warm smile, extending my hand first to Mrs. Foster. "How do you do, Mrs. Foster? Mr. Foster?" I shook both hands, in turn, trying not to register the shock that both attempted to hide. "It's a pleasure to meet you both; Davis has told me so much about you." The long agony of that moment and the consternation playing on both faces posed a great challenge to my composure. But my upbringing at the exacting hands of Emerson and Miranda Atherton-Page stood me in good stead under trying circumstances like these.

Never let 'em see you sweat, Luckie.

Emmaline was visibly disconcerted but rallied quickly, clearly possessing good breeding of her own to draw on. She smiled tightly at me and gestured to the two remaining chairs at the table. "I'm afraid we can't say the same, Miss Page; why don't you both join us?"

Ouch. The point goes to the home team.

After only a split second of looking like a deer paralyzed in headlights, Mr. Foster pulled out a chair for me, murmuring, "Here we are, Lucinda."

The dining room was relatively quiet with only a low buzz of conversation and the unobtrusive waitstaff to cover the uncomfortable silence threatening our table, but Emmaline came to the rescue. "Lucinda, I trust Davis has been taking the time to show you the best parts of our beautiful, historic city. He's a native, you know. Savannah's blood runs through him." She turned again to her son, patting his hand. Davis looked uncomfortable, but I wasn't completely sure why.

"Yes, ma'am; he's been the perfect host." I murmured my response even though she was pointedly ignoring me now. Turning, I sent Mr. Foster another wide smile. "I'd love some wine, Mr.

Foster; do you have any recommendation for a girl with a rack full of big Cabs at home?" His demeanor lifted immediately, and I relaxed. I could play this one like a piano, even if he didn't like the color of my skin. The ego of a good ole boy, monied or not, made him no match for me. Walk in the park. Davis's mouth cocked in a crooked little smile, alerting me that he was watching the show. Mr. Foster opened the leather-bound wine list, studying it with a smile on his broad face, so I turned my attention to face the much larger challenge at my right hand.

Mrs. Foster watched her husband's fascination with the wine list with a mildly sympathetic expression. She could probably see right through me, but perfect manners restrained what she would say or do about it. I double-checked my pleasant smile and addressed her. "You would be proud of Davis, Mrs. Foster; he's been the perfect ambassador for your city. Not that I wasn't in love before." I shot Davis a mischievous grin. "With Savannah, of course."

She didn't know exactly what to make of me, and her eyes betrayed the confusion. Her husband was an effective distraction as he made a bit of a show ordering a bottle of the 2010 Chappellet Signature Cab. "Well, that's lovely, dear. I'm glad he's showing you around…around town. I trust you've made it by SCAD? And Bonaventure, obviously."

With the addition of excellent food and good wine, the bumpy path dinner previously traversed smoothed somewhat. Davis's dad was quite the storyteller, launching into lengthy and often humorous accounts from his early married life with Emmaline and from Davis's childhood. It was easy to see the affection Davis had for his parents, especially his mother who he endearingly called "Mama." His parents were obviously proud of their only child, often sharing in the story-telling details and fondly recalling his childhood. Dessert and coffee had arrived before I knew it, and the end seemed in sight. Davis laughed and smiled throughout the meal, often watching me with undisguised affection. I felt a good deal more tranquil than expected as I excused myself for a nose powdering and to allow Davis a private moment with his family.

Upon my return, Davis and his father were engaged in the traditional well-mannered tug-of-war for the dinner check. Emmaline turned primly in her chair and looked me up and down surreptitiously. "Lucinda, my dear, we'll be hosting a small gathering of our closest friends Saturday evening in Davis's honor. I thought it would be such a pity for him to return home only to work and have no opportunity to see those closest to our family." She lowered her voice. "I don't know that he's told you, but Davis has very deep roots here. Very deep indeed; Savannah has been our family's home for generations now." She settled back in her chair, shooting a quick glance at her son, still engaged in conversation. "The gathering is black tie, darling, and I know that's burdensome, given you came to town unaware." She leaned forward slightly, feigning concern. "Men don't have such issues when it comes to dressing for an occasion, do they?" She waved her hand dismissively. "Half a dozen tailored tuxedos, a couple pair of Ferragamo loafers? Voila! It's different for us, though. A lady must concern herself with designers, fittings, accessories." She sighed with affected chagrin. "I understand you'd feel uncomfortable with nothing appropriate"—her eyes gave me another once-over—"nothing appropriate to meet Savannah society. There are expectations here, as I'm sure you're aware, Lucinda."

She paused, sipping her wine and studying my expression. I met her eyes with a small smile, careful not to allow my composure to slip, but didn't respond. Emmaline blinked first, fidgeting with her napkin, and hurried along, trying to close the deal. "I knew you wouldn't want Davis to feel uncomfortable, so I took the liberty of arranging for you to enjoy an opening at the Telfair Museum. It will be a lovely evening out solo, and you'll find a ticket at the will-call window under your name. Davis has formal wear at our home, of course, so I'll have it couriered to his hotel."

So, there it was. Emmaline had done her due diligence and covered the bases preparing for the very likely event the out-of-town girl was unacceptable. The opera-length gloves were off, and she'd done it without the knowledge of either her husband or son.

Well played, Emmaline Foster.

All the niceties, the endearments, all the charm and hospitality pointed my way this evening was only eyewash for the real subtext. To be fair, Davis had warned me that his parents were predisposed to dislike me because of my skin color. But appearances were too important to this woman for her to risk an overt move. She wanted to trip me up and cause me to embarrass myself publicly. No woman, regardless of her background, would issue a black-tie invitation to an event this important with only two days' notice. The fact that I was away from home and caring for her injured son was inconsequential. She'd concocted an airtight scenario with both outcomes weighted heavily in her favor. Either I'd send Davis to the party alone, indicating his family and friends were unimportant to me, or I'd fail to turn myself out acceptably, causing him embarrassment. And, more importantly, he'd realize I could never fit into his family or the social circles in which they traveled.

I smiled coolly. "Will you be choosing a floor-length gown, Mrs. Foster, or is cocktail-length more locally appropriate?" I could tell my composure caught her off guard. Surprise and disappointment registered on her face. She'd had every expectation of winning this round, but Emmaline Foster had no idea whom she was dealing with. I was cut from the upper crust myself, at least the old iteration of me was, and I had a few tricks up my sleeve.

"Floor-length should do nicely, my dear." She smiled, but her tone was cold. Less than forty-eight hours and a formal event with the requirement of a floor-length gown? It would have reduced a lesser woman to tears. Davis and his father were oblivious, engaged in conversation and taking care of the check. Just as well. This was work for Emmaline and me. She stood, followed immediately by her husband and son. I took my time, then stood and addressed her, still careful that my tone was cordial.

"It's so kind of you to include me, Mrs. Foster." I turned and touched Davis's father's elbow. "Mr. Foster. I am anxious to see your lovely home, and I do enjoy a formal event; seems they're few and far between these days. Davis and I look forward to seeing you Saturday evening."

Goodbyes were quickly pronounced, and Davis kissed his mother's cheek before they swept out the door of the grand old house. I helped him with his crutches, and we stepped out into the blanket of night. We turned down Bryan Street, strolling along in silence for a few minutes before he glanced my direction. "I thought things went well tonight; my dad's quite the storyteller, don't you think?"

I tried to plot the best course through this situation. Our relationship was fresh and untested; and he had an obvious bond of affection with his parents, despite their flaws. This was not the hill I wanted to die on. I could handle Emmaline without his help and, hopefully, without his knowledge. I silently debated exactly how to proceed, pretending to study the moon peeking between the live oaks. But Davis spoke up again.

"At least I *thought* things were going well until I overheard my mother sabotaging you."

My head whipped around to see his mouth set in a grim line. "She waited until Daddy had me engaged in talking about these hand-rolled cigars he loves, thinking my eye would be off the ball." He shook his head and rolled his beautiful green eyes heavenward. "You gotta hand it to her—she's a pro. Air-kisses and compliments while she sinks a knife in your back. Wish I could say I'm shocked, but she's ruthless when it comes to getting what she wants."

Not for a moment did I think he was aware of the corner Emmaline was painting me into. "I didn't think you heard her. And, frankly, I didn't think you'd see the difficult situation this could put me in. Stab in the dark here: this is no small gathering of your nearest and dearest either, is it?"

Davis laughed, but the smile on his lips didn't meet his eyes. "Hell, no. I'd guarantee she's invited every mover and shaker from Port Royal to Sea Island. And she's going to paint me up as some kind of hero because I had to punch out of a crippled jet. The broken leg will be the cherry on top and garner lots of sympathy for the alleged wounded hero. I'm gonna look like a big asshole in a tux with the leg seam split. Pretty sure we won't be able to get me into that monkey suit any other way." He sighed, disgusted. "And now this. I didn't do the math on what a fix this is for you until I heard her spelling dress-code requirements like it was the fucking Met Gala." Sarcasm crept into his tone, along with an engaging smile for my benefit. "What's wrong with you anyway? Did you pack for a work trip to Savannah and forget all your vintage Dior gowns?" He stopped abruptly under the glow of a streetlight. "Don't worry, Peaches. I wouldn't hang you out to dry on this; we just won't go. I'm never in a hurry to strap myself into a tux. Spending an evening eating pizza and watching *CSI* beats the hell out of seafood towers and jazz trios anyway."

I rose slightly on tiptoes to kiss his delicious mouth. "You never stop surprising me, Davis Payne Foster. But this time I'm the one with a wicked curveball."

He raised one eyebrow and palmed my ass, pulling me closer. "What do you have up your sleeve, young lady?"

"Don't you worry your pretty head about it, Tarzan. Just find someone to open the seam on your tux pants; I have a few favors to call in. Your mama just bought herself a front row ticket to my A game."

Chapter
TWENTY-FOUR

"Born on the Bayou"

Lucinda

I breathed a genuine sigh of relief, closed my eyes, and smiled, tucking my phone between my shoulder and ear.

"I can't thank you enough, Anna. You're a lifesaver, woman. I'll Venmo the bucks over for express delivery as soon as we hang up. Best to Harry and hugs to those beautiful grandbabies. Mmmkay. You too, love. Bye now." I hung up and was engaged in my lewd version of a happy dance when my dreamboat emerged from the bathroom, dressed for work in his flight suit. His eyes lit playfully.

"Is it time for lap dances? I can be late." He pulled up the long zipper and began stuffing half a dozen pockets all over the garment with pens, scraps of paper, and other detritus from the desk near the door. "What's got you so full of life at this early hour?"

I'd been driving Davis to and from work each day, often joining him for lunch so we could hit a little midday physical therapy. Normally, his day began early. I had never been a morning person; all my co-workers knew about my two-cup minimum and poured coffee into me before attempting conversation at the beginning of the shift. This morning was an exception.

"I had an idea last night about how to solve the formal-wear dilemma but couldn't follow up until this morning." I pulled on a tee shirt and shorts for the quick drive to Hunter. "Anna Van Horn is an old friend of my mother's. She worked in a major design house during the years I was a teenager. I loved going to the studio when my mother was being fitted or consulting for a gown for an important event. Anna was always so kind to me; she'd let me try on some of the designs and pretend to model. I still see her occasionally when I'm in Manhattan. As she approached retirement age, she and her husband, Harry, moved into a smaller condo near Bryant Park and the Garment District, and she opened a little boutique business renting designer wear. It's grown due to the contacts she maintained in the rag trade, and I threw myself at her feet."

As we boarded the elevator and made our way to the rental car, I noted how dramatically Davis's mobility had increased since our arrival. Bibi would be very pleased with his progress. I continued the story after we were underway. "Anna has my measurements on file, so that makes everything easier. I told her the story, and I've gotta tell you, she had some choice words to say about what's going on down south. She's second generation American. Her parents emigrated from Russia—it's Anna Ivanov Van Horn—and she makes me look like an amateur when it comes to profanity." We both laughed, but I was glad Davis hadn't heard the things my friend said about his dear mama. He might not have found humor in the creative ideas Anna had for how Emmaline should be dealt with.

"Anyway, she knows my taste and picked out a brand-new Badgley Mischka gown for me. It just came in three days ago. Dark floral print, ruching at the waist, chiffon…plunging neckline." I was gone down the rabbit hole already. For a girl with a soft spot for fashion, I'd picked a hell of a profession. Baggy cotton scrubs left everything to be desired in the haute couture department. This development had me practically bouncing in my seat as I told Davis about my good fortune. "She insisted on sending it gratis after hearing about the drama, so it's coming overnight. The only puzzle I have to put together is a bag and shoes, but she sent a photo of the gown to help. It's devastating."

Davis leaned over, planting a soft kiss on my mouth while we stopped at a traffic light near the airfield. "You're amazing, Lucinda; I never had a doubt you'd figure a way to own this town. And I damn sure can't wait to walk into my childhood home with my beautiful woman on my arm. You're breathtaking when you wake up in the morning, wearing nothing but my old tee shirt, but you're going to stop traffic tomorrow, baby."

I pulled along the curb so Davis could have the shortest walk into the building where his temporary office was located. I pulled him close and kissed him goodbye. "You can take that to the bank, Captain Foster. But I don't care what anyone thinks about me or how I'm dressed. I just want to have you fighting off a hard-on all night until you can get me back to the hotel, pull that gown up around my waist, and force your big cock into my slick little pussy." I kissed his nose. "Have a good day at work, Davis."

He groaned, palming his dick. "Fuckin' A, Peaches. You don't take it easy on a guy, do you?"

I was stepping out of the shower when I heard my phone. Bibi's name on the screen was a surprise, but a welcome one. "Hey, Beeb…what's up?" I was glad to hear another woman's voice on the line. A friendly woman's voice. Evidently, I'd missed the companionship of my girlfriends more than I'd thought.

"Hello, sweet cheeks. How are you holding up in the swamp?" Her deep laugh was warm and infectious. "Look, I'm busy like a one-legged man in an ass-kicking contest. My waiting room overfloweth at present, so I'm cutting to the chase. Chuck and Davis had coffee this morning, and the whole seething mess that is your man's mother's bullshit came pouring out of him. Rather unexpected for a male to share, don't you think?" I could hear her gulping coffee, but she didn't wait for a reply.

"Look. Here's the thing. My aunt Mary Crawford is expecting you for lunch. I know that sounds effing crazy as shit, but just listen. Mary Crawford's lived in the quagmire outside Savannah since the Lord Jesus was a child, and she has more money than His daddy. She eats bitches like Emmaline Foster for tea, but she's the salt of the earth, Luckie. I love her like tequila. I don't know the whole story, but this I do know: Mary Crawford—we call her MariSee for short—is a thousand years old and has a collection of vintage everything that is not to be believed. I called her on a whim, and she insisted you come out to see her on Wilmington Island and stay for lunch. I know you need to accessorize the Badgley Mischka, and my hunch is you won't need to hit the department stores. MariSee will load you up. Just don't have too many scones with lunch, or you'll never fit in that dress. Even at her age, she's probably the best cook on the planet. Chuck told me he's going on a juice fast when he gets home." She snorted with laughter.

I was breathless. "Damn, Bibi. I don't know what to say. I mean, thanks, girl. I'm getting dressed—can you text me the address?"

It was a short drive to the address Bibi sent me, no more than twenty minutes, but I detoured slightly to drive by Bonaventure

Cemetery. Davis and I hadn't visited, but the haunting beauty of the live oaks shading the site made me decide we'd have to find time before our departure to do just that. I continued along the Island Expressway for a short distance until the GPS guided me onto progressively narrower roads and finally a gravel road. An imposing iron gate no less than ten or twelve feet tall stood open on one side, the scrollwork across the top proclaiming it to be the home of the Asher family. More likely an estate, I thought, squeezing the rental car through the partially open gate.

It was easily another half mile along the gravel road before a sweeping curve opened, revealing a rambling old brick mansion. I parked and walked the mossy brick path leading past gardens bursting with huge azalea bushes, gerbera daisies, and fat purple hydrangeas. The grounds stretched long arms around to the rear of the house, plantings hugging the foundation, and ended at the river. I must have stopped, unconsciously lost in the beauty, because I was startled by a wiry figure striding rapidly across the yard in my direction.

Aunt Mary Crawford Asher couldn't have seen five feet or a hundred pounds in any of the thousand years Bibi had reported her walking the earth. Catching a glimpse of her wrinkled face under the big straw hat that shaded her from the midday sun, I speculated Bibi had underestimated her age. I walked toward her across the velvety lawn, extending my hand. "How do you do, Mrs. Asher? Thank you so much for your gracious invitation."

The tiny woman reached for my hand and stared up with the palest blue eyes I'd ever seen. "And you must be Lucinda, my dear girl." She pumped my hand, gripping it like a politician. "I'm glad you could join me. And it's Aunt Mary Crawford. In full, Mary Crawford Buckalew Asher. But kinfolks and friends call me MariSee. Hell, my husband's people procreated at such a rate, everyone in Chatham County probably is blood kinfolks. Goddamn bunny rabbits, those Ashers."

It was already clear why Bibi was such a force of nature, I thought. But Aunt Mary Crawford was striding back across the yard like her little ass was on fire. Having no better idea, I gave chase.

"Come help me get the wagon in, Lucinda. You look like a big, strong girl, and nice curvy hips. Good breeding stock was what we used to say, but I'm told that's in poor taste these days. Whatever the hell that is."

Rounding the corner of the house, we encountered an old wooden wagon filled with cut flowers, most from the expansive rose garden that spilled along this entire side of the home. "Mrs…MariSee, these are stunning. You have quite the green thumb." I grabbed the handle and started for the front door, but she motioned toward the back.

"This way. We'll get them in through the kitchen wing." She led the way, arms full of gardening tools, and I dragged the wagon directly into an expansive mudroom with brick floors, long marble countertops, and a trio of sinks. MariSee used a step stool to find a dozen or so old cut glass vases, setting them on the counter before shedding her gloves. "Wash up here, Lucinda, and I'll find us something cold to drink. Lunch will be a little minute, so you can help me get these flowers arranged."

That was entirely open for debate, I thought, keeping it to myself.

She was back in no time with two big Mason jars of very sweet tea. She handed me a pair of garden shears, grabbing a menacing looking pair for herself, and set to work clipping leaves from the mountain of flowers in the wagon. I emulated her, watching from my peripheral vision and trying not to betray myself as a rank amateur. "I like to have fresh flowers about the house, Lucinda. It makes a house smell like a home instead of a hospital where an old woman's busy dying." I didn't have any idea what to say, but she didn't leave me out on the limb alone. "We're all dying, you know. That's why it's important to know who you are. And who you're not, Lucinda. So you can live until you die." She fixed me with those piercing blue eyes. "Do you understand, young lady?"

I didn't.

But I pulled leaves and nodded my head adamantly. "Yes, ma'am. I think so."

"You'd damn sure better know who you are if you're going up against Emmaline Abbott Foster. I understand from Bellamy the two of you crossed paths last night for the first time."

So Bibi had clued her in, but I had a hunch MariSee knew stuff anyway. If she did, it was a good idea to keep arranging flowers in my own skill-free way, listen and learn. "We did. We had dinner, and I thought everything was going well. The conversation was enjoyable, and Davis seemed very relaxed. Then, at the end of our meal, she told me about the expectation to make an appearance at this black-tie affair. But I'm sure Bibi told you."

She peered at me, silent for a second. "So she did." She continued to prune a few more roses, then selected a big crystal vase and began to effortlessly arrange a huge pile of blooms into a casual work of art. "Lucinda, you're not from these parts, but that's something many can forgive." She smiled at her own joke. "I'm only teasing you, dear girl.

"I was born in this house and raised here too. When I married my Mister Asher, I insisted he come here to live with me. And live with me he did. We were in love from the day I set him in my sights at the Catholic church when I was fourteen. And blissful together until the day the angels took him from me back in nineteen hundred and eighty-six. There was only one heartbreak in all the happy years we shared, and that was that I couldn't give Mister Asher children." She smiled, stopped clipping, and stared beatifically out the window. "But we adopted eleven beautiful babies."

Eleven children?

"Not all babies, mind you." She worked skillfully with gnarled fingers, creating a third masterpiece in an aluminum watering can. I had given up the pretense of arranging florals and leaned on the countertop, soaking in every word.

"Three little girls, two white and one precious little cocoa-colored sweetheart who didn't speak a word until after her seventh birthday." Her eyes grew misty for a moment. "Eight handsome little boys, three of mixed race, one little white child whose goddamn mother nearly starved him before Mister Asher and I brought him here, and four of the prettiest little black boys you ever saw. Three were brothers whose mama died in childbirth; they lost their daddy in a car accident the next year. Two were fresh from heaven when we picked them up at the hospital, but six of the boys were almost ready for school before they came to us. They're all grown now, of course, but those were challenging days, Lucinda. So many little ones, but I knew we were fortunate to have the resources. We could give them everything they needed, most importantly, the love of a mother and a father who didn't care about the color of their skin."

Her hands stilled, and she turned to look at me. She didn't have an uncertain bone in her body. She looked right into me, as if seeing everything although we'd just met. She was shrewd and perceptive, but not without affection. Her small, arthritic hand reached out, touching my arm.

"You love him, don't you, my dear?"

My eyes puddled immediately. Was it painted all over my face? I nodded mutely, unable to speak.

She lifted her chin, but the wrinkles around her eyes crinkled with kindness. "You're a black woman in love with a white man from a prominent, old family in a very Southern city. Perhaps one of the oldest families. And perhaps the most Southern city. Surely you saw the difficulties you might encounter."

I exhaled hard, willing myself not to unravel in the mudroom of the most formidable dowager I'd ever met. "Yes, MariSee. Well, no, I suppose. Not exactly."

She patted my hand and resumed her ministrations with the flowers. "But that just brings us back to where we began, you see? Do you remember what I said, Lucinda? You must know who you are. And who you are not. Once you know those things, no one can shake you. I raised beautiful little black babies in a town where no one had ever heard of interracial families. The only saving grace we had was a bank account that brought the snobs in this city to their knees. You know what they say, don't you?" She grinned playfully. "Money talks and bullshit walks. But money talks and talks and talks. The people who wanted nothing to do with my babies couldn't ignore the piles of it Mister Asher brought home, spoiled us with, and gave away to every disadvantaged person he could find. And, as much as the financial plenitude eased our path, the joy of my life is and has always been my beautiful family. I knew who I was; no one could shake that foundation. You will not be moved either, my dear. If it's love, you will stand firm against the adversity. No one wields a power greater than love. Not even the likes of Emmie Foster."

I'd barely spoken while she'd poured a wealth of wisdom into me, all the while constructing a roomful of fresh florals. She shot a sideways grin my direction. "As I mentioned, I like to have fresh flowers about the house. Now let's see that gown. I have four cedar closets full of shoes and bags. Collecting dusty old things was one of my delightful pastimes that amused Mister Asher. Let's have a look before we wash up and have lunch. I have shrimp and grits. Or she-crab soup, if you prefer."

Chapter
TWENTY-FIVE

"How Will I Know"

Lucinda

I'd been like a kid in a candy store as MariSee and I picked through the four cedar closets where an array of her vintage dresses, shoes, and handbags were stored. Each dress or blouse or shawl was hung carefully on a padded hanger, and the shoes nestled in tissue paper, most in their original boxes. "Easily eighty percent of what's here was mine or belonged to my sister, Alice. We were the only two girls in our family, and I'm afraid we were both spoiled clotheshorses." She smiled, holding up a white Halston jumpsuit that must have been altered to fit her petite frame. "Bellamy said she thought you wore a seven or seven and a half?" I smiled my assent, having already noticed most of the shoes to be in that size range. "Well, now, aren't we fortunate? My sister and I vacillated between a six and an eight over the years and the course of her pregnancies." Her eyes brightened as she pulled a Yves Saint Laurent shoebox from a low shelf. "Then, in the nineties, I discovered eBay and what a delightful diversion that is. No need to load up in the Lincoln and scout the estate sales." She peeled the lid from the box, revealing a gorgeous pair of black, silk slingbacks with a jeweled detail. I reached in to pet them.

"Oooh, they're stunning, MariSee, truly. They'd be perfect." She held one out with a smile, and I slid it easily onto my foot.

She motioned for me to follow her after handing me the box. "Shoes down and a handbag to go. And we don't even have fit to consider." She opened the third door, ushering me into a room holding mostly jewelry and handbags of every description. My eyes flew over the shelf, taking in designers from the era of Jackie O to treasures that appeared to be almost current. Scanning the shelves, my eyes lit on a black silk bag. Examining it more closely, it looked antique but was in perfect condition and had a sterling silver frame adorned with emerald-cut aquamarines, yellow topaz, and several small sapphires.

"You have an excellent eye, my dear. I carried that bag only once, in the mid-nineties to a ball honoring John Berendt when he was a finalist for the Pulitzer Prize for *Midnight in the Garden of Good and Evil*. Now, here in Savannah, we just call it 'The Book.' I found this little bag at an estate sale out on Green Island Road, and it spoke to me. Pity I have no idea how old it is."

I gathered my booty, thanking MariSee for loaning them to me and casting a final, longing look toward the magical closets before starting down the stairs. The house must certainly have been the size of a football stadium, I thought, to have space for such a luxury. Any one of the closets would dwarf many of my friends' apartments in Manhattan.

Once downstairs, MariSee settled in a petite needlepoint rocker near a window overlooking the river and extended a hand, indicating I should join her. "Let's speak for a moment about the Foster family, Lucinda." She cocked her head, looking out across the water to Skidaway Island in the distance. "The Fosters have lived here near the river damn near as long as the Ashers have. I'd like to say I have no quarrel with either Emmaline or Davis, but raising a family with eleven children the shades of the rainbow colors your perspective, pardon the pun." She laughed at her inadvertent slip.

"And, mind you, this was the sixties. There were still separate washrooms in many places, not that I gave one damn. Money gives you the latitude to do things your own way, and my children went to the restroom where I did. No one in this town would've dared cross me. And it's as wrong as the devil himself that the black mamas and daddies in this town had to suffer the 'separate but equal' absurdity." She sighed and smiled longingly out at the vista over her backyard. I imagined the yard crowded with shouting, laughing kids. "Our babies brought wealth to Mister Asher and myself that eclipsed our material blessings by far, but it also provided us with clarity on issues of racial inequality decades before many others of our generation." She turned away from her water view, face serious.

"Let's be honest, Lucinda. Many of my generation, especially those living in the Deep South, still have no clarity. Ignorance and hate are never uglier than when they're trained on innocent children. Some people hold hate in their heart, carefully tending to it like a flower, year after year. Taking satisfaction in watching it flourish. But many more just allow the ignorance of racism to continue, never opening their minds to the God's truth that we're all created in the image of our Maker. That the color of our skin is of no more consequence than the color of our eyes or hair. The Fosters fall into that second group. They would deny to their dying day that they're racist. But I imagine you saw the truth of it firsthand."

She touched my hand. "You will go to their home tomorrow night, and you will be elegant and poised, like a queen above the fray. Your composure will reassure your Davis, and he's bound to need that. Beyond that, Lucinda, you will allow him to tend his own garden. And we'll pray he does what's right."

We sat in the breakfast room, early afternoon sunshine painting the charming nook with warmth. "I have to be candid, MariSee. Bibi told me you were the best cook in the family, and I'd need to watch myself at your table or risk needing double Spanx to make the dress work." I rolled my eyes and teased the last vestiges of grits from the old Wedgwood bowl. "But I didn't have any idea food could be *this* good. I didn't even know my life had been empty and meaningless without cheese grits. I'm a New York girl, born and bred. Do you think I can learn to make these?"

The little old lady rose, clearing our plates, and laughed heartily. "Of course, dear. Grits are no hill for a climber, as we say, but you'll need to follow the directions precisely. I'll send them along to you in the post. I'm warning you, though. The authentic, original recipes used by most of the locals don't have the cheese. That's just the way I prefer it. Along with all my boys, including Mister Asher. The children would always go out with their father on the boat and try to catch shrimp, so I'd make this for their supper. He had to cast the net when they were little, of course. But my boys grew big and tall, stronger than their father. The children adored him; we all did." Her eyes clouded over again briefly. "I miss him every day since he left."

I joined her at the sink, grabbing a dish towel to dry the bowls and cast-iron pot she'd made the shrimp and grits in. "How did you know he was the one for you, MariSee?" It was a ridiculously intimate question for a woman I'd only just met. But I couldn't imagine an older female figure in my life who could neatly field such a question.

She put down the cut crystal glass she was washing and turned to look at me, piercing me again with her canny gaze. "When you can't see your path progressing without him. When you want to wander the corners of his mind, hear his thoughts, bear his burdens, walk through any pain he encounters so he doesn't do it alone. When you feel wild and free and, what's that term you young women are so fond of?" She closed her eyes, thinking for a few seconds. "Empowered. That's it. Free and empowered and encouraged to be exactly who you are when he's at your side." Her face softened. "That's when you've found the one your heart loves, child." She turned her attention again to the glassware. "Bellamy tells me you've been with him nearly every minute since that awful accident happened. Did you give any consideration to stepping back after you almost lost him?"

I stopped drying and thought. "Not for a second. I never thought of leaving for a single minute, MariSee. I ran to him and stayed there."

She moved to the table, wiping it with a soapy cloth. "I think you already have your answer, Lucinda. Bellamy is Alice's granddaughter, so I'm really her great aunt, you see. But Alice passed when Bibi was a baby, so I treat Bellamy like my own. She's something special, that girl. And I love her Charles, too. I'm having the time of my life cooking for him this week. You talk to her; she knows Davis Foster. And she knows a thing or two about love and the care and feeding it requires."

I helped MariSee place the arrangements throughout the house, rolling the wooden wagon behind through the expansive hallways of the house at her behest. She regaled me with history of the old place, the ghost that allegedly appeared occasionally in the boathouse, and even showed me the secret room used to shelter slaves before they were spirited away along the Underground Railroad toward freedom further north. We carried the last half dozen arrangements up the massive horseshoe staircase and placed them in two of the seven upstairs bedrooms.

"Now, Lucinda, dear. The party is tomorrow evening?" I nodded affirmatively. "You have everything you need now to look the part of a beautiful woman deeply in love with a very handsome young man. Pity I had to send my regrets, but I can't abide Emmaline." She chuckled. "No matter, of course. She certainly can't abide the likes of me."

She had been invited? So much for nearest and dearest. The jockeying for position among the social register in this town was beyond me.

The hours flew, and I found myself disappointed about leaving, but Davis's workday was coming to an end. As we said our goodbyes on the expansive front stoop, I put my arms around her tiny frame, giving her an affectionate hug. "How can I thank you for today, MariSee? I feel I've been given a precious gift in meeting you."

She waved one twisted little hand. "Your company was my pleasure, Lucinda. You tell that niece of mine to find some time to fly out and see her old auntie. Or maybe I'll just jump on an airplane myself. Two of my sons live in Scottsdale; they may be due for a visit from their mama."

One thing was for sure. If Mrs. Mary Crawford Buckalew Asher graced Arizona with a visit, I was clearing my calendar.

Chapter
TWENTY-SIX

"Black or White"

Davis

The broken leg had been damned inconvenient, but never more so than now.

Luckie looked ridiculously out of place behind the wheel of our serviceable rental car, the dark chiffon of her full skirt puddling on the carpet beside her feet. She should've been peeking through demurely lowered lashes at the press just before ascending the stairs at the Cannes Film Festival, pausing halfway to allow photos of her elaborate shoes and elegant bag. Instead, she was following my directions as we wound closer to my childhood home, lost in thought between turns, a knitted brow gently marring her beauty.

I placed my hand gently on her thigh. "Try not to worry, Peaches. You're so jaw-droppingly gorgeous tonight, and I don't just mean the clothes. I have to keep reminding myself that you're really mine, and I couldn't be prouder or more anxious to show you off to the whole city tonight." I grinned. "That's probably who my mother really invited, you know. There'll be a cast of thousands in the front yard when we pull up." That elicited a smile.

"I don't really care if the party's large or small. It's just that I'm in love with you, and I wish that was the only thing giving me butterflies tonight. We shouldn't have to wonder if I'll be accepted by your family and friends—and most of all, your mom and dad—just because my skin's darker than yours. What a terrible, ludicrous thing to concern ourselves with in this day and age." She shook her head but turned to me with a brave little smile. "I'll make you proud, Davis Payne Foster, I promise you that. I..." Her lip quivered a bit.

I caught her right hand, bringing it to my lips, and kissed it. "You already make me proud, Lucinda. Proud and grateful and so happy. I couldn't give one flying fuck what anyone else thinks. Anyone at all, and that includes my parents, as much as I love them. I swear, Luckie, what we have belongs to us alone. We are going to take the time to nurture this love and see where it leads. Don't forget, Peaches. I choose you."

We pulled into the driveway of the rambling, white Gothic Revival house where I'd grown up, parking a hundred yards or so away since cars already clogged the motor court and front drive. The long walkway was glowing with low-profile landscape lighting, and the sunset cast the chalky exterior of the house in pale pinks and purples reflected from the water nearby. I was a comedic figure, mostly dashing in my Ralph Lauren tux with a large helping of absurd in the form of the split leg seam flapping wildly to accommodate my cast. Lucinda walked regally at my side, giving me an occasional concerned glance as I maneuvered along the darkened drive with my crutches. She was tall and impossibly slender with perfect posture. Grace personified. Her gown was the perfect complement to her dark skin, all frothy, billowing black with vivid flowers decorating the fabric. It swirled around her legs and floated behind her in what she informed me was a small train. My mother, along with the rest of Savannah society, was going to be knocked out. I could barely breathe when she walked out of the bathroom an hour ago.

We made our way up the front steps, and I paused in front of the mammoth oak door, burnished with age. My mother found it at Red Baron Antiques in Atlanta, dragged it back to Savannah, and hired a contractor to tear open the front of our house. He redesigned it to make the door its centerpiece. Daddy had a kitty cat about the entire ordeal, but even he knew not to cross Emmaline on that one. In the waning light of sunset, I turned and took Luckie's hand in my own once more.

"Thank you for standing by me, literally and figuratively, for these past weeks. It's been a little like falling in love in a pressure cooker, hasn't it?" She smiled, looking into my eyes. "I do love everything I see in you, Lucinda Page. Now let me kiss that perfect mouth once more before I have to go inside and be a good boy for a few hours."

I pulled her into a tight embrace, and her soft breasts pressed so close I could feel our hearts beating out their cadence between us. My lips were on hers, exploring and nipping softly until she softened in my arms. My cock thickened, and she rocked her hips gently against me and opened her mouth to the demands of my tongue. One of her hands grasped my ass, caressing and then pulling me closer so she could move rhythmically against the length of my hard-on. Just as my brain entered the final stages of powering completely down, the hefty door creaked and swung open.

There, dwarfed in the yawning doorway, was Mama, nearly purple with rage. She was obviously wearing high heels judging from the way she almost reached my shoulder, and was swathed in a floor-length Bordeaux-colored gown, expensively under-stated, as usual. Because of the lack of available blood flow to my brain for higher decision making and the obvious tent I'd pitched in my tuxedo pants, the best idea I could produce at that moment was to hold Luckie tightly to me. Adding to my list of issues was the fact I'd abandoned my crutches to play grab ass, and balance was a serious problem.

"Evenin', Mama."

She hissed under her breath, aware of the half dozen or so partygoers who'd gathered in the grand foyer where champagne was evidently being served. "Davis Payne. What in heaven's name has come over you? Making out on my front porch like common trash with this…"

Uh-oh. I interrupted before she could burn it to the ground. "Mama, you remember Lucinda." Luckie turned in one agile motion, moving in front of me to simultaneously greet my mother with an offered hand and shield the onlookers from the aforementioned tent in my drawers. Not ever having been at the mercy of a public woody, she didn't know the appearance of one's mother was the ultimate antidote. I reached for my crutches and saw my mother compose herself, offering Luckie a smile that didn't reach her eyes.

"Well, of course. Lucinda, please come in, dear. And welcome to our home."

Rearranged and balanced on my crutches, I tugged on the ridiculously gaping pant leg and followed Luckie into the house. The marble foyer held maybe fifty or so guests enjoying champagne, likely Krug, Mama's favorite and her signature at her parties. A few waitstaff passed hors d'oeuvres unobtrusively among the crowd, and the predicted jazz trio churned out Duke Ellington's "Take the A Train" from their position in the formal living room. Probably one of the most useless rooms in a house full of useless rooms, I thought. That group of musicians had probably spent more time in that room than our family combined. My mother's voice, filled with affection and excitement I knew she was fabricating, broke in on my musings.

"Look, darling…Davis, look who's here. It's the Hope-Armstrongs. So good of you to come." My mother had an irritating habit of referring to families by both surnames in cases where she'd known the woman before her marriage and therefore knew her maiden name. I held out my hand to our longtime neighbors.

"Aunt Nonnie, Uncle Heywood, it's so good to see you both. May I present my girlfriend, Ms. Lucinda Page of Manhattan?" If Luckie was put out by the archaic display, not a flicker of it showed on her face. She extended her hand.

"What a pleasure to meet you, Mrs. Hope-Armstrong. Mr. Armstrong." Damn, I thought, shooting her an incredulous look. Her Old South game was strong. I engaged our neighbors in a bit of conversation, swiping champagne at the earliest opportunity for Luckie and me before Mama tugged me away. Before leaving, I noticed Aunt Nonnie reaching for Luckie's hand and giving it a squeeze. She stood on tiptoes to reach her ear and whispered barely loud enough for me to hear.

"So pleased to meet you, my dear. It's bound to be an interesting evening for you in the company of all these old fussbudgets, but something tells me you're equal to the task. If you survive the sheer boredom, bring me a spot of champagne later and tell me all about it." Her old eyes twinkled, and Luckie promised to do just that.

Daddy joined us, giving Luckie's knuckles a perfunctory grazing kiss and regarding the whole scene with curiosity. It occurred to me that Mama was driving the boat on the party, and I wondered if she'd read Daddy in on her purposes, dubious or otherwise.

"Davis, it's the Forsythe-Gannons. And, look, the Iversons and the Kirschbaum-Kleins." My mother's continued tour of the room left the impression that none of these people had ever darkened our door. In reality, I doubted it had been three months since they'd hosted the very same group. Same party, different day. Luckie somehow managed to look as if it was the most delightful company she'd ever had the privilege of enjoying. She laughed, flirted, and worked the room like a pro, charming the ladies and gentlemen with equal ease.

My filthy-mouthed girlfriend, with her mouthwatering tits and slick, needy little pussy morphed smoothly into a blue-blooded aristocrat. In only a short time, she had the cream of Savannah's upper crust eating out of her hand. I stole away from Mama to eavesdrop as she held court.

Dinner *and* a show.

"Now, Mrs. Havis-Murray, I absolutely insist you tell me everything I need to know about making grits. I'm not from around here, in case you can't tell…" The group laughed appreciatively at her self-deprecating tone. "…and I didn't even know I loved them until I got here. Imagine my surprise."

Ernestine Havis-Murray laughed and patted her hand, passing along all her secrets for turning out perfect grits. I didn't have the heart to tell her I loved the instant grits I bought in the box. Had she known, Aunt Ernie would surely have left me for dead at the city limits. From the corner of my eye, I noticed my mother sweeping by with a fresh flute of champagne, watching Luckie unobtrusively in her peripheral vision. I felt a hand on my shoulder and turned to see Daddy standing there, two glasses of whiskey balanced in one hand.

"Macallan. The good stuff, Son. You had enough bubbly?" I grinned, setting my half-full flute on a passing tray. "Come on, Davis, walk with me. Nobody's out on the dock yet. The breeze should keep the skeeters at bay for now." After whispering my destination in Luckie's ear, I followed my dad across the marble expanse of the foyer, through the kitchen where caterers worked steadily on a variety of platters, and onto the screened porch running the length of the house. The sun was gone now, lights on the long dock offered the only illumination in the backyard.

"Your mother always wanted a pool back here, but I couldn't bear losing the lawn. I somehow always pictured this yard full of a big white tent and you dancing with your bride at a wedding reception designed to bankrupt the bride's daddy and me." He chuckled at himself, taking a generous sip of whiskey. "Not sure why I'd think about such a thing. Weddings are what women dream about, not men." Daddy was in a reflective mood, though I couldn't tell exactly why. We reached the dock, walking its length, and I stared down into the water of the river.

"I didn't know the details of the dreams you had for me, Daddy." I didn't look at him, but I sensed he listened intently to every word. "I just knew you expected me to join you at Foster and Sons at the earliest opportunity." I fortified myself with a sip of Macallan; the moment would never present itself more clearly than it was doing right now. "But that was never what I wanted."

Daddy sighed and took a healthy slug of whiskey. I allowed the silence to hang heavily, resisting the urge to soften the blow. "I am so proud of you, Davis. Always have been. I didn't want the two of us to follow the path I did with my daddy—to keep you at arm's length and be a stranger to you on the day I died. But it's true I never asked about the dreams you had for yourself. I was proud when you told me you wanted to serve in the military and attend The Citadel, but I assumed you were doing it because of family tradition. Me, and your granddaddy before me. It fell in line with what I'd hoped, that you'd want to do what I did. Stay here. Work in the family business every day with me. Find a nice local girl from a nice local family and settle down." The silence stretched as I took in this unfamiliar side of my father, regretful and off balance.

He turned and took my measure with a face that suddenly looked weary. "I tried to force you into the mold of my expectation, and that was wrong of me. The fault lies entirely with me, a man who was set in his ways but loved his son."

I took a deep breath. "I didn't give it too much thought over these past years. I just poured all my energy into flying and my military career. You know how much space that can take up in your life." Daddy nodded his assent. "I've learned to enjoy the company of people who are different from me. I hope it doesn't hurt you and Mama, but being far from Savannah and the South…" I took another big sip of the Macallan for liquid courage and continued. "It's made my world a bigger place. A better place."

Daddy rocked back and forth on his heels, his brow furrowed. "Things haven't been real pleasant around here since your mama found out you were dating a black woman."

So. We're going to go there.

"I'd imagine not. But you and Mama need to understand something very important here." My voice bordered on stern, a tone I had never taken with my father. He looked up, meeting my steady gaze. "It's serious; I love Lucinda."

His face softened slowly, and then he surprised me by raising his glass with a hearty laugh. "Well, God help ya, boy. When you fall in love, all bets are off, and you can take that to the damn bank." He took another swallow of the whiskey and cleared his throat. "The world's changing, kid, and your dad's a dinosaur. I wouldn't call your mama a dinosaur to her face, but the shoe fits; just don't tell her I said so." He laughed again, then sobered, staring across the water.

"I could tell when I met her that you two were…that you felt something for each other. And your mama knows, too, Davis; she's scared shitless. This isn't how…when we were coming up, it wasn't done this way." He was struggling, both with what he felt and the delivery, but I let him flail.

"We didn't raise you this way, but I'm hard-pressed to understand why we believed what we did. It just…it ain't Christian to judge a book by its cover." He shook his head hard as if trying to dislodge the ingrained wrong there. "She's having a hard time—we both are—but we'll get there. Old habits die hard, but we'll get there."

My throat was tight, and his unexpected words were the culprit. "I was afraid you'd make me choose." I was surprised to hear my voice break with the words.

He turned to me, his face questioning. "Choose?"

"Pick between you and Mama...and the woman I love." My throat burned, and my heart pounded at the thought. With all their significant faults, I loved my parents. Daddy's arm was around my shoulder, and he pulled me closer. When he spoke, his voice was tinged with emotion too.

"There's nothing more important than love, Davis Payne. Hell, I've loved your mama for more years than I can remember now, and we've made each other very happy. And very unhappy. But I wouldn't trade what we have for anything. Nothing will bring you soul-deep joy like the love of a good woman. You ever been in love before, Son?"

I shook my head. "No, sir."

He broke into a wide grin. "You're in for the ride of your life."

Chapter
TWENTY-SEVEN

"Waiting on the World to Change"

Lucinda

I wasn't sure why Davis had been gone for so long and fretted that things between his father and him might have gone sideways. I tried to focus; I had to keep my A game front and center. There was no margin of error with the older generation that swirled around me. They seemed unusually adept at extracting information. The party had moved further into the house, expanding throughout the formal and informal areas of the downstairs. There were two open bars, one at each end of the sprawling living area, and a lavish buffet sprang up like a mushroom out of the ground, winding through the dining room and into the foyer.

Mrs. Hope-Armstrong approached stealthily, like a genteel little terrorist, from behind me and touched my elbow. "I took the liberty of coming to find you, Lucinda; it appears your popularity may not diminish any time in the near future." She held up a tall glass filled with a frosty, fruity concoction. "Why don't you join me for a nip of planter's punch? It's just fruit juice, really, with a splash of dark rum."

I took the glass with a smile and thanks, trying a generous sip. Holy hell. These people must have really known how to hold their alcohol because the "splash of dark rum" probably comprised half of the tall glass. I coughed delicately. "Why thank you, Mrs. Hope-Armstrong, it's so thoughtful of—" Before the thought could be finished, however, she'd locked her arm with mine and was squiring me to a quieter corner of the living room.

"Now, my name is Mary Glen Hope-Armstrong, my dear, but you must call me Aunt Nonnie as Davis does. All the young people do, although we're not proper blood kin. It's just our way. Emmaline throws wonderful parties, you know, and I'd never miss one. Always at the ready to host charity events…she does so much good work with the Savannah Women's League." Nonnie was a plump little blue hair, perfectly turned out and wearing a king's ransom in sapphires around her chubby neck. She punctuated her speech with theatrical hand gestures, and I wondered how long it would be before one of us was wearing the planter's punch.

"But, Lucinda, I must tell you: there's been a wait list for this particular affair since Lacie Hammond-Marsh saw you with Davis at the Kobo Gallery Sunday afternoon. She knew you weren't from around here because Lacie knows everybody in Georgia." She ticked them off on her bejeweled fingers. "The Carters, Anne Cox Chambers, the Candlers. Why, I believe she even met that handsome Mr. Tyler Perry once." Nonnie took a long drink of her punch and patted my hand. "You must feel like an exotic creature on display at the zoo. Tell me, dear, how are you holding up to all the gawking and speculation?"

The plot thickens.

Emmaline had known about me before Davis came clean over the phone Tuesday. It came as no surprise that she was a couple of steps ahead of us.

I laughed gently, wondering if Nonnie's candor was second nature or alcohol induced. "Actually, everyone's been welcoming and gracious, and really quite magnanimous considering they have a Yankee in their midst, asking for recipes and tourist advice."

Nonnie chuckled, but her demeanor took on a more serious tone. "I'll be frank, Lucinda. Enjoying the company of a charming, beautiful young woman, even one as cultured as you are, is a treat we are gladly accustomed to in our fair city. There's a high premium placed on what we like to call 'good breeding.' But when that splendid, polished creature has caught the eye of one of our favorite sons—and she happens to be black—someone's liable to get trampled on the way to the carving station."

You had to hand it to her, I thought with an indulgent grin. All fortified with rum, Nonnie didn't pull her punches. On the other hand, her outspokenness was tempered with what felt like genuine affection. The fact-finding mission she'd embarked on didn't seem malicious. Additionally, there was no need to concern myself with holding down my end of the conversation; the spirits evidently turned the little old socialite talkative. I wouldn't have to strain the gray matter deducing the undercurrent in the room; Nonnie laid it all out on the table without hesitation. Wind her up and watch her go.

"I hope you're not put out with me for bringing up race, my dear. It's just not in my nature to be coy, and I can't imagine it hasn't been on your mind as well."

I surveyed the room, populated with the lily-white elite of Savannah, and wondered how many of the conversations revolved around me. Around Davis and his upbringing. The color of my skin. Returning attention to our conversation, I decided Mrs. Hope-Armstrong deserved to know I didn't have a shy bone in my body either.

"Since you've done me the courtesy of being plainspoken,

Aunt Nonnie, I'll gladly return the favor. I've not spent much time in the South, though my visits here have been so thoroughly enjoyable. I love your city—the history and architecture and the kindness of the people. And don't even get me started on the food." I rubbed my ever so slightly rounded tummy, glad the dress was somewhat forgiving. "But I know the attitudes of many people here surrounding race, especially interracial relationships, differ from my personal viewpoint. And, as long as we're being direct, they differ from most of the rest of the country." I took a sip of punch, weighing my words. "I can't bring myself to be swayed by, or even interested in, the opinion of anyone foolish enough to judge a person by the color of their skin. It flies in the face of reason. And it causes me to doubt the character of the person who espouses it."

Nonnie's round little face unexpectedly broke into a brilliant smile. "I knew I liked you, Miss Lucinda Page, and I should've known the Foster boy would bring home an interesting woman." She leaned closer to me, as if to whisper in my ear, despite a height difference that approached a solid foot. "You're not at all wrong about the racial issues the South still struggles with, but don't misunderstand. We're not all cut from the same cloth, and even some of the old dogs have learned new tricks." She raised her eyebrows, taking a long draw on her punch.

"Yes, I believe I met one only yesterday," I murmured, sipping.

Her eyes danced. "Yes, I believe I heard something about MariSee having you for lunch, didn't I? Now, Lucinda, don't look so surprised; you're the most interesting thing happening in Savannah this week, so I made it my business to watch the show from the sidelines." Her laughing eyes softened, and she lowered her voice again. "MariSee is one of my oldest friends; we began primary school at Massie together many years ago. She and I are two of the old dogs I referred to before. Her second eldest son, Tanner Burton Asher, is my godson. Fine, strapping boy with bright brown eyes and a sharp mind. So handsome, that one. He's a barrister in Scottsdale now."

Had I not believed the gospel of small-town America before, I certainly did now. Mary Glen Hope-Armstrong let me in on the fact that all of Davis's family social circle had me in their sights, but for a variety of reasons. I'd been pleasantly surprised twice in twenty-four hours by two elderly local women, each lending wisdom and support in their own unique way.

"Now, I'll not be guilty of whitewashing the truth, as we say down here," Nonnie said, continuing my baptism by fire. "No one's perfectly enlightened, and some don't bother to be enlightened at all. Judging by the wide berth Emmaline's been giving you all evening, I'll venture to say she's not among your biggest fans."

It wasn't posed as a question because Nonnie already knew the answer, but I took care to be intentionally vague. "I'd say the jury's out, Aunt Nonnie. We only met on Thursday for the first time, and there hasn't been much opportunity for us to get to know one another."

She nodded approvingly. "That's a good attitude and a generous one. Emmaline and I go way back, too, and I'll lift the veil on that only enough to say she had a very hard time of it coming up. She was the youngest of five, the only daughter of Harrison Hoyle Abbott, probably the wealthiest man in these parts in the day. Harrison's daddy's people had slaves when he was a child, and he made sure his children all believed 'The War of Northern Aggression' had wrongly taken away their God-given right to keep slaves."

The War of Northern Aggression? What fresh hell was this?

"I know it's shocking, Lucinda, but this was how people actually thought. How they talked. Harrison was an angry man, bitter that something he believed he deserved had somehow been taken from him. As if God Almighty ever ordained that one human being could own another, never mind abuse and disparage that child of God based on the color of their skin. Although the Abbotts had more material wealth than anyone for miles, Emmie's daddy had a cold heart, all bound up with hate.

"Then, when Emmie was about ten or eleven, her sweet mama could take no more. She swallowed all the pills she could find and took her leave from this life and the five babies who needed her so. I won't torment you with the ongoing details, but Emmaline takes care to hold herself well removed from people with very few exceptions. In many ways, she has never grown beyond the heartbroken little girl who desperately need-ed the mama who left her. As sad as it is, none of us can grow or progress without people around us who care enough to speak truth into our lives."

I think my mouth was still open, poise utterly departed in the presence of a woman I'd completely underestimated. I'd seen a comical little matron, kind and a bit melodramatic. But I missed the prudence and savvy worldview, probably a result of carefully observing the occupants of the fishbowl she lived in. "Aunt Nonnie, you mentioned there were exceptions when it came to Mrs. Foster's cloistered existence."

"The two that come to mind are the men whose home this is. There's J.R., of course." My face registered the question for me, and Nonnie responded. "Everyone close to the family, kin or otherwise, calls Davis's daddy J.R., for Junior." She looked thoughtful. "Not everyone, I suppose, because Emmie calls him Payne, and his daddy was Senior, of course. J.R.'s daddy, I mean, not Davis's. Davis is a third, but he didn't abide the nickname Trey, even as a little boy, so he turned out to be the only Davis of the lot. It's very simple, really."

Simple was not the word I'd use, but I could ask Davis later.

Nonnie was continuing, and I needed to pay attention.

"J.R. is a formidable man who has a soft spot the size of Texas for that little woman, and she worships the ground he walks on. When little Davis came along, they'd all but given up on having their own babies. I don't know that I've ever seen parents so affected by the birth of a child. She loves him deeply. Emmie may be damaged goods, much like the rest of us, my dear, but don't count her out. If there's hope for any of us to change, it's all rooted in the love we have for other people."

I saw Davis and his father emerge from the back porch, obviously returning from a walk by the river. His eyes swept the room, settling on me. He had a quick word with his dad, moving quickly across the room to join me. He wrapped an arm around my waist from behind, squeezing gently, and placed an affectionate kiss on my cheek. "Hi there, Peaches." He rumbled a little in his throat, speaking so low only I could hear him, and then he turned his attention to Nonnie. "Aunt Nonnie, you're looking radiant as always. Are those shiny baubles from Uncle Heywood or one of your other admirers?" He grinned, indicating the sapphire display around her neck.

"Hush up, Davis Foster. That's a fresh mouth on you; you're not too big for your mama to switch you. If you don't think I'll tell her, you've got another think comin'." Even as the threats flowed, she smiled fondly. "I've taken it upon myself to acquaint Miss Page with the finer points of our beautiful city's residents, Davis. I knew you wouldn't mind."

Davis rolled his eyes, sighing at Nonnie. "Goddammit, Nonnie. Could you cut a guy a break? Can't you see I'm already out of my league here?"

She sipped the nearly empty vat of planter's punch, lowering her face with the demure look she'd recently denied possessing. Looking up through her lashes, she offered him her empty glass. "Now be a dear and get me a refill, Davis. It's been a warmish evening, and I've got a terrible thirst." As Davis smiled and took her glass, she sent him with one final piece of instruction. "Be sure and ask Balfour to add an extra shot of that dark rum; it's a tad watery if you ask me."

Holy shit. These old ladies are no joke.

Chapter
TWENTY-EIGHT

"Moves Like Jagger"

Davis

The Tominac Fitness Center, which looked a lot like a gym to me, was the rallying point early on this Thursday morning, and Dawg offered me a hand as I maneuvered myself from the seat of his lifted pickup truck. "What moved you to acquire this hayseed limousine, Dawg? Last time I saw you at DM, you had that sweet '67 Mustang with the cherry restoration job. Whatever happened to her?" I reached to the floorboard and grabbed the briefcase I'd been using to corral paperwork for the past couple of weeks, and we made our way toward the front door.

Dawg guffawed loudly. "Victoria Marie Court happened, that's what. When I popped the question last summer, she didn't want a diamond. She wanted the 'Stang." He sighed, but the big grin never left his face. "Deliverance, love makes you do some crazy shit, man. Besides, when in Rome, right? I've always wanted a pickup, and living in the South gives me the best excuse I'll ever have."

Tom "Dawg" Vanderbilt was from Miami and the sole heir to a huge real estate enterprise. Like me, he'd been dodging his birthright in Uncle Sam's Flying Club, and his parents were almost as pleased about it as mine were. A chance meeting at the O'Club one Friday night and a few too many beers revealed this common ground, so I was especially glad to see him again. He was currently assigned to Fort Stewart, the hosts for this exercise, as a Brigade **ALO**, but he'd been at Davis-Monthan and a Scorpion when I arrived there. Dawg earned his tactical courtesy of the wide stubborn streak he'd evidently exhibited since childhood. His mother said he was "like a dog with a bone" when she sent him for golf lessons at the country club. Despite a complete lack of aptitude, he eventually mastered the game, and he brought the same dogged determination to his flying.

Dawg and I had spent a long night in his office breaking out the **Air Tasking Order** to find specifics applying to the Scorpion mission in this "war." The **Frag** from the **ATO** usually consisted of an **Initial Point**, a time to arrive on target, desired weapons load, and the radio frequency to be used in communications with the **FAC**. While the aircraft would not employ live ammunition or ordinance, the artillery and armor would. Ft. Stewart, with its extensive maneuver areas and live fire ranges, was ideally suited to host this large-scale exercise. The goal was the closest simulation of World War III we could produce, complete with armor, artillery, infantry, and air power. The A-10 was practically custom-made to accomplish the CAS mission. Its ability to support ground troops in contact with the enemy was unparalleled and undisputed in the Army community.

The gym, which Dawg also refused to call a fitness center, had been converted into a briefing facility for the air component of this year's "Georgia Reforger" exercise. Rows of chairs were unimaginatively set up in front of a seventies vintage lectern equipped with a microphone. Dawg and I poured large paper cups of coffee from the urn set atop a wobbly card table. "The Army really needs to take some procurement lessons from The Big Blue Team," Dawg cracked. "Didn't realize how spoiled I was until I got temporary billeting on base when I arrived." He grimaced. "Harsh, D. I don't even think the thread count on the sheets was up to snuff." We shared a laugh and turned to see the remaining Scorpions, similarly attired in flight suits, near the front of the room. They were also drinking coffee, being entertained by Rock, mid-anecdote.

We approached the group, and I handled introductions. Dawg extended his hand to each man, in turn, welcoming them with a wide grin. "Great to have you guys here; Colonel Fitzpatrick has been pumped about having some real CAS for this exercise; the Hawgs are a badass addition to the lineup." A few additional pleasantries were exchanged, coffee was refilled, and the Scorpion pilots busied themselves annotating their maps until the briefing began.

Fitzpatrick walked to the podium with his own bulging briefcase and a mug of coffee resembling a tankard, stopping to shake my hand heartily along the way. The mass briefing was comprehensive, covering time slots, radio frequencies, ingress and egress, restricted areas, and safety, safety, safety. The Colonel repeatedly emphasized the security of people and assets, repeating himself so frequently that even he eventually had to laugh. "I hear it too, people, and I know I sound like a damn broken record." He laughed easily, taking a big slug of coffee, then sobering. "But nothing we do here today is worth endangering a single life. So use an abundance of caution—and have some fun, for God's sake. I plan to." With that, the mass brief broke up, and Coach gathered the Scorpions for a squadron brief. He grabbed a chair, turning it backward, and sat facing the small assembly.

"Georgia Reforger assumes a resurgent Russian military. As you're aware, the threat dictates our tactics, and this exercise was organized to test and stress those tactics. The threats today are **SA-16 Gimlets** and **SA-8 Geckos**; the Army has acquired a number of SA-8 systems from former Eastern bloc countries for training. The SA-16 will be simulated with "**Smokey SAMs**." Our weapons load is entirely simulated, guns and **Maverick missiles**, as well as **AIM-9 Sidewinders** for self-defense. Of course, the SA-8 dictates an extremely low-level ingress and egress with minimum time pop-up engagements and weapon delivery."

The briefing was completed, and the group dispersed. Coach and I walked together out of the gym, and I grabbed my crotch with a wry grin. "All this talk about low-level and min-time delivery's giving me a hard-on."

Coach clapped me on the back with a sympathetic laugh. "Your day's coming, D. Soon enough, you'll be back in the cockpit, and this will seem like a bad dream."

I knew he was right, but that day couldn't come soon enough. For now, I'd have to be content to watch my buddies play in the sun.

Coach had decided on a two-ship employment concept to cover as much of the frag as possible. Many of the **IPs** were close enough together for a pair of two-ships to coordinate a combined attack on a group of targets as the ground battle progressed. His voice crackled through the radio as Dawg and I careened through a rocky creek bed in our old Humvee.

"Coach check…two-p."

Coach checked his flight in on the FAC frequency. "Dawg, Coach, two A-10s, IP709, gun and four by Mavericks, authenticate Alpha Delta." Having requested confirmation of the controllers on the other end of his radio transmissions, he waited for the coded response.

Dawg keyed the mic. "Coach, Dawg. I authenticate Foxtrot November. Your control today will be provided by Deliverance, stand by for **Nine Line**."

I could hear Coach's laugh, muffled by the oxygen mask. He would have never compromised his professionalism by saying anything over the radio, but I knew very well what was running through his head: *Deliverance, you pathetic bastard, were you so desperate to get in the middle of the action that you risked the wrath of your woman and mine?*

I was exactly that pathetic. Having burned the midnight oil with Dawg breaking out the frag, I hopped a ride with him into the thick of "battle" and was now bouncing wildly through rough terrain, carefully protecting my mending left leg from any unfortunate outcome. If Bibi found out, she'd kill both of us.

"Coach, Deliverance. Ready to copy Nine Line?" Even in the age of digital transmissions, this remained the most reliable way for the FAC to communicate with the pilot. As I spoke, he would scrawl the particulars in grease pencil on the glass canopy of his jet, ready for quick reference.

"Coach: Line, Shooter-Shooter, Maverick."

The target was a company of tanks just beyond the tree line on the far western end of the maneuver area. Using a scant few words, Coach had neatly conveyed his plan of attack to his wingman, Boo. They would ingress, line abreast for maximum mutual support, then simultaneously pop up and employ Maverick missiles to eliminate the threat. Piece of cake.

I watched as Coach expertly maneuvered his two-ship into line formation at the ingress point, pushed the power to maximum, and descended to two hundred fifty feet **AGL**. His **RHAW** scope was lit up with SA-8 and air-to-air radar, indicating a search from the Red Air fighters overhead. But no one had locked on them. Yet.

"Deliverance, Coach. IP inbound."

"Coach, Deliverance. Cleared hot."

Our voices retained the trademark "fighter pilot cool," but my heart pounded, glad to be back in the game, if only on the sidelines. The jets were relatively lightweight, carrying only a fraction of the weapons load a Hawg was capable of lugging into battle. Combined with the cool morning air, this meant Coach's jets were tickling three hundred thirty knots. The Maverick's TV camera was displayed on a cockpit screen for targeting, ready to meet the threat with deadly force. Coach's terse words bit through the radio.

"Coach, action. Now."

At the desired range, the hulking jets rose in an arc over the battlefield, popping up from terrain that had hidden their presence, and visually acquired their targets. The **HUD** in Coach's cockpit allowed him to set an aiming reference on one of the tanks. Glancing at the monitor, he could use the miniature joystick on the throttle to control the TV camera and direct, then lock the missile. Having exposed his aircraft to the enemy for less than five seconds, Coach's practiced hands had locked and simulated the launch of the missile. He and Boo broke hard off the target, straining against the G-forces, dispensed **chaff and flares**, and dove for cover. I watched them descend back into the terrain, egressing to the south, as briefed. I knew Coach would clock the two "Smokey Sams" when he checked six, but they were out of range. Coach and Boo were out clean.

Marilyn checked in with Coach as they egressed, deconflicting their altitudes, and Coach briefed Marilyn on the target and threat status. Coach and Boo had enough fuel for one more attack before retiring to Hunter for the day, so he and Marilyn crafted a more complex plan on the fly. The multiple ingress/egress points and weapons worked together seamlessly, treating our hosts to an impressive show of firepower.

I couldn't wipe the shit-eating grin off my face as Dawg sped along the rocky trails, driving more like a teenage boy than an Air Force major. Cold beer would be flowing freely at the debrief, and a party was in order. The Scorpions were well represented today and gave our Army brothers and sisters some quality training and entertainment. Although I sorely missed flying, they made me proud to have a part to play.

And, like Coach said, my day was coming.

Chapter TWENTY-NINE

"Flirtin' With Disaster"

Lucinda

I'd taken the morning after dropping off Davis at Hunter to indulge in a long walk, wandering into any shop or bakery that struck my fancy. It seemed there was no end to establishments that met this description, and I was in retail heaven. I'd wandered far enough from the hotel to need an Uber when it was time to return in order to pick up Davis on time. He'd be plenty tired after today. It was the day set aside for the CAS exercise, the focus of his work and the main reason the other Scorpions had come across the country TDY.

In the aftermath of the party at his parents' house, his relief was palpable. He was relaxed, smiling and laughing more readily. I attributed the change partially to an obvious increase in mobility and the fact that Dr. Taft had given him permission to begin walking for ten minutes at a time without crutches. The brace he wore changed and physical therapy continued unabated, but he was increasingly free of the limitations his injury had originally placed on him. This progression also moved him ever closer to climbing back into the cockpit of his airplane, and although Davis didn't complain, I knew the longing was there.

He didn't grumble because the monster he'd struggled with in the aftermath of the accident was finally gone. After suffering a traumatic event like an aircraft accident that could have been fatal, most people would have grappled with their mortality. Or perhaps fear of disability, whether physical or emotional. Davis had struggled mightily with the possibility that his ability to fly could be taken from him. Having lived under the lifelong expectation of his family—and their dream he'd return to his home and the family business—he'd only recently found the place he belonged. He'd shared this with me in the darkness of one long night a few days after returning home from the hospital. The minutes had stretched to hours as I struggled to control his pain, so I passed the time at his bedside asking him about his love of flying. He'd found what he was born to do, where his strengths lay. Then, as his abilities matured, it became apparent he was not only a gifted pilot but one who loved teaching those less experienced than he was. It was an unusual combination, and it energized him.

Now he saw his goal on the horizon, maybe even sooner than we'd expected. He worked tirelessly, treating his recovery like a job and constantly pushing himself to achieve goals ahead of schedule.

I knew there was also tension building in anticipation of my meeting his parents for the first time, an occasion he expected to go very badly. That heaped additional pressure on our fledgling relationship and potentially placed Davis in a position of having to choose between his parents and me. He hadn't admitted until we returned to our hotel from the party that he'd feared that eventuality more than any other. My gut told me he had shouldered significant stress with these scenarios playing out simultaneously, and I did my best to reassure him. I would never knowingly endanger his relationship with his parents. Now subject to a distant and permanently cooled relationship with my own mother and father, I knew the value of preserving what he had, no matter how imperfect.

Now I happily combed the shelves of the crowded antique store, weighing the idea of buying an additional bag to stuff with treasures I'd collected on this trip. A move like that was tantamount to admitting I'd shopped too much. *As if that's even a thing.* I dismissed it out of hand. Stopping at a shop charmingly named The Vicar's Wife, I squinted against the bright sunshine to study the contents through the store window.

Vintage jewelry. Score.

I pushed the door open, greeting the friendly proprietor, and eagerly examined a pair of delicate earrings. Aquamarine, perhaps? Maybe blue topaz. My eyes darted around the corners of the shop, spying glassware, some lighting, and mirrors. Most of that was too large to consider; my bags were definitely at their limit.

I almost missed her, hidden away at the rear of the space, studying a truly enormous architectural remnant. It could've been a large part of an iron gate or fence; I couldn't be certain. But the woman considering it was absolutely Emmaline. Her chic dark hair was touched with silver, her small frame beautifully attired in a posh little peach-colored pantsuit. The bag she carried was a Hermès Birkin, easily worth more than my BMW. But it was her hands that gave it away, almost birdlike and fluttering over the gigantic piece as if sizing it up to take home. I considered slipping out quietly, but discarded the idea and approached.

"Hello there, Mrs. Foster." I tried to force a happy smile into my voice, moving to touch her elbow lightly.

"Oh, what?" She whirled around, a bit off balance, and I caught her elbow more firmly.

"Mrs. Foster, it's Lucinda." I smiled again, trying for light and relaxed. "Lucinda Page. Davis's…" *Easy there, Luckie.* "Davis's girlfriend, remember?" It took just a second too long for recognition to dawn, I thought. I wondered if this was her version of passive-aggressive; that did seem to be one of her long suits.

She arranged her face in a careful smile. "Yes, of course, Lucinda. I was just lost in thought there for a second. How have you been, dear?" She extended a hand to shake mine, but the Birkin hit the floor.

I squeezed her hand gently and retrieved the bag, handing it back. "I'm soaking up every part of the city I can, trying to make the most of the short time we have left." Her smile faded a little, and she suddenly looked frail and a bit lost. My heart went out to her, despite everything. She probably thought she saw the writing on the wall and was about to lose her only son. I took a chance and reached for her other hand. "Say, Mrs. Foster, I don't suppose you might have time to join me for lunch? I noticed a darling bakery across the way, and I'm famished." She seemed far away once again, so I smiled broadly. "I saw a sign out front about cupcakes." Finally, a little grin surfaced.

"I'm not feeling so well, and perhaps I could use a little tea sandwich or some such." She nodded and gathered her bag, bidding the owner goodbye. We walked across Bull Street in silence, and I scolded myself silently for being so impulsive. This had the makings of a supremely uncomfortable meal. I encouraged Emmaline to take a seat at the table near the window and went to place our orders. Returning after a few minutes, I placed the mug of hot tea she'd requested in front of her, depositing sugar and cream nearby, along with a teaspoon.

She regarded me uncertainly and reached for the spoon, missing on the first try. *She's such a little slip of a woman…she must be suffering from hypoglycemia.* I never had much difficulty with my own weight, but I was what could be charitably termed a hearty eater. To maintain the willowy slim figure Emmaline did,

I guessed she didn't eat much at all. I reached for the spoon and sugar, handing it to her carefully and smiling warmly. I didn't want to embarrass her, but she probably needed to eat something sooner rather than later.

"I ordered us the rosemary chicken sandwiches; they sounded so delicious. And maybe a cupcake to split afterward?" I was beginning to feel the weight of carrying the entire conversation on my shoulders. Emmaline hadn't spoken a word since we left the antique shop, I realized. I looked up sharply just in time to see her struggling with the sugar packet and focused more carefully on her. She looked ill at ease, confused. And her motor skills seemed to be failing her.

"Emmaline." The nurse hat was on, and I was working, studying her. "Reach out and grab my hands." I held two hands across the table, palms up. She reached for me and touched my hands wordlessly. "Now grab my hands, Emmaline. Pull hard." She grasped me, still uncertain, but the left hand was almost limp. Glancing up, I could now see the left side of her cheek and eye drooping, nearly imperceptibly. But it was definite. "How do you feel, Emmaline? Tell me." My voice was gentle but directive.

Her brown eyes stared into mine, panic leaking in. Her lips moved—she was trying, but she didn't speak. I squeezed her hands gently, placing them on the table. "Don't you worry about anything, Mrs. Foster. Everything will be fine; I'll take good care of you, I promise." Without allowing my eyes to drift from her face, I reached out, grabbing the apron of the older female employee who'd taken my order. Turning to her, I kept my voice low and calm. "I need you to sit right here with my friend Emmaline. She's not well, and I need to call an ambulance. How far is it to the hospital?"

I stood, switching places with the older woman. "Why, it can't be more than three miles to Candler, and Memorial's right next door to that." She reached for Emmaline's shaking hands. "I'll sit right here until you get back." She had a comforting, motherly demeanor and spoke quietly to Mrs. Foster. I stood and fished my phone out of my purse, dialing 911 as quickly as I could. Pushing open the door, I slipped outside onto the sidewalk.

"Nine-one-one. What's your emergency?"

"My name is Lucinda Page; I'm located at the Back in the Day Bakery on Bull Street. My companion is a sixty-year-old Caucasian female in apparent good health who is probably experiencing an acute CVA. I need an ambulance, please."

The operator collected additional data, calling for the first responders in the meantime. As I relayed information, I watched through the window, seeing the bakery employee soothe and calm Emmaline. The sound of sirens was almost immediate, reassuring me that the hospital was closer than I had dared hope. More than most healthcare emergencies, a CVA, more commonly known as a stroke, was a situation where time was critical. Early treatment with so-called "clot-busting" medications could frequently prevent brain damage, heading off further complications and speeding recovery. When the operator finished collecting the information she needed, I requested a call transfer to the ambulance, adding that I was an emergency department nurse.

The paramedic answered, identifying himself as Jeff, and I strained to hear his voice over the roar of the siren. "I'm Lucinda Page, and I was at lunch with your patient, Jeff. I'm an emergency department RN in Tucson, Arizona. I want to let you know this is a probable CVA, so please call back to the department—they'll need to have tPA ready. I'm not well versed in her history, but I'll contact the family when you pick up. Odds favor an ischemic episode, as I know you're aware. I'll be out front, Jeff."

I'd barely hung up and dropped the phone into my bag before the ambulance rounded the corner, lights and siren cooking. In moments, Jeff and his co-worker rolled a stretcher into the front door of the bakery and began to move a terrified Emmaline onto the bed. I soothed her, noting the wild, panicked look in her eyes, and spoke quietly.

"I'll ride with you to the hospital, Emmaline. And I'll call J.R. and Davis. They'll be there in no time at all, I promise. You're going to get the very best care, and the people in the emergency department will work hard to find out what's wrong and fix it." I squeezed her hands again, very gently, and climbed into the back of the truck behind her. "I'm right here, Emmaline."

Jeff pulled on my blouse. "You can't ride with us, Miss Page; you're not family."

I leveled a stern look at Jeff, the very nice paramedic. "Jeff. I'm family. I'm not going to cause trouble or get in your way, but time is absolutely of the essence." His face looked a little desperate, so I brought the brief discussion to its conclusion. "Close the fucking doors, Jeff." I sat down, again taking Emmaline's cold little hand. "Let's roll."

Chapter
THIRTY

"Moon River"

Lucinda

D avis and I had been walking quietly for half an hour now,
taking in the dark beauty of the famous Bonaventure
Cemetery. Yesterday had been an impossibly long day
followed by a terribly long night in the hospital. The doctors
determined Emmaline's stroke was indeed ischemic, and the
medications worked as advertised, effectively destroying the clot
that plagued her. After speaking to the attending at length, I was
able to convince J.R. and Davis to go home and rest. I remained
at Emmaline's bedside, even though she was heavily sedated, in
case she awoke. Dozing in the bedside chair yielded about an
hour of sleep as the day wore on, but Davis needed the rest much
more than I did. I seemed to spend quite a bit of time sleeping
in chairs beside hospital beds, I'd thought ruefully. Only weeks
ago, it had been Davis's bed; four years ago, it was Camille's. I
shivered at both memories.

Davis arrived back at the hospital around dinnertime, bearing pure comfort in the form of shrimp and grits delivered to his

hotel room by none other than MariSee. She'd evidently bribed the desk attendant at the hotel for our room number and pounded on the door until Davis answered, disheveled and sleepy. She waited while he showered and dressed, and then drove him to the hospital at an alarming rate of speed in her 1961 Lincoln Continental. How she knew of Emmaline's stroke or where we were staying, he never found out. She'd thrust a large container of the shrimp and grits I loved so much into his hands at the hospital's porte cochère and instructed him to "Tell Emmie I'll be saying the Rosary tonight and lighting candles for her."

J.R. arrived within the hour, and we decided he'd stay the night. The vat of shrimp and grits was a gracious plenty, as MariSee said it would be, for the three of us, so I rounded up bowls and plastic utensils from the nurses. We ate quietly, watching Emmaline for signs of wakefulness. Davis and his dad said their goodbyes, and I gathered our things to go, sending a wave and small smile to J.R. Then, unexpectedly, I felt big arms around my waist.

Turning, I saw fear in J.R.'s eyes and tears wetting his cheeks. He gathered me in a tight embrace and whispered brokenly, "I don't know what would have become of her, Lucinda. What if you hadn't been there? What if it had been someone else?" He pulled away slightly and stared at me. "You saved her, Lucinda. She's my everything, Emmie is. Well, my Emmie and Davis. I don't know what…" Emotion choked away the sentiment, so I wrapped my arms around him and whispered back into his ear.

"I'm glad I was there, Mr. Foster. And I have a good feeling Mrs. Foster will have a very successful recovery. She arrived at the hospital quickly, less than fifteen minutes after the onset of symptoms and the medicine was ready when we arrived."

"All thanks to you, Lucinda. I don't know any way to express my gratitude." His voice was stronger, but tears flowed unabated down the proud man's face.

I straightened and patted his shoulders. "You get whatever

rest you can, Mr. Foster. She'll be awake in the morning, I'd wager, and she's going to need you beside her, strong and ready to help her get better."

He nodded, hugged his son again, and we were gone.

After retrieving the rental car from hock in the parking lot, Davis directed me toward the Wilmington River, and I found an empty space near Bonaventure. We walked hand in hand, no conversation disturbing the silence and beauty of the cemetery painted by streaks of waning light. I sensed he was still processing the events of the past two days, so I waited. He found a low brick wall, settling slowly and leaning forward to rest his elbows on his knees.

"I keep wondering what would've happened if you hadn't seen Mama and invited her to lunch. Even if it had been someone else, she might have been able to sell the story that she was just hungry or hadn't rested well the night before." His eyes were tired, and creases etched by worry sullied his handsome face. "Daddy's right, Luckie—you really did save her. She might have survived; I know that. But the damage could've been so much more severe. She might have—"

I reached a hand across, resting it on one muscular forearm and interrupted. "There's no way to know, Davis. It's just not the way of fate to allow us a window into 'what if.'" I patted his arm until he turned his eyes to me again. "And you know what? I'm glad. I can't allow myself to fall into the abyss of worrying about what might have happened to you when the cockpit you were strapped into was torn off your airplane and you had to eject. I don't let myself think about what might have happened if I hadn't found Camille, all broken and bleeding in the gravel behind the dumpster." I patted his arm and leaned on the strong shoulder of the man I loved. Once again I was trusted with the privilege of caring for someone I loved in a season of pain and crisis.

"The odds are that someone would've helped your mom even

if I hadn't been there. And it's perfectly normal for you and your dad to be frightened and to wonder about a thousand possibilities, because that's the nature of grief. Just don't allow it to control you. Focus on the good and be a strong support as she faces recovery. It can be overwhelming; you know that better than most people, Davis."

His lips were warm and soft on mine, and I marveled at the tenderness of the man I'd fallen for. His hand cupped my face, pulling me closer and guiding the kiss as his other arm rested on my waist. Our tongues touched and caressed in the way of lovers who knew one another well but longed for the sweetness of contact just the same. After thoroughly making love to my mouth, he pulled away slightly, eyes still closed, and rested his forehead against mine. "I love you so much, sweet girl. You're every single thing I hoped I'd find and a hundred things I hadn't dreamed of. The story of you and me has been nothing but pressure and catastrophe and disaster. You've been thrown every curveball in the book, but you never failed to rise to the occasion." His eyes opened and pulled me into their depths. "Thank you for being here, for taking care of my dad and me. Daddy's always called Mama his everything, ever since I was a little boy. I didn't know what that meant when I was a little guy. But when he said it in the hospital room, I had a moment of lightning clarity, Lucinda. I understand now. I know exactly what he means." He took my face gently in his hands. "You're *my* everything, Luckie. Thank you for being that for my mama and daddy, even though they haven't shown you they deserve you."

I smiled and stood, taking his hand. "Come on—let's walk. I want to see Johnny Mercer's grave." He was moving really well without crutches now, so I only needed to slow my pace a little to allow him to keep up. "I've given all this a lot of thought, Davis. The racial thing with your parents, all the friction." He turned to look at me, the worry showing clearly, but he let me speak. "The issue isn't yours to arbitrate, Tarzan. Nor is it mine." I swallowed and plunged in.

"If we continue forward and our love continues to grow, we're going to be taking steps that will require them to deal with their positions and feelings. And their reactions aren't yours or mine to shoulder. We know what we have is authentic. The steward-ship and care of what's between us are our responsibility. That other issue belongs to them."

He walked along quietly, occasionally stopping to read a plaque or grave marker before finally responding. "It feels heavy, like I need to fix it. But you're right. And if things begin to change with them, I want to know it's genuine. I could force the issue, but I don't want that."

We walked together a while longer, visiting the final resting places of several notable residents including Johnny Mercer. In the distance, the rising moon's splintered reflection shone off the river. Reluctantly, we turned our backs on the light and started back. Davis was much quieter than I'd become accustomed to. I broke the silence in the cemetery myself this time.

"Promise me one thing, Davis. Just keep walking through it with me, not ahead of me." He stopped in the path we walked, looking at me with a question in his eyes, so I explained. "We've made it this far together. I don't want you to run ahead, trying to fix everything because you're afraid of your parents hurting me. I'm a strong woman. I've faced difficulty and misunderstanding before. And I really believe, in spite of everything, that good will win out in the end. Don't force it on my behalf, Davis; stand by me and love me. Let's let fate do its work."

His mouth on mine told me, once again, everything I needed to know.

Chapter
THIRTY-ONE

"Roar"

Davis

M ama had returned home from the hospital three days
ago, a day earlier than her doctor originally said
he'd allow, but she was accompanied by an army of
healthcare professionals. Daddy was mired in irrational guilt
and was taking it out on his checkbook, paying for much more
full-time care and assistance at home than either the physician
or Luckie thought necessary. Mama had been settled into one of
the ground-floor suites and was sleeping, utterly exhausted from
visits from the physical and occupational therapists Daddy had
hired.

Luckie and I lunched on the porch overlooking the river. I
was starting to notice the affinity she had for water, although I
wasn't sure she knew she had one. Given the opportunity, she
would gravitate to the outdoors and a water view every time. I
thought it a little unusual for a Manhattan girl, but New York had
plenty of stunning water views as well. I looked for chances to
give her things that made her happy, and this was one.

Nathan was one of the first people Luckie read into Mama's situation, and he'd immediately made accommodations to my schedule and travel plans before I could ask. He texted to communicate the good wishes sent from all the Scorpions right before he and Coach launched the TDY contingent on their return trip to Davis-Monthan. Additionally, he asked me to take a couple of days to watch Mama's progress before making any decisions about my return. And while I was grateful for his generosity, I had a big appointment coming up with Dr. Taft—not to mention that Camille and her staff were probably running themselves ragged covering Luckie's shifts. We needed to get home at the earliest realistic opportunity.

Because nothing could go to plan, a tremendous ruckus set up in the foyer, just out of my line of sight. There was a scuffle and a loud voice shouting instruction. Just as I rose to investigate, Aunt Nonnie strode across the family room toward our table on the screened porch. She was attired in tight, floral capri pants, a cotton shirt, and a large straw hat that looked as if she'd purchased it from the foreman of a rice paddy. In one hand, she balanced four Tupperware containers stacked precariously on one another. In the other, she held a thick rope functioning as a leash, attached to a truly fearsome dog. It appeared to be a two-hundred-pound cross between a Shar-Pei and a Brahma bull. The gargantuan animal had a wide smile on its face and cheerfully dragged Nonnie across the room in our direction.

"Well, good morning, Aunt Nonnie." I took a step her way, wondering if I should attempt to assist with the dog. Nonnie somehow reined in the slobbering beast who went to Luckie like a marlin to a gourd. She offered her hand for him to sniff. Then she nuzzled his wide, wrinkled face and scratched his head enthusiastically, much to his delight.

Nonnie kissed my cheeks and gripped my face, studying me. "Davis, my darling boy. You have suffered far too much of late.

The stress is too great for any one family; I can't bear it." She indicated the stack of Tupperware. "I brought pie, of course. And this…" She gestured in the general direction of the massive animal snuggling Lucinda. "This is Scarlett. She's my new rescue Neapolitan mastiff and a bit unmanageable at the moment. But she's a lover, not a fighter." Nonnie petted her head affectionately. "Sweet little angel. Now sit for Mommy. Sit."

Scarlett thought not. She ignored Nonnie, continuing her courtship of my girlfriend. Luckie spoke up between the kisses Scarlett lavished on her. "Nonnie, that's so thoughtful of you; I can't imagine how delicious these must be. But I'm afraid Mrs. Foster is on a pureed diet and probably won't be able to eat these." She popped the top on the first container, and a mouthwatering aroma escaped. Luckie groaned. "Double crust cherry…my favorite, and it's warm. Maybe you'd rather take them to someone else who can enjoy them?"

Nonnie rolled her eyes. "Nonsense. Emmie wouldn't touch a piece of pie with a gun to her head, even if she was fit as a fiddle. A sad little bag of bones, she is, as I've told her many times." She harrumphed. "The woman has to stand twice to make a shadow. The pie is for all y'all."

She stepped forward and laid her hand on Luckie's shoulder. "Let me enlighten you, sugar. In the South, when someone takes ill, we'll fry down a chicken or two to drop by. You might bake something, too." Luckie's face betrayed confusion, clearly unsure of the distinction between frying and baking, but Nonnie continued. "If their mama's traveling away out of town, we'll take food by, a casserole or a crock of file gumbo for the gentleman of the house and the children.

"But now if someone passes—God forbid—the family will have their quiver slap full of company for a week, maybe two. In that case, you get up early and make up everything you've got handy in the Frigidaire. Chicken-fried steak or a country ham with red-eye gravy and field peas or a Hoppin' John, a mess of collards, grits—of course—a skillet pone of cornbread and a couple of pound cakes or chess pies. Well, off the top of my head." She fussed with her pocketbook while Luckie shot me an expression of pure astonishment.

Daddy strode into the room and greeted Nonnie who had already made herself at home in the kitchen, dished up the pie for everyone, and tucked into a sink of dirty dishes. "Mary Glen, you stop foolin' with those dishes now; I've asked Helen Louise to come every day for a while. She'll put the kitchen in order. When this is over, we'll probably never get back to having her just twice a week." He laughed unconvincingly. I wondered if he doubted Mama would be herself again.

We ate pie and ice cream together, with Aunt Nonnie feeding Scarlett nearly an entire piece off a spoon from Mama's extensive service of Old Master sterling flatware. It was a mercy that Mama slept through this particular travesty. She would've had a cow. After visiting for a few minutes, Nonnie offered to do everything from the laundry to the marketing and was rebuffed by Daddy at every turn. At last convinced she'd done her due, she bid us a pleasant afternoon and left with Scarlett trotting along at her heel.

Daddy closed the front door and turned to me, wiping his brow with a hankie. "I hope your mother doesn't find out Mary Glen had that horse in her marble foyer. She'll have a cow."

Luckie and I planned to depart Savannah for Tucson after breakfast in the morning. It had been less than a week since her stroke, but Luckie's rapid diagnosis and action assured a far better than average outcome for my mother. Additionally, she was relatively young and in excellent health otherwise, so the prognosis was encouraging. She could speak without noticeable difficulty, and her facial features looked quite the same to me. Her issues were mostly related to fine motor skills like feeding herself and brushing her teeth. We were treating her unaffected walking and swallowing with caution, but the therapists were optimistic. Her strength seemed to improve daily, although she continued to sleep more than usual.

During the days since Mama came home, Lucinda spent much of her time researching issues related to her recovery, discussing the plans for care with the therapists and other caregivers, and teaching both Mama and Daddy everything she could to help after we'd departed for home. She frequently sat at my mother's bedside, reading or catching up on emails with Cami while Mama watched her "stories." She'd been a devotee of *Days of Our Lives* and *General Hospital* since I was a child, and that was unlikely to be affected by the inconvenience of a stroke.

On this final afternoon at home, I heard voices in the sun-room on the rear corner of the house near Mama's bedroom suite as I cleared away her lunch dishes. Stopping to investigate, I saw Luckie seated on a stool near my mother's miniature wingback chair, bent close to her and speaking softly with a gentle smile on her face. She held Mama's left hand, helping her touch each finger, in turn, to her thumb. "You see, Mrs. Foster, this is an important exercise. You want to practice it so you can begin to feed yourself reliably." Frustration showed on Mama's face as she struggled with the previously simple task. The first two fingers touched her thumb with little difficulty, but the last two were an obvious effort. The pinkie finger wouldn't cooperate at all.

But Lucinda smiled at Mama. "You're doing so much better; even better than yesterday, Mrs. Foster. I can tell you're improving. And Aunt Nonnie says you need to eat more, so we can't let her down, can we?" She laughed her big belly laugh, patting

Mother's hand, and even Mama had to let fly with her slightly lopsided grin. The laugh died away, and Luckie took a big breath before she addressed Mama. "You're going to be okay, Mrs. Foster. You're doing so well, so I need you to be brave for Davis and J.R., and work diligently on all the things we've talked about." She sighed. "I wish I could just stay here and look after you myself, but Mr. Foster and Helen Louise will be right here. And Nonnie and Miss Clara. You'll be good as new in no time—I know it."

The lump in my throat was colossal, and I fought back tears watching my girl repay my mother's scheming with kindness. I felt a hand heavy on my shoulder and turned to see Daddy there, swallowing back the emotion that played across his face. I felt paralyzed, not sure what to do or say now that I'd come face to face with the injustice I'd seen since our arrival. Playing out right before my eyes was proof Lucinda had risen above it all, her actions powered by her love for me.

But Daddy wasn't paralyzed. Not at all.

He moved past me into the room, the seriousness in his eyes trained on Mama. His voice didn't convey anger, but the tone was far firmer than any I'd ever heard him use to address her. "Emmie, Lucinda is leaving tomorrow morning. I would certainly think, after everything that's happened here, you'd have many things to say to this fine, beautiful young woman. I know I do, but you may well owe her your goddamn life, Emmaline. Use that voice God spared you for something meaningful."

The air was heavy in the room as Mama regarded my father with wide eyes. I felt sure he'd never spoken to her like that, certainly not in front of others, and her expression betrayed as much. Her throat worked visibly, and she stared at her lap where her hands twisted nervously. I looked at Lucinda, seeing her face reflecting nothing but compassion for the woman next to her.

Then Mama straightened, looked at my girl, and sighed. "Lucinda, my dear, I'm so sorry. I've been wrong, and J.R. is right. I hope it won't hurt you if I'm direct, but I decided not to care for you because of the color of your skin. I wanted to distance you from my son because I never pictured him bringing home someone who looked like you."

Luckie's chin lifted and one corner of her mouth tilted up almost imperceptibly. "You mean you never pictured him falling in love with a black woman?"

Mama's face softened, breaking into a genuine smile, her eyes shiny with tears. She looked between Luckie and me several times. "You're in love? Of course, you are." She blinked, and a tear spilled over. "I've waited so long to see who would win your heart, Davis Payne. I've always hoped you could find someone who would love you like I love your daddy." She reached for Luckie's hand. "I'm truly...just so happy for you both, my dear. The only thing tarnishing this moment is the stubbornness of a foolish woman. How could I ever have judged you based on something neither of us controls? And then you return my behavior with selfless kindness. I do owe you a debt, Lucinda. Can you possibly forgive the contemptible behavior of a ridiculous old woman?"

Luckie's response was immediate. "Of course, Mrs. Foster."

"After all we've been through, Lucinda, it's Emmie." Her hand reached tentatively to stroke Luckie's face. "You are a truly stunning woman, inside and out. No wonder my Davis is in love with you."

Luckie laughed again, reaching up to touch Mama's hand on her face. "Now, Emmie. If I hadn't spilled the beans, would you have known?"

Mama's grin returned, this time trained on Daddy and me. "A mother knows these things. There's nothing more heartwarming than when your child falls in love; I've waited my whole life to see it in the eyes of my baby. I've always wanted his happiness above everything else."

Lucinda reached forward, brushing a kiss across Mama's cheek. "Then we're on the same page, Emmie. I promise you I'll do everything I can."

Chapter
THIRTY-TWO

"You Shook Me All Night Long"

About Five Months Later
Lucinda

"I just need to know something, Cami." Viv picked her head up from the spot where she'd rested it on the break-room table. Her green eyes stared, half-mast, around the table, finding Camille. Vivvie shook her head as if clearing the cobwebs away. "How is it possible that only a few years ago, we did this three nights a week?"

Camille twisted her wavy blond hair into a complex knot, securing it with an oversized plastic clip, and yawned. "Can't believe it myself. How the hell did I stay up—working even—all night long? I think Luckie and I did it for three and a half years, Viv. And I don't know whether to be grateful or irritated at how quiet it's been since midnight." She raised her voice, enunciating the word "quiet." Every nurse knew saying that particular word was pushing your luck; an easy shift was an infrequent occurrence and was not to be questioned.

"Doesn't matter." Samanthe spoke from her position on her

knees in front of the fridge. She'd unloaded its contents and was keeping busy cleaning it out, a chore that looked to be months overdue. "It's all for a good cause, and this is the best wedding gift we could've given Lorraine." She pulled off a pair of latex gloves, jumped up, and dumped the basin of bleach water she'd been using into the sink.

With a good deal of help from Vivianne, I'd performed a minor miracle on the monthly schedule and swapped the day and night shifts for a singular Saturday evening. Lorraine Jefferies was the universally beloved night shift charge nurse, ridiculously competent, generous to a fault, and funny as all hell. She'd found the love of her life and tied the knot around eight p.m. the previous night, with, among numerous others, her many night shift friends in attendance. That meant our crew was suffering through an interminable night shift for the first time in several years. To add insult to injury, the patients had been variously dealt with—admitted or **OTD**—by around midnight. Our group mostly failed at sleeping before the shift began, but it seemed Viv was suffering the most.

For my part, I'd opted to help Sam by going through the contents of the dozens of Tupperware containers that crowded the fridge, making life and death decisions about what could be cleaned and what had to go in a biohazard bag for immediate disposal. I peeked warily under the lid of an ancient Cool Whip container, resealing it at once. "Holy motherfucker. I just threw up a little in my mouth; that's a prize winner right there, Sammie." I lifted the lid a bit to show her; she shook her head sadly. "Which fuckwit left this science project here, and what makes food grow green hair, anyway?" I tossed the entire container into the large red bag nearby.

Grace stood in the corner, stretching and twisting her lithe body into various yoga poses. "We need something exciting to help us wake up. Come on, Luckie, give up the goods on Tarzan.

We need details about the trip to Georgia; even before then, you were practically on lockdown with your private duty gig." She giggled a little, sliding into warrior I. "I think Davis may have benefited from more than excellent nursing care during his recovery."

I tossed a stack of nasty Rubbermaid containers into the sink filled with hot soapy water, and pulled on a fresh pair of latex gloves. "You girls know I'm no shrinking violet when it comes to sex." Viv picked her head up off the table where she'd dozed off, made the universal gesture for "gag me" and promptly flopped her head back down. "Suffice to say we found creative ways around the various torture contraptions Dr. Taft had Davis restrained in."

I scrubbed the filthy storage containers, thinking about the past few months. The quiet in the room was interrupted only by my splashing in the sink and the occasional gagging sounds Samanthe made when she encountered a particularly disturbing container of leftovers. When I spoke, my voice was softer than usual. "You know, it's surprising how it happened, when I consider how it all started." My cheeks heated, and a dull throb set up between my legs as I remembered his hands on me that first night. The words he'd whispered in the dark. *I won't take advantage of a lady, no matter what my dick thinks... Take my cock, Luckie...* Snapping back into the moment, I cleared my throat and scrubbed harder.

Camille jumped up, hand cupping her little belly, and stretched out in downward dog next to Grace. I smiled, as I always did when I saw her pregnant tummy; the impossible had happened, and Camille was expecting Nathan's baby in the early fall. She'd shared the news with me early, around the end of her first trimester, but no one else knew until earlier this month. The abundance of blessings Cami and Nathan were enjoying was celebrated almost continuously within our circle; we were all thrilled about this baby and the pregnancy, completely unremarkable thus far.

Cami shot me a mischievous look. "Do you mean how it started with Davis?" She craned her head to check that the hallway was still vacant. "Like in a dark closet with you riding him like a rented mule?" This brought Vivianne back to consciousness, chortling.

"Oh, sure." I arched one eyebrow and pinned them with a fake haughty stare. "I'm going to be cowed by a break room of dick-swallowing cuntcakes. I do not think so, ladies." I pointed accusingly at an adorably pregnant Camille with my little finger. "Everybody knows you fuck, young lady. The proof is filling out your scrubs and making you spend more time peeing than working." I sighed melodramatically.

"Anyway, you make it sound so dirty. I'll have you bitches know that Davis made sweet, sweet love to me in that closet." Even I had to join in the laughter at that one as I rinsed the stack of dishes with water so hot it burned my hands through the gloves. Cleanliness was a powerful concern when it came to the break-room fridge.

That gave us all a good laugh, and there was no better way to fight off the lethargy. Sam piped up, but she was hard to hear since her head was in the back of the fridge. "This relationship of yours has been like a roller coaster that you forgot to buckle into before the train left the station. You should've known it wouldn't be normal when you had to Heimlich somebody on your first date."

I sighed with a smile. "Yeah. That was the omen I missed, Sam. From anyone looking in, it must look like a nuclear-powered clusterfuck. We barely had any time to get to know each other and be a regular couple before the accident blindsided us. That was like pouring gas on a fire. The Savannah trip felt like a pressure cooker with the friction with Emmie and J.R. Then the stroke happened…"

Vivvie turned abruptly from her perch on the chair she used to reach her locker, almost falling off in the process. "Shit. Almost fell—again. Has anyone seen my bandage scissors?" She peered at me from above, brow furrowed. "Wait, Luckie, since when are you on a first-name basis with Deliverance's parents? I must have missed a chapter somewhere along the way; I thought the evil queen of the swamp despised your Nubian beauty."

"No, no, no, Viv; your info is past its expiration date. I told you to ignore the trash that beautiful brother of yours tries to pass off as good, quality gossip." Vivianne's brother, Jacob Travis, was a looker. All "just-rolled-out-of-bed" blond hair and blue eyes. He and Vivianne did a hilarious straight-faced shtick posing as twins, but they never fooled anyone. At least no one smart.

Grace looked up from her triangle pose, a little smile touching her lips. "He may not be much of a gossip, but he sure is easy on the eyes." She stared hazily at nothing, and her voice dropped to a whisper. "Those arms, you know. They're as big around as my thigh."

Vivianne grinned at Grace; she was so sweetly innocent, mouth open and a blush spreading across her cheeks. "Down, girl. Keep your man-eater claws out of my virginal brother." Cami guffawed, then clapped her hand over her mouth, eyes wide, when Viv shot her a mock warning look. "What? He's totally celibate and devoid of impure thoughts. As far as I know."

Viv was hilarious when it came to her brother; the man practically reeked of sex. Any female in a half-mile radius was in danger of falling into the snare of Bash's pheromones. "Yeah, Viv. Everybody's aware that Jacob's never had carnal knowledge of a woman. And nobody's ever pictured him naked. Especially not all of us." Cami snorted again, and Grace blushed a deep pink that went to the roots of her hair.

Vivvie sniffed contemptuously. "My big brother doesn't even

have any…you know…boy parts down there." Her hands waved around in the general area of her lap. "He looks like a Ken doll naked. Not that I've looked. I just know."

Grace probably didn't mean to whisper loud enough to Camille for us to hear, but I shut off the water just in time. And everyone heard.

"I'd volunteer to investigate that issue."

Vivvie's and Grace's hands flew simultaneously to cover their faces, and there was a lot more laughter.

Eventually, Viv cleared her throat and grinned at Grace, shaking her head. "Okay, Luckie. Back to you and Tarzan, since we're discussing the fine-as-hell male population of the Scorpion squadron. How are you two weathering the storms that keep making landfall on your doorstep?"

I pulled my gloves off and walked across the room, grabbing a couple of towels from the linen cart in the hallway. I threw one to Viv who joined me at the sink, and we began to dry the mountain of mismatched containers. The whirlwind of the past few months played across my mind like a movie on fast forward. "I wouldn't wish what's happened to us on anyone, especially on two people trying to get a relationship off the ground, but we did fall fast and hard. I think we're more sure of our feelings than we'd probably be otherwise." I sighed. "But I wouldn't want to do it again."

Vivvie snapped her damp towel at my legs, missing entirely. "What do you suppose is wrong with the damned clock? It can't just be five a.m."

A collective sigh went up from the whole group.

Vivianne had issued a prior invitation to our sleepy group for breakfast and a sleepover, assuming we survived our first night shift in years. Stumbling through the back door of the ED and into the bright sunlight, everyone searched their bags for sunglasses and parted paths at the parking deck. Viv had closed on her first home only four months ago and was eager to show us "The Dump," as she fondly called it.

It was an old adobe style ranch on Craycroft in need of the tough love only Viv could administer. She was a Pinterest master and fearless do-it-yourselfer who saw the pink-tiled baths and dark paneling throughout the house as a canvas on which she could work her particular brand of magic. The house's most important feature and the pièce de résistance, was a big swimming pool with an adobe privacy wall. A pool would normally have been hard to come by at a lowly nurse's price point, but the crumbling ceilings and overgrown yard put most people off, rendering the asking price within reach.

Pulling into the driveway, I noted Vivianne had been hard at work. The yard was tidy, with the weeds and brush already pulled up and hauled away. The detritus of a Pepto pink bath was piled into boxes in the carport, all ready for disposal. Vivvie had been a busy girl. We parked our cars in the driveway and along the street, wandering toward the house like the walking dead. Inexplicably, Samanthe wore bunny slippers and a long Power Rangers sleep shirt, her hair braided and her face scrubbed clean of makeup. In her hand, she carried an electric toothbrush. Looking up to see the group staring at her in the driveway, she shrugged.

"What? I always changed at stoplights when I worked nights before. I'll be asleep three or four minutes before you guys; and with the way we feel right now, you can't honestly tell me those three minutes don't matter."

It was hard to argue with that logic in our condition. Hell, it was hard to drive the scant two miles up Craycroft to Vivianne's front door without getting a hotel room. The house was cool and dark, all the blinds and curtains closed in preparation for our sleepover. Viv locked the door and looked at the clock on the stove. "Okay, it's seven-forty a.m., so let's say brunch around the pool starting between two and three? Cami and Luckie, take the king bed in the front bedroom; Gracie and Sam, twins in the back. The A/C is set to stun, so let's hibernate, girls."

The group dispersed almost wordlessly and wandered to sinks in the kitchen and the small bathroom, brushing teeth and washing faces. Scrubs were discarded on the floor for retrieval later. Sam's weary voice called from down the hall. "See, I told you bitches. I'm already asleep." She giggled.

I climbed between the cool sheets where Camille was already curled up like a cat and tucked in tight, spooning her and giving her a quick squeeze. "I missed ya, girl. Thanks for everything you did for Davis and me. Starting with hauling his busted ass off that medivac. You know I love you, but that's just one more reason."

There was no response from Cami, and I grinned. The girl could really sleep, although being five months pregnant probably made it even easier. I wasn't sure I wanted kids, but watching Camille carry her miracle baby made me just about as happy as anything could. She would be a great little mommy. I grabbed my pillow, snuggling in and waiting for the first snore. Instead, her voice drifted through the cool silence.

"Are you happy, Luckie? Do you think Davis…is he the one?" She flipped over, combing her thick blond mane away from her face. "It's almost too much to hope for, isn't it? Both of us, I mean."

I looked at my friend, tired but more content than I'd ever seen her. This baby wasn't the only miracle. "Yeah, that would be something, wouldn't it? I am happy, Cam. *So* happy. And he might be the one; I know I love him. I wasn't even sure I'd ever feel this for somebody."

Camille yawned and rubbed her belly. "You're way too lovable not to get this far. Something told me what you two had might be the real deal."

"Night, Cam." I rubbed her tummy. "Beanie." That was my pet name for the baby until we knew the sex.

"Night, Luckie Lady. Love you."

Chapter
THIRTY-THREE

"Soak up the Sun"

Lucinda

My phone said ten past two when I rolled over, all alone in the bed. Sleep after a night shift was more like a coma than a restful night, but it was only designed to bank enough sleep for the remainder of the day until normal people crawled back in the rack. I sat up, draining the water bottle at my bedside and padded toward the kitchen.

Camille stood between the yawning doors of the refrigerator and studied its contents as if they held the secrets of the universe. Her free hand rubbed her bump unconsciously. I reached past her, snagging the orange juice, and searched for a glass in the cabinet. "I take it The Bean needs a feeding?"

She whirled on me, eyes wide. "Luckie. You have no idea. This kid is not that big, but I eat like I'm carrying a litter. My ass needs a 'wide load' sign." She shook her head, smiling. "Nathan thinks the whole package is cute. His words. He can't keep his hands off me."

I sneaked a cheek up onto the countertop after draining my

glass and refilled. Why were they so small anyway? "In fairness to Nate, the titty fairy was quite generous; and you know a lot of boys love a girl with an ass." I made a show of examining her from head to toe. "Which you have, in spades."

Sam lollygagged into the kitchen looking impossibly beautiful in her worn nightshirt and bunny slippers. She was a freak of nature, to be sure. "So, Camille. Is it true what they say about second trimester? Are you making Nathan feed the kitty twice a day?"

Camille stood up suddenly from her mission of foraging in the crisper drawer, banged her head slightly, and looked at Sam with confusion.

"You know, Cami. Afternoon D. Calling a Joint Session of Congress." Sam dropped into a deep bend, ass almost to the floor and twerked her tight little behind right above the fluffy bunnies. "Bow-chick-a-wow-wow…"

"What the hell is going on in my house?" Vivianne stood in the doorway wearing a long, lacy gown that showed off her amazing rack. Her hair was lustrous and perfect, and even without a stitch of makeup, she looked runway ready. Bitch.

Understanding dawned on Camille's face. "Oh, yes. *Fucking.* I know I'm supposed to say making love because we're getting married and having a baby. But sometimes…really lots of times, it's absolutely *fucking.* He told me the other morning with a completely straight face I had to climb off his dick because he was late for work." She shrugged her shoulders and gnawed on a handful of radishes she'd retrieved on her foraging mission. "I just need it. A lot."

Vivianne wrinkled her nose at Camille's choice of snack and busied herself making a big pot of coffee. "Don't eat too much, preggo. I made brunch."

I drained the last of the OJ from my glass, finally feeling human. "I'm changing into my suit and jumping in that pool unless you need my help, Vivaroo." I raised my eyebrows. "Can I give you a hand—please? Let me help you." I wondered briefly how Vivianne had avoided starving since leaving home. Dreadful as her cooking was, the tricky part lay in the fact she considered herself the modern version of Julia Child.

"No need, Luckie." Vivianne opened a cabinet, producing half a dozen open boxes of breakfast cereal, each with more sugar and artificial dye than the last. She pulled a five-pound canister of sugar from an upper cabinet, a quart of almond milk from the fridge, and waved one hand gracefully at the atrocity. "Brunch is served."

Sam mercifully leaped in the silence that ensued. "Oh, my. Too much to choose from; I'm not sure how much I can eat so soon after waking up." She had the panicked look of a wild animal caught in a snare.

Cami held up a handful of greens. "I'm all full of radishes."

"Hey, I almost forgot." Viv pulled a Crock-Pot out from the corner of the countertop. "I made this, too. Cream of Wheat with chorizo." She smiled and wiggled her eyebrows. "And peas. I made the recipe up myself; fuck Food Network."

Camille's eyes flew open wide, and she clutched her stomach as she jogged toward the bathroom. "Oh, God, girls…gotta pee. Right now."

The five of us lay on mismatched loungers around the cool, aqua oval of the backyard pool soaking in the sun's warmth. Vivianne and I had discarded our tops since our privacy was ensured by the wall around the yard, and Cami was busting out all over. Her tankini looked much more like an ill-fitting bikini, but she hadn't yet swapped to a maternity bathing suit.

Grace rolled over, flipping a mass of curly dark hair off her back. "All ready for the big day, Camille?"

Cami groaned. "I can't wait to marry Nathan, but the planning and details are pretty tedious." She hadn't opened her eyes so far. "And I'm tired. I'd rather sleep than discuss seating charts with the event planner. Naps are the shit."

The doorbell sounded from inside the house, but our drowsy collective didn't budge. Finally, Grace stood with a groan, tying the string of her halter suit around her neck and arranging her breasts in the suit's confines. "I'll get it, Viv. Does anyone want a refill?" Vivianne was a decent bartender despite her lack of culinary skill. She'd managed a couple of excellent pitchers of Bloody Marys that nearly made up for the horrifying cereal and chorizo debacle earlier. I stood up, stretching.

"I want a refill, but I'll get it." I pulled my bikini top on over my head and followed Gracie inside. As I slid the long glass door closed to keep the glorious air conditioning inside, I saw who'd come calling.

At the front door, Grace's small form was dwarfed by one Jacob Travis, towering over her like a beast considering options with his prey. One bulging arm held two large shopping bags from a bakery down the road, the whole business adrift with delicious aromas. Grace had clasped her hands behind her back and was shifting her weight nervously, but Jake seemed perfectly at ease. His voice was deep and his smile wide and disarming as he murmured quietly to her. He didn't seem to notice anyone else was home.

I sauntered into the kitchen, grabbing the pitcher of Bloody Marys and refilled my glass. "Can you join us for a drink, Jake?" He lifted his gaze reluctantly from Grace who continued to stare up at him as if her life depended on it. "It looks like you may have come on a mission of mercy, so it's the least I could offer."

He returned my smile and walked toward the breakfast bar, gently urging Grace along with one hand splayed on the small of her back. She looked a little breathless to me. "You cracked the code, Lucinda. How are you?"

I rummaged in the cabinet for a glass. "From the looks of the takeout you brought, I'd wager you know exactly how I am. How we all are." I checked quickly that Viv was still by the pool. "We're fucking starving."

He nodded knowingly. "I heard the scuttlebutt from Happy this morning. We hit the gym early, and he told me that you guys covered the night shift for your buddy so all her friends could go to the wedding." He looked down at Grace who looked down at her feet, embarrassed at having been caught staring. "That was really great of you, but Nate was worried about Camille working all night. He told me about the sleepover—good idea to stay close by, but I was worried about everybody too, same as Nate. Different reasons, though. Can't let the do-gooders starve. Especially the knocked-up one. Nathan doesn't know about my twin sister's challenges in the kitchen."

"Jake!" Vivianne appeared in the doorway. "Hi there, big bro. I didn't know it was you; good thing I put my top back on." She laughed uproariously.

"Not funny, Vivvie. Far as I know, you don't even have boobs. You're not even a girl," he sniffed. "Look, I brought breakfast… more like brunch, I guess." He unloaded several large takeout containers. "See? Crêpes, all kinds, from that French bakery you like down by the mall. And thick-cut bacon."

"Oh my God. Did you say crêpes? Hi, Bashful." Cami walked through the door, belly still sticking out of her tankini, her mouth agape.

"The boss said you like chocolate." Jake held out a smaller container with Cami's name on it. "Don't forget the bacon, Camille. It's the best—I may or may not have sampled some on the way over."

"I doubt anyone's very hungry, brother of mine, although it's nice of you to bring this by." Viv gestured toward the kitchen littered with cereal boxes. "We already ate."

"No, that's alright." Cami snatched the box from Jake, smiling at him. "Thank you, Bashful. The Bean and I can't ever seem to get enough to eat."

"Hate to see you eat alone, Cam." I flipped open a box, groaning at the sight of the delicate crêpes variously stuffed with bananas and cream, strawberries and chocolate, and wafer-thin apple slices with caramel. Soon we'd served up several plates heaped with sweets and were enjoying a real brunch by the pool. At least almost all of us. Viv, Cami, Sam and I slipped back onto the patio after thanking Jacob and bidding him goodbye, but Grace remained behind.

After a few minutes, she returned with her own plate, a telltale blush coloring her cheeks. "You are so goddamn adorable, Gracie. I swear I could just eat you up with a fucking spoon if my belly weren't full of apple crêpes." I licked my lips and smiled widely at her. She was the singular shy member of our tribe and too much fun to tease. "Did you thank Jake properly for his generosity?"

"Ahhumm. Nope." Grace's big violet eyes looked at her teeny little feet as she sat on one of the loungers. Her blush was once again in full bloom. "No special thanks. Just the regular kind. Of thank you, I mean."

Vivianne shot me a conspiratorial look, smirking. "Did my brother wrap his big ol' arms around you and give you a long, wet smooch, Gracie?"

She scanned the group with wide eyes. "No, no. No kissing, Vivvie. I wouldn't, you know…I mean, I would. I guess."

Camille reached over and patted her knee. "Don't you worry about these busybodies, Grace. It's nobody's business anyway. Kiss whomever you like."

Everyone joined in the laughter, even Grace, as Sam steered

the conversation back toward the wedding festivities, now only three weeks distant. "I heard there's a big bachelor party road trip laid in for Vegas next weekend, Camille. You good with that?"

Camille rolled her eyes with a smile and licked the last of the chocolate from her fingers. "Of course. I'm not the least bit concerned about Nathan, and Chuck will be along to keep all the buffoonery in hand. You guys know Bibi doesn't suffer fools in any form; Chuck's her other half in more ways than one."

"Well, I'm much more excited about what we have planned than any stupid sausage party the boys might be having. La Paloma's the bomb. We're gonna pamper you and The Bean so good you won't know what hit you, Cam." My heart was full thinking about all the good finally coming home to roost for my friend. As her maid of honor, I was in charge of the bachelorette weekend, and it had been more fun than I'd expected to plan it. "Everybody remember we're meeting at the Trattoria for dinner and drinks at seven. Spa treatments start the next morning at ten."

Vivvie rubbed her hands together. "Can't freaking wait. I'm going to find some huge masseur to pummel the ever-living fuck out of me and a little lady with a paintbrush and a bucket of green gunk to paint my naked bod and wrap me in seaweed or something."

Camille stood up, a thoughtful expression on her face as she gathered dirty dishes. "Mmm...seaweed. We should get sushi."

Samanthe's gaze followed her as she left the patio. "I don't even want to think about how much we'll have to feed her when The Bean gets bigger."

Chapter
THIRTY-FOUR

"Fly Me to the Moon"

Davis

The alarm jolted like a lightning bolt, yanking me from a deep sleep, but something felt different today. Sitting up and looking around, I smiled with soul-deep satisfaction. This morning would be my first time in the cockpit since the sunny morning last summer when one split second changed everything.

I stretched carefully, but the leg was strong. Both Doc Taft and Bibi were confident I was ready. I knew I was past ready. These months had been eventful, both in terms of learning about myself and in my relationship with Lucinda. My cock hardened at the thought of her.

My juicy peach.

Our schedules didn't often allow sleepovers, and I missed her warmth and sweetness when she wasn't wrapped in my arms at night. What we were together had been tested in the fire, and it confirmed what I'd known for months. She was meant for me, and I was her man. I wasn't sure what the past months would have looked like without her beside me—encouraging me. Nurturing, scolding, and comforting me.

Loving me.

It happened almost without our knowledge. We fell in love in the eye of a hurricane, with a hundred things swirling around us. Pressing in, pushing us together, pulling us apart. A hundred things threatening to crush my dreams. A hundred things we'd never dreamed of, conspiring to show us the soul of the other and open the door to love.

Today was the day I'd waited for anxiously since awakening in the PACU with Luckie's sweet voice calling me back to a new reality. We'd been given a test to master, and we'd passed. My eyes swept around the room and landed on the engraved plaque Mama gave me when I finished pilot training. It was inscribed with John Gillespie Magee's celebrated sonnet, "High Flight," ubiquitous in the flying community. I read the words, almost able to recite them from memory, but some passages rang truer in the light of this new day.

Today I would rejoin the tumbling mirth.

I stepped out of the Jag and into the quiet of early morning just as Bashful parked his beat-all-to-hell pickup in the adjoining space. The sun was just peeking over the flight line, and soon the entire area would buzz with the activities of a busy workday. For now, I sat on Bash's bumper, tightening the speed lacers on my boots. Bash joined me, frowning at the stiff leather as I worked the laces.

"New boots, Deliverance? You look like a fucking rookie, dude. **Unsat.**"

I grinned wryly. "Yeah, you're gonna have your hands full this morning; I've definitely got the look of a Sunday driver. Thing is, they insisted on issuing a new pair because they couldn't find part of the old left one. And what was left was full of blood after the whole parasailing incident at Ajo."

Bash grimaced. "Gnarly. I hate blood and guts, man." He looked thoughtful. "Does it ever strike you as strange that Luckie is so feminine and all…but she works around all that gross medical shit? I mean, I took crêpes and breakfast stuff to the girls after their night shift. They were staying at Viv's new place on Craycroft, and she was feeding everybody breakfast and…"

I interrupted, alarmed. "Vivianne wasn't cooking, was she? Luckie didn't mention it, or I would've, you know, done something."

"No way, man." He laughed, and I relaxed; everyone knew about Vivvie's culinary ineptitude. "Don't flip your wig; I got 'em fed. Viv's my sister, so I bear part of the responsibility for the havoc her food can wreak. I should've taught her how to make PB and J or something when we were kids. Anyway, they're all just so nice and so girly, and it doesn't seem like the kind of job… Is it me, or is it kind of weird?"

I watched him carefully. "Are we talking about anyone in particular here, Bash? Who did you see yesterday at Vivvie's?"

"They were all there. You know; Viv, Cam, Luckie—the usual suspects."

I squinted at him. "Dude. Who?"

He sighed. "Grace Marshall. She's soft and sweet and kind of defenseless. Or something." Bashful looked all knotted up; it was completely atypical. "I mean she's obviously a smart, capable woman, or she wouldn't be doing such an important job. A hard job. But there's something about her." He frowned, staring at the ground. "I want to throw her over my shoulder and take her home with me."

I shook my head, at a complete loss to explain why Bash and I were discussing women. "Jake, man, it sounds like you need to ask her to dinner. Get to know her better."

"Yeah, well, that's not all I wanna do. This is uncharted territory; you know I don't roll this way with the ladies, D." He lifted an eyebrow in my direction.

He was right; he didn't roll this way. Jacob Travis dated very infrequently, but it wasn't for lack of attention from the female population. He was never at loose ends over a woman. He exuded sex appeal and was the kind of good-looking that was undeniable, even to me. Not that we fucking talked about it. I punched his shoulder amiably. "No matter what you want to do, dinner's probably the first step."

He leered at me. "Word on the street is that dinner isn't *your* opening move." He shrugged. "But no harm, no foul, D. It's sure working for you; Luckie's an awesome girl."

"Okay, Jacob. I won't smash your face in. This time. Let's go flying." He'd called over the weekend to let me know he'd be flying with me for my check out, my first time back in the cockpit.

Bashful clapped me on the shoulder as we walked together through the front door of the squadron building. "You could've checked out with any of the flight commanders or instructors, but I asked Happy if I could do the honors. In fact, I asked him in the waiting room at the hospital while we waited for Luckie to bring us news after your surgery." I glanced at him, surprised. "I've been looking forward to this since I left Ajo on Miles's wing headed for DM; I allowed myself one last look at you on the desert floor before we turned to go. I promised myself right then you'd be back—better than ever and kickin' ass. So this is kind of my way of making good on that promise."

With so many people in my corner after the accident that almost took it all away, failure had never been an option.

The A-10 was one of only a few aircraft in the Air Force's inventory with no two-seat versions. Most single-seat fighters had a "family model" with two seats so an instructor could ride along with a trainee to offer instruction and assure safety. But not the Warthog.

So, on this bluebird April morning, eight months after Ajo, I taxied the big jet onto the end of the runway accompanied only by my thoughts and a profound sense of gratitude. Blue sky stretched out forever, and everything seemed possible again. The left leg was strong, and my feet easily held the brakes as huge engines roared on either side of my cockpit, readying for takeoff. I was glad the oxygen mask on my helmet obscured the wide grin I couldn't seem to wipe away this morning; that might have fucked up the "cool fighter pilot" thing I was supposed to have going. Taking a deep breath, I released the brakes, and my Warthog began its takeoff roll, the runway disappearing behind me. The lumbering aircraft—so ungainly on the ground—accumulated speed rapidly, seemingly anxious to take me flying. Bashful was ten seconds behind me, just dropping his brakes; he would chase me on this ride and put me through my paces. I glanced skyward, pulling the stick between my legs steadily, and the jet rotated effortlessly. We easily escaped the ties holding us, and the ground fell away. I recalled the words engraved on the plaque of my bedroom.

…I have slipped the surly bonds of earth…

Beginning with my first Cessna solo ride as a teenager at the Savannah airport, and on every flight since then, my heart leaped a little at the moment the laws of flight won their battle with the law of gravity. The moment the bonds of earth were temporarily broken represented something even more precious than freedom to me. It meant endless possibility. Like many pilots, I fell in love with flying at an early age, reading everything I could get my hands on and studying all the materials for my private pilot's license well before my first lesson at age fifteen. On my seventeenth birthday, I completed the final required flight and was granted a private pilot's license. But it was well before then, buzzing over Coastal Georgia with my instructor in our local aero club's tiny Cessna, that I determined flying would be my life's work. From that day, all my best efforts were aimed at making that goal reality.

Having that prize ripped from my grip for the better part of a year made today all the more sweet. I sucked up the gear and flaps, arcing into an unhurried turn to the west, and watched Bash accelerate. He turned across my flight path to take his position on my wing for the trip to the area where we'd work. Bash keyed the mic.

"Bottom of the ninth, Deliverance, the score's tied. Time for the big one…you up for this, D?"

"Walk in the park, Kazansky; let's go do that pilot shit." I saw Bashful shake his head and imagined his rueful expression.

"Can't believe we're quoting that goddamn movie, man."

Chapter
THIRTY-FIVE

"Your Heart Will Lead You Home"

Lucinda

"**A**re you sure it's normal, MariSee?" I peered suspiciously into the pot. "They don't look thick enough to me. They're kind of soupy." I held the phone between my ear and shoulder and stirred the grits again.

"Cover them up, child. Stop worrying them. Fry down your chicken like I told you, and check them right before suppertime." MariSee's voice was patient, but I was sure she was rolling her eyes. "If they're still not to your liking, just add a little more cheddar or Colby all grated up. Davis will love them."

"Yes, ma'am." There was a smile in my voice, but I really was grateful to MariSee for coming to my rescue. It was for damn sure she was at the head of a very short list I could count on to school me in the food of Davis's childhood. I said a fond goodbye and set about coating his previously tidy kitchen with a thin layer of flour as I shook the chicken pieces in a brown paper sack per MariSee's instructions. Just finding a brown paper sack was no small feat, and she'd nearly swooned when I suggested the use of a plastic grocery store sack.

This Southern fried thing was very serious business.

Davis slipped into the kitchen and wrapped his arms around my waist, nuzzling my neck affectionately. "Have I ever told you that I find a beautiful woman frying chicken utterly irresistible?" I turned away from the pot of grits I'd just thickened with cheese as MariSee suggested and wrapped my arms around Davis, smelling vaguely of jet fuel, and looking positively eatable in his flight suit. That ugly khaki bag did things for his ass that did things to my lady parts. His mouth was on mine, gentle and persuasive, before pulling back a millimeter and licking my lips suggestively. Blood rushed between my legs and tempted me to abandon dinner altogether.

"I'm not frying chicken, Davis, not presently. These," I motioned to the pot on the stove, "are grits to go with the chicken I've already fried. I couldn't even with the collards, so we're having green beans." MariSee had been unhappy with my substitution.

"It smells like Mama's kitchen in here, Peaches." I raised my eyebrows with the obvious but unspoken question. "Believe it or not, that little woman can cook up a storm. I don't think she ever ate a damn bite of any of it, but Daddy and I sure did. She always had that diet plate—he air-quoted it—with the hamburger patty and cottage cheese with a tomato slice." He grimaced. "How anyone could eat that when there was fried chicken in the house, I'll never understand." He shook his head sorrowfully.

I squeezed his waist. "Let's have a beer before dinner, Tarzan. I want to hear about your soiree."

Davis guffawed as he took two bottles from the fridge and swatted my ass. "Did you mean my sortie?"

I sniffed haughtily. "Of course. Whatever."

He smiled warmly and opened the patio door, motioning me into the warm springtime air and onto one of the cushioned chairs there. "It was everything I've waited for, Lucinda. So worth all the therapy and disappointment." He took a long drink of the cold beer, his throat working. He was so fucking sexy; it just never got old. "I can't even tell you how much it means that you walked through this with me. I won't ever forget it." His eyes were locked on mine during the last words he said, and I couldn't tear my eyes away.

"I could never have imagined it could be like this, Davis. I wasn't looking for Mister Right, but now I see I've been waiting my whole life for you." I smiled mischievously. "MariSee says the way to a Southern boy's heart is through his stomach. Let me see if I can win your affection with cheese grits." I stood to move toward the kitchen, but he caught me by the waist and growled in my ear.

"There's another path to my heart, Luckie."

I smiled and kissed his cheek, untangling from his embrace. "Yeah, MariSee had some pointers on the alternate route, as well."

We lolled on the sofa, full of good food and basking in the waning light of the best day in many months. He stroked my bare thigh thoughtfully. "I spoke to Mama today; she remembered this was the first day I'd go flying since the accident, but she still calls it a crash." Davis laughed, but sobered quickly, turning to me. "I can't remember a time before today when she remembered an important milestone related to my flying." He was quiet for a second. "She didn't come to my UPT graduation because there was a fundraiser for the Women's League."

I turned to look at him, eyes still far away. "I didn't think about much today except what the everlasting fuck was wrong with my goddamned grits." I laughed and reached out to touch his face. "Things are different now with your mama and daddy. You see that, don't you?" Another moment passed. "She called me, Davis."

His head whipped around. "She did? When?"

I hadn't said anything yet, waiting for the right time. Which was apparently now. "Yesterday. She wanted to thank me again. And she asked about you." I polished my nails on my tee shirt. "We're kind of BFFs now, if you weren't aware."

He returned to his previously thoughtful state but pulled my head into his lap, stroking my cheek. The silence stretched for a minute, then two. Finally, Davis rose, locked the front door, and closed the drapes. He scooped me into his strong arms with no hesitation, a rare occurrence for a girl as tall as me, I thought.

"You're it for me, Lucinda Page. The whole package. There doesn't seem to be an end to your generosity or kindness, especially when it's directed at me or the family and friends I love so much. You even learned how to make cheese grits and fry chicken." A little smile danced along the corners of his mouth briefly, but he quickly sobered, eyes darkening. His voice was low, cutting through the quiet.

"And you're so goddamned beautiful, I want you wrapped in my arms and full of my cock every minute of the day." He growled in my ear as his head dipped and nipped the soft skin of my neck. "I'm taking you to bed, Lucinda."

His long, hard body was relaxed, sitting straight up against the headboard, and he stared at me with eyes like a thunderstorm. I knelt, straddling his thick thighs and working his straining length into my pussy. He laced his fingers behind his head and slowly painted me with a cool gaze. "Take all of it, Luckie, all my cock. I want to feel my balls tucking up against your bottom, pretty girl." It was a bit more difficult than usual to take the final couple of inches from my position, and my face must have betrayed the struggle. Taking that in, his hands settled gently on my shoulders, eyes still zeroed in on mine. "Your tight, wet little cunt belongs to me now, Lucinda. And every inch of my dick is yours. Relax and take it, Peaches." He pulled me closer, rested my head on his shoulder, and applied steady, firm pressure to my shoulders. He continued, pushing me slowly downward until I could feel the fat mushroom head of that glorious cock tuck itself into the dimple of my cervix. It ached deliciously, and my clit throbbed with the painful pleasure of it. His kisses peppered my neck and he breathed hard a couple of times, lifting his hips slightly to seat himself even more deeply inside me. "Love your snug, perfect pussy...hugs me so tight, Luckie." His voice was urgent now. "I need you to feel how much I need all of you...need you to take all of me. Every drop of my cum in your tight pussy. You're all mine, baby."

His hand slipped between us, one finger finding my center, swelling and slick. He held himself firmly against my cervix and stroked my clit gently with a fingertip. His touch was featherlight and agonizingly sweet. My core swirled and dipped, tighter and tighter, and I moaned into his neck, licking and biting. One of his big hands palmed my bottom, working me slowly up and down the length of his cock, impossibly deeper each time. I groaned, begging for more, but the sound seemed far away, as if I was floating. His touch was constant, bringing me so close...closer still, and I dug my nails into the muscles of his wide shoulders.

"Take it, baby. Just for a minute let me have you, balls deep. That pussy's so tight around me...just let go. Come on my cock, sweetheart; I'll catch you."

And then I was falling, the most brilliant orgasm rippling and fluttering effortlessly through me. Davis groaned as I convulsed around his hardness and continued the unrelenting rhythm, pushing his thick cock in and out. Circling the wet, pulsing knot of my clit. "I can feel you, sweet baby; hot little pussy sucking my cock. Begging for my cum. Do you need it, Luckie?" Seconds passed, and I clutched him, holding on desperately and panting while pleasure bathed me. Just as the orgasm began to loosen its hold and my head cleared, Davis's big arms lifted me, flipping me onto my back and pushing my knees wide. He drove himself in deep and pushed with his hands on the back of my thighs until the tops touched the bed.

His strokes slowed, then stopped, and I was full of him as the last traces of my orgasm fluttered and faded. His intense gaze was fixed first on my face but dropped to where our bodies joined. "I love feeling you come on my cock, Luckie. I'll never stop needing that, wanting to give you that." He dropped his big, hard body over mine, resting on his elbows beside my face, and allowed the instinctive rhythm to take over again. It felt raw and unguarded, the way he fucked me—staring into my eyes and letting me see the desperation in his. He lowered his face; lips brushing but not kissing mine. He groaned and whispered the filthy, possessive thoughts crowding his mind as he took me.

Without warning, he pulled himself from my body and rose to his knees in one swift motion. He looked like a fucking god, towering over me. Sweat slicked the planes of muscle, and his breath came in ragged gasps. With one hand, he held my knees wide, exposing all the swollen, creamy wetness between my thighs. His other hand fisted his slippery length, webbed with ropy veins. He stroked hard, once, then twice, grimacing when his fist encountered the angry, purple crown. My fingers replaced the void his cock left at my center, the middle two filling the aching emptiness and spreading wetness across my clit. "Marking you, Lucinda…you belong to me." His voice was a quiet growl, all possessive need, and he stroked himself several more times.

My body felt his focus and words as intensely as a caress, and my second orgasm tore through me as I stared, whispering his name.

White-hot ropes of semen lashed the bare lips of my pussy, and Davis roared his satisfaction, hips snapping upward. His gaze dropped between my legs, and we watched together as his thick cum shot across my body, washing my clit with warmth. His strokes slowed, and his eyes looked up to hold mine steadily until our breathing returned to normal. Then Davis lowered himself, giving me his weight and exploring my mouth leisurely with his tongue. "Love you, Lucinda...all of you, baby." His lips moved across my face and neck, kissing and licking as if he wanted to spend the remainder of the night examining every curve. He sucked each sensitive nipple into his mouth in turn, gently treating each to his tongue's warm attention, and then moved across the flat plane of my belly. Kissing, tasting, exploring.

And then, oh my fuck. The flat of his tongue licked languidly across the bare part of my mound, cleaning his warm cum from me, and then bringing soft lips to mine for a kiss, deep and slow. He continued to move between my pussy and my mouth, licking and gently sucking his warm offering from my skin before returning to share it with me. Our tongues tangled, savoring the taste of us, until he'd thoroughly bathed me, leaving my center wetter than before.

There were no words that night, nothing I could muster was sufficiently profound to tell Davis how his love had changed me. So we wound our naked bodies around one another and drifted away contentedly in the dark.

Chapter
THIRTY-SIX

"Life is a Highway"

Davis

"**D**ude. I dunno." Hung's eyebrows snapped together, expressing the concern we all felt. The group stood in Coach's driveway, the rallying point for the long-awaited bachelor party trip to Las Vegas. Nathan's wedding was still two weeks distant, but the prevailing cooler heads dictated a fortnight for hangover recovery. I was sure this was an excellent idea.

It had been months, maybe even a couple of years, since the Scorpions had an opportunity to celebrate with the party marathon accompanying a wedding done right. Camille was almost six months along with Happy's kid, but that was doing nothing but piling happiness on top of the joy they already felt at finding one another.

Bachelor weekend planning was enthusiastically embraced by the LPA in the absence of Happy's best man, Bam, whose own wife had just delivered their second son. But the weekend was off to a questionable start this spring morning when Rock, self-appointed director of transportation, pulled up in front of Coach's house. The vehicle's door swung open with a loud thunk, and a large piece of rubber window trim fell to the ground. The silence was deafening for a full minute as we stared in disbelief at the eyesore. Finally, I cleared my throat to break the awkward silence.

"Umm, Rock, it's like…a little school bus."

It was, indeed, one of those shortened school buses, easily thirty years old and suffering from acute neglect. The paint had been so long absent, it was impossible to tell the original color; though I assumed it had been school-bus yellow at some point during the Summer of Love. It boasted only one hubcap, and at least two of the windows were missing glass. They had been economically repaired with duct tape and black garbage bags.

Boo squatted in the middle of the driveway, littered with a ragtag collection of luggage, and dug into the cooler. Eventually, he produced two cold cans of beer and tossed one to Happy. He toasted Rock and the heap of junk, remarking cheerfully, "It was a little school bus when Nixon was in the White House, D. Now it's thirty bucks cash—tops—at the salvage yard."

Bashful bent to check the cooler's contents. "To be fair, it's also a probable fire hazard, Boo."

"Excellent point, my man." Boo raised his beer again. "Cheers."

Nathan looked at his lieutenants and raised his unopened beer with a questioning look. "Gentlemen. It's oh-nine-hundred hours."

Boo remained upbeat in spite of the obvious transportation disaster we faced. "Relax, boss. Natural Light's a breakfast beer. Or brunch. As the designated alcohol officer, I insist on Nattys for the first cooler of the day; it's all about hangover prevention, friends. Besides, Nattys are trendy."

Nathan seemed to consider his rationale, glancing again at the rusty minibus, and popped the top. I figured it was time for a grown-up to investigate; luckily Coach stepped forward, brandishing the largest coffee mug I'd ever seen.

"Hayes, son, tell me exactly how you came to be in possession of this…" he pursed his lips and squinted at the atrocity blocking his driveway, "…vehicle."

Rock jumped from the top step of the school bus with a wide grin, oblivious to the skepticism. "Morning, all." He rubbed his hands gleefully together. "Everybody ready for the Scorpion Vegas Soirée? I hear that what goes on there, stays there, friends—and I intend to have carnal knowledge of at least one lucky young lady before the sun rises. Load 'em up, everybody."

Coach raised one bushy eyebrow when no one moved. "Rock, focus. The bus?"

Rock's signature grin remained intact. "Coach, my uncle Sonny knows this guy. He got me this thing for the weekend. On the cheap." He slapped one rusty fender. "She's solid as a rock; Mel says so. He does a run to Vegas every other weekend for the VFW gambling junkets. Fifty bucks cash, round trip—you guys should go with us sometime." His enthusiasm was warming the crowd's dampened mood now. "Those old dudes know how to party, man. I'm up two and a half large for the year, and that includes the cost of four up with the room discounts at The Oasis."

"Two's in." Torch nodded his approval, noticing the side-eye I shot his direction. "What? I'm a great gambler, D. Teach you to count cards this weekend if you want."

Bibi appeared in the driveway during Rock's explanation, bearing a coffee pot. She refilled Coach's mug before retrieving a Natty from the cooler for herself, popping the top and taking a healthy swig. She regarded Miles, resplendent in her well-worn running shorts, hoodie, and hot-pink Chuck Taylors. "Morning, Charlotte. Are you sure you want to accompany this shitshow to Vegas?"

Miles nodded, grinning. "Nothing's too good for our revered

leader, Bibi. And somebody has to wrangle the animals, you know? No better candidate than the marginally reformed version of yours truly."

Bibi nodded slowly. "You would've been welcome to join us at La Paloma, but I understand. Try to keep the sausage party in hand, so to speak." She guffawed at her joke and took another long drink of the beer before turning her attention to Rock. "Am I to understand you've personally ridden on this bus to Vegas, Hayes?"

Rock nodded vigorously. "Yes, ma'am. Several times."

Bibi stared at the train wreck parked in front of her house for a few seconds, then took an additional drink of her beer. "Right. Off you go, then. Get this thing off the street before the sky cops show up. There's bound to be some sort of regulation we're violating." She planted a long kiss on Coach's surprised face and slapped his ass soundly. "I've got a bachelorette spa weekend to prep for. Thanks for the beer, guys." She turned and walked back into the house.

We watched her go, then looked around at one another. Coach shrugged and downed the remainder of his coffee. "Okay, then. Let's load up and hit the road."

Rock was a competent driver, and the Rusty Little Bus That Could put miles in our rear view at a respectable clip, accompanied by an alarming variety of noises. It even managed to exceed the speed limit handily, resulting in some quality entertainment as Rock smoothly talked his way out of a speeding ticket outside Sun City.

"It's fucking crowded in here." Torch was cranky as hell, and the predictable absence of air conditioning was not helping. "And I'm fucking hot." The seat he had settled on initially was rendered unserviceable when we discovered the nails holding it to the bus's metal floor were loose. He'd been forced to double up with Boo who passed him a beer and pretended to snuggle him in the small seat they now shared.

"Aw, princess. Don't be premenstrual; I love spending special time with you." Boo batted his eyes. "I even showed my love by pulling the garbage bags out of your window, so you could enjoy the cool desert air."

"Piss off, Boo. And don't paw me like an animal. Fucking perv." Hung, Miles, and the remainder of the well-lubricated group found this hilarious and took up the cause, irritating Torch. It was one of the squadron's favorite pastimes. Coach and Happy held down the two back seats, sipping beers, and I'd taken up residence in the seat just ahead of Coach.

"So, Deliverance. Not that I need to ask, but how's life now that you're back on flying status?" Coach's relaxed smile reminded me that he and Bibi had been among my greatest cheerleaders and advocates during the long months after the accident.

"Everything I knew it would be, Coach." I felt more than relaxed, and this third beer was making me a little philosophical. "Bibi and Luckie took such good care of me, and I felt good from pretty early on about the odds I'd recover and return to flying. But, you know, I think everything would've been alright either way."

Happy shot me a sideways grin. "You're being cavalier about flying because your ass fell in love." He chugged the last of his Natty and signaled Boo. "Do we have any man beer, Boo?" He turned his attention back to me. "Don't be embarrassed, D; it happens to the best of us. I didn't even know I could be this content."

Coach nodded sagely. "That's what I was trying to tell you when Bibi and I visited the day you moved in, Nate. It's hard to overestimate the wealth of good that a woman's love can bring into your life. Just don't let any of the peanut gallery hear us talking about it, for God's sake." He gestured to the seats ahead of us where Miles, Torch, and Boo huddled around Rock in the driver's seat, deep in discussion about craps strategies. Hung, Marilyn, and Bashful napped in the middle seats.

"So. What exactly is it the happily married, the almost married, and the happily accompanied do in Sin City?" Nathan gestured to the three of us, in turn. "I know it's all about the sinning, but I've gone cold on any woman—beautiful or otherwise—who isn't carrying my baby and warming my bed."

"Valid question, boss. The last time I had a boys' weekend in Vegas, my life was in a different place." The group I'd traveled with chased pussy relentlessly all weekend. Unsuccessfully too, if memory served. I gambled a little, drank too much, and took in a show the night everyone else spent the entire day in bed battling hangovers. I was fine numbering myself with the "old married farts." Lucinda Page had already become my everything. "I'm gonna miss her this weekend—three measly days; does that make me one of you guys?"

They both smiled, but I could tell we were in the same boat. Got it bad.

Soon I was in the process of waking Hung, Marilyn, and Bashful. The barren desert landscape continued to roll by, but we were nearing the southern edge of Vegas. I marveled silently that the vehicle had almost succeeded in getting us to our destination. *So much for judging a book by its cover.*

Just then a loud pop sounded, instantly grabbing my attention. The noise was deafening and accompanied by an impressive show of steam and water emanating from under the hood of our little bus. We coasted to a stop along the shoulder of the interstate; the cars whizzed by, seemingly oblivious to our fate.

Boo sat up suddenly from the seat where he'd been snoring for the past hour, hair wildly askew and obviously quite drunk.

He took in the scene for a moment before loudly making a declaration. "Could be a hose." With that, he fell back into his seat, asleep and snoring again within seconds.

Hung was sarcastic but good-natured. "Ya think? Hey, Rock, want me to call triple A?"

Rock nodded, dejected.

Bashful was on his feet right away, clapping Rock on the shoulder. "Don't give it a thought, man. The old girl almost got us there; we'll get a tow and be partying on the Strip before you know it."

Hung tapped his phone to end the call with AAA. "He's right, Rock; don't listen to my dumb ass. This trip is gonna set records for **Hog Log** write-ups. It will be the most legendary bachelor party in the history of bachelor parties. Our children and their children will talk about this weekend, dude. It'll make *The Hangover* look like *The Sound of Music*."

Then he just had to fucking say it.

"All our bad luck is officially behind us now."

Chapter
THIRTY-SEVEN

"Pocketful of Sunshine"

Lucinda

"**G**irl. This is the life we were born to live."

My eyes were screwed tightly closed, but Camille's answering groan assured me she was still with me. We'd arrived at the spa early for an additional massage before our night out with the rest of the gang. Camille opted for a pregnancy Zen massage—whatever the fuck that was—that rendered her euphoric and dopey. A beautiful, evil little Latina lady was up to her elbows in the knots around my shoulders and upper back. The magic her hands worked caused me alternately to curse her and see God. My bachelorette weekend experiences to this point had been the "drunken girl squad wolf-whistling at the male stripper" variety, so I was somewhat stymied at the prospect of hosting one for a pregnant bride-to-be. But this celebration might well win me over. If this afternoon's spa experience was any indication, I'd crossed over to the dark side. In fact, I'd completely lost interest in the nude male body with one dramatic exception.

The impossibly taut frame of the man I'd fallen for, artistically wrapped in long, sinewy muscle. The penetrating green stare. Thick blond hair, boyishly tousled. I dreamed about him even as I slept securely wrapped in his thick arms. Fantasized while we cuddled on the sofa watching football. Over the past several months, the love growing between us had matured in the light of blissfully ordinary circumstances. Life and work proceeded uninterrupted by the stress and adversity that marked our first months together, and we were both relieved and thankful for the respite. Now it was time to celebrate the life Camille was about to begin with Nathan, and I wanted all the focus to remain on them, right where it belonged.

As Miss Isabella worked her sorcery, I considered the group we'd join tonight to celebrate. Our little girl squad was more than simply the sum of its parts. The complex, chameleon-like personalities seemed to weave themselves together effortlessly. The strength of that bond brought an abundance of love and support I could never have imagined. Now I couldn't conceive of my life without it.

Cami was the beating heart and soul of us, gentle and compassionate but with enough grit and moxie to keep things interesting. She'd suffered heartbreak in a way few had, and it made her at once gentle and tough. It also made her the perfect charge nurse—and my wonderfully perfect best friend.

Vivianne was the standard bearer. On the surface, she could be critical, uncompromising, even difficult. She held us all to a line in the sand that seemed impossible to toe, but only because she held herself there first. In some ways, she may have been the most unprotected of all, because she appeared to require no shelter. Viv was a fierce advocate for those who needed her defense, and she was a consummate truth-teller. It didn't matter who crossed her path; she was fearless, especially where we were concerned.

Grace was our soft underbelly. Kind, sweet, empathetic. Most people probably mistook her for naïve, but we'd gradually learned better. Anyone who sold Grace short did so at their own peril. She, too, had a past littered with difficulty she didn't readily share. Her quiet personality and penchant for making the burdens of others her own shifted focus from the hardship she'd shouldered during her formative years. It was impossible not to adore Grace. The only glaring flaw was her deficient profanity skills. She sucked, and I really did need to set to work on that, in earnest this time.

Samanthe had a wealth of stunning beauty and intelligence in a group of women who lacked neither. She was sophisticated and well-read, even beyond that of the average educated professional. She seemed entirely assured of what she wanted out of life, possessing unusual self-confidence from a young age. I fretted Sam would never find her equal; it was hard to think such a man existed.

And me? MariSee was right—it's essential to know who you are. I was the mama bear. Protector and educator of the pack, entertaining and guiding with wit when I could and an unparalleled foul mouth. Moderating Vivvie and drawing Grace out of the woodwork. Caretaking and healing, whether at work or elsewhere. I'd never given a moment of serious thought to the notion I'd fall irretrievably, hopelessly in love. But here we were. Cami knocked up, and both of us head over heels in love. Camille's take was right on the money—it seemed almost too much to hope for.

An insistent elbow digging into my lower back dragged me out of my head with a hearty groan. I turned to face Camille, draped in a sheet, arms and legs so relaxed she was probably in danger of rolling off the table. Nathan would be pleased to see her in this state, I thought with a smile. His protective instincts were already laser-focused on his fiancée, but they'd kicked into overdrive with the news she was expecting their child. In the aftermath of the attack she'd suffered years before, surgical intervention saved her life but left her unlikely to conceive. Her pregnancy was a gift neither of them dared to hope for, especially after Amos's death. Now Nathan's alpha male spidey senses were on high alert, bordering on being an ass pain. He was only slightly annoying until I allowed myself to remember all she'd been through. Then I just loved him all the more and worked overtime to hide it. That fire didn't require tending.

"Wake up, mamacita. The girls will be here in an hour. We've gotta get you dolled up to hit the town." She opened one eye, looking drowsily in my direction and pulling her limbs slowly back onto the masseuse's table. Her eyes slammed shut.

"I see literally no reason at all to get 'dolled up,' Luckie." Her fingers lazily quoted the words. "I'm pretty sure I've got more cock on lock than I can fuck in a lifetime."

It was a tribute to the professional tormenting my lower back that the suffering didn't abate for even a moment. "Baby girl. I think you're endorphin drunk, even though you're not exercising. Let's strive not to use the term 'cock' around anyone we haven't worked with for the past several years. Mmmmkay?"

She opened her eyes only to roll them in my direction. "This is a very low-key weekend, Luckie; I think anything I do or say is small potatoes compared to what the boys are up to in Vegas."

Her eyes closed again, and her limbs relaxed toward the table's edge. I noted movement at the door of the open-concept spa and turned in time to see Viv and Sam appear. They toasted me silently with hotel water glasses almost filled with what I guessed was Cuervo Silver. They downed the shots, and then Sam doffed her bikini top, sliding into the bubbling water near our massage tables with a groan.

This bachelorette party was definitely breaking new ground, and I liked the change. This might be the new bachelorette gold standard.

Chapter
THIRTY-EIGHT

"Born to Be Wild"

Davis

I stepped back onto the rolling rust bucket after generously tipping the AAA mechanic who'd expertly taken care of our blown hose. The whole affair cost us less than an hour, and we had Rock laughing about it in no time. He revved the cantankerous engine and lurched into traffic, sending me scrambling for a seat.

Miles stood and turned to face the sweaty, mildly buzzed assembly with a giant grin. "Back on track and only an hour till we reach the carefully-chosen Scorpion bachelor party headquarters."

Coach's bushy eyebrows arched in mock amazement, and he aimed the question at no one in particular. "Miles is in charge of lodging?"

Rock chugged his energy drink, high spirits restored, and smiled widely into the rear-facing mirror. "Stinger LPA has a firm policy of equitable labor division, Coach. And, you know, from each, according to his or her ability and questionable contacts and secret talents to, uh…" he frowned briefly, "…to everybody else, according to whatever they need. Or don't have. Like, presently."

Torch raised his beer. "With liberty and fraternity for all."

Miles toasted with Torch, calling out to Rock, "Play ball!"

Coach spared me a sideways glance. "So Miles is the billeting PROJO."

I sighed and searched the dwindling beer supply. "Dammit. No more Sam or Amstel; only PBR. What the fuck, Boo?"

He cut his eyes briefly in my direction. "D, have some faith. Leave the alcohol to the experts. Like Natty, PBR is a light, trendy brunch beer. It's a marathon, not a sprint, dude. Resupplies will be accomplished in good time, but my goal is maximizing our Vegas fun with targeted blood-alcohol-level maintenance over the course of a twenty to twenty-two-hour day. And yes, Coach, Miles is in charge of lodging. See also: Rock's mention of secret talents and questionable contacts."

Miles had stretched her slim frame across the aisle, effectively taking up two seats. This didn't settle well with Torch, who still doubled up with Boo; although his more well-lubricated status mellowed the response considerably. A spirited discussion of Miles's suitability to procure lodging continued while she dozed and Torch studiously tied the laces of her Chucks securely together.

At last, the skyline of Sin City loomed, awash with garish promise. A mildly tawdry weekend with the Stingers, celebrating and making questionable decisions seemed the perfect way to mark Happy's nuptials. I helped Boo load the empty cans littering the bus floor into the beer cooler while Miles swore a blue streak and vowed retribution as she loosened the knot in her sneakers.

"You miserable motherfuckers are so lucky I didn't face-plant when I stood up." Her eyes narrowed and swept the sweaty, disheveled assembly. "You reek, you know—every one of you." Her nose wrinkled in disgust. "I'll find out who did this, and they will regret the day of their birth when I'm done. But you're all complicit." She finished tying the untangled laces with a flourish. "You don't even deserve the great hotel I've lined up. But I'll show my superior breeding by showering your clammy, loathsome asses with undeserved generosity." She swept the group again with her disapproving glare. "Actually, showering should be the first thing on the agenda."

Torch sniffed his armpit furtively, knit his brow, and burped loudly. Miles shot him a poisonous look. "It was you, Torch Thomas, you worm. I know it. You'd better sleep with one eye open, assclown."

Torch burped again, then snorted loudly, effectively outing himself. Just in time to save him from certain death, Rock threw the bus into park and announced, "We're here!"

Hung whistled low, and we all stared up at the golden facade of the massive Mandalay Bay Resort. "Miles, you've totally vindicated yourself. I've gotta admit, I didn't see this coming in at our price point—Mandalay Bay?"

Miles grunted in disgust, grabbing her backpack from the overhead rack. "Not there, Hung; over here." She pointed to the building whose parking lot we currently occupied, directly across the street from the gleaming resort. A derelict sign, partially lit with neon, depicted a giant rabbit-like critter, formally attired and playing a quarter slot machine with apparent delight. We all stared at the sign, but Bashful summoned his powers of speech first.

"The Laughing Jackalope." He made an indecipherable noise in his throat.

"Bar and Grill!" Boo stood and high-fived Miles, gathering his bag. "They've got twenty-four-hour video poker, man. Let's do it." He jumped off the bus, followed by the remainder of the LPA.

Coach looked at Hung, Happy, and me, his face an implacable mask as he pointed to the sign. "And there are vacancies, gentlemen. Imagine our good fortune." We gathered our belongings and followed the LPA off the bus. The peeling stucco was the color of the desert around it and pockmarked with sizable holes. The glass in the door leading to the lobby had been replaced with plywood adorned with spray-painted instructions: No Soliciting. Miles pulled a yellow legal pad from her backpack and studied it momentarily before motioning for our attention.

"Okay, gang, here are the room assignments."

Torch cleared his throat. "I'm not sleeping with a dude. Or you, Miles; no offense."

Miles waved her hand as if swatting an annoying fly. "None taken; nobody's sleeping with any dudes. Or me, you fool. There are two beds in every room; Coach, you're with Happy. Torch, Rock, and Boo together—that room has an extra bed; Hung, you're with Bash. And Deliverance, that leaves you with me."

In other company, there might have been commentary about my bunking with Miles, but not here. "Let's get checked in, everybody. Then showers and we hit the Strip." Miles threw her bag over her shoulder and started for the front door. I fell into step alongside her, and she looked up through the dark lens of her aviators with a wide grin. "Just so you're aware, I ran this by Luckie yesterday, D. Keeping it above board and all."

I laughed. "She knows we're buds. What'd she say?"

She snorted as I opened the lobby door for her. "She said you monopolize the bathroom and snore like a freight train, and then she recommended I do whatever I could to pawn you off on someone else."

"I won it in a poker game." Miles was seated between Coach and me at a blackjack table at the Flamingo. I was in the process of motioning the waiter for another round when her pronouncement stopped me in my tracks.

"What do you mean, won it?" Coach and I were thoroughly confused, and the third round of Tanqueray and tonics wouldn't help things at all. "Are you telling me you own the Laughing Antelope?"

"The Laughing Jackalope, Deliverance. And, no, I don't own it." Miles picked up my drink and took a swallow, grimacing, before returning to her draft beer. "You might wanna slow down there, big guy; I think that pine tar's killing brain cells. First Thursday of the month, I play poker with some of the ladies." She thought for a moment, ticking off the participants on her fingers. "There's Patricia, the high school teacher who gives all the boys boners; Gemini, the MILF who lives next door to me; and Gen, the travel agent." She paused, thinking. "Both of the college professors, Dawn and Leigh, three pilots: Barbara and Michelle from over at the 354th and Laura from the 357th. Oh, and Bibi."

Coach's eyebrows lifted in question. "Bellamy doesn't play poker." He thought for a moment. "Just Bunco once a month."

Miles shot him a wide smile. "First Thursday? I hate to rat out my friend, but that Bunco evolved in short order. Into poker night." She placed her bet. "Last month, Patricia threw a weekend in Vegas in the pot. Lodging for ten, Blue Man Group, and drinks at the Peppermill—that's where we're headed next. BMG is gonna be a hard pass. Anyway, I kicked ass in Follow the Queen and took that trip right off Patricia's perfectly manicured hands." Miles took a long drink of her beer. "And Coach, if you don't think Bibi plays poker, I'd recommend you steer clear of any game she's dealt into. The woman's a fucking shark."

Coach shook his head in amazement. "After eighteen years, you think you know a girl…"

Having solved the mystery of the lodging officer, we left the table to round up the gang and head for the Peppermill. We discovered Happy and Torch at a craps table where Torch was losing his ass—so much for the vaunted gambling expertise. The residents of **The Land of No Slack** pummeled Torch's ego endlessly as we headed north along the Strip in a cramped minivan cab, but he'd been rendered bulletproof by Boo's carefully orchestrated alcohol regimen and insisted tomorrow was his day. Happy seemed relaxed, living up to his ironic nickname for once. According to Luckie, Happy's protective instincts escalated to weapons-grade the moment Camille told him they were expecting. The company Camille was keeping this weekend at the spa bachelorette party was likely the only thing that got him out of town. Some of the best nurses in the city were with her every moment, and they had seen her through unspeakable tragedy long before Nathan or I arrived on the scene.

Miles tossed her ridiculous mane of red curls accidentally in my face as she turned backward on the sidewalk, taking stock of our group. "You guys. Where's Boo?" She stopped in the center of the crowded sidewalk just outside our destination, a retro confection of velvet, neon and throwback cocktails. Bashful grabbed her by the arm, dragging her out of the path of half a dozen Elvis impersonators. I could only see one who was probably male.

"Boo said he'd meet us here. He met somebody." Bashful finger-quoted the "somebody" part dramatically. "He said she was a fourteen on a scale of ten; he's bringing her here for a drink. He thinks the company he keeps is a plus in this situation, but he's dead wrong about that." A cab pulled up to the door of the bar as we approached and—speak of the devil—Boo alighted with his "date." Still a hundred feet or so away, we stopped in our tracks.

Clearly a male in drag.

Good looking, to be sure, but Boo didn't bat for that team. Ever.

Miles, probably the most sober of the group, spoke first: "Well, fuck me in the ear sideways on a Tuesday afternoon."

Conversation broke out on every side, everyone shouting to be heard over the melee.

"I don't care what anybody says, I'm absofuckinglutely not…"

"This should be a rank situation. I'm junior here…"

"Miles, you're a woman; he'd be less embarrassed if you…"

"You don't think he's paying for it, do you?"

I groaned. Happy shouldn't have to deal with this, what with it being his bachelor party. And, from the thousand-yard stare Coach was sporting, he was in no condition. I turned to Miles. "I'm not forking over for this hooker, Miles; let's divide and conquer here. I got 'Dude Looks Like a Lady,' you break the bad news to Boo. He's got a hot date tonight, alright. But it's with Rosie Palm." As we walked away to separate Boo from his date, Hung was laughing so hard, he could barely remain upright.

The pretty raven-haired waitress served Boo's third Long Island Iced Tea with a generous side of cleavage, but it did little to bolster his sodden spirits. Torch leaned in, wrapping him in a whole-body hug. "Boo-Boo-Be-Do. Is my precious princess feeling sad? Don't you worry, sweetheart. I'm here for you. I'll wrap you all up in my love and my big, hairy man body tonight until you forget all about your…girl." He rubbed Boo's knee and batted his eyes in faux seduction. "I love to spoon."

Maybe it was the late hour—or the alcohol—but even Boo had to burst into uncontrollable laughter. "If you dickless motherfuckers write this up in the Hog Log, I swear I'll rip your balls off and stuff them down your throat."

I toasted the group with the dregs of my final gin and tonic. "If it happens here, it stays here, friends. Unless something even better happens tomorrow. And here's to Happy and his girl."

"Hear! Hear!" The glasses were raised in unison just as Torch slumped onto Boo's shoulder and began to snore loudly.

Nathan sighed and signaled the waitress, rolling his eyes. "Check, please."

Chapter
THIRTY-NINE

"Benediction"

Lucinda

"I don't understand." Davis and I snuggled in the corner of the booth at the Doghouse Saloon, enjoying our second prickly pear margarita and awaiting the arrival of the prospective bride and groom. It was finally the night before Nate and Camille's long-awaited wedding; the Scorpions were gathering, along with other family and friends, at the lovely Tanque Verde Ranch. Davis was regaling me with the long version of Boo's lost Vegas love. "Even if he was around the bend, surely he could tell…"

Davis shook his head with mock melancholy, interrupting. "Nope, he couldn't tell. I'm not sure Boo could tell his ass from a hole in the ground by that point. His patented program of blood-alcohol-level maintenance let him down."

"It's gonna be hard to look him in the eye with a straight face." I shook my head with a smile. "And how did you get elected to give the hooker the heave-ho? I would have paid money to be a fly on the wall for that conversation."

Before Davis could answer, we were interrupted by the bois-terous laughter of a group outside. The door swung open, ad-mitting Vivianne, Bashful, and their very tall, very handsome British cousin. His arm was around Viv, and they were all talking at once. Spying us in the corner, they strode toward our table. Davis stood, extending his hand.

"Oliver, right?" They shook warmly, and then Davis reached for my hand and pulled me close to his side. "This is Lucinda Page." His gaze warmed me, and the other occupants of the room disappeared for a split second as I basked in the light of his affection.

"So good to see you both again; it's Luckie, isn't it?" Oliver's accent was crisp and light. A guaranteed leg-spreader, I thought. Vivvie crushed me in a big hug and grabbed my hand from Davis, pulling me back to the cozy booth where we'd been sitting for the past hour. The men took their seats with Davis at my side and Bashful next to Viv.

The bartender took our order as the chatter resumed. "Where are the lovebirds?" Viv helped herself to a slurp of my margarita, then changed her order to a prickly pear marg. "I thought they'd be the first ones to check in, but we didn't see them in the lobby or walking over to the bar."

Bash grinned. "He's probably holed up with her in their fancy casita, reciting sonnets to her beauty or writing poetry about his undying love. I swear, if the man didn't fly and fight like a god, I'd lay money he had no testicles at all."

Vivianne swatted him. "Shut up, twin brother. Someday you'll find a beautiful girl who rips your heart out of your chest and takes you home to meet her dad and makes you knock her up with a dozen babies. Then you'll laugh about your hard-hearted bachelor ways."

Oliver's pale blue eyes sparkled as he sipped his whiskey and regarded his cousins. "If you ask me, Jacob's heart may already be in danger."

"Well, no shit." Davis turned slowly to Bash. "*Do* share with the group, *Jacob*."

Bash slid Oliver a venomous glare. "I don't respond to that name, cuz. It's Bash or Bashful. Jake in a pinch."

Oliver and Viv rolled their eyes. "Brilliant redirect, bro, but it'll all come out in the end."

The bar filled steadily as members of the wedding party and guests arrived, ordering drinks and munching on delicious homemade tortilla chips and guacamole. Bibi appeared with the entire LPA who'd evidently given her a lift. Coach had to work late buttoning up the squadron for the weekend. Hung and Marilyn slid an additional table up to the two we'd already joined and tore into a couple of enormous plates of fish tacos they'd picked up from the dining room en route to the bar.

Hung, who was seated next to Bibi, gave her a big hug. "Coach said to tell you he'd be on the road by 1800 hours, Beeb. He also said some real dirty stuff about his intentions this weekend, but I'm not gonna repeat that to a lady."

Bibi looked suspicious. "He didn't really say that to you, Hung. Did he?" They shared a laugh, but I noted the question went unanswered.

The room was warmed with friendship and camaraderie, and I felt contentment swell in my chest as Davis gathered me into his big arms. One of the cattle hands came in to lay a fire in the rustic rock fireplace, quickly chasing away the chill of impending evening. The noise level and laughter grew, and someone began playing an acoustic guitar in the corner, singing an old western ballad. We surveyed the scene with our faces almost touching, catching snippets of conversations here and there. My head rested against his broad shoulder, then he spoke.

"Is this what you want, Lucinda? To be a part of something this big and noisy and intrusive?" Conversations faded into the background as I considered his question. His breathing and the beat of his big, generous heart were the only sounds I heard. "This life isn't for everyone. And I can't say for sure, at least not beyond the next few years, but I think it's for me. The way these people surrounded me and let me lean on them after the accident... Hell, they picked me up and carried me when I didn't have enough strength to keep going." His voice faded, and I let the quiet stretch. "It's not just the flying and the fun and parties. Serving together—doing something that really matters—it ties you together and gives you a good look at what your friends are made of. Gives you a front row seat to watch them at their best and worst."

I turned to smile at him, still not breaking the silence.

A wide grin broke slowly over his face. "But you already knew that, didn't you? You and your girls are that to one another. Like family."

My head rested on his shoulder again. "More than family, Davis. Camille and I really only had each other in this world, for all practical purposes. We've seen it all together and gotten each other over the mountains and through the darkest valleys. I get it, honey; I really do."

His voice dropped lower, as if we were alone together. "That's why I need to know if this..." He held up his hand, indicating the room filled with our friends. "If it's what you want for yourself. Because they're so important to me, Luckie." He sat up straighter and took my face in both of his huge hands. His eyes were soft, and he looked completely purposeful. Intent. "They're important, but there's only one person I can't live without. More than the next breath I'm going to take, Lucinda Dominique Page, I want a forever with you." My heart pounded so loudly I was sure everyone in the room could hear, and it was so damn hard to breathe. "I don't want an answer here in this crowded room; I just want you to know what my heart and my head are telling me. I need you, Peaches. And I love you like I didn't even know I could."

I lifted my face closer to his. "Everything in me, Davis. I love you with every ounce of me." His mouth was soft on mine, the tip of his tongue barely sliding along the seam of my lips. It was a kiss to seal the deal. All the details remained, but I knew this gentle kiss was his oath, a promise that we belonged to each other.

A whoop broke the solitude between us. "Get it, D!" Rock, Boo, and Torch had been joined by Miles at some point as we'd taken our temporary leave from reality. Now Boo and Rock were locked in a mock lascivious embrace, awkwardly pawing one another, eyes and tongues lolling. Miles was standing on her chair, grinding her hips in vulgar circles. She held Vivianne's head in her hands, inches from her writhing form, approximating a sexual act I was certain neither of them had engaged in. Vivvie twerked her perfect little ass enthusiastically, carefully holding her margarita clear of the shenanigans.

Bashful pressed two fingers into his temple, exhaling loudly as he watched his sister. "I'm going to need a lifetime of therapy after this. Who bought her the third drink?"

Hung's crooked grin was wicked. "I did. And I'd do it again." He settled back into his chair, sipping a bottled beer and laughing quietly with his gaze fixed on Vivianne.

Davis whispered in my ear. "Holy shit. Look at Oliver, Peaches. Is he looking at Miles?"

Oliver's stare was heated and definitely glued on Miles's gyrating hips; his regard didn't waver a millimeter even as he spoke briefly to those around him. When the buffoonery seemed to be winding down, he stood and offered Miles his hand. She allowed her lashes to sweep down with a demure smile, looking more flirtatious than I'd ever seen her. Then she stepped to the floor where her diminutive frame was utterly dwarfed by Oliver, easily the tallest man in the room. He leaned down to whisper in her ear, then brought her hand to his lips and brushed it with a quick kiss. Miles looked up through her lashes with a little smile.

Davis made a sound of undisguised disgust deep in his throat. I shot him a questioning look, wondering what I'd missed.

"I've never seen Miles do that."

"Do what, Tarzan?"

He wrinkled his nose. "You know. Act like a…a girl. It confuses me." He lifted his chin in the direction of the door. "Possible additional arrivals."

In the front doorway of the bar, Grace and Samanthe stood, surveying the scene. The slack jaw on Sam told me they'd caught at least part of the floor show; she spotted me, waving. Bashful was fast on his feet and striding quickly in their direction. When he reached them, he greeted Sam briefly then turned his full attention on Grace like a laser beam. A shy smile spread across her face as he stepped closer to engage her in conversation.

Davis turned an accusatory glare on me. "Did you know about this?"

I shrugged. "I know a lot of things, Tarzan. A lot of things."

Another hour passed, food and drinks flowing freely. Coach had just arrived, greeting everyone and pulling Bibi into his arms for a quick kiss. The room was romantic, lit by the fire's glow and the alcohol was doing a fine job of social lubrication. There were several intimate conversations in progress. Here and there, knees and hands brushed casually. Hung brought Vivianne a soda from the bar and sat down close by, his arm stretched over the back of her chair. Something on the other side of the bar caught his attention, but before I could look, his face broke into a huge grin. He shouted his greeting above the low roar of conversation and laughter.

"It's the boss and Camille, everybody. Happy, where the hell you been, man?" There was an outcry of agreement. But I knew where they'd been.

Nathan and Camille stood in the door, awash in the obvious glow of their shared love and affection from their friends. They moved among the tables, shaking hands and hugging and greeting. Eventually, they made their way to the back corner where we were seated. I stood and embraced them both, focusing my attention on Camille and resting one hand on her bump. I leaned in, speaking to her alone. "How's the baby?"

Nathan took her back, wrapping her in both arms and smiling like an idiot. "She's beautiful. Everything's perfect."

I couldn't contain my glee. "She? *She?*"

Camille smiled too, rubbing her round tummy gently. "It's a girl, honey; her name's Lucinda Hope." Her eyes lifted and held mine. "Our precious little Luci, whose namesake is the best girl I know."

The room blurred, and Davis's strong arms again embraced me; it was impossible to digest it all. "I don't know what to say, sweetheart. I don't. It's too much heaven."

It had been four years since the heartbreaking death of Camille's son, Amos. He was only hours old, his death the result of a **cord accident**. Her water broke very early in her pregnancy, at only twenty-three of the expected forty weeks. Monday had marked the beginning of Camille's twenty-third week, and she'd been increasingly uneasy as the week wore on. Cami's beloved obstetrician, Lee Scott, worked her into the afternoon schedule today for an extra checkup and ultrasound.

The arrival of Nick and Candace Bamford from Maine was the final one for the day. Nick, whose tactical was "Bam," was Nate's pilot training roommate and best friend. Candace embraced Nate upon their arrival, obviously emotional. Nathan was the best man at their wedding three years ago and had learned of his fiancée's death during their festive reception. Nick grabbed a napkin from the table to wipe Candace's tears as Nate gave her an affectionate peck on the cheek.

"Sorry, everybody," she dabbed her eyes and smiled at the group assembled at our table. "New-mama hormones in the house. The truth is, I'm just devastated I won't ever get my shot at this big guy." She gave Happy a good-natured punch on the shoulder. He gave her a little twirl, dancing and singing a few painfully off-key bars of "I Only Have Eyes for You."

Davis's drawl was thick. "Don't quit your day job, Happy."

Bam and Candace pulled up extra chairs to join Nathan, Camille, Davis and me. Bam signaled the bartender for yet another round, and I surveyed the happy scene around me. Not every day would be filled with this kind of joy, but today was, and I wanted to soak it in. My hand moved to rest on Cami's little bump and was soon covered with her own slim hand. The baby hiccupped, and Camille laughed. Davis's hand squeezed my thigh, and his lips brushed the skin below my ear. "Love you, my beautiful girl."

So much wonder. So much good. A hundred blessings I hadn't ever dreamed of. After the seemingly endless chapters of loneliness, loss, and tragedy with this sister of my heart, tonight was our benediction.

Chapter FORTY

"I Choose You"

Lucinda

The pink adobe Nathan and Camille shared sat at the top of a hill with a stunning view of Saguaro National Park. Nathan had soundly rejected the idea of not seeing his bride before the wedding, opting instead to spend the night before the ceremony together in their casita. When it was time to dress, however, I insisted he go join the men in the wedding party, most of them lodged in the salas down the hill.

Just before noon, I kissed Davis goodbye and walked across the grounds carrying my garment bag and toiletry case. It might not have been the brightest idea, refusing to allow Tarzan to give me a lift. Springtime in Tucson brought very warm days, and there was a significant hill to climb en route to Cami's casita. In addition, every square inch of me from my kiss-swollen lips to deliciously aching pussy was feeling Davis's possessive lovemaking from last night. He had been at once tender and unyielding, attending my need with his mouth and fingers for well over an hour before I begged him to fill me. We slept soundly, tangled around each other as usual until the hour before sunrise when I awoke with him, hard and thick, inside me. I was happily sated as I climbed the steps of the casita, stopping to drink in the view.

Murmured voices came from the inside, and I turned to see the front door open a few inches. Looking into the living area, my heart skipped a beat. Camille stood on the thick rug in front of the fireplace clad in lacy silk panties that hugged the under-side of her round tummy and her favorite old silk dressing gown, opened to reveal her pregnant form. On his knees before her, Nathan knelt with his lips pressed to her belly; Camille stroked his head, whispering something I couldn't hear. I fought off a big lump in my throat before knocking softly.

Camille turned to me, smiling and motioning for me to come in. She bent to cup Nate's square jaw, kissing him as she closed and tied her robe. "Come on in, Luckie. Nathan was just leaving, weren't you, sweetheart?"

He frowned a little but stood, gathering his own bags and giv-ing me an affectionate hug when I approached. "I want to have a word with the perpetrator of this 'no seeing the bride before the wedding' bullshit. I should damn well be able to see my beautiful wife anytime I want."

"Valid point, Nate, but that's the thing. See, she's not official yet." I patted his back fondly. "Why don't you get the hell out of here so we can work on getting that underway? I think every-body's ready for this train to leave the station." He didn't look much happier, but he did kiss Camille long and hard once more before he finally left, grumbling under his breath.

I laughed as I closed the door behind him. "Alpha much? He's got a bad case of you, girl. Maybe you should just go ahead and marry the lovesick pup." I poured us cocktails of sparkling hon-ey limeade picked up en route from the kitchen and toasted my dearest friend. "A lifetime of joy, love, adventure, and friendship continues today with the happy addition of a wonderful man who loves you more than his own life. I'm so happy for you, baby girl. Here's to you and Nathan."

We sipped, laughed, fussed and primped for the next couple of hours, leisurely enjoying one another's company and excitedly reviewing the wedding details. Once her hair was in rollers, I insisted Cami lie down for a quick power nap. I grabbed mint lotion stashed in my purse for the occasion and treated her to a foot rub until her breathing became deep and even. I set the alarm on my phone for thirty minutes and settled into a plush old leather chair to text Davis. He was, loosely speaking, in charge of the group of Scorpions who would form the saber arch often seen at military weddings.

Me: What's happening, Tarzan?

Davis: Sword wrangling lessons in progress. The LPA is a clusterfuck wrapped in a shitshow. They learned how to do this at some point in school or **OTS**, but their brains must be sieves. Miles is particularly entertaining.

Me: They'll come through in the clutch, I'm sure. How does the front lawn look? Did the florist make it on time?

Davis: Everything looks nice; the chef just brought the wedding cake out of the kitchen. It tastes great. The florists are here, and Vivianne's flogging them like a rented mule.

Me: You do have a way with the Queen's English, Tarzan. Wait. How do you know how the cake tastes?

Davis: Viv says to tell you she has it all under control.

Me: I have no doubt. I'll tell sleeping beauty when I wake her up. See you soon, handsome.

"Ready to do this, Cami?" I carefully handed her the armload of flowers the florist had delivered to us at the casita a few minutes before. Her bouquet was an artfully arranged confection of long-stemmed wildflowers with a heaping helping of greenery. She put them to her nose and smiled.

"They smell so sweet. Does everything look all right, Luckie… do I look alright? Are my boobies out too much? Is my dress caught in my panties? Holy shit, the baby's going berserk; my butterflies must have her wound up."

Nerves. Completely natural. I grasped her shoulders, giving them a squeeze. "Breathe, Camille. You look like a beautiful, ethereal bohemian princess bride. So pretty you take my breath away. Don't you think about one damn thing except Nathan Morgan. After what I saw this morning, I have no idea how he'll react when he gets a load of all this beauty." I smiled at her, and her shoulders relaxed. "But if his heart gives out, I'll do compressions while you walk down the aisle."

She was the loveliest version of herself I'd ever seen. The gown was perfect for her on this day, in this place: a billowing ivory silk gauze confection that gathered into an empire waist under her breasts and fell behind her two or three feet in a sweeping train we'd be pinning up for dancing. Hand-tatted lace adorned the bodice and train of the dress; the short sleeves fluttered with the slightest breeze. Only a few wildflowers were woven artfully into her hair—we had Samanthe to thank for that bit of magic. It was Nathan's one request: no veil. He asked that nothing obscure the sight of his fiancée's face as she walked toward him.

I was her lone attendant. "You're all I need, Lucinda," she'd said when she asked me. "You're all I've ever needed, and you've always been beside me. The day I marry Nathan, you're the one I want next to me."

She hadn't asked her father to walk her down the aisle, having felt the absence of her parents more acutely over the past months of the engagement and pregnancy. In the end, they postponed meeting Nathan several times, and then declined to attend the wedding when Camille told her mother she'd decided to walk down the aisle alone. The feelings I had about that turn of events didn't merit a mention on this perfect day. I would be anything and everything she needed from me, and now she had the love of a good man who would be all of that for her as well.

"I love you, Camille." I gave her a little air-kiss, careful not to smudge anything. There was a brisk knock at the door of the casita. "That's our ride, my sister; let's go." I fussed with her hair for a few seconds, then grabbed my own gorgeous bouquet and opened the door. On the front porch stood Lieutenant Colonel Chuck Ditka, resplendent in his dress uniform, with Bibi at his side. His eyes grew shiny as he looked wordlessly at Camille. Then he bent at the waist, took her hand, and brushed it with a kiss. "You are a vision, my dear. May I have the pleasure?" He offered her his arm, and Bibi relieved her of the flowers as we made our way to the car, settling in for the short ride down the hill.

I stood at the door leading out to the terrace where all the wedding guests were gathered. Idly, I wondered if it was a coincidence the wedding florals matched the dress Cami had given me free rein in choosing. "No reason not to wear what you love," she'd said. "You have the best taste of anyone I know. Anyway, you're my one and only." I'd selected a dress of similar fabric to hers, light enough to float on the afternoon breeze and sleeveless. It was a rosy beige with a high, ruffled, Victorian-style neckline and complemented with a bouquet of wildflowers similar to Camille's. I wore the sheer joy my heart felt all over my face, almost too much to bear as I watched the beautiful, blond bear of a man in the front row turn and capture me with his stare. A few minutes ago, he'd paraded by the door to the small room hiding Camille and me as we peeked out to watch the proceedings. He led the procession of saber bearers, marching with perfect precision in their navy blue dress uniforms; Bashful, Marilyn, Hung, Miles, Rock, Boo, and Coach.

Adam Roberts, who'd celebrated his eighth birthday yesterday, was the very reason Camille and Nathan met on the fateful day Adam required a visit to the emergency room. Now he was handsome as could be, all decked out in a navy vest, bow tie, and long pants; he'd been tasked with wrangling Mayze down the aisle. It was universally agreed that Solomon was too much of a wild card to attend the service, but Mayze seemed to be handling her appearance with aplomb. She lumbered down the grass path at Adam's behest and allowed Nathan to scratch her ears affectionately before settling in with a huff at the feet of Rick and Michelle, Adam's parents and Nathan's next-door neighbors who were seated in the third row.

The strains of Pachelbel's "Canon in D" floated across the terrace to meet my ears, and I surveyed the crowd—a sea of happy, familiar faces—as they turned to look at me. Then I stepped out the door and onto the grass aisle.

Chapter
FORTY-ONE

"Come Away with Me"

Davis

It all faded to black. Amid the beauty of the desert and the company of so many good friends, all I could see was the person I needed more than life walking toward me. She looked more beautiful than I'd ever seen her. It wasn't just the perfection of her face or the pretty dress swaying gracefully around the curves I loved. It was contented joy that radiated off her in waves. At least until our eyes met. When that happened, her gaze heated, and I was instantly transported back to our room before the sun rose this morning. Fortunately, the walk down the aisle was short, affording us a mercifully brief time to embarrass ourselves in public.

She took her place near the altar opposite Bam after stopping to touch Nathan's hand and speak quietly to him. Chaplain Larry "Apollo" Creed stood behind the assembly, smiling broadly as he saw the bride appear and motioned the congregants to stand.

Camille looked so small standing all alone in the massive doorway of the rock building, delicate in her wispy lace gown with a bouquet of flowers so large I wanted to offer help in carrying them. Then she took a step out of the building and onto the soft grass aisle, dropping the enormous bouquet to her side and holding it in her right hand. She laid her left hand with its sparkling engagement ring across her softly rounded belly and lifted her eyes to meet Nathan's.

He stepped into the aisle and extended a hand toward her. She smiled and walked slowly to him and straight into his embrace. The entire row where I sat with the other seven saber bearers erupted with sniffles and cleared throats; Miles reached for a tissue she'd wisely concealed in her breast pocket. I knew then I wouldn't rest until I saw Lucinda Page walking down an aisle toward me. That Nathan was one lucky motherfucker.

Nathan and Camille eventually untangled themselves and made their way forward, still holding hands. Apollo grinned at them, having apparently expected something akin to this. Clearly not his first rodeo. His greeting to them and those gathered meandered along familiar paths, and my focus drifted back to Luckie. Nothing particular gained my attention until Apollo inquired, of no one in particular, "Who giveth this woman to be married to this man?"

Oh, hell no.

I had gleaned an important tidbit from a long breakfast conversation a couple of weeks ago with Luckie: this familiar portion of the ceremony would absolutely not be playing out at Camille's wedding. There had been a good bit of spirited monologuing from Lucinda on the offensiveness inherent in the verbiage; a woman was her own person, not the property of her family or anyone else. This archaic nugget of sexism deserved permanent banishment. She was very clear on her thoughts about "giving away" the bride. And she shared with me that Camille's feelings on the issue were even stronger.

They shouldn't have skipped the rehearsal. Now the reverend has well and truly stepped in it.

The words hung in the air for only a split second. General O'Cherry, seated in the second row across from the saber guard, stood and turned slightly to address the bridal party. He was similarly attired to the other active duty members in his crisp navy blue mess dress, but the medals that covered much of his chest distinguished him from the rank and file. That, and shoulder boards covered with silver metallic braid and adorned with a star, indicating his rank as a general officer. He spoke in a commanding voice, tinged with emotion. "She, alone, gives herself to this man in marriage. But she is loved and supported by a legion of loyal friends, both new and old, and welcomed wholeheartedly into the family of the United States Air Force."

Camille turned to his voice, mouth open, as he began to speak; then her face softened, and she smiled happily, mouthing "thank you" as he sat.

The vows were of the traditional variety. I vaguely recognized the words as they drifted into my consciousness, a bit at a time. "...from this day forward...holy estate of matrimony... pledge thee my troth...'til death do us part." I'd never listened carefully to the vows at weddings I'd attended over the years; the ceremony was merely a ticket to be punched on the way to an open bar and tipsy bridesmaids. But today was entirely different, and I tried to steal glances at Luckie without garnering extra attention. I was lost in thought when Bash's elbow dug deep into my side.

"You too busy to help out? That was our cue." He was hissing under his breath.

Dammit.

We stood, and I gave the verbal command loudly enough to be heard only by the eight of us. "Detail, carry sabers. Forward march." We filed into the aisle, forming two rows.

Apollo's hands covered Nathan and Camille's clasped hands.

"In as much as you have thus consented in holy matrimony and have witnessed the same…"

"Detail, halt. Center face." The eight of us turned crisply to face one another.

"By the authority vested in me by God Almighty and the United States Air Force, I now pronounce you husband and wife." He lifted his hands high in blessing with a broad smile to the couple. "And what God hath joined together, let no man put asunder."

"Detail. Arch, sabers." My voice was low so as not to pull focus from everyone's favorite moment of the ceremony. We brought our sabers to chin level, then snapped them into place overhead, forming an arch over the aisle.

"Colonel Morgan, you may kiss your lovely bride."

From the periphery, I could see Happy whisper a private word to his glowing wife before sweeping her into an affectionate embrace and kissing her thoroughly.

"Ladies and gentlemen, is it my great pleasure to present Colonel and Mrs. Nathan Morgan."

Despite cheers from the audience, Nate's and Cami's eyes never left one another as they began their journey back up the aisle, passing under the sabers. Then, as they cleared the final pair, Coach executed a firm swat to Camille's behind with his saber, carrying out an old military tradition. "Welcome to the United States Air Force, ma'am."

The reception was in full swing. A nine-piece band ably covered everyone from Garth Brooks to Earth, Wind & Fire and kept the dance floor crowded as a purple and orange sunset cast the scene in romantic light. Eventually, velvety darkness blanketed the desert, and twinkle lights presided over the dance floor and surrounding tables. The wedding cake was layers of chocolate, lemon, and strawberry; I took it upon myself to sample all three flavors liberally. The entire cake was swathed in smooth frosting and decorated with colorful flowers and bright red fondant scorpions. Boo perched one of the candy scorpions on his shoulder as he danced with Happy's mom.

Hung and Miles led the crowd in learning The Wobble with a big assist from Luckie. I was so transfixed, watching her hips sway that I almost didn't notice Bibi leading me onto the floor to join the fun. The Electric Slide followed, then a two-step to "My Maria."

Luckie found me and grabbed my hand. "Come on, I need a Southern boy to teach me how to two-step." I swung her close to me, mumbling instructions as Boo and Rock led the crowd at large in a comically inaccurate instructional. After a couple of verses of heresy, Happy's parents came forward to provide a proper demonstration. Ordinarily, it might not have caught my attention. But tonight I was transfixed watching this couple in one another's arms, having spent three decades together doing "for better or for worse." My gaze traveled across the floor to see Happy and Camille fumbling their way through a two-step; they laughed and held one another, occasionally stopping to laugh at a shared joke. Having never seriously considered the idea of forever with one person, it suddenly all seemed possible.

Yeah. This is for me.

Lucinda's body was soft against mine, all wound up in my arms. Adele's bewitching voice swirled around in the black night punctuated with twinkling lights overhead. My voice was a poor substitute for hers, but I sang softly in Luckie's ear. The lyrics spoke to the magnitude of my devotion and the lengths my heart would travel to assure her of my love. My Peaches picked her head up from where it rested on my shoulder and leaned in, dancing on her bare tiptoes, until our foreheads touched lightly.

"I know you would do anything, go anywhere for me, Davis. But there's nothing you need to do—nothing more. Nothing beyond being who you are; it's enough simply to let me know how you love me." She kissed my mouth sweetly, and I knew I held more in my arms than I'd ever thought would be mine. I swallowed the emotion gathered in my chest.

"Then it's time to start walking our path together instead of separately, Lucinda. Come live with me. Let me love you all the time, and let's make plans for our forever."

One tear welled, falling to wet her cheek, and she nodded. "Yes. I'm ready to start forever with you, Davis Payne Foster."

English is pleased to request the pleasure of your company for the continuation of Davis and Lucinda's forever in the novella,
The Night the Lights Went Out in Georgia.
Coming in the winter of 2018.

I'd love to let you know about future news in the Hard Broke series. Please subscribe to my newsletter here
mailchi.mp/065247279da1/newsletter-landing-page
Or
Visit my website anytime for updates: englishmichaels.com

The Hard Broke Series chronicles the adventures of the Scorpion squadron and the emergency room nurses who cross their paths and change their lives. Follow along as their fortunes unfold and they encounter life and love along the way.

Surly Bonds (Book One)
Nathan and Camille

A Hundred Things You Haven't Dreamed Of (Book Two)
Davis and Lucinda

Untresspassed (Book Three)
Oliver and Charlotte
Coming Winter 2018

For an author, an honest review of their work is a precious commodity. If you would kindly consider leaving a review, however brief, at the vendor where you purchased my book, I'd be very grateful.

About the AUTHOR

English Michaels is a wife, mom, and recovering registered nurse. Several lifetimes ago, in a galaxy that seems very far away, she was a wide-eyed newlywed, just married to a freshly-minted U.S. Air Force pilot. The first years of married life afforded her a look behind the curtain into the realm of one of the most elite—and least understood—communities in the military, the intriguing world of the fighter pilot.

English is an inveterate Pinterest junkie who has spent a king's ransom on paint and craft supplies. She's mostly disillusioned with television and waging a low energy battle with a Diet Coke addiction. She isn't going to mention that she enjoys travel, because who doesn't? She makes her home in the southern U.S. with Mister English and a whole lot of leftover paint. *Surly Bonds* is her first book, the result of a long-awaited evolution from real person to writer.